Playing with Fire

"Are you coming down with a fever, Miss Castle?" Jake lifted his hand and laid it against her cheek. "You feel kind of warm."

"So do you," she whispered.

The warmth radiated from his body, heating up her front as though she stood before a hearth. He slipped his hand to the back of her neck, driving his fingers through the abundance of her hair.

Antonia didn't wait for him to tilt her head to receive his kiss. She lifted her chin, all but asking him to bend down and meet her offered lips. All her instincts told her that Jake wanted to kiss her. So what was taking him so long?

Jake remembered a lake out in the middle of nowhere. He'd been riding through the heat of the day for hours. His horse had caught the scent of the water and galloped hard toward it. Jake remembered he hadn't even waited to dismount, but had dived in from the saddle. Antonia's eyes were the deep clear blue of that paradise of water. It would be so easy to drown there. . . .

HEART STRINGS

LYDIA BROWNE

DIAMOND BOOKS, NEW YORK

This book is a Diamond original edition,
and has never been previously published.

HEART STRINGS

A Diamond Book / published by arrangement with
the author

PRINTING HISTORY
Diamond edition / September 1993

ISBN: 1-55773-941-2

Diamond Books are published by The Berkley Publishing Group,
200 Madison Avenue, New York, NY 10016.
DIAMOND and the "D" design
are trademarks belonging to Charter Communications, Inc.

PRINTED IN THE UNITED STATES OF AMERICA

10 9 8 7 6 5 4 3 2 1

Dedicated
with love to my husband

HEART
STRINGS

Chapter 1

Jake Faraday stopped in the center of the double doorway of the Grange Hall. He should have come earlier. Every bench was already occupied by a line of male rears, and even the aisles were chockablock with men, some cursing, most spitting, and all of them expecting to be titillated.

Somebody pushed his shoulder, almost a blow.

"Git out of the dang-blasted way!"

Jake turned and the man hastily lifted his shapeless hat. "Sorry, I didn't know that was you, Marshal." He showed brown teeth in an ingratiating grin.

When it seemed annihilation was not to fly immediately from the powerful body he'd so foolishly shoved, he replaced his hat. With a look behind him he said, "Come on, boys." A gang of rowdies followed him in, every man jack avoiding Marshal Faraday's cool gray eyes.

Jake flicked back the sides of his brown wool coat and slid his fingers into the front pockets of his pants, his hogleg in a black leather holster on his thigh. He hoped to God the only place he'd have to put a bullet tonight was in the ceiling.

Though the main aisle was crowded, he had no trouble walking toward the front. Men stepped out of his way, the more respectable muttering, "Evenin', Marshal."

The stage was still empty, except for a lectern and a

1

table with a bowl of flowers, a pitcher with water, and a couple of glasses. Jake stood with his back to the stage, looking at the shiny, hot faces and listening to the crude jokes.

"Your old lady send you out here to learn somethin', Osgood?"

"Not mine, yourn!"

Someone else said, "I heard she done gave a special talk to Miss Annie's girls."

"Aw, nobody could teach them girls nothin'." And the man gave a rebel yell that silenced the hall a second.

When whistles and catcalls broke out anew, Jake glanced up at the stage. A man, whose bald head gleamed as brightly as the silk hat under his arm, smiled around and waved at the crowd. As he came down the three steps at the side of the narrow stage, he gave back as good as he got until he reached Jake's side. By common consent, the standees moved back to give the judge and the marshal room, and privacy to talk without being more than somewhat overheard.

"Expectin' trouble, Jake?" Judge Cotton asked, with a glance at the exposed pistol.

"Nope. This bunch won't do anything to end their fun early. As long as these folks can stand up to it and not go runnin' off, or the boys might decide to break up the hall just on general principles."

"Will you be able to stop them?"

"Nope. It'd be like putting out a prairie fire on my lonesome. And my deputies are all trying to talk their lady friends out of comin' down here."

"And the girls have the deputies where they can keep an eye on 'em." After looking around at his noisy friends and neighbors, Judge Cotton changed the subject. "Mrs. Cotton made me be sure to tell you she wants you to come for supper on Tuesday. I daren't go back if you don't say you will."

For a man accounted the wiliest justice in Missouri, Judge Cotton had astoundingly innocent eyes. Despite the whiskey flask that bulged in the pocket of his black silk coat, there were no red lines marring the serene blue and white. His small, round face was as merry as a baby's.

"Who's she got coming this week?"

"It'll just be the three of us."

The marshal's lean jaw tightened. "Are you sure Mary Lou Ginnis isn't coming to copy out a recipe your wife promised her? Or Widow Nichols to talk over some legal tangle only you can fix up? Only she spent the whole jeezeldy evening battin' her eyes at me and Mary Lou never went near the kitchen or a pen."

"Well, you can't blame the ladies for trying, Jake. A fine, handsome fellow like you oughtn't to be walking around without a fine-looking wife and four or five young 'uns. Mrs. Cotton's been talking to me about it, and I see her point of view."

"Did you ever hear about the rabbit who wanted all his brothers to lose their ears 'cause he'd lost his own? You put all the men you want away in the calaboose, Judge, but no life sentences for me."

Even before he finished speaking, he was turning once more to face the stage in response to the deafening whistles that now broke out. Since he was tall, he could easily see above the level of the stage. Walking toward him were two women, their skirts dusting the boards, and a man.

One woman was pretty but nothing special and the fellow was the sort of namby-pamby skinny-boy Jake never cared much for. He could dismiss them in one glance, just long enough to realize that they were shaking with nerves. The second woman, however, merited a longer look. She approached the unruly audience with such confidence he almost overlooked her beauty.

And she was beautiful. Under smooth brows, her eyes were large and thickly lashed. Though her mouth was primmed up in response to the rough reception, there was still fullness in the pink lips under a short, straight nose. Her neatly bound hair was the gold of braid on a cavalry uniform, which her severe navy-blue dress resembled. The dress pleased his male eyes, with a simple flowing skirt unlike the dresses of other ladies he knew. Her dress outlined her waist and bust like theirs did, but with more to show for it. Jake felt like letting loose a timber wolf's howl himself.

Antonia Castle approached the lectern. Her two assistants were noticeably nervous. She could only hope her own stage fright was not so obvious, though she had as much reason as Henry and Evelyn to tremble. This crowd was wilder, more prurient-minded than the audiences she was accustomed to addressing in Chicago or Kansas City.

Though in agreement with Mrs. Lloyd Newstead's opinion that the message of enlightened sexual education must be brought to the masses, Antonia was sure Mrs. Lloyd Newstead had not meant the Great Unwashed to be *this* unwashed. She was almost grateful for the strong smoke of their burning cigars, lying like a blue quilt in the air before her.

Antonia raised her hand for silence. "Come out behind that box, honey!" a loud voice called. "We can't see your . . ."

Fearing she was turning pink, Antonia could not but rejoice that the rest of the sentence was lost in the sealike roaring of the crowd. She doubted he'd used the proper anatomical term anyway. There was much laughter at her expense.

Her smile seemed to do more to calm the crowd than her gestures. "Good evening," she began, her voice raised with ladylike strength to compensate for those who still continued to talk. "I am Antonia Castle and—"

"I don't care what your name is, little darlin'. How much for the whole night?"

"Whativer he's offerin', I'll double it!"

Antonia fought to control the quaver in her voice and

went on. "Tonight I would like to talk to you about the most beautiful and tender gift God made to humanity. The love between man and woman is—"

She was roused from her set speech not by any vocal interruption, which she could just as well ignore, but by the slamming open of the double doors at the far end of the hall. At first glance it seemed to Antonia as though a row of perambulating bonnets had entered the hall.

Looking again, Antonia could see the sturdy black-clad bodies beneath the ribbon-covered straw scoops. At some hidden signal the women marched forward. There must have been twenty of them. Arms swinging in unison, they paraded down the aisle of the Grange Hall and came to a stop at the benches, third row from the stage.

The lead woman poked the man sitting at the end. Antonia saw him flinch. "Git up, Jem Roberts, and give me your seat."

The now silent men scrambled to get out of the way. When every woman had a seat, they folded their arms. Each woman seemed to have but one bosom, straight across. Except for the first, they had said nothing. Under the riotous bonnets, their faces were identically grim. With one exception.

On the end of the first row was a woman—little more than a girl—somewhat different from the rest. Her dress was less severe as a tiny frill of white lace edged the placket. Honey-brown hair in soft curls peeked out from beneath her bonnet. Squinting a little, Antonia felt instinctively that here was someone not entirely hostile to her message. If her words could sway this one woman, perhaps the others could be made to hear.

More confidently Antonia continued from where she'd left off, addressing this woman particularly. Smiling again, she saw at once the tiny flicker of a like reaction, instantly smothered. Often, on other platforms, she had felt as though her voice reached out like a warm hand to touch another person. This time, however, that sensation had no chance to grow.

"The love between man and woman ought to be tender, loving, and without fear. But how often—"

"Jezebel!"

"Temptress!"

"Comin' here to corrupt our menfolk!"

All of a sudden the air was full of red fruit. Antonia ducked behind the lectern, more from instinct than experience. Several of the projectiles exploded on the stage near to her. Obviously tomatoes still grew in Missouri, despite the approaching autumn. With a glance over her shoulder, she saw that Henry and Evelyn were on the floor. She motioned them to stay down.

Rising from her crouch, Antonia said, "Yet, so often, we find that ignorance—" The tomato that struck her shoulder did not hurt. She felt only surprise, and that could not keep her from speaking out.

"Ignorance prevents the spirit from seeking its true—" The next bomb splattered her face. She wiped thin seeds and stinging red juice from her cheek even as she went on. "Seeking true independence from the narrow confines of—"

"Scarlet woman!" One of the ladies in particular had a piercing voice. "Brazen hussy! Stealing our men. Taking away the love of our sons. You should be horsewhipped!" She had a wicked aim as well.

Antonia ducked too late. Really, it hurt no more than being struck with a hard snowball. More painful was the loss of any chance at restoring order so that she might continue to deliver her useful and important message. The woman she'd singled out held a tomato in her hand, but had not hurled it thus far.

Despite this encouraging sign, Antonia felt disheartened as she wiped away the mingled tomato juice and tears. None of her other meetings had degenerated like this. She really did not know what Mrs. Lloyd Newstead would say.

Peering around the base of the lectern, Antonia saw, surprisingly, that the men who had been teasing her before were doing the most to calm down the women. Their efforts were not enough.

Several of the women seemed to be trying to reach the stage, clawing at the men in their way. They continued to shriek biblical epithets at the forlorn figure behind the lectern, so that the very air seemed to ring with condemnation.

All at once a man stood beside her. Antonia got off her knees, prepared to defend herself. Henry and Evelyn would come to her aid if she could hold him off for even a moment. But the man did not even look at her.

"That's enough," he said in a voice that silenced all, even the most hysterical woman. "I'm goin' to declare this meeting closed. You all go on home now."

It was not possible for the Grange Hall to be completely empty almost as soon as he'd spoken, but that's how it seemed to Antonia.

"By what right do you close my meeting?" she demanded, thinking that he was too big. One of the difficulties, she had found, of being only five feet, five inches tall was that it left her little recourse when some overgrown male started heaving his authority around. Sometimes standing up to an oaf surprised him so much he would back down.

The big man turned to face her. His movements were slow yet an internal certainty told her he could move with great swiftness when necessary. His chest was deep, his torso long, and his thighs broad and strong looking. Though these impressions flashed through her mind in an instant, it took her a moment longer to register the star on his chest and the gun at his side.

"I'm the marshal," he said, sticking his hands in his pockets. "This meeting is a public nuisance. Go on back to Miz Fleck's boardinghouse, Miss Castle."

"How did . . . ?" Of course, there was probably only one boardinghouse in Culverton. There was probably no more than one of *anything* in Culverton. Dismissing that, Antonia went on, "I still maintain you have no right to close this meeting."

Insultingly he turned away. "Go ahead and give your lecture to the hall, then. Miss Castle."

She watched him step down from the stage as if the distance from boards to floor was no more than a single riser. He walked away up the almost empty aisle, stopping to talk a moment to an older gentleman in a black silk coat. They left together.

She decided that the worst thing was that his gray-green eyes had been emptier than the hall when they'd rested on her. Antonia prided herself on never using her femininity to wheedle men. Such tricks only held back the progress of the ideals she supported. Yet she was not used to being looked at with no interest whatsoever!

After a moment she could not help smiling, if grimly. No doubt ripe tomatoes did little to improve her appearance. Under his eyes, she'd forgotten the stains of her humiliation.

"Are you all right, Antonia?"

"Yes, I'm fine, Henry," she said mechanically as her assistants stepped forward. Evelyn shyly offered her pocket handkerchief. "I hope you weren't too frightened," Antonia said, smiling again as she wiped away the tomato juice.

"Oh, no," the girl said. "Henry sheltered me from the worst of it. Turn around and show her, Henry."

Square in the middle of the thin young man's back was the wet splotchy mark of a direct hit. "At least it was ripe," he said, adjusting his spectacles. "I imagine a green tomato, as would be thrown earlier in the summer, to be quite painful."

"Oh, Henry, don't be so silly!"

Evelyn was pretty, with glossy brown hair and white teeth. Henry, too, was attractive, in a way that brought out the mother instinct in older ladies and the helpful friend in younger ones. It was Mrs. Lloyd Newstead's contention that young and attractive persons made the best lecturers on the subject nearest her heart. Not, however, it would seem in Culverton, Missouri.

In a few minutes they left the Grange Hall by the backdoor. Antonia had hid the worst of the stains with her mantle and tucked up her disarranged hair under her blue felt hat.

All the nervous energy that should have been released during her talk remained in her system. She walked quickly, Henry keeping up by virtue of his long legs, but Evelyn had to scurry along. All Evelyn's clothing was elegant with the now fashionable tied-back petticoats, which meant short strides at best, like a hobbled horse.

Hearing a disturbance in the street ahead, Antonia paid it no mind but kept on walking, her thoughts busy with the fiasco of her meeting. It was not far to the boarding-house and she was determined to ignore anything that might come between her and a bathtub. Tomato juice, it seemed, turned sticky with time.

Henry, however, laid a restraining hand on her arm. "Maybe we ought to take another way, Antonia."

"I'm sorry, what . . . ?" She peered down the street.

A crowd of men swirled around, most likely the same ones who'd just been driven from the Grange Hall. They seemed interested in a large yellow wagon, promises in gaudy paint on the sides, which stood in front of an imposing columned building, the only one of its kind in Culverton. The lettering above the pediment that pro-claimed it to be Quincannon Memorial City Hall was still fresh and sharply chiseled.

"Typical!" Antonia said. "Allowing a cheap medi-cine show in front of their new city hall, but a perfectly respectable lecture is closed down by the marshal."

Heedless of Henry's restraining cough, Antonia went closer. Now she could hear fast fiddle music. What had seemed to her a string of bright beads bobbing up and down revealed itself to be five dancers, all female, oddly expressionless. They wore short spangled skirts that showed off their somewhat heavy legs. Paper lanterns, orange and red barred with black bands, burned in the still air.

Walking up, Antonia stood on the edge of the crowd, just out of range of the circles of lights shed by the lanterns. The men did not notice her, being too busy staring at the women kicking up their legs on the makeshift stage of the wagon. Strangely there was none of the good-humored chaffing here that she'd heard in the Grange Hall. These men watched with intense concentration, their feelings betrayed only by the liquid glitter in their eyes and by their mouths hanging wetly open.

Then the dancers were finished, bowing to no applause. They stepped out of sight and a man came to take their place. His coat was off, showing his grimy shirt, dark sweat circles under the arms.

He hooked his thumbs in his braces and leaned back, saying, "Well, boys, I'm glad you've come. Now, before we get on with the rest of the entertainment, I just want to have a few words with you. I know that a good few of you is married and I know that some of you is thinkin' of gettin' married. That's the way of the world."

Antonia hardly had time to wonder if "Prof. Prospero," as the man was described on the side of the wagon, was also interested in sexual education before he continued.

"But there's a problem with gettin' married and any married man'll tell you true . . . it's the women!" A few laughs echoed through the crowd, but most of the men just stood and watched the man on the stage. He was handsome in an unshaved way, but Antonia disliked his pomaded hair and the way he leaned down toward the crowd without taking his hands from his bright blue suspenders.

"Now, medical authority, famous men from Germany and France, tells us that women have none of the feelings of a man. Their needs are not our needs." Here, he made a gesture with his fist that Antonia did not comprehend. "And they can make life pretty tough for a fella interested in a little warm companionship." His voice rose in falsetto. "Not now, you bad man! Oh, just wait till I tell Mama!"

At this bit of histrionics, there was laughter from more than a few throats. Antonia had given enough speeches to know when an audience's attention had been caught. The showman on the stage had diverted the men from their contemplation of the girls, so that they were interested in what he had to say. He held up his hands for silence, though it meant disentangling them from his braces. She did not see where he got it from, but a bottle appeared in one hand.

"Now, I have a solution to this problem." He tapped the flat bottle. "Professor Prospero's own secret formula, developed over years of trial and error. The Shah of Persia himself swears by it—I send him a supply with each new jewel in his harem. And let me tell you, boys, I've dispatched over one hundred bottles this year alone! Just two little tablespoons in any liquid taken before bedtime—cocoa, tea, or coffee! And your little bird will nestle sweetly against your bosom. She can deny you nothing and best of all—"

"I'll take a bottle."

"Best of all, come the dawn, she will become her sweet, innocent self again, with hardly a memory of the pleasures shared in the night. Now, who'll take a bottle? A mere four bits for paradise!"

"Of all the revolting . . . !" Antonia circled around to the wagon. Gathering her skirt in her two hands, she stepped up onto the stage. Looking out proudly over the men's heads, she said, "It never occurs to any of you, I suppose, that a little kindness, gentleness, and restraint might make your wives and sweethearts feel like showing you affection! Oh, no! You've got to sneak down here and buy some magic potion—"

"That ain't all they're buying, sister." The showman had her by the elbow and hissed in her ear. "Get out of here before you skew my pitch.'' He tried to hustle her forward, but Antonia jerked her arm free.

"I will not leave! Gentlemen, listen to me, please!" They were looking at her but not with sympathy. Antonia wondered if she'd made a mistake by haranguing them instead of appealing to their better instincts.

"If this stuff's as good as you say," a voice called, "why not try it out on her?"

Antonia could just make out who was speaking. He was a short man wearing a broad-brimmed hat that made him look like a mushroom. He did not look away when she glared at him, but leaned forward, excitement glistening in his protuberant eyes.

"Yeah, try it out on her!" he repeated, and the shout was taken up by other rowdies.

"Don't be ridiculous!" She tried to step down, but the showman had her once more by the arm and rough, anonymous hands pushed her. Glancing wildly around, she glimpsed Henry, trying to reach her but blocked by the contracting crowd.

Antonia called out to him uselessly. He could not help her. She would have to help herself. Turning to face Professor Prospero, she demanded, "Let me go at once!"

But he only laughed and pulled her into a confining embrace. The smell of his sweaty body sickened her. Panicking, she kicked and tried to bite.

"Come on, boys, she's a handful! Who's gonna help me?"

A hand in her hair jerked her head back. She only hurt herself when she tried to shake loose. Then the bottle was above her face and they were forcing open her mouth. It smelled like coal tar and tasted like molasses and paregoric.

Antonia gagged and coughed and, finding herself freed, stumbled blindly about. The worst was that they were laughing at her helplessness. She felt anger and fear, fear of the vast creature waiting in the darkness beyond the lanterns, waiting to see what she would do.

Then her eyesight cleared. She was on her knees at the edge of the platform. Her pride forbade such a humbled posture. She stood up. Feeling a tug, she pulled her skirt loose from a protruding nail. The sound of the tearing cloth was clear and loud. "That's right, darlin'! Take it off!"

"Nothing is coming off!" she shouted back. Henry called her name and the men in the square all craned their necks to look at him. Single voices leaped up from the din.

"That must be her fella!"

"Skinny, ain't he? And four eyes!"

"Git him up thar, too. Hey, Professor, that brew of yourn work on men?"

"He ain't a man, he's a plucked cock!"

Antonia shook her head then squinted across the street. Toward her came a phalanx of bonneted women, their arms swinging in unison. With a sharp cry of "There they are!" the respectable women of Culverton broke into a trot. "Hussy! Strumpet!"

"Wait a minute. . . . It's not . . . !" Then Antonia realized she was hearing the plural of these pejorative terms.

From behind her she heard a woman say, "Come on, Professor, let's get out of here!" Looking, she saw a half-dressed female, no doubt one of the dancers, peering out at the dazed showman. The Professor nodded and ran for the head of the wagon.

Antonia put out her leg. He went sprawling, clutching at her skirt. The already tortured cloth ripped loose at the waistband. As Antonia jerked away from the showman she fell over into the audience below.

The night became a mad jumble of impressions, of women screaming, of cloth tearing, and of personally being involved in at least three separate scratching, clawing fights. It seemed to be largely a female affair. Or so she thought, until she felt herself captured by hard male hands, while another man reached out greedily to rend her bodice. She screamed then herself.

At first Jake had no intention of joining in the free-for-all. If it had been a regular saloon brawl, he'd have cleaned it up in five minutes. He'd done it before. But though he'd taken part in suicide missions and impossible sorties as an Indian fighter, he'd never been trained to battle women. It wasn't until the pretty brunette he'd seen on the Grange Hall stage waved madly at him that he took part.

"Oh, please, sir," she said, waddling over to him as quickly as her confining skirts allowed. "You must help him!"

"Who?"

"Henry!" she said, as though it were obvious. "He went to save Antonia, but I can't see him now."

With a frown Jake said, "Miss Castle is mixed up in this? Figures." Grimly he turned to wade into the battle.

If the combatants were two men, he left them alone to fight it out. If two females were fighting, he'd shake them gently by the scruff of the neck until they were too dizzy to go on. But if he came upon a man fighting with a woman, or more than one, he'd grab the man and hurl him away like a broken tree branch. All the while he was looking out for a golden head. The noise grew less and less, until a scream shredded the air, a scream that seemed to reach into his soul.

He reacted without thought. Swatting away the two men who held her by the arms, Jake bent and scooped her up, one arm under her knees and the other supporting her back. She resisted his tender embrace as though continuing the fight.

"Hush now, Miss Castle. Hush now."

Looking down on the two prone men, he saw that they weren't farmers, weren't anybody he knew. "Git out of town," he growled, "and you'll live. Maybe."

Grateful, she leaned comfortably against his broad

shoulder, very tired. His face was close to hers as he carried her away. He smelled like coffee, smoke, and soap. She studied his tanned skin, as smooth as a coat of paint, except for the sun crinkles about his eyes. A faint haze of whiskers over his chin and cheeks echoed the dark brown of his hair. She sighed and snuggled against him, feeling as much at ease as she ever had in her life. Where had they met before? Surely she could recall such an attractive man.

The pleasant haze that enveloped her ended when she felt a strange breeze. Looking at her knees, brought close to her eyes by her position, Antonia was horrified to see white cloth and a tiny edge of lace.

Somehow her skirt and petticoats had come adrift and she lay in this man's arms clad in nothing but her knickers and her tailor-made bodice. Immediately she stiffened, trying to hold herself with some distance from the broad torso thrumming beneath her own. He tightened his arms, though he did not turn his head to look at her.

"Thank you for rescuing me," she said in her quick voice, somewhat more breathlessly than usual. She removed her hand from where it had slipped between his coat and his white shirt. "Those men . . ."

"You were doin' all right."

"No, it was good of you. But, if you please, I'd like you to put me down now."

"Nope."

"I beg your pardon?"

"Can't do it."

"But my friends . . ." Antonia twisted to look back at the wagon over his wide shoulder. She couldn't see Henry or Evelyn anywhere. "Please, I must see to my friends. I insist you put me down."

Tensing, for there was a chance he could be just as barbaric as those other men, despite his badge, she struggled in his arms. "I insist!"

Jake tossed her up to resettle her. The feel of her small

body squirming against his chest made it damned difficult to keep one foot going down in front of the other. And her freed hair tickled his nose with a scent he couldn't identify.

"Never mind about your friends. That boy came out of the brawl with more clothes on than you've got. And that other little gal wasn't in it at all. She's got some sense, I reckon."

"I'm glad to hear it." Well, Antonia thought, calming down, at least he can say something beyond "Nope."

Her struggles against his body had told her that she had bruises, but surely she wasn't incapacitated. "All the same I don't think you have to carry me. I'm not hurt. I can walk."

"Nope."

Antonia sighed, exasperated.

"No shoes," he said.

Her feet did feel cool. "Never mind that. Put me down."

"Can't."

"Why not, for goodness' sake?"

"You're under arrest."

Chapter 2

"And just what am I charged with?"

"Disturbin' the peace. But if you don't settle down, Miss Castle, I'll add resistin' arrest."

What good was resistance? He was too big, for one thing, and her position too insecure for another. So Antonia did her best to ignore him, though this was not easy when his breath mingled with hers from nearness.

Though she bit her lips, she could not repress bitter words. "What about all those other people? I suppose they were just standing around peaceably! Why don't you arrest them?"

"I will, as soon as I get you to the jail."

"Jail!"

"Where'd you think I was taking you?"

"My hotel. I can't spend the evening dressed like this!"

"You're right. I'd hate to add indecent exposure to the charges. We got blankets over at the jail. Too bad Quincannon City Hall isn't ready yet. Could have saved me all this walkin'. You're not as light as a feather, you know."

He turned his shoulder to nudge open the door of a strong-looking stone building. Entering a plain, white-washed office, he called, "Caleb? Pete? You back yet?" Bending, he set Antonia on her feet.

17

"That you, Jake?" a thickened male voice called from the shadowy back of the building. "I was just havin' a little lie-down."

Obviously, Antonia thought, others were about to witness her degradation. Disdaining to protect her modesty, she stood in the middle of the floor, her hands clenched into fists at her sides. Her stockinged toes curled, too, from contact with the cold stone floor. She did not regret the loss of her elastic-sided boots, for she now recalled that she'd removed one to strike someone, though she was not certain what became of the other.

Antonia's thoughts turned to the description of this outrageous arrest she'd give to Mrs. Lloyd Newstead on her return to Chicago. Obviously the strategy for bringing enlightenment to the back of beyond would have to be altered.

With a sympathetic glance, not unmixed with laughter, Jake opened a cabinet and brought out a rough plaid. When she'd been in his arms, he'd had a hard time keeping his eyes from the hints of skin exposed by her lack of clothes. Now that she stood up, he found it awful tough to look anywhere but at the soft roundness of her rear end. Her skin seemed to have a kind of glow, so that it shone through the thin white cloth of her knickers. He liked the lace and the pink ribbons, for that seemed more delicate and feminine than black satin and red bows.

He realized he was staring at her now, as he had managed not to do before. Thrusting the blanket at her, he averted his eyes once more. It was a shame to cover it all up, but somehow he didn't like the thought of anybody else seeing her this way, not even harmless old Pete.

"Here you go, Miss Castle."

She snatched the blanket from his hand and wrapped it about her waist, tucking in the ends to form a more or less useful skirt. Sweetly she said, "I suppose you'll have to lock me up now? I'm such a dangerous felon."

"Yup."

He took down a jangle of keys from a hook on the wall. Standing back, he indicated that Antonia should walk before him down the corridor that led off behind the office. Her head held high, she brushed past him.

A grizzled older man, yawning and stretching in the first cell on the right, stopped with his hands above his head to stare after her, his mouth hanging open.

"Evenin', Pete," Jake said. "You ready to head out with me? There was a ruckus over at the Hall. The Professor's come back. Right on schedule."

"Did he bring them girls?"

"'Course." Jake opened the cell door. "You'll be all right in here, Miss Castle." She swept into the cell as though into a box at the opera, bestowing on him a brief glance of utter disgust. Her anger burned her cheeks, half-hidden by the tangled looseness of her hair.

Pete was chuckling to himself. "I bet Miss Annie's goin' to have something to say to the Professor! But you done warned him off the last time he came through town." He peered at Antonia. "She don't look like no fancy-piece."

"Nope, not exactly." Jake closed the cell door with a ringing bang that made Antonia jump. She refused, however, to waste another look on him.

Instead she studied her new surroundings. The square cell was as plain as the office, one wall only iron bars set in from floor to ceiling. Two bunks were built against opposite walls, and a pail sat on the floor. A small window, also barred, was the only interruption in the blank wall. Unfortunately this ventilation could not compete with the stale odors of alcohol and long use of similar pails.

It was quite some time before she was disturbed again. Jake disappeared without saying another word to her, taking Pete along. Perhaps, she thought bitterly, he'd gone to arrest some more villainous characters. She just knew this was all a feeble attempt to prevent her speaking out, even as his unwarranted interruption of her meeting had been.

Well, perhaps he had had a right to end her lecture. It hadn't been conducted as she'd hoped it might be, or, for that matter, as the Society for Social Harmony suggested such a meeting should be run. But to arrest her now, when she had been the insulted party, was too much!

Rather than plan what she'd say to Mrs. Lloyd Newstead, Antonia began mentally to write the telegram she'd send, expressing her outrage regardless of expense. After all, what was the use of having a generous trust fund if she could not send telegrams that said exactly what she wanted them to?

Antonia was polishing a sentence that began "petty prejudices and dirty-minded dullards" when the marshal came back. She had not even reached her description of him as yet, so she studied him anew to get her insults correct. Goodness, but he was a *big* man!

Ahead of him came a bedraggled figure only just recognizable as the once dapper Professor Prospero. He stumbled along, clutching his head and moaning piteously. However, he stopped in his tracks as he passed Antonia's cell.

Pointing a wavering finger at her, he said, "That's her, Marshal, that's the ornery female who busted up my lecture! I was minding my business when she got up on the stage and started in to hollerin' at everybody. You ask 'em, they'll tell you the same as me."

"I did nothing of the kind," Antonia fired back. "I simply made plain certain facts, or tried to, when this person laid hands on me."

Jake poked the professor in the back with one finger. "Move along," he said. "The judge'll work it all out in the morning."

"The morning?" Antonia cried. "You can't expect me to stay here, in prison, overnight?" Jake only shook his dark head at her and escorted the professor to his cell.

As he returned, Antonia held out her hand to him

through the bars. "Please," she said, "at least send a message to my friends so they know where I am. I know they must be concerned."

"Already did it," he muttered, without stopping.

"Thank you so much!" she flung at his back as she flopped down on the bunk. Instantly she sprang up again, for the surface was painfully hard.

Pulling back the rough gray blanket, she saw a cotton mattress no thicker than her hand. She saw no sheet and no pillow. Thinking with regret of her boardinghouse bed, not that it had been anywhere near as deep and comforting as the one she slept on in her own home, Antonia lay down, her head decorously toward the open side of the cell.

Not even the sound of Jake and Pete ushering in a body of whores disturbed her, though the other women wondered stridently at Antonia having a cell all to herself when they had to share. Pete stayed behind to chaffer a little with the girls, enjoying having all their attention to himself, for whatever reason. Jake stopped in the corridor, just to check up on her, he told himself.

Her face was crumpled in intense concentration, as though it took great effort to sleep. Her hands served her as a pillow, and he thought with regret of the one he kept in the cupboard for his own use, during the long shifts of the night. He hadn't thought to get her a sheet either.

Jake's gaze passed along the half-turned form of the woman. That rough blanket must be scratching her delicate skin. He found that his eyes were lingering on the gentle curve of her hip, thrown into high relief by her position.

He did not take much time with women. The respectable ones wanted to get married first, and with him serving as marshal, the nonrespectable ones were strictly hands off. Every year or two he took himself off to Kansas City, where nobody much cared what he or anybody else did. He'd rather not pay for it, as it left him feeling uncomfortable in his mind. The act, he'd found, seemed kind of overrated anyway. Yet Jake found his gaze returning once again to the curves beneath Miss Castle's blanket.

He made an effort to think of Antonia as the interfering, misguided do-gooder he knew her to be, and yet the memory of his instinctive reaction to her scream worried him. He was content that Judge Cotton was sure to order her out of town on the first train tomorrow. An exquisitely tiny and golden-haired idiot was the last kind of trouble he needed, especially the kind that looked so innocent when asleep.

Hearing Pete bid the ladies pleasant dreams, Jake tore his eyes from Antonia's face. He hurried ahead of his deputy to the safety of his office, where he spent the remainder of the night studying the faces of bristled desperadoes on wanted posters. A few hours of that and he'd see a mean and miserable soul lurking beneath the smile of the sweetest grandmother on earth.

Antonia woke up when she tried to snuggle deeper into the blanket, but only succeeded in exposing her toes to the chill air of morning. She lay on her side, blinking at the wall. Someone had drawn a rough sketch there. Staring at it dully, in a few moments she realized it rudely represented the focus and core of an incarcerated man's thoughts.

"Oh, my heavens!" she exclaimed, and sat up.

The events of last evening came rushing back. Standing up, she snatched at her blankets, and with them draped about her, Antonia went to the barred door. Someone had better bring her some breakfast and quickly, or she'd have something to say about it. "Hello? Marshal?"

The voice that answered her, however, was not the rich, low voice of the rude and overbearing man who'd arrested her.

"Antonia!" Evelyn cried, coming at a trot down the corridor, her silver earrings dancing beneath her elaborately coiled hair. She struggled with a small traveling case, clasping it in both hands.

"We were so worried for you. No, Henry," she said, looking back. "You stay there. We don't want you."

"What time is it?" Antonia asked as her insides rumbled from hunger. She'd been too nervous to eat before the lecture and there'd been no chance afterward.

"Eight-thirty. Oh, Antonia, I can't believe you're in jail!" The brunette's green eyes began to fill with tears.

"I can hardly believe it myself. Have you sent a telegram to the office yet, telling them about all this?"

From behind her handkerchief, the girl said in a quavering voice, "No . . . no. We . . . that is, Henry and I weren't sure . . ."

"Yes, Evelyn?"

"We weren't sure you'd want them to know. I mean, a riot and your being arrested, and all this, it just doesn't look right, Antonia. I don't know what Mrs. Newstead is going to say about it. You know what a stickler she is for the proprieties. Why, when Mr. Brown and Lucy Arkwright even drove together from his talk in Oak Park, you know what Mrs. Newstead said. Lucy wasn't allowed in the same office with Mr. Brown, and after they'd been doing such good work together."

"Yes, I know. I sent them a silver epergne for their wedding gift. But as none of this was my fault, I doubt Mrs. Newstead can claim I have poor judgment. I suppose we'll be leaving Culverton this afternoon. I'll send her a notice that we are cutting our lecture tour short and returning to Chicago. Unless you and Henry feel like going on?"

"No, Henry wants me out of harm's way, as he put it." Evelyn's smooth cheeks became suffused with rose. "He was so brave, Antonia. He plunged right in among all that crowd to save you. I was never in any danger."

The girl sighed and then went on, "Oh, I almost forgot. I brought you some clothes. I found your hat after

the . . . um . . . you know. But I don't think you're
going to want to wear it again.''

"I'll take the clothes, at any rate. Did you bring my
brush? Bless you; my hair is one enormous knot. You
wouldn't happen to have a few cookies or an apple?''

While she was changing into her traveling dress
behind the blanket Evelyn thoughtfully held up before
the bars, Antonia asked, ''Did the marshal give you
permission to see me?''

"He talked to Henry early this morning.''

Antonia adjusted the scarf necktie that tucked into the
throat of her more-or-less male-style coat, buttoned close
to her neck. She was glad her brown-and-orange-checked
skirt was not wide, for there would have hardly been
room for it in the cell. ''I'll see Henry now, then. Perhaps
the marshal told him when I'll be getting out of here.''

"Poor Antonia,'' Evelyn said, sniffling. ''How dreadful to be forced to spend a night in prison! You're a
heroine! I know I should never have borne it.''

Antonia hardly knew what to say to that. To agree
would be vain, to disagree vulgar. She could only give a
weak smile and hope Evelyn would restrain her dramatic
tendencies. It made her an effective speaker but a
wearying companion.

Fortunately Evelyn did not seem to require an answer.
She flounced prettily down the corridor, calling out,
''Henry! You can see her now.''

Henry sported a black eye that put Antonia in mind of
the shifting, mysterious colors of changeable silk. She
was about to offer her sympathies when he grinned at
her. ''It looks worse than it is, and I laid out the man that
gave it to me.'' He showed her his right hand, wrapped
about with a handkerchief.

"Good for you!''

"Antonia! How can you say so? I've been scolding
him half the morning.'' Noticing the fond look Evelyn
bestowed upon him and the besotted gaze the young man
returned, Antonia realized the attraction growing be-

tween them on this trip had blossomed into true affection.

Antonia could not restrain a sigh. Though she had no need to marry, being well supported and really entirely independent, it seemed somehow a shame that the only eligible man she'd ever gone on a lecture tour with had been fifty-seven and she closely chaperoned.

Having now herself reached the age of twenty-five, and as Mrs. Newstead considered her levelheaded to the final degree, Antonia was supposed to be chaperon for Evelyn. She could hardly wait to return to Chicago and be free of the ungrateful responsibility of keeping Henry and Evelyn apart, a task she'd failed in last night.

If she had a suspicious mind, she would wonder what transpired after the young couple had returned to the boardinghouse. But, recalling Mrs. Fleck's hard, keen eye, she knew no practical application of their sexual-education message had occurred.

Returning to the business at hand, Antonia asked, "Henry, are they planning to let me out of here sometime today?"

"Marshal Faraday came by the boardinghouse this morning to tell me we are going to be asked to leave town by the first train. But it went an hour ago, and we couldn't leave without you. The court's in session across the street."

"Court? Already? Has my case been called?"

"No," Henry said, looking uneasy. "All sorts of people have been going in and out for the last hour or so."

"*All* sorts," Evelyn put in. "Some sadly fallen, I'm afraid."

Henry gave her a sharp look. But Antonia said, "You mean, Professor Prospero's . . . ah . . . ladies? We've met. What was their sentence?"

"The judge ordered twenty-dollar fines, and they are to leave town. Apparently this is not the first time this particular—how shall I say?—that this organization has come to Culverton. They seemed to enjoy meeting His Honor again. One woman called him . . ." Henry cleared his throat. " 'Droopy drawers.' ' "

Evelyn giggled and Antonia tried to look disapproving, though she knew her lips were twitching. "I fear Mrs. Lloyd Newstead herself should have come this time. I am not equal to the challenges of a small Missouri town, it seems." She paced back and forth before her friends. But, protest to them as she would, there was nothing to do but wait.

After a long, weary while Henry volunteered to go and see what was happening in Judge Cotton's court. When almost half an hour had passed without his return, Evelyn impatiently went in search of him.

She did not come back either. Fed up, Antonia listened beneath the window. All seemed silent. Reaching up, she could just grasp the bars with her gloved hand. Shaking the bars did nothing but free a little dust.

Antonia wrinkled her nose and sneezed. Stumbling back from the window, she kicked over the galvanized pail, sending it rolling over the hard floor with a tinny rattle. Luckily she'd not been able to bring herself to use it. In a moment it was upside down and she was standing on it. By pulling herself up by the bars, she could just see the alley outside. It was empty, save for a dog trotting quickly past on private business.

"Plannin' a jailbreak, Miss Castle?"

"I had thought about it," Antonia said with great self-command, although he'd startled her, sneaking up so irritatingly. She supposed a marshal must move as silently as an Indian. It was probably part of his job. Though she supposed she must respect him for it, this talent did not make him more likable.

She stepped off her bucket and took up from the bunk her hat, black with gold braid about the edges, matching her dress. The long hat pin neatly skewered the hat to her hair.

"I'm ready now, Marshal." At his blank look she

said, with more than a trace of impatience, "Aren't you supposed to take me to see a judge? If you have such a person in this . . ." Antonia tried to think of a word sharp enough to express her emotions. "This dreadful town?"

This morning he'd been tempted to let her go and the hell with it. As marshal, he had a certain leeway in the performance of his duties. Drunks, after drying out, were rarely charged, nor, for that matter, were saloon brawlers, after they'd come around. If Judge Cotton hadn't been so particular about holding court early today, Jake thought, he would have let her out first thing in the morning, with a strict warning not to come back to Culverton.

But he'd been kept so busy, running between the jail and the judge's front parlor, giving testimony, that there'd hardly been a minute to put on a clean shirt or to talk to her. Jake had hoped a night in jail would knock some of the arrogance out of her and that she'd be becomingly grateful to the man who let her go free.

But here she was, wearing as mannish a dress as he'd ever seen, laying down the law to him. He could almost bring himself to forget what kind of underpinnings she wore. Not that she still wasn't the prettiest thing he'd ever seen in jail. Why, when she'd put her hands up to her head to fix that hat, he . . . Sternly Jake shook his head.

"No?" she said. "You're not going to take me to be sentenced? Well, I'm very grateful. No doubt trying to spread enlightenment is a capital offense in Culverton."

"Ma'am, I was just wonderin' how a woman can be so ornery first thing in the morning." He unlocked her cell and swung open the door. Standing back, he motioned for her to come forward.

"You keep using that word. Ornery. What on earth does it mean?" Nothing good, she was sure, though she doubted this yokel could give her any other meaning.

Jake thought, It means, you spitfire, that you are

perverse, disobedient, and ill-tempered. Aloud he said merely, "I dunno, ma'am. Just means ornery, I guess."

Walking out, Antonia was taken anew by his immense size and thought what a pity it was that so handsome a man should be as stupid as two stones! He hadn't struck her that way at first, when he'd so officiously broken up her meeting, but he seemed to become thicker and slower each time she spoke to him. No doubt she'd seen him briefly at his best. Remembering suddenly the impact of his broad chest as he'd picked her up, she realized how splendid his best must be.

"Well, shall we go? I suppose I can come back for my . . . no, never mind. I shan't have any use for those things," she said, throwing a look back into her cell. She scooped up her traveling case, which contained her brush and her scent.

Without waiting for him, she marched away down the corridor and through his office. On reaching the street, she asked, "Which way to the courthouse?"

"There ain't no courthouse. Yet. We're goin' to the judge's house."

Funny, she couldn't remember his having said "ain't" before. She glanced up into his face, but his black, low-crowned hat shaded his eyes, so she could not guess at their expression. "Well, which way do we go?"

"Right 'cross the street."

"Oh." The street was unpaved and extremely dusty, save where a horse had gone by. She grasped the cloth of her skirt and raised it to keep it clean. With great bravery, she stepped down onto the street.

Looking down, Jake could glimpse one trim foot in a tight leather boot. He could not help being disgruntled that the girl had pretty ankles. Why couldn't she have been a slab-faced hen with hands and feet to match? Then he might find her antics amusing. He walked around behind her and swept her up against his chest.

She squeaked with alarm but settled down almost at once, her back straight and hard in his arms. Somehow it pleased him that she was just as stiff this morning as last night. Her next words surprised him so much he almost dropped her.

"Thank you," she said. "I was hoping you'd do that."

Instantly Antonia was ashamed of herself. She shouldn't have said it. Thanks would have been enough. To say more might give him the notion that being held by him like this was a pleasurable experience, which it certainly was *not*! The bulge of his arm muscles against her upper body was no more than a phenomenon of aesthetic interest, like looking at sculptures of Grecian heroes, splendidly naked in marble.

On the other side of the dusty street, he put her down gently on the boardwalk, little more than fences laid end to end on the ground. Both she and Evelyn had caught their heels in the gaps more than once. She thanked him with a second glance and a short nod. "Which building is it?"

The old jail was in the heart of the town. Along both sides of the street were clapboard buildings that showed the signs of hasty and probably moneyless erection. Three different stores seemed to share a single facade, they were built so closely together. A few homes and stores stood alone, yet still leaned slightly toward the others. It seemed as if the town huddled together out of fear of the vastness of the country that surrounded it.

As though to deny this cowardly appearance, bold signs declared in the simplest terms the business carried on within. Planks painted bright colors hung out over the uneven boardwalk proclaiming SALOON, BANK, and GENERAL STORE—POST OFFICE.

The judge's house, like the others along this main street, showed it was a private home by the whitewashed fence and the brave display of flowers set out in a broken square around the front door.

Jake held open the iron-hinged gate for his prisoner, and she stepped up the three steps to the covered porch with her head held high. A motherly woman of about fifty opened the door with a bright smile for Jake.

"Hello again, Marshal. My, what a busy mornin' it's been. Oh, my. Oh, yes. I haven't got on with a single thing I mean to do."

"Miz Cotton, this is Miss Antonia Castle."

Antonia found herself looking into a twinkling pair of brown eyes, whose lashes, despite the woman's gray hair, were still dark and long. She was short and round in her calico apron, like a homemade doll. "How do you do, Mrs. Cotton."

"Well, I'm just fine, Miss Castle. 'Scuse my not shakin' hands, but I was rolling out some biscuits when I heard you come up. I swan if it ain't the first thing I've turned my hand to today. Go straight on in to the parlor, Miss Castle. The judge'll see you there."

Much of Antonia's nervousness evaporated at Mrs. Cotton's welcome, until she reflected that all the wrong-doers of Culverton must pass through her front door on the way to judgment. She doubted Mrs. Cotton could fail to be friendly even to a hardened murderer.

Entering the parlor with her guard behind her, Antonia no longer wondered at the disappearance of Henry and Evelyn. They sat on curvy chairs pulled up close to a round table covered with a crocheted tablecloth, flowered china, and breakfast.

Henry stood up when Antonia entered, hastily wiping biscuit crumbs and butter from his chin. His glasses were fogged from the steaming coffee. Evelyn only smiled and lathered a warm round with sweet butter, sliding it onto a plate and handing it to Antonia.

Evelyn tossed her head and affected not to notice Marshal Faraday. Lifting the heavy china coffeepot to fill another cup, she said, "I told you she was hungry, too, Henry."

Antonia seated herself at Henry's vacated chair. It took all her self-control not to shovel the food in her mouth as fast as she could, while a sip of hot coffee helped to clear her head.

"Where is the judge?" she asked at last, turning around to look at Jake. He just shrugged his square shoulders.

Henry answered, "Mrs. Cotton said he'd be right back. Someone wanted his opinion about a pig."

"A pig? And I'm just supposed to wait around until he deigns to return. I tell you, Evelyn, I can barely stand to wait until we can leave Culverton."

Mrs. Cotton bustled in with the chipped iron kettle in one towel-wrapped hand. "More biscuits'll be ready in a minute. Have some more coffee, do. Didn't I tell you Liza Fleck's biscuits ain't a patch on mine?"

"Yes, ma'am," Henry said, but the lady of the house had already turned to Jake. Mrs. Cotton giggled just like a young girl when she cast her eyes up to the marshal's face.

"You set yourself down and eat a morsel. Your young lady ain't goin' anywhere, not until the judge gets back. You can keep an eye on her from across the table." Going up on tiptoe, she whispered in a voice that carried across the room, "She's right pretty. I'd keep both eyes on her, if I was you."

Antonia suddenly found the flowers on the plate before her very interesting. She thought the least the marshal could have done was to continue to stand out of her sight. But he took up another chair from against the wall and set it down right next to her.

She froze, and inched away from the large thigh suddenly close to hers beneath the blue fringed cloth. He hung his hat on the back of his chair. "Excuse me," Jake said, reaching across her for the coffeepot. He said it again when he put it back.

But that was not the end. He reached out for the ruby-red jam and Antonia snapped, "Can't you ask for what you want?"

"Easier to put out my hand for it," he said, and his

arm touched her shoulder, making her jerk away. It was only a miracle that she did not spill her coffee in her lap. She was certain he bothered her on purpose.

Just as she sipped the last of her coffee, which she had to admit was very good, the front door opened, setting up a breeze. Antonia jerked around, hoping to see someone judgelike.

Instead there stood in the hall a small woman in a stiff black dress. When she glimpsed the group in the parlor, her black eyes went wide. "You!" she declared in outraged tones. "You evil, wicked—"

"Now, Miz Dakers . . ." Jake said, rising, his napkin still tucked into the collar of his shirt.

The woman pressed her hand against her heart. "No," she said, "I must command myself." The fascinated strangers stared at her, until Antonia realized that this was one of the women from last night's meeting, the loudest and most hysterical of all those who had come to condemn her message unheard.

"More coffee, Henry? Could you manage one more of these wonderful biscuits, Evelyn?" Her two friends jerked their attention away from the woman in the hall and followed Antonia's lead. It was impossible, however, to pretend this was an ordinary breakfast.

The woman walked into the parlor, twitching her skirt away so that it came nowhere near Antonia. With pointed attention, she studied a framed sampler on the wall.

Under her breath she read the motto aloud, "Even a child is known by his doings, whether his work be pure, and whether it be right."

Evelyn took a fit of the giggles, smothered in her handkerchief. Antonia did not feel like smiling.

Then, somewhere out of sight, a door slammed and the floorboards of the house shook to an approaching step. A bald-headed older man bounded into the room, but stopped short.

"Mother!"

Mrs. Cotton appeared.

"Mother, how in the name of Sweet Fanny Adams am I supposed to run a courtroom in the middle of a consarned ladies' tea party?" he asked, pointing a plump finger at the parlor table.

"Oh, hush, I've never seen a man to carry on so," Mrs. Cotton replied with a disgusted glance. Without haste, she began to clear the table.

When Antonia made a move to help, Mrs. Cotton pressed her fingers onto the girl's shoulder and said, "No need for you to stir yourself. Just sit."

With a quick glance, however, she seemed to draw Evelyn up out of her chair. "D'you mind carrying this tray for me, Miss Bartlett? And Mr. Layton, I got a big old sugar sack that wants shiftin'." Henry and Evelyn exchanged glances and stood up.

The judge and Marshal Faraday were standing with their heads together by the mantel. Mrs. Dakers shot suspicious glances at everyone, though her eyes did not stay long on Antonia. The judge chuckled and pushed his fist against Jake's arm.

Then Judge Cotton turned to Antonia and an unconvincing frown came between his brows, as though he were an amateur actor beginning a play. "Miss Castle, this court is convened to inquire into a charge brung against you by the honorable citizens of Culverton."

Antonia felt as though she were glued to her chair. Though she wished to stand up and with a scoffing laugh walk out of this parlor/courtroom, somehow she did not seem able to do it. It was not the thought of the marshal, leaning against the wall with his arms crossed, that restrained her. Perhaps she simply had too much respect for the law, in whatever absurd guise it appeared.

"As soon as you tell me what the charge is, I'm sure I can refute it completely. I have done nothing wrong."

"We'll see 'bout that. Now, I just want to tell you this isn't exactly a formal court, more like a discovery. We're going to try and discover a little bit of truth before we come to the regular hearing. You wouldn't be afraid of answering a couple of harmless little questions?"

"Of course I'm not afraid." She straightened her back and looked the judge in the eye. Her perfect attitude was spoiled by Mrs. Cotton coming in to take away the cover from the table.

"I'll be out of your way in a minute, Vernon. You don't need to go lookin' at me that way." In a whisper, she said to Antonia, "Don't you let that old man bullyrag you."

"Mother! Don't prompt the witness."

When the woman left, after making a terrible face at her husband, who pretended not to see, the judge said, "Now, Miss Castle, I take it you're a spinster. Of what state?"

"I live in Chicago. Illinois."

"That's not what I mean. Where were you born?"

"Minnaqua, Connecticut."

"Mina—what?"

Antonia spelled it, though there was no clerk to take it down. The judge seemed to notice that, too, for he brought out a messy sheaf of papers from one pocket and called, "Mother! What'd you do with my pen?"

Mrs. Cotton came hustling out, shaking her head, a long pen in one hand and a bottle of ink in the other. "There. If you ain't a baby, then I never seen mud. Jake knows where everything is in his house, I'll be bound."

"He ain't got no woman to mess around with his business," Judge Cotton replied, but not until his wife was out of the room.

Jake coughed, and Antonia glanced at him. His eyes were raised to the ceiling, a look of complete disinterest in the squabbles of judge and spouse. Yet something like a smile had left traces behind in his expression.

"Now, what'd you say the name of that town was? Where is that?"

"It's not far from Mystic, Connecticut, on the Atlantic seaboard."

"Your pa a sea captain, maybe?

"No."

"What he do?"

"He is . . . employed by a shoe-manufacturing business." Castle Shoes were famous in the East but as yet her father had not begun selling them this far west, except to the army. Until three years ago, when her grandfather and founder of the business had died, her father had been a mere employee, working his way up through the ranks as her oldest brother now did. So she did not lie, not really.

The judge wrote for a moment on the topmost piece of paper. He looked up and coughed before he said, "You ever bin married, Miss Castle?"

"No."

"You know, you're supposed to say 'Your Honor,' but let it go, let it go. Now, are you engaged, maybe to some nice feller in Chicago?"

"No. Your Honor."

The judge smiled at her before seeming to remember the seriousness of the business in which they were engaged. "Now I'm goin' to call a witness. Miz Dakers, I wonder if you'd be willin' to say what you saw last evening."

The woman in black hunched over in her corner, like a child in disgrace at school. She mumbled. The judge looked over at Jake, who said, "Now, Miz Dakers, don't be afraid."

The marshal smiled and Antonia was astonished. When his lips curved, his face became warm and friendly, showing just the right number of clean, white teeth. He looked almost . . . intelligent. She jerked her eyes away from his face just before he looked at her. Her heart beat strangely fast and she put it down to the tenseness of the moment.

Mrs. Dakers seemed to respond to the marshal. "The forces of darkness gathered over Culverton last night, Judge Cotton," she said in a voice suddenly vigorous.

"This wicked girl came before us to spread evil and corruption to the pure hearts of our young men. Salome dancing before Herod. I saw; I witnessed." The woman's head sank onto her bosom, the fire fading from her eyes.

"Thank you, Miz Dakers. You can go on along home now," the judge said, standing up.

When the woman had slunk from the room, he sat down and scrawled some more lines on his papers. Then he put aside the pen, folded his hands, and leaned forward. "There you have it, Miss Castle. I reckon that's pretty near conclusive evidence."

Antonia could not believe that any rational person would take the ravings of an obviously deranged woman as evidence. Her eyes flicked from one man to the other. The marshal wore a satisfied smirk.

With a contemptuous sniff, Antonia decided that if Mrs. Dakers ever changed her mind about sexual education, she'd make a more effective speaker than Mrs. Lloyd Newstead herself. "Very well, Judge, pass sentence."

"Now don't be in such a dang . . . in such a rush, Miss Castle. Like I say, this ain't a trial. Just a way of seein' the truth."

"If you think that display was the truth . . . !"

"Now, now. I think I got a way of figurin' this thing out. The way I see it, everything depends on you. What kind of person are you, Miss Castle? That's one of them questions you don't got to answer." He held up one hand.

"If you're a nice girl, well, it's pretty clear what Miz Dakers said is just a . . ." He tapped his temple, then held up his other hand. "If, like she says, you're a corruptin' 'fluence, well, I guess you'll have to be tried, proper, and sent maybe to the Women's Home up to Missagoula." The judge shrugged.

Jake moved from his position against the wall. Up to now he'd been kind of enjoying seeing Miss Castle get her comeuppance. He had thought, however, that a fine and an order to leave town would be the extent of her punishment. After all, Professor Prospero's good-time girls had got that much.

"Wait a minute, Judge," he said.

"You just stay out of this, Jake, and stand ready to carry out my judgment."

Judge Cotton cleared his throat. "Here goes. In order to find out about you, I, in the power of this here court, order you, Antonia Castle, to spend thirty days with a morally upright and single man between the age of thirty-two and thirty-three. If, at the end of this time, you are still a virgin—as certified by a competent medical authority, I mean—then your school, or whatever it is, can open a branch in town and I won't go giving you a hard time. Not legally, though I don't approve of what you're tryin' to do."

"Judge," Jake asked evenly, "what kind of hooch you been drinkin'?"

"I never heard of anything more preposterous," Antonia said, not requiring a champion. Despite her principles, she was a little shocked to hear sexual terms applied to herself.

Her statement was echoed from behind her as Evelyn and Henry entered the room, Henry still rolling down his sleeves from the washing he was somehow inspired to do. He strode forward and said, "I've attended law school and I cannot . . . Where did you learn your law, sir?"

The judge winked one wily eye. "Like most stuff, I make it up as I go along. Now, hush up, or I'll give you contempt of court, Mr. Law School."

He looked over at Antonia. "If you'd druther, Miss Castle, I can sentence you to thirty days at Missagoula, just as easy."

"Very well." Steaming, Antonia realized she was forced to concede. Besides, humiliating as the judge's terms were, she could not imagine a man in Culverton attractive enough to tempt her from her maiden status. As a lady, born and bred, she could simply ignore whoever she was to stay with for the duration. With a secret determination, however, she declared herself woman enough to make that thirty days living hell for whatever unfortunate male the judge inflicted on her.

This question seemed to interest the marshal, too. "Judge," he said, "what poor bastard . . . ? The only man that old who isn't married or engaged is . . . well, there's Poot Harvey, but he's a couple boards short of a shed, and I guess the bartender at the Silver Spoon is about that old. . . ."

His words faded as he realized Judge Cotton was looking at him with an even more peculiar expression than usual in his innocent, laughing eyes. "Oh, no."

"Never!" Antonia added a moment later.

Chapter 3

Marshal Faraday chuckled quietly, such an unexpected sound that Antonia jumped as though pinched. He said, "C'mon, Judge, what are you really goin' to do with her?"

Judge Cotton's fluffy pale brows drew down over his eyes. "Now, you listen up a minute, Jake. This here's my court and I done give you an order. You're a sworn marshal. You got to do what I say. You take that young lady along to your place and you keep her there thirty days. What's the matter? Don't you reckon you kin keep your hands to yourself that long?"

"That's not the problem," Jake said quickly.

"I can assure you that will *never* be a problem."

Now Jake regarded her with the steady gaze of a wild wolf, his eyes a flat pewter gray. Antonia did not flinch. He was nothing but a big, raw yokel without a single redeeming quality. Keeping him at arm's length would be the easiest task she'd undertaken in years.

However, when she let her eyes drop down over his hard, lean body, doubts came to chip at her confidence. He was awfully tall and she knew already the strength of his arms. The size of his thighs in the tight-fitting wool pants told her they were no less strong. All the authorities agreed that men had less self-control than women. What if he couldn't keep his passions in check and took advantage of the situation the judge had forced upon her?

There had to be a way out, but at the moment she couldn't come up with one. Perhaps it would be best if she pretended to go along with this preposterous business.

She said, "If Your Honor is really intent upon this 'discovery,' it seems I have no choice but to submit. Are you certain thirty days will be enough to determine my character?"

Jake mumbled, "More than enough."

Antonia glared at him.

More loudly Jake said, "Are you sure about this, Miss Castle? Your reputation won't be the same."

"I'm not concerned with what the people of Culverton think of me. And I'm sure my friends wouldn't dream of spreading this sordid affair around."

"I won't say a word," Evelyn vowed.

"You can rely on me," Henry added. "But don't you think I ought to tell Mrs. Newstead? I know she'd have a lawyer here within a week to get you out of it."

Rising, Antonia crossed the room to talk to them. "No, Henry, I don't think Judge Cotton would listen to anyone. You can tell Mrs. Newstead the truth, though. It will make an excellent article for our next pamphlet. I shall write down everything that happens while I am forced to remain here."

"I'll go immediately." But Henry's voice lacked enthusiasm. He looked at Evelyn. "I don't like to leave you."

"Evelyn," Antonia said, "had much better travel with you." When Henry exclaimed in shock, she went on, holding up her hand, "Well, she can't stay here alone in a boardinghouse, and I don't think Marshal Faraday would be very welcoming."

"I ain't got room," a deep voice answered.

"There, you see?" Antonia said. "He ain't got room."

"But if we travel together," Evelyn put in, blushing, "I can't think what Mrs. Newstead would say. I mean, without you there, Antonia. It doesn't seem . . . that is to say . . . is it proper?''

The judge said, "You know, I kin marry people, though Preacher Budgell may not like it.''

"I reckon you've done enough, Judge," Jake said.

Henry grasped Evelyn's hand ardently. "Marriage would protect you," he said. "But I don't want to take advantage. I hoped that someday . . . but not like this.''

"Don't you want to marry me?" Though Henry seemed unable to answer, Evelyn apparently had no doubts about his feelings. Her eyes glistening, she said, "Oh, Henry, I'd be so happy.''

Antonia stepped back, feeling like an intruder. She met the scornful sneer of the marshal and the bright interest of the judge. "If court is adjourned, Your Honor," she said, "I suppose you could ask the minister to come by. If you think he really would marry people he doesn't personally know. I can vouch that neither of them is married, if that helps.''

"I don't guess Mr. Budgell would kick up much of a ruckus, Miss Castle. Now, let me see. Today's Saturday?''

Judge Cotton hauled out a heavy silver hunter from his pocket and compared it with the wooden case clock ticking in the corner. "If you kin marry up by one, there's a train out at three, which'd give us just 'bout time for a little bit of a shindig. Yep, Jake. You go fetch the preacher.''

"Not so fast. What about . . . I can't live with that girl!''

The judge banged the table with his fist. "Court adjourned.'' He got up and walked out, stuffing his bits of paper into his pockets as he left.

"Consarn it, Judge," Jake called after him. "You can't leave it like this.''

He gave Antonia a quick up-and-down glance. She felt a snake or a rat would have received a more sympathetic look and returned the expression, raising her eyebrows for good measure.

"For God's sake, Judge!"

The only answer he got came from down the hall like an echo. "Court's adjourned, Marshal."

"Damn that old man!" Jake said.

"There's no need to swear, Marshal," Antonia answered. So that's the kind of man he really was! Given to foul language at the slightest setback.

He opened his mouth as though to speak, but sighed instead, shaking his head. Snatching his hat from the table, he jammed it on his dark head and said, "You best come with me, Mr. Layton. You're gonna have to git a ring and then Preacher'll want to see you. Jaw at you awhile, most likely."

Jake gave Antonia one more look, as if he couldn't quite believe she wasn't a figure from some horrible nightmare.

How word got out so quickly that the two young strangers were getting married, Antonia never quite knew. Perhaps Mrs. Cotton had been listening to developments in court from behind the kitchen door. But no sooner had Jake taken Henry down the street to find the preacher than the Cottons' door began to resound with knocks.

The women of Culverton came to the house in twos and threes, each bringing some token for the bride. A group of young girls, almost but not quite women yet, slipped upstairs, each with a bud or two of wildflowers, which seemed scraggly and dry to Antonia. It was easy to promise herself, however, that only compliments and delight would pass her lips, for Evelyn's sake.

Another knock sounded at the front door. Antonia, isolated in the parlor, suddenly felt sure it was Jake coming back. Nervously she smoothed the upswept hair at her temples. She could face him; she had to get used to it.

Entering the hall, she jerked open the door. The

woman on the step appeared to be younger than the other women who'd entered wearing wedding rings, and prettier, too, with light brown hair curling softly against her cheeks under her black bonnet.

Antonia decided there was no possibility she was disappointed not to find Jake's large frame filling the doorway. The momentary sensation that her heart had dropped several inches must be due to some other cause, like indigestion.

She smiled graciously and said, "Won't you come in? Everyone's upstairs."

"Oh! No. I . . . this is for the bride," the girl said, thrusting a brown box into Antonia's hands. She hesitated and then turned away.

"Wait," Antonia said. She recognized the girl as the only even slightly friendly face at the lecture. "Please come in."

"No, no! I got to get on home."

"Who's that, Miss Castle?" Mrs. Cotton asked, squinting a little as she tried to see into the sunlight from the dark hall. "Jenny! Come on in, girl. What'd you bring?"

"I . . . I thought, seeing as I was last to marry up, I'd . . . well, a bride oughta have a veil, I guess."

"Why, if you ain't the sweetest thing! Miss Bartlett'll be tickled to have the use of it. Won't she, Miss Castle?"

"Absolutely. I know she wouldn't have felt like a bride without it. Won't you come up and give it to her?"

Jenny pulled at her fingers. "I gotta get home to my chores."

"Don't worry 'bout that, child. Ain't nothin' gettin' done today. I don't know what the menfolk gonna eat for supper. Warm water and stale bread iffen they're lucky. You come on in and set." Mrs. Cotton took the girl's arm and all but hauled her over the threshold.

"Git on up them stairs and give that poor girl some hints on marryin'. Everybody else is, even them as never had a man so much as to call."

The young woman was obviously longing to go up, but at that moment a burst of laughter from the second-best bedroom seemed to frighten her. "No, best not . . ." she gasped. With a swift glance toward the stairs, she fled.

Her hands on her hips, Mrs. Cotton shook her head. As if to answer Antonia's unspoken questions, she said, "That girl, I swan, was the purtiest, liveliest thing you ever hoped to see when she first came to this town. Now she don't seem able to say boo to dead goose."

"Is her husband so brutal?" Antonia thought of the broken, bruised women who sometimes came to the Society's shelter for a word of comfort before returning to violent men. Men were by their natures unpredictable.

Would Jake Faraday take his frustration at the judge's ruling out on her? He might do it. When he looked at her with such dislike, she could believe him capable of cruelty. She wasn't sure she wouldn't prefer being the object of a man's uncontrollable lust than the victim of brutality.

"Miss Castle, that boy is so crazy in love for her, he'd eat dirt to please her and call it rum puddin'. Nobody knows what the trouble is and Jenny ain't one to talk about herself." Shaking her head, Mrs. Cotton bustled back toward the back of the house.

Antonia carried the box upstairs, toward the laughter. When she pushed the door open, she was greeted by silence and sidelong looks.

Evelyn danced forward. "Darling, darling Antonia! Everyone's been so sweet! Just look at this, and this, and this!" Quickly she showed Antonia an elegantly embroidered handkerchief, a sachet to pin inside her bodice, and the assembled bouquet of wildflowers.

A murmur, as though of whispered apology, went around the seated women. "Weren't nothin'."

"Someone else sent you something, Evelyn, though this is only a loan." Antonia took the lid off the box. Fold after fold of white tulle edged with lace exploded softly upward.

Evelyn reached out with a shaking hand to caress the veil. Pulling it from the box, she placed one end onto her head. As though trained like a rose vine to climb only where it can be most beautifully shown, the tulle fell in an elegant drape behind the bride.

Her eyes wet, she said to the strangers gathered about her, "I just don't know how to say thank you."

Antonia found herself outside as the women came forward to arrange the veil. She discovered she did not miss the elaboration of satin, lace, and dressmaker's artistry that she'd always thought the apex of the wedding day. Perhaps the explanation was simply that every bride, no matter what her circumstances, is more beautiful than any other seen before. Antonia wondered if the miracle would ever be worked on her.

Downstairs in the hall, a boy of about fifteen stood thoughtfully scratching his sandy-colored head.

"May I help you?" Antonia asked.

"I just come from Miz Fleck's. There's all of them grips there. She don't want me to take 'em to the depot without Mr. Layton knowin' 'bout it."

"Yes, the baggage." Suddenly Antonia was struck by an idea. It meant being nice to Jake for a few hours, but it also might mean freedom.

It was all she could do not to smirk as she said, "By all means, take their bags to the train. I'll tell Mr. Layton myself. Let's see, they were staying in rooms twenty-four and twenty-nine, right?"

"Yes, ma'am."

"Then take those bags. *All* of them." Antonia reached in through the side slit of her skirt and took out two nickels.

"Here," she said, offering them to the boy. He looked at them rather suspiciously. "In Chicago, all the hotels employ bellboys. They always take gratuities. Now, you will take care of this matter yourself?"

Slowly he reached out to take the coins. "I guess it'd be all right."

"Of course. I suggest you take everything down right away so there's no danger of their bags missing the train. It's not too big a job for you, is it?"

"No, ma'am. I'm awful strong."

"I'm sure you are."

Antonia watched the barefoot errand boy dart away. Closing the door, she leaned against it a moment, her eyes alight with excitement. That'll show Mr. Marshal Jake Faraday, she thought.

Jake stood in the church, flapping his hat across his thighs. As soon as Henry said what they'd come for, Preacher Budgell had dropped to his knees and started to pray as if God were deaf. It amused Jake that Layton looked around helplessly when Mr. Budgell began praying. He obviously hadn't wanted to join in but did anyway.

Jake was grateful that the polite upbringing he had been given had all but worn off. The experience of a wild lifetime came in handy when telling people what he thought of them. He'd have to come up with some rude things to say to Miss Castle when he took her to his place tonight. It was kind of fun seeing her light up like a firework.

He ran a thumb along his jaw, trying to remember if his house was fit for company. What the hell, he thought, I didn't invite her. Let her clean up if she doesn't like it.

When the light through the red-and-blue-glass circle above the pulpit had moved across two planks of pine flooring, Jake cleared his throat. "Maybe you want to talk to Mr. Layton about a couple of things, Mr. Budgell? You know the kind of thing I'm talking about?"

"Never mind," Henry stammered. "Perhaps it would be best if I just declared my single state and—"

"Amen!" Despite this, the preacher did not stand up. He bowed his head to continue silently.

Henry, on the other hand, seemed only too happy to get off the hard floor. He sagged at the knees, as though his legs were asleep, and Jake stepped over to prop him up. "Thank you, Marshal. Um, Preacher? I wonder if we might . . . ?"

The young minister unfolded his hands and stood up. "A man is a source of wisdom to his wife. He must not despair when applying gentle correction to her words and deeds."

"Mr. Budgell isn't married," Jake said out of the corner of his mouth.

"He shall be a lamp unto her darkness and her wayward nature checked by his hand."

"I'm afraid I don't conceive of my marriage to Evelyn as being along those lines, er, Reverend." Henry coughed as he received an elbow in the ribs.

"Keep jawin' like that and your gal may not get a church weddin'," Jake muttered. "You really hanker to be married up by Judge Cotton? Think it over."

"That is to say, er, Reverend, I'm very interested in your point of view. Would you mind explaining that part about, ah, woman's wayward nature?"

Jake listened absently to the preacher's replies. He wondered how any man could doubt what women were really like after spending five minutes in the company of Antonia Castle. Probably Layton was so busy making eyes at that other girl he hadn't noticed. Or maybe Layton's taste didn't run to blondes, even those with just the right kind of figure.

It wasn't decent, come to think of it, the way she never let her corset bones show. Made a man think she didn't wear one. He realized he'd been trying to puzzle that out ever since he'd picked her up last night. It sure hadn't felt as though she were wearing much under her top, and he knew what she wore underneath her skirt. As he remembered the details of what he'd seen, and imagined what he'd missed, the rest of the preacher's lecture passed him by.

Somehow or other Jake found himself Henry Layton's best man. Under the long rectangular windows, the pews were filling up. Children had been sent hotfoot for their fathers to come in from the fields. Jake saw a lot of wet collars and hair slicked down on heads that had been hastily pumped clean.

Justice having been served this morning, he overlooked the scraped knuckles and contusions on half the people who faced him, just as he'd ignored the shiner on the groom. Jake doubted the preacher, who had missed the aftermath of the meeting, even noticed that his congregation resembled the Yankees a day after Chancellorsville.

Beside him, Henry muttered, "I don't know about this."

"Too late now." Jake smiled knowingly at the assembled people and at least three women dropped their prayer books.

"I'm certain I'm rushing her into this. Why, I've never even told her I love her."

"You kin do your courtin' later on. Seems to me, wives mostly complain men don't do it no more after they say 'I will.'"

"I agree, Marshal. On the other hand . . ."

Jake gave Henry a direct glance. "Straighten up, boy. She said she'd have you. Pretty little gal like that must have a whole swarm of yahoos after her. Tell her you love her when you get to a smart St. Louis hotel and then . . ." Jake winked and Henry drew himself upright.

"I shall, of course, allow a proper interval to elapse before . . . is that how you'd treat a woman who has honored you with her highest regard?"

"Yup." Jake noticed a stir of excitement at the back of the church. "Bet she's comin' now."

Antonia was already inside the church. In the last backless pew, she could hardly see the marshal. Those glimpses she did get between the heads in front of her amused her. How disgusted he looked by everything! No doubt he thought women were for momentary pleasure only and that any man who pledged himself for eternity was an idiot. How often had she met with that attitude in single men.

A poke in the side made her glance up. Mrs. Cotton whispered, "Miss Bartlett's lookin' for you."

"Is everything all right?" Antonia asked, rising to follow the older woman.

"Oh, my. Oh, yes. She's just a mite twitchety."

Judging by the way her bouquet shook, Evelyn seemed on the brink of complete collapse. All her color had fled, leaving her as pale as though she were sick. She reached out and grasped Antonia's arm, her fingers digging deep. "How . . . how do I look?"

"Lovely. Simply lovely. I've never seen you more radiant."

Casting a glance around, Evelyn bent her knees and scooped up her trailing veil. She led Antonia out of earshot of the remaining women and girls. "Oh, Antonia, I don't know if I want to do this! I mean . . ." Her face crumpled with worry and strain.

"Goodness, Evelyn, you don't have to, you know. You can change your mind."

"But I want to marry Henry. I . . . love him and I look forward to being his wife."

"Is it . . . is it tonight that bothers you? I know Henry won't do anything to distress or alarm you."

Evelyn shook her head. "Of course not. I know as much about . . . that . . . as you do. It's just . . ."

"You don't have to marry him just to be correct on this trip, Evelyn."

"But I can't travel for days on a train without a husband or a chaperon!"

"You won't have to. If my valises, as I hope, have gone with yours and Henry's to the station, I'm halfway to getting on the train myself. All I have to do is accompany you, as though to see you off, as any friend would. I imagine all of Culverton will follow you. In the confusion, I sneak on board the train and hide until we pull away. What could be easier?"

"But if you're caught, the judge said he'd put you in that awful place! Missagorilla."

"I'm not going to think about getting caught. And once I'm back in Chicago, it will be very difficult for Culverton's law to catch up with me. If they should pursue this nonsense, a competent attorney will soon make a fool of the marshal. I mean, the judge."

She must flee. The thought of endless days spent in Marshal Faraday's company made her feel distinctly odd. Her hands were cold, but at the same time she was far too hot, as though an unquenchable furnace had been ignited somewhere deep inside her.

"What if your baggage isn't on the train?" Evelyn wailed in a whisper.

"It should be, but I don't care if it is or not. I told the boy from the boardinghouse to collect everything from our room. But even if it isn't, I'm getting on that train!" She offered a reassuring smile to the women waiting for Evelyn.

Evelyn's forehead wrinkled. "Would it be easier if you were my maid of honor? Oh, please say you will. I meant to ask before, but you never seemed to be around."

"Then you still want to marry Henry? My plan will work whether or not—"

"Of course I do, silly. He might change his mind and not ask me again." But she still looked distressed.

"Then what is the matter?"

Running her hand over the fine twill of her blue dress, Evelyn asked, "Do—do you think he'll like me? I don't look at all like the brides he's used to."

"How many has he had?" Antonia laughed and then said, "You know men never notice clothes. Ask him in a year what you wore today and he'll probably say white organdy and orange blossoms."

Evelyn giggled. "Or he'll say I dripped with diamonds and lace. Do you remember how Nora wore that awful . . ." Talking on her favorite subject, her glow restored, Evelyn walked back to the church door. Mrs. Cotton waved a handkerchief just inside and singing voices filled the air.

As Evelyn fussed a last moment with her veil, Judge Cotton came dashing up. "Just a minute, honey," he said. "You ain't goin' nowhere without this piece of paper, 'lowing you to get hitched up. It's your marriage license. I wrote it up myself. My old schoolteacher said I had the best handwritin' he ever did see."

Handing it to Evelyn, he crooked his arm. "Now, it's my privilege t'give the bride away, seein' as you're marryin' up 'cause of me."

His wife came forward, hands on hips. "What are you talkin' about? She don't want to walk nowhere with you."

Evelyn smiled on the judge and said, "I'd be so happy."

Antonia walked slowly up the uncarpeted aisle of the church. The congregation sang aloud, a hymn she did not recognize. Halfway toward the minister, Antonia lifted her eyes from her fingers, folded at her waist. For all she noticed, Henry might have found himself a suit of scarlet satin to be married in.

Jake drew all her attention. He was so busy looking everywhere except at her that she knew he was vividly aware of her approach. At last she met his eyes and could not look away as she came nearer and nearer. The brilliant light in the church made his eyes appear to be as green and velvety as moss. Antonia was fascinated by the change.

At the same time she wanted to laugh aloud. Her lips twitched and she smiled happily at him, acknowledging a certain fellowship with the marshal. No doubt he'd be pleased when she escaped, though he'd undoubtedly try not to show it.

Gently she took the bouquet from Evelyn's nerveless fingers. It smelled wild and fresh, like the open air where the flowers had grown.

She looked up when the bride and groom stepped forward on the judge's affirmation that he gave the bride to her husband. A mist rose before her vision and she blinked hard, trying not to give in to the sentimental tears she always wept at a wedding.

The youthful minister earnestly recited vows for the groom to repeat. When he came to the part about "with my body, I thee worship," red flared in Antonia's face.

She knew Jake scrutinized her and tried to keep her attention focused on her friends. Her eyes, though, turned irresistibly toward the marshal. Antonia relaxed again when it seemed he had not, after all, witnessed her strange reaction to those tender words. But why was he breathing so hard?

When she took his arm at the end of the ceremony and walked out behind Henry and Evelyn, she remembered her plan and said pleasantly, "Don't you love weddings? I do."

"I thought your kind didn't believe in 'em."

"*My* kind?"

"You know, people who come 'round lecturin' other folks."

"We . . . I just don't happen to think everyone should be completely ignorant! Unlike some people who seem to enjoy it." Antonia tried to tug her hand free from where it was tucked between his elbow and the heat of his body. Somehow he kept hold of it, despite her best efforts.

"Behave. We gotta walk together to the judge's place. And smile again. Everybody's lookin' at us."

Antonia arranged her expression into a rigid grin, which she flashed around for a moment before saying, "I suppose every person in town knows all about this disgusting arrangement the judge has forced on me?"

"Well, I sure didn't tell 'em." He began to walk faster, and Antonia had to hang on to him to keep up.

"I didn't think you had. It was probably Mrs. Cotton.

After all, you're not any happier about all this than I am.''

She considered telling him her plan. Her escape would be to his benefit as well. Perhaps he could even make matters easier for her. But at the last moment, even as her mouth was opening, she remembered he was a lawman. She hoped she could manage to be nice to him without being sick, but she had to persuade him not to take her to his residence until after Evelyn and Henry left for the train.

They only stayed at the Cottons' home a moment. When they came out, Jake carried a large basket and Antonia balanced a cake plate on her upturned hands.

"Where is this creek?" she asked, striving to keep her chin out of the white frosted angel cake that Mrs. Cotton had conjured up from her pantry. "If it's fair . . ."

"Ain't too bad. A couple of minutes' walk. At least you don't wear them stupid tight dresses."

"My goodness," she muttered. "A compliment."

Jake toyed with the idea of sticking one foot out in front of her. A little trip and a lot of frosting and maybe some of the starch would go out of her. But he rejected the notion with what he thought of as great forbearance, even chivalry.

In the bright sunshine, the green grass was a blanket patchwork. Laughing children raced about. A tree with leaves just turning from light green to gold seemed to be at the center of their games. Its knotty roots poked down though the bank to the sun-sparkled water. The breeze that rustled among the leaves brought with it the intermittent strumming of a guitar and the intriguing smell of wood smoke. Women half reclined on their blankets, sometimes scolding, but more often smiling as their children raced by.

Immediately under the tree stood a table, made from two sawhorses and a plank, bent in the middle from the weight of baked goods. Apparently everyone brought their own main dishes and shared dessert.

Antonia put Mrs. Cotton's cake down and asked Jake dazedly, "What kind of weddings do they put on for people they know?"

"Yoo-hoo!" A woman kneeling on a blanket to one side of the table waved at the marshal and he turned toward her. Unwillingly to let him out of her sight—purely for safety's sake!—Antonia followed.

He did walk well, with long, powerful strides and straight back. She supposed only men who lived an energetic life developed shoulders like that. The bodies of the city men she knew seemed thin and flabby by comparison.

The Widow Nichols didn't give Antonia a second glance when Jake introduced them. "I'm saving this spot for you, Marshal. And I remembered to bring my special beet pickles. You know how you loved them at the Fourth of July. So don't wander away, you greedy man!"

"Shouldn't we find Henry and Evelyn, Jake? We must give them our congratulations," Antonia said, again slipping her hand beneath his arm. Thinking of the way he'd look when he learned she had escaped, Antonia's smile was real.

"Yup," he said at once. "''Scuse us, Miz Nichols."

The glances she received as she strolled on the marshal's arm did not seem so cold as they had this morning. A few women even nodded at her, though without smiling. The men who were there stared openly. Antonia was used to that. There were always some who thought any woman who talked candidly about the sexual life must be perennially available. Ignoring such boors was commonplace for a traveling lecturer.

She was glad that she did not see the men who'd attacked her last night. Her self-control might snap, and she'd hate to become involved in another riot during Evelyn's wedding picnic. Not that Jake would let things go that far, she thought confidently, pleasantly aware of the firm muscles under her fingers. Perhaps other people were aware of his muscles, too, for certainly everyone was strangely polite.

Henry looked as though he'd been struck over the head from behind. He blinked a lot and didn't seem to know who he was talking to. When Antonia went to him, he simply said, "So good of you to trouble."

Evelyn divided adoring glances between her new husband and her ring, the best the town's general store had to offer. Antonia laughed and kissed them both, before walking off again with Jake, who was still carrying Mrs. Cotton's basket.

"You've known them a long time?"

"I've known Henry longer than Evelyn. She only joined the Society two years ago."

"And when did you join up? God, it sounds like the army."

She ignored that and answered simply, "When I first moved to Chicago. I've only lived there four years."

"You said your daddy was still livin'?"

"That's correct. My mother, too."

"Why don't you live with 'em?"

"Really, Marshal, I don't think . . ." She remembered her resolve and the necessity for it. She mustn't irritate him, or he might want to leave the picnic early. "I simply felt I no longer wished to live in Connecticut."

"Bet it was 'cause of some man."

"No, that had nothing . . . Look, there's Mrs. Cotton. I'm sure she must be starved by now. Whatever's in that basket certainly smells delicious."

The grass was cool and spongy beneath her shoes. She was almost reluctant to stop walking, but they should give Mrs. Cotton her basket. Perhaps a little later they could wander down to the creek's edge, where it was cool and shady. Quite a few young couples were going that way.

Mrs. Cotton offered to share her fried chicken with

Antonia and Jake. Antonia sat beside her on the blanket, and after a moment Jake did, too. He sat Indian fashion, his legs bent under him, his pants straining over the width of his thighs. Antonia found she was staring at the brass tongue and loop of his belt buckle. Suddenly the breeze that touched her cheeks had no power to cool her. She tried hard to concentrate on the chicken wing in her hand.

After acknowledging Antonia's compliments on the food, Mrs. Cotton asked, "How old might you be, Miss Castle? Not that it's any business of mine."

"I'm twenty-five." Would Mrs. Cotton think of her as an old maid? Jake definitely would, especially after his question about a man in her past. He probably already thought of her as a dried-up, interfering spinster, which, she reminded herself, was all to the good if it restrained his baser instincts. She reminded herself it didn't matter what the rest of Culverton thought of her.

Mrs. Cotton got a faraway look in her eyes and she moved the fingers of one hand restlessly. "A seven-year gap is just about right between husband and wife."

"But Evelyn's only three years younger than Henry."

"That's all right, too. Now Vernon and me are just the same age, to the month. I remember what he was like when we first married up. Oh, my. Oh, yes. You wouldn't think of it now, what with that stomach and no hair to speak of, but he was the handsomest, charming-est boy you'd ever want to meet. Why, he'd take one look at me and my insides'd turn to water." Her voice dropped to a whisper as she said to herself, "Tell you true, they still do, sometimes."

A shadow fell across the two women and they looked up. "What in tarnation do you want now, old man? If you et any more of that sour-apple pie, you'll be out in back all night long."

The judge left his fork sticking straight up out of the filling. "You seen that Ransom boy, Mother? How 'bout you, Jake? The young 'uns want to start dancing and we can't do without a fiddle.''

"Get Hiram to do it. He's always lookin' to show off."

"I guess. But he can't play like the Ransom boy."

"You want me to find him, Judge?" Jake asked. "He's been spendin' a lot of time with that red-haired kid of Miz Fleck's."

Dismissing the men, Mrs. Cotton turned back to Antonia. "You all right, child? All your color's gone."

"No, I'm . . . that is, yes, it's rather warm. Jake, do you mind if we go for a walk? I . . . I think that would be refreshing."

The older woman gave the marshal a push. "What you dreamin' about? Git up and help the lady. Take her down by the creek. And you, Vernon, are you goin' to stand around all day? Them young folks want to start dancin' and you ain't found 'em a fiddle player yet."

Jake stood up and held out his hands to Antonia. Their warm, rough clasp closed over hers and he drew her gently upward. For what seemed a long time she left her hands in his while she was fascinated by the discovery of a cleft in his chin.

His gaze seemed transfixed by her mouth, and though she knew she should not do it, her tongue crept out to shine her lower lip. She watched fearfully as some slow fire came to smolder in his sea-gray eyes.

"You know," she said, panicking, "I feel better now. And this chicken's so good, I can't resist another piece."

"Me, either," Jake said. Was there the slightest tremor in his voice?

Her legs felt as though they would not hold her up and she dropped back down beside Mrs. Cotton. More than ever it was vitally important that she get out of Culverton. She must leave before she wanted to stay.

Mrs. Cotton said, "You girls always do lace too tight. No blood gits to your head and you come over faint. Seen it happen a hundred times."

Antonia was willing to address the human body from a stage to hundreds of people, but she was not used to hearing underclothing discussed in mixed company. She looked at Jake from beneath her eye lashes. He caught her eye and grinned at her, shaking his head slightly. Remembering in what state of undress he'd seen her last night, she became scarlet.

"There now, Miss Castle," he said. "Your color's come back a treat."

When they heard the fiddle music start, Jake asked, "If you want to dance . . . ?"

Regretfully, Antonia shook her head and said, "I'd rather not. Thank you."

Dancing with him would be too dangerous. He was so large and yet moved so silently. She wondered what it would be like to move in rhythm with him, joined into one body moving through space. She knew she wondered about it too much.

Mrs. Cotton said, "I'll bet that man of mine will be steppin' on all the purty gals' toes."

As it turned out, it was wise of the judge to keep an eye on his watch. He started trying to round up the bride and groom at two-twenty, but they were dancing and paid him no mind. Then, when he was able to attract their attention, they said good-bye and thank you to every citizen over the age of twelve. Judge Cotton must have hauled out his watch twenty times in the next half hour. At last he appealed to his wife.

Mrs. Cotton said, "Miss Bartlett, or Miz Layton, as I should say, you best give me that veil. I'll see Jenny gets it. You write me a letter sometime so I know how you gettin' along. Quit yer fussin', Vernon. The three o'clock's never on time."

"Where's Antonia?" the bride asked.

"I'm here," she said, parting from Jake. "Do you want me to come to the train station with you?" How did actresses manage to sound natural? She felt as though everyone were staring at her, but she dared not look to see if Jake was aware of her performance.

Evelyn started at her question, turned three shades of red, coughed, and said, "Yes, please."

Evelyn and Henry led a large group toward the train station. Antonia walked beside the bride. She'd moved quickly to avoid Jake. Fortunately the widow had latched onto him as soon as he was alone. Antonia forced herself not to walk faster than the newlyweds. If only Evelyn could take a full step!

A black engine, all geometry, stood at the head of five red cars lined with black and yellow. The windows were open and the train was mostly empty.

Trying to behave normally, Antonia glanced about her. Everyone clustered around the bridal couple and all eyes were on them. All eyes except for a gray pair, narrowed with suspicion. Antonia smiled at the marshal and waggled her fingers at him cheerily, though her lips were dry. There had to be one moment when she could slip on board unnoticed—there had to be!

"Marshal Faraday," Henry said, putting out his hand. Jake felt he had to shake it. "I want to thank you for helping me and for being my best man on such short notice. I hope we may have the pleasure of seeing you if you are ever in Chicago. The university can always find me."

"Thanks," Jake said, wondering where Antonia had gotten herself to.

Evelyn glanced flirtatiously at the handsome marshal. "I know Henry wouldn't mind if you gave me a kiss. It's supposed to be very good luck to kiss the bride."

Though Widow Nichols sniffed, Jake disengaged his arm from her grasp. Taking off his hat, he leaned down to brush Evelyn's cheek with his lips. Then he straightened and glowered at the applauding crowd.

Antonia only heard a raucous cheer and guessed it meant Henry had embraced his new wife on the platform. At that moment she was scrunched down between two seats, her head on her knees. She'd pulled off her hat to prevent it from showing in the window frame. Under her breath she counted the seconds. Even if this train were chronically late, the delay couldn't possibly last much longer.

Ticket counterfoils and candy bags littered the dusty floor. She hoped there were no crawling insects and gathered her skirts more tightly against her ankles. Every nerve straining, she listened for the grunting chuff of the engine, waited for the violent back-and-forward motion of the train moving out. She felt an almost overwhelming need to relieve herself, just as when she'd been a little girl playing hide-and-go-seek in the big house her parents still lived in.

There was a noise but not a train noise. She ducked down further and peered under the seats. Black boots, dulled by a film of dust, slowly approached. Tan pants outlined long calves. Antonia kept her head down. If she didn't even breathe . . .

"Miss Castle," Jake said, "I think you better come on out of there."

Chapter 4

"**N**ow look," she began heatedly. Then she remembered an old adage about flies and honey. Antonia bestowed upon the lawman a winsome smile. "Surely you don't want me to stay?"

"I got my duty to do, Miss Castle. You heard the judge."

"But think a moment, Marshal." She increased the earnestness of her smile in the hope of softening his heart. "If you let me leave on this train you won't have to share your house with me. You'll be free, the same as I will. I don't mean to offend you, but I do not want to stay with you, or in Culverton for that matter, for another thirty minutes, let alone thirty days."

"No offense taken. Are you coming out of there, or do I have to drag you?" She did look kind of adorable, Jake thought, sitting on the floor with her knees tucked up and her hair all every which way. Especially when she began to spark.

"Don't you understand?" she said slowly, as though speaking to a child. "Just get off the train, turn your back a minute, and I'll be out of your way."

"Well, it's mighty tempting, Miss Castle."

"Oh, good." She relaxed.

"Are you coming out of there, or do I have to start dragging you? I got a duty, Miss Castle." The thought of the Widow Nichols and Mary Lou Ginnis gave him more incentive to do his job than Judge Cotton's righteous anger if he didn't. Thirty days with Antonia would, for all its attendant horrors, mean a month without hot-eyed pursuit. Also, though this was of no importance, Antonia was mighty easy to look at. Jake dismissed these distracting thoughts and concentrated on his duty. He walked forward slowly.

Antonia saw herself distorted in the brass mirror of his belt buckle and involuntarily let her eyes drop before snapping them closed. She knew what a gentleman kept in his trousers, but to see a buttoned fly so near shocked the sensibilities of even an enlightened woman.

His warm fingers closed around her wrist as he lifted her right arm. She jerked it free. He said, ''Now come on, Miss Castle. You're getting off this train. You might as well walk.''

Mute and stubborn, she shook her head. She felt that he'd withdrawn, and opened her eyes to see if he was baffled. Tilting her head back, she avoided the sight that so alarmed her. ''You can't force me to go.''

Jake sighed and shook his head. Then, swiftly, he bent and grabbed both of her ankles. When he pulled, Antonia came sliding out from between the seats on her back.

She yelped. Grabbing at the seats' support, she tried to hold on. But he kept pulling. She kicked, doing him no harm. She found that she could do little but strive to keep her skirts from riding up any farther than they had already. To keep her modesty, she had to let go of the seat. When she lay in the aisle, he stopped.

Holding both her ankles in one large hand, he turned away from her. Placing her feet on his hips, he said over his shoulder, ''I can drag you like this, Miss Castle.''

''You . . . barbarian!''

Jake shrugged and began to walk forward.

''Stop!'' The floorboards bumped her and her jacket rode up in the back. She knew he meant what he said.

''You'll walk then?'' he asked, looking behind again.

''Yes!''

"I'm right glad you can see reason." A glimpse of a red petticoat underneath her white one pleased his eyes. He realized even a bad job could have elements of enjoyment.

When Jake let her feet fall, Antonia sat up. "I'll never forgive you for this . . . outrage!"

"When a woman says she'll never forgive, she's halfway to doing it, or so my father used to say."

"You *had* a father?" Antonia asked as nastily as she could. Maddeningly, he only chuckled. She burned for revenge like the barbarian she'd called him. If only she could chop him down to her size!

Disdaining the hand he held out, Antonia scrambled to her feet by leaning on a seat. She picked up her hat and beat the dust out of it. Despite its looking as though a cow had worn it to a stampede, she skewered it to her hair.

"Your hair's a mite untidy."

Were there justice, the look she gave him now should have shriveled him where he stood. But she'd learned already that justice didn't exist in Culverton. Let the people of this town know just how badly she'd been treated.

Catching sight of herself in a window, she thought about Evelyn and Harry. If they saw her looking like a scarecrow after a sleepless night, they might not leave. Antonia could only hope they would send her a lawyer to get her out of this predicament as swiftly as possible.

"Have you a pocket comb?"

Jake fished his from his pocket. So she was vain, after all. He wasn't surprised. He'd never seen a beauty yet who didn't feel more concerned over her looks than anything, or anyone, else around her.

After a moment's neatening Antonia returned it to him, still without looking in his direction. "Shall we go, then?" she asked, her chin held proudly.

"After you, Miss Castle."

The crowd that had seen Evelyn and Henry off had

dispersed. No one, except the station manager, saw Antonia get off the train. Hardly had the marshal stepped to the ground behind her when the whistle blew and the chuffing of the engine increased.

"An engineer," Jake said as if to himself, "likes to stay friendly with the law, in case of a train robbery."

Antonia rolled her eyes and kept walking ahead of him.

"No, this way, Miss Castle." He took her arm and guided her around to the side of the station. A horse and buckboard stood beside the platform. "I usually just walk, or ride, to my house, but I didn't think you'd fancy it. And then all that baggage."

In the back of the wagon were several valises, all of which were very familiar to Antonia. Seeing them, she came very close to using her only swear word.

"Mr. Layton said Miz Fleck's boy had made a mistake, and he didn't want you to be left with nothing. So he separated your bags from his and his missus's."

Oh Henry, Antonia thought. I hope Evelyn burns every dinner for the next fifteen years!

"Hop up, Miss Castle." He stood by the horse's head, waiting to untie the reins from the fence.

Antonia looked around for inspiration. With the train gone and the street all but empty, her spirits sank to the soles of her brown leather boots. There seemed to be no help for it; she'd have to go with him, for one night at least.

When she considered what one night could mean, if he turned out not to be honorable, her stomach fluttered with what she was almost certain was fear. She scuffed a toe into the dirt beside the wagon's big front wheel and looked at Jake from the corner of her eye. Of course she felt fear; what else could she feel when he stood there, so intensely masculine and so big?

She quickly glanced away, and then couldn't be certain how she came once more to be caught up in his arms. Her gaze flew at once to his face, so close to her own she could count the green flecks in his gray eyes. He grinned down at her shocked expression.

"It's a good thing you're so small. I'd be in a fix right enough if you were stubborn *and* big as a horse." He set her down in the buckboard's seat. "Stay put," he said, walking back to the horse's head.

Antonia could think of nothing to say to him that would express her true feelings at this moment. She kept silent all the jouncing way to his house. As near as she could judge, his property was about a mile and a half from the railroad station, on a spur running off from the rough main road. Reaching the house itself tried her bouncing rear end the most.

The small house, of white painted clapboards, stood on the edge of a wood. As she waited for Jake to swing her down, she could hear water trickling as though a spring or creek flowed nearby.

"Step on the spoke of the wheel, Miss Castle. I can't do everything for you." He had already opened his front door. He entered, carrying in one of her valises.

The long windows and door made his house look taller than it was. A single stovepipe stuck up from the shake roof. Antonia set her teeth and stepped down, her small feet feeling for the spoke beneath them. Mud from the wheel stained her dress. If she'd been less ladylike, she would have given in to the temptation to rub her sorely tried derriere. A gravel path kept her boots clean while a rock border contained only more dirt.

Antonia wondered if, in the spring, the marshal occupied his off-duty hours with gardening. She thought not. No doubt broken blossoms such as Professor Prospero's girls were more appealing than the sweet flowers that nature provided. Expecting the worst sort of disorder, she stepped a cautious foot over the threshold of the house that she would be sharing with Jake.

She caught him in the act of picking up a pile of yellowed newspapers. "Nothing like a newspaper to start a fire," he said.

"Of course."

Jake watched her carefully, waiting for her to whip an apron out of her pocket and start cleaning. Every other woman that had come to his home, even those who'd stopped by with a husband, couldn't seem to hold back a minute. Let him leave the room and he'd come back to find her neatening and straightening. They'd plump pillows when he'd just gotten them to fit his kinks, brush down the curtains, which were doing no harm, or wish aloud for sand to clean his floor, when he wanted to be at his ease in a house that wasn't so clean a body couldn't stand it.

This one showed no signs of incipient neatness. Neither did she look as if she were holding herself in to keep herself from catching something. All the same Jake glanced at her with his suspicions plain on his face. "Well?" he asked.

Antonia decided that on the whole it could have been worse. There were no paintings of lolling women in undress, no cuspidors, and no visible underclothing, soiled or otherwise.

"Am I to sleep here?" she asked, turning toward a closed door in the middle of the left-hand wall.

Jake stepped quickly over and stood in the doorway. "That's the only bedroom, and it's mine. You're not to go in there, do you hear?"

What did he expect her to do, break down the door? "I assure you, Marshal Faraday, that I have no intention, now or ever, of entering your sacred domain. I merely want to know where I am to sleep."

"All right. Just so long as we're clear about that. You don't go in there. Don't be like Psyche."

"Psyche?" Antonia repeated, amazed. "What do you know about Greek mythology?"

"I mean . . . Psyche MacDougal. Another girl who never did what people told her. She went on into a man's bedroom when he said not to, and I don't reckon I have to tell you what happened to her. You being a lecturer and all.'' Jake managed to stretch his face into a leer.

Antonia turned away in disgust. ''I suppose I shall sleep on this,'' she said, walking to the sofa. Bits of stuffing showed through the faded red damask cover. When she bent over and patted, some of the gray fluff floated to the floor and the wood creaked and squeaked. ''Noisy,'' she said.

''That shouldn't trouble you,'' Jake said without thinking. ''You're a quiet sleeper.''

Her eyes narrowed. ''How do you know that?''

''You're forgetting, Miss Castle. This isn't the first night you've spent under a roof of mine. I saw you, at the jail.''

A slow, rising tide of color washed over her face from the neck of her jacket to the roots of her hair, ''Did you charge admission?''

''You were in my charge; I had to make sure you were all right.''

''That doesn't give you permission to ogle me!'' Antonia could have said more. The words were pent up behind her tongue, ready to be thrown at him in hurtful volleys. But what was the use? Until the next train came through, by which time she hoped to persuade him to allow her escape, she was stuck.

''Let me see the rest of the house, besides your precious bedroom.''

Jake admitted that you had to admire a woman who could control her temper at least some of the time. Unaccountably, however, he felt cheated. When Miss Castle got mad, her eyes glittered, her chest rose and fell to faster breaths, and she almost seemed to grow to twice her size like an angry cat. Jake wondered how much stroking it would take to bring her down once she got good and riled.

''There isn't much more to the house,'' he said. ''Just the kitchen, through here.'' He opened the second door to the living room, opposite the front door.

A stack of dirty dishes sat in the dry sink. Two flies buzzed happily among the sticky remains of several meals. With a movement so fast Antonia couldn't follow his hand, Jake captured the insects. Opening the back-door, he let them fly free.

He turned a sheepish face to Antonia. "Guess I've gotten a little behind in the housework. I'll wash 'em. You dry." He tossed her a dish towel.

An oaken bucket sat on the floor. He picked it up. "I'll say one thing for the man that built this house. He put in a good, big cistern. I'll get some water. Be right back."

Antonia shook her head over the ideas a man could have about neatness. Not that she had exalted ideas about the state of the homely temple, but she'd have discharged her cook in a minute if her kitchen became filled with unwashed dishes.

Jake came back and, after dumping soap flakes over the dishes, poured in the water.

"Aren't you going to heat it first?" Antonia ventured.

"Nope. Cold gets 'em just as clean. Besides, my stove's a mite fidgety. Takes a while to get it going. But you'll soon get the hang of it."

"I?"

"I was thinking . . . I usually come home for dinner around twelve—depending on how busy we all are down at the jail. And if you want to make supper for about six, that's fine with—"

"You expect me to cook for you?"

His big shoulders lifted and fell. "I got a fry pan here somewhere and a big cast-iron—"

"You expect *me* to cook for *you*?"

His own temper began to rise. "As long as we've got to live together, we might as well make the most of it!"

"It seems to me you *are* making the most of it." Antonia flicked a glance around the kitchen, taking in the temperamental stove, the dirty plates and cups, and the man. With an exasperated huff, she slammed open the backdoor and dashed down the two steps. In a moment she was out of sight.

Jake caught up with her five minutes later. She walked so fast he could follow the dust trail she kicked up. It had taken Jake five minutes to dry his hands and to turn around the wagon. Ordinarily, he knew, these things wouldn't have taken more than a minute, at the most. But he'd sat in the wagon for a while in stunned consternation when he realized that when Antonia Castle flew into a passion, he wanted to kiss her until she melted into another kind of passion. Either that or to beat her; he didn't know at the moment which notion had the upper hand.

Dang it, he thought, watching her small yet stalwart figure marching along, it's been too long since I visited Kansas City. Much too long.

Jake let the horse draw up slightly past her and let the animal ramble as slow as it pleased. "Going to Culverton?" he asked.

Antonia pretended she walked all alone in the midst of the vast wilderness. Not another human made a footprint on the virgin terrain, or ever had, she told herself. Not a white man, not an Indian, especially not a too-big lawman with the mental capacity of a . . . dandelion.

"You must be thinking something mighty hard about me, Miss Castle, judging by the sour look on your pretty face. Why not climb up here and tell me all about it? You know you'd enjoy being nasty to me."

My, she thought, isn't it peaceful here, without another soul for miles and miles. His slow, rumbling chuckle came softly to her ears. She remembered how his broad chest had thrummed against her body when he spoke. What would it be like to be very close to him when he laughed? Not that he ever seemed to laugh aloud, she noticed, and wondered why.

Shaking her head as though she were bothered by a fly, she continued walking as if there were no one for a hundred miles. The metal rings on the horse's harness jingled. Suddenly Antonia's nose tickled as the swifter pace of the horse kicked up dust, leaving her sneezing as Jake drove past. "Bless you," he said as he drove away.

Jake took the rig back to the livery stable. The owner, Paul Dakers, came out of his forge behind the stable at Jake's whistle. Though no more than twenty-five, Dakers had the mighty frame of the born blacksmith, and Jake always grinned a little at the difference between this red-skinned giant and the small women in his life.

Mrs. Dakers, who'd so memorably helped the judge condemn him to thirty days with Antonia, and Jenny, Paul's wife, were both on the petite side. The difference in size between husband and wife was even greater than that between himself and Antonia. For the first time Jake thought of this difference less as a joke than as a problem in maneuvering. How did a man kiss a woman who barely came up to his shoulder?

Paul wiped the back of his neck with a spotted handkerchief and drew it across his wide forehead under the thick blond hair. "Well, you were right, Marshal. You didn't need it but half an hour. Tell you what, I won't unhitch ol' Grifter here yet."

"Why not?" Jake asked, waiting for the joke.

"Well, taking a look at that woman, I'm gonna need this here wagon to bring your body back tonight, after she kills you. That's one angry gal." The blacksmith nodded toward the dusty figure of Antonia Castle striding down Main Street. Several women stood in front of Wilmot's General Store, talking fast and furious about the newcomer.

Jake asked, "Could you have Attila ready for me in about five minutes?"

"Right. Sure you won't need the wagon? Well, you don't weigh much. I can carry you to the undertaker's."

"I don't guess I'll be bothering Jeff tonight." Feinting a blow at the massive man's midsection, Jake walked out of the stable yard.

Where was that woman going? She walked past the

general store, past the dressmaker's, and past the Cottons' place. Watching the switch of her hips as she strode along, Jake almost didn't care. He felt willing to follow for quite a while.

When he realized, however, that she was heading back to the depot, Jake's mouth fixed in a hard line. Persistence in a man might be an admirable quality, even if his friends called him pigheaded. A woman, however, ought to pay attention when she's told something, especially when it's for her own good.

He quickened his steps to come up behind her. Reaching out, he brushed her back. Antonia stopped at that feather touch and turned, insolent patience in every line of her body. Jake tried to speak calmly. He put a hand on her shoulder in a fatherly way, as he told himself. He said, "There won't be another train until the one you missed today comes back down the line."

"The one I *missed* today?"

"So come on back home, Miss Castle. You can't live at the depot. Mr. Grapplin won't like it."

"Will you kindly take your hand off me? I'm not under arrest now, I believe." She knocked his hand away. "If you'll excuse me . . ." Antonia started for the station once again.

He stepped around her. "You are the stubbornest woman!" His grin held triumph. "Remember, I've got the cure for that." He started to reach for her, to lift her high in his arms once more, to feel her small but perfect body against his.

Antonia kicked him, her foot landing square against his tall leather boot. It jarred her toes but, she was glad to see, hurt him, too. His eyebrows went up and his mouth opened. She swung her hand around, aiming high for his smirking face. With speed that dazzled her, Jake caught her hand.

He held her arm out at full extension and swept his free arm about her waist, pulling her in so that no room existed between their bodies. She strove to break free, full of defiance, until she glanced up.

His eyes met hers with a strange intensity. He frowned, but she began to burn with a slow, devouring radiance. No other man ever looked at her that way, as though he would discover every secret she kept. Under his eyes, changeable as the sea, Antonia longed to reveal everything.

Then he released her and stepped back. Without thinking, Antonia raised her hand again and half slapped, half pushed his face, knocking his black hat to the ground.

"Don't you ever dare to touch me again," she said in a low voice, sincerity throbbing in each clear syllable.

Jake raised his hands in mock surrender. "Yes, ma'am. You're safe from me. But there ain't a train for two days."

Ignoring his feeble humor, Antonia stalked up the depot steps and into the station. The scrubbed pine boards gave out a fresh scent that survived even the smells of peanuts and perspiration that seemed ingrained into every waiting room across the Middle West.

She'd been in enough of them on this and other lecture circuits to last a lifetime. Culverton only made her more determined to ask Mrs. Lloyd Newstead to assign her to the committee that, rumor had it, was to petition Washington to overturn the revolting Comstock Act. Named for Postmaster General Anthony Comstock, whose campaign to suppress vice had censored the U.S. Mails, even prosecuting those who mailed medical textbooks, this act forced the Society to send out lecturers rather than pamphlets. Antonia felt she could now plead a case to make even that hardened gentleman weep.

Remembering how proscribed the mails were, Antonia approached the wizened stationmaster. As it was impossible to express her outrage fully in a letter—for her depiction of Jake Faraday alone was certain to fall foul of the law—she would do better under the forced restraint of a telegraph form.

The stationmaster peered out at her from between the bars of the ticket window, as a sad-faced monkey looked at the world from a cage. He nodded at her, the apple in his skinny neck bobbing up and down.

"Ain't no train for two days," he said. His voice, along with the poor grammar and scratchy tone, still held some flavor of Germany. "I can sell you a ticket now, if you want."

"No, thank you. I should like to send a telegram. *Two* telegrams. The first to Mrs. Lloyd Newstead, 505 Augustine Avenue, Chicago."

A good half hour later Antonia emerged from the station, replacing her small leather coin purse in the pocket of her skirt. She glanced toward the marshal, who sat in a rocking chair beside the station's main door, and wrinkled her nose as though some strong odor offended it. Tossing her head disdainfully, she set out, once more, for Jake's small house, trying to walk stiffly, for she did not want him ogling her from the rear.

Jake thoughtfully scratched behind his ear with one finger. Then, stretching, he stood up. "I want one of these," he said to himself, touching his toe to the rocker. He opened the glass-and-wooden door and went inside, saying, "Mr. Grapplin?"

"Mr. Marshal?"

"How's the wife?"

"Good, good. She make me a *kuchen* yesterday. Good as my mother's. You come over for a piece?"

"I think I had some at the wedding."

"Nice wedding. Reminds me of my own, when Maisie and I married." He grinned reminiscently, but Jake knew Mr. Grapplin didn't have that much married life to remember as he and his young bride were only wed a year ago. Maisie Shaw had been another of the town's seemingly endless supply of single schoolmistresses. They came, they saw, they married. And the town sent for another nice young girl to teach the kids.

Jake asked after Mr. Grapplin's new son. "What is he now, three months old? Doesn't time fly?"

"Fine boy I got. But he's four months old. Who could

know?'' Mr. Grapplin shined his ridged nails on his shirtfront and then passed his hand through his grizzled hair. "Fine boy,'' he repeated, grinning even more broadly.

"Uh, Mr. Grapplin, that young lady that was in here just now . . .''

"She is the one that gives a dirty speech yesterday.''

"Uh, that's right. What did she want?''

"To send telegrams.''

Jake leaned on the counter. "Who to?''

"I can't tell you that, Mr. Marshal. I got regulations.''

"Yeah. Well, all my best to Maisie and your son . . . what's his name then?''

"Hank. For Maisie's father.''

"Hank. I'll see him around, I'm sure. Bound to be a born chunk of hellfire.'' The father looked proud at the prospect. Jake touched two fingers to the brim of his somewhat dusty hat and turned to leave.

"Mr. Marshal!'' Grapplin pulled down the ticket window's blind. In a moment Jake heard the scratching of a key and the office door opened. The stationmaster beckoned.

He looked both ways as Jake came closer and then whispered, "I shouldn't say nothing, but one of that lady's telegrams went to another marshal.''

"*Another* marshal?''

"Yes. Marshal Fields. Chicago.''

Jake ran over in his mind a list of all the federal and state lawmen that he knew personally or had ever heard of. "I don't know any Marshal Fields. What did she—''

He caught back the rest of his question. The stationmaster had already half betrayed his trust and looked pretty nervous about it. "Thanks, Mr. Grapplin. I won't tell anybody that you said anything to me.''

"You are the marshal . . . you I maybe can tell. I will look in the regulations.'' He poked forward his hand, which Jake shook. "I say hello, Maisie.''

"Thanks.'' Jake left the station and walked up Main

Street, thinking. Though Antonia had denied any romance when the judge asked her about men, Jake knew all woman turned coy when asked a direct question of that kind. Most pretended to have more "friends" than less, but he'd never known any to refused admitting to at least one.

Of course, to admit to a gentleman friend might have subjected Antonia to a humiliating medical examination, instead of putting it off to a distant date, from which experience she might still be saved.

Jake stopped in the middle of the street and only just remembered to put down his lifted foot. The judge had said something about verifying Antonia's virginity by a qualified medical man. That meant Doc Partridge. Jake felt his face set in the kind of frown his mother used to say would stay forever.

The thought of any man putting his hands on her little golden figure made his heart turn to stone, but old Doc Partridge who never took a bath but when Miss Annie's girls insisted and who stayed drunk three days out of five . . . Jake began to regret not letting Antonia escape by train this afternoon. Well, there was another on Monday. He'd see her aboard it himself, Judge Cotton or no Judge Cotton.

He became aware that someone called his name. Blinking, Jake looked around and realized he'd been standing in the middle of the street for heaven knew how long.

Dakers stood in the shade of his livery stable and said, "Man, I thought you had taken a fit standing out there. Attila's ready, if you want to take him."

The blacksmith was so big that Jake almost overlooked his horse. Attila, though black as the heart of the Hun, had a patient, almost placid nature. Jake had found, in the course of his duty, that speed could not compare with a steady animal that could work for hours and travel long distances without rest, no matter how slowly. Attila might not win many races, but like his namesake, he'd travel from the steppes of Russia to the banks of the Danube, given time.

Jake occupied the journey home with thinking out a story to explain his mount's unusual name, should Antonia hear it and wonder. Every time Antonia showed him what an unschooled farmhand she thought him, Jake felt like laughing up his sleeve. If she only knew . . .

Antonia came back to Jake's house to find Mrs. Cotton sitting at the small wooden table in the kitchen. A basket, covered with a checked cloth, sat on the table in front of her. The dishes had been done and the room redd-up and scrubbed down.

"Thank you," Antonia said, from the depths of her heart.

Mrs. Cotton smiled and put her worn leather Bible away in her pocket. "Least I could do. There's man-neat and there's woman-neat, and for someone that ain't used to man-neat, it can wear you down. Now you can start fresh, Miss Castle, seeing what that old man of mine has let you in for."

"I can't say that I'm pleased with the judge's decision. . . ."

"No, now why should you be? Ain't it a man all over, though? I been saying for I don't know how long that a man like Jake Faraday shouldn't stay all alone . . . not when there's women hungry for a husband."

Antonia sniffed. "Who'd want to marry him?"

"Half the single girls in the state, believe me. Why, if I didn't have the judge, who's to say I wouldn't try for the marshal myself? I mayn't be the best-looking gal in the West, but I'm a good cook, if I do say so myself."

Wishing she dared kiss Mrs. Cotton's cheek, Antonia patted the older woman's hand and said, "I think you're one of the most beautiful women I've ever seen."

"You're a liar, but I thank you. I won't say the judge don't agree with you." Mrs. Cotton primped the collar of her plain brown dress.

"But dang that old man anyway! He just can't bear to

see nothin' going to waste. He's always poking in my kitchen, saying can't we save this bit of gravy, or 'lowing how his mother could of made three meals from a moldy heel of bread and two flakes of turnip! Why, you got to see that the notion of a full-grown man that ain't married just started worryin' and nigglin' at the judge until he got to do something with him or bust!''

"But why me? Why . . . ?" She gestured toward the kitchen and, by extension, the whole house and the man who owned it.

"Jake Faraday won't look at no other girl in this town. Why, Mrs. Lucas even brought out her sister's gal all that way from Sterling, Arkansas, and Jake wouldn't hardly say hello. Just as well . . . turns out she had a fella already. It goes to show, though, don't it, what the judge is up against?"

"I'm afraid I still don't understand why the judge should choose me to try to change the marshal's mind about women. *I* certainly don't want to marry him!"

"As for choosing you, I guess you ain't looked in your glass much. I reckon Judge Cotton thinks that if Jake has a good-lookin' gal like you around, cooking for him, making eyes at him, plumping up his pillows, he might get to where he likes it. And then Mary Lou, or one of the other gals, can stop sighing and nab him. You can git on back to Chicago not a hair the worse for it, and it'd be the makin' of the marshal. Man shouldn't live by his lonesome. Ain't natural."

Mrs. Cotton stood up. "I put you up some odds and ends, seeing as you've hardly had the time to find your feet. That man didn't have nothing in the house but beans and bread. And coffee. You never saw such a man for coffee."

"Can't you stay? I know the marshal would want to thank you, too, and . . . I . . ."

Patting her shoulder, Mrs. Cotton said, "Don't you worry 'bout Jake. He's just as scared of you as you are of him. It's like havin' a new dog in the house, 'cept Jake won't pee on your rosebushes. 'Least, I don't think he will.''

As much as she wanted to, Antonia couldn't keep Mrs. Cotton. After the door had shut behind the older woman, Antonia sat and listened to the silence. Insects, out in the woods, made noises as though they were learning to imitate crickets, inexpertly and all together.

Out the window she saw that the light had deepened into dusk, though it would not be dark for some time yet. Antonia liked having a good-sized window in the kitchen, and felt she would have liked this little house on the edge of the woods, if Jake had not come with the building.

Maybe he'd gone to the saloon and would come back roaring drunk. Even if he just sat and gambled, he might not be back for hours, longer if one of the girls at the bar had taken his fancy. Antonia struggled to dismiss this idea, and the image of herself, dressed in feathers and silk, taking Jake Faraday by the hand up rickety stairs.

What difference did it make to her where Jake Faraday spent his evenings? With any luck, a band of desperadoes needed rounding up and he'd spend the entire month in the desolate wilderness. But Antonia could only then imagine him lying out there somewhere, his chin pointing at the sky, after meeting an outlaw with faster hands than himself. She preferred the image of him in a darkened bedroom, slipping off his gun belt.

She flung herself out of her seat and went into the living room. Wasn't there a book or a magazine to take her mind off these bizarre images? She looked for the newspapers Jake had picked up, but he'd tidied them away too well. Even housecleaning failed as entertainment, for Mrs. Cotton had busied herself in this room as well as in the kitchen.

When she'd exhausted all her options, and was thinking of going to sleep to pass the time, she heard slow-clopping hooves in the yard. Peeking out past the plain muslin curtains, Antonia saw Jake dismounting

from a black horse. He led the animal away and Antonia
followed him, looking out each window as he passed
within its range. His shoulders were broad, his back
straight, his waist slim, and he possessed a remarkably
compact . . . Antonia covered her eyes a moment to
regain her sanity.

Around the side of the house was a shed of white-
washed boards. Jake led his horse in there. Antonia kept
watch. A long time went by before he emerged. Hastily
Antonia arranged herself on the sofa, leaning her forehead on the fingers of her right hand, as though she were
deep in thought.

"Why don't you light a lamp? Darker than the armpit
of hell in here." A moment later a match flared and a
kerosene lamp flickered into life.

Antonia looked up at him, startled, though she'd heard
him coming in. Had it really been less than an hour ago
that she'd brawled with him in the open street? She
wanted very much to apologize, but she didn't quite
know what to say. "Um . . . Mrs. Cotton dropped by a
basket for us."

"She's a good woman." Did she know that the
lamplight brought out a certain sparkle in the golden
floss of her hair, even while her eyes grew brilliant in the
sudden light? He told himself she did know and would
not scruple to call attention to her hair with some little
gesture. Taking off his coat and hat, he hung them on a
peg driven into the wall.

"Yes. I . . . I like her very much."

"Even though she's from Culverton?"

"I don't hate everything about Culverton. I don't hate
anything about it. My mother told me I should never hate
anything or anyone."

"Not even the men that tore your clothes all to flinders
yesterday?" He remembered how she looked, wearing
nothing much beyond knickers but still full of fight and
vinegar. Jake turned away from the light as though to
cough, hiding a smile.

"I hope I shan't ever meet them again, but if I did, I should try to conduct myself as a Christian woman and forgive them." Antonia fought to keep her voice level, but the memory of those horrible moments when she was at the mercy of the rabble came back as the worst experience of her life.

Jake heard the quaver and mentally kicked himself. He came and sat beside her on the sofa. She drew her shoulders up straight and half turned to face him. "Most of 'em were nothing but cowpokes and drifters. They'd heard about the Professor coming into town and just came in for the fun. Miss Annie doesn't let any old cowboy into her place and the Professor's girls . . . they don't just dance."

"I know. Remember, we shared living quarters, briefly."

Her smile had returned, if still a bit tremulous. "I'm kind of sorry now that I locked you up . . ." he began, starting to make a joke of it.

"No sorrier than I," Antonia said, standing up. "We should eat and then I, for one, am dreadfully tired."

"Suits me." For the first time Antonia saw Jake unbutton the top button of his shirt after undoing the black stock tie he wore, its edge just showing under his collar. She felt she should reprove him for this informality, but her mouth had gone too dry to form words. When he reached down to untie the string that held his holster against his leg and then put his hands to the tongue of his gun belt, Antonia became very much interested in the stitching of her sleeve.

As though by common consent, they said little during their meal of salt pork and biscuits. After supper, he stretched and yawned. "Well, it's been a busy day. I don't often round up vicious criminals anymore."

"Did you ever?" Antonia did do the dishes tonight, but only because she couldn't bear the thought of Mrs. Cotton's hard work being ruined.

Jake smiled. "Ever hear of the Waterson gang?"

"No. Are you in the mood to boast? I doubt I'll be impressed, but go ahead."

"You are the most contrary woman! I joined the Confederate army when I was sixteen, 'cause they were runnin' short of men by then. After that, I came west and joined up with the cavalry. After a high old time fighting the Indians, I joined the federal marshals. While chasing a group of horse thieves out of Kansas, I passed through Culverton and I liked it. They didn't have law here then. I changed that! As a matter of fact, I took care of the folks that were burnin' and panickin' this town about once a week. Impressed?"

Despite herself, Antonia was. But she tossed her head and said, "How interesting," in a tone that made a lie of her words.

In a disgusted tone, Jake said, "I'm going to bed. Keep the lamp burning in here, in case you've got to go out back in the night."

"Thank you," she said freezingly.

"You're welcome." He was ashamed of himself for boasting. He'd never done anything like it before, but the cold disinterest in her eyes had been a challenge like one he'd never met. Jake knew he'd wanted to see her coo with admiration for his exploits. Other women were always trying to get him to confide in them, asking flirty questions to draw him out and looking disappointed when he remained reserved.

Antonia sat on the sofa again, waiting for his noises of preparing for bed to cease. She heard both boots hit the floor and several sighs, along with one or two growls that sounded like muffled comments. Until she felt certain he was asleep, she did not want to make a single move toward getting ready for sleep herself. How could she possibly disrobe knowing he lay awake, perhaps naked, on the other side of a thin door?

Only then did she notice that she had no bedding. She couldn't ask him for any, but neither could she sleep on the sofa in the middle of the room without some covering. What if he should walk through and see her in her nightgown? True, he'd already seen a great deal of her person that she'd never shown to another living human. However, the difference between daytime attire and nightclothing was vaster than the mere change might at first account for.

Antonia mentally reviewed the clothing in her valises with an eye toward improvisation. She had no voluminous crinoline skirts, no fur-lined opera cloaks, or even any winter mantles. As she wished for the wardrobe she'd left in Chicago, the door to Jake's bedroom opened a crack.

She saw one gray-green eye. The door closed for an instant, then reopened. A brown, muscular arm appeared, flung a dark gray blanket into the living room, and vanished.

Chapter 5

Compared with the mattress at the jail, the old sofa seemed like a bed from an Arabian fantasy. Yet Antonia could not sleep. She would doze, think she heard a noise from Jake's room, and bolt awake.

Sometimes she even dreamed that Jake came out. Once, he stood beside the edge of the sofa, looking down at her with the same intense gaze that had so shaken her in the street. Antonia regretted waking from that dream.

She shifted onto her side, reclaiming the bolster that had slipped from beneath her head. All she usually had to do was lie still, think deep, slow thoughts, and sleep gathered her in. Her mind now, however, raced with thoughts of Jake Faraday. He stood between her and her rest, and she resented him for it.

Sitting up, she glared at the closed door between them. *Now* she could hear his voice, a low rumble like distant thunder. Did he talk in his sleep? Antonia suspected that she was as much on his mind as he was on hers. If she crept to the door and listened, would she hear her own name muttered on a sleeping sigh? And if she could hear him now, might he have heard when she'd awakened with a whispered ''Jake''?

Antonia blushed in the darkness as she lay down once more. It stood to reason that a person wasn't responsible for what happened in her dreams.

Then the inner door did open and Jake strode into the

living room. Other than that he wore clothes, he looked precisely the same as in her dream. She sprang up, clutching her blanket to her chest. "What . . . !"

"Don't get het up, Miss Castle. I don't have time to dally with you now. There's a fire over at the livery stable and I've got to go. Can't you hear the rifles?" He lifted his hat and coat down and put them on.

"When will you be back?"

"When the fire's out." He left. She heard him call, "Be with you in a minute, Bob. Let me get saddled up." In no time at all the sound of hooves rumbled away.

A fire? She could hear far-off shots now, two at a time and then a pause. Rising from the sofa, she wrapped the blanket more securely about her, reinforcing the yards of white cotton batiste that made up her summer nightgown. She drew back the curtains in the living-room window. The sky in the direction of Culverton was dark, for there were no gas streetlamps here to burn through the night.

It must be a small fire, Antonia thought. Despite that, she began to dress in the slightly bedraggled clothes she'd worn all day. As she pinned on her hat she wondered that it had been only a single day since she'd put on this brightly checked suit at the jail.

Once outside, she became aware that birds talked and fluttered in the trees though the dark had not yet lifted. For that matter, it couldn't be much past midnight. Antonia told herself that no possible reason existed for her to walk all the way back to Culverton. No one needed her there. The sensible thing to do would be to go back to sleep. She began walking.

The light of the new moon scarcely illuminated her path, but the dusty road seemed to shine of its own. In the dark the country seemed as large and as lonely as she'd imagined it to be this afternoon. The fields to either side were waving in the wind, as though troubled by a giant hand.

At one point she heard a rustle in the anonymous grayness beside the road and paused, petrified, while a black-masked creature peered out at her. The raccoon decided, apparently, that she was neither edible nor interesting and turned its wide, hunched back to her. Antonia tiptoed past and ran on until a stitch ate at her side.

As she came closer to town the smell of smoke surrounded her. A dull orange glow hovering in the sky and a massed confusion led her to the stables. The heart of the fire seemed to be around to the rear. Antonia stood and watched the efforts of the citizens, feeling out of place and useless.

A bucket brigade had formed, the men splashing and cursing as they threw the heavy buckets from hand to hand. Women and children held brooms and dripping sacks, leaping upon any falling spark. Two children rushed past her, carrying a pail of sand and shovels. Antonia noticed their quick-pattering feet were bare.

Someone touched her on the shoulder. She turned to see Judge Cotton standing beside her. He'd left off his black silk coat, but his tall hat still reposed upon his bald head. ''I told 'em we shoulda bought that hand pump the last time the salesman come through, but no . . . they wanted a city hall to hold their heads up. Fat lot of good it'll do 'em if it burns.''

He spat in the direction of the fire. ''At least Wilmot stocked extra of them fire grenades, though he only did that after he run through an ordinance that every house-hold had to have 'em.''

''What can I do, Judge?''

''Get yerself a wet gunnysack and beat out anything that looks like fire. We've got to save the stables—the smithy's burning now and nothing to be done.''

''I suppose they've already taken the animals out?''

''Jake and Paul are doing that now.''

No sooner had the judge spoken than a cry went up. ''The roof's on fire!''

Reflexively everyone looked up. A demon of fire danced upon the ridgepole. Already the dry shingles

hissed and crackled, the resin whining a song of defeat.
Antonia could, in just this single moment, see the fire
spread, devouring the roof.

"Damnation!" the judge said softly. "We don't have
a ladder that tall. The stable's a goner. I better tell the
boys to hurry them hosses."

He started away toward the entrance of the barn.
Antonia followed, quivering with a sudden consuming
fear. Fear for the man she disliked more than any she'd
ever met.

A tormented scream tore the night, followed at once
by another and another in an appalling chorus. Antonia
froze for an instant, then forced her feet onward. She'd
heard frightened horses before, as a girl, and knew with
what violence they could act against the very people
trying to save them. There had been a flood once, in
Minnaqua. . . .

The large double doors of the stable stood open. The
judge walked in, calling, "Jake? Paul?"

"Over here!"

Bits of the burning roof had tumbled into the interior.
Antonia saw hay burning, turning itself to brief gold, as
though a devilish miller's daughter sat and spun. Bits of
blue glass were a danger on the floor while flames licked
at the interior supports, but had not yet taken a firm hold.

Above the increasing roar, the screams of the horses
continued. A pair of hooves lashed out and Antonia
jumped for the center of the stable where the fires were
the hottest. A flame reached for her long skirt. She
gathered the fabric in and went to stand beside the judge.

"Don't you boys have any better sense . . . " the
judge began until he saw what had kept them.

"Thank God," Jake said, looking around. "I didn't
dare leave him to get help."

The huge frame of the blacksmith lay spread-eagled
on the floor. Fast-welling blood saturated the bandanna
Jake pressed to Paul Dakers's shoulder. He also had a
large abrasion on his forehead and burned holes in his

clothing. The man groaned, unconscious but evidently in pain.

"What happened here?" Judge Cotton demanded.

"We were getting a horse out when I turned and saw Paul had collapsed. Everything was on fire around him, so I think some of the roof fell on him. Go get some help, Judge. I can't carry him alone and I can't leave him."

Antonia dropped to knees beside the fallen giant, putting her fingers over the bandanna. "I'll hold that. Judge, you get help. Jake, you start saving those horses!"

"What? What the devil are you . . . ?" Jake sputtered, obviously seeing her for the first time.

"Never mind." She pushed his hand away and placed her hand firmly over the sodden cloth, wincing at the heat of the blood between her fingers.

"Judge . . ." She looked over her shoulder. The judge already picked his way over the burning debris that now littered every inch of the center floor. She smiled grimly. At least one man here knew how to obey.

Some flaming shingles dropped near her. Though she hissed through her teeth, she instinctively leaned over the prostrate blacksmith to protect him.

"Get out of here!" Jake demanded, forcing her chin up with his reddened fingers.

"The horses!" she yelled back, meeting his eyes steadily. "They'll go mad!"

She saw him search the heavens for an answer. He must have seen only the burning rafters. He leaned forward and, grindingly hard, crushed her lips with his for a single instant. Then Jake leaped up and vanished into the smoke and flame.

Dumbfounded, Antonia stared after him, her free fingers pressed to her mouth. There'd been no reason for him to kiss her that she could see. More debris showered down around her and she put his kiss out of her mind, to mull over later.

She coughed as her eyes began to water. With her free hand she tamped out the sparks that fell ever more thickly on her patient. A cinder burned her cheek and she wiped it away. It seemed twice an eternity before anyone came to help her.

The men that came had sopping cloths tied around their heads, protecting their mouths and noses. The judge, whom she knew by his hat, handed one to her. She held the blessed cool moistness to her face, but kept the pressure on the big man's wound, even as they lifted him up.

"Where's Jake?" she shouted, but the judge only shook his head. A new fear, worse than fire, leaped up. Had she sent the marshal to his doom?

Running along with the men, she caught swift sights of the burning interior, images she'd never forget. A swirling vortex of fire consuming a stall, a wagon all brilliant in fire like a setpiece at the Fourth of July, and a burning rake, the wooden tines twisting like a devil's claw, flashed past her.

Outside, in the relative quiet of sheer human pandemonium, Antonia asked the judge again, "Where's Jake? Is he safe?"

"I haven't seen him since I left the stable, honey. Look out now, here's Doc Partridge."

A scruffy little man came up, smelling strongly of alcohol. Antonia had had nothing but the reek of fire and smoke in her nostrils so long that even whiskey was welcome. The doctor lifted off Paul's bandanna and whistled.

"Lookit this, Judge. He's got a nail in here. Right in the shoulder."

"A nail?" one of the bearers said in a Southern accent.

"Yup. Must of fallen off the roof. Pity it wasn't hot—would of cauterized the veins as it went in and there wouldn't be all this blood. 'Scuse me, miss," he said, reaching back for his bag. "Reminds me of the war—them Rebs'd shoot just about anything at us that'd fit in the muzzle of a gun."

Antonia turned away, feeling sick, while the bearer said, "I sure do remember that. Why, my cousin, what was in supply, paid fifty cents for a barrel o' rusty nails when we run out o' bullets. Jist as good as a minié ball."

How could men be so callous? Despite the insensitivity of the sex, Antonia knew she'd give a great deal for a sight of Jake. His kiss hadn't meant anything, she knew, being an expression of general frustration and perhaps of anxiety. If nothing else, she wanted him to be alive so she could tell him she understood that. She did not want to think of the chances that he might still be in the flaming stable.

The building was nothing now but a frame. The walls and roof were only resemblances sketched on sheets of fire. Antonia stood and watched that roaring maelstrom, realizing nothing could have lived through it.

She heard a shriek, louder than the fire, less unearthly than the screams of horses. "Paul! Paul!"

A slight figure in a filthy yellow dress ran toward the huddled group of men. Antonia stepped out and caught the girl. She recognized Jenny, who had given Evelyn her veil, though terror distorted her face.

"Wait," she said, holding on to the thin shoulders. "Wait until the doctor is finished with him."

"Doctor?" The staring eyes blinked. She ceased struggling against Antonia's gentle grasp. "He's not . . . dead?"

"No," Antonia said, shaking her head, though she could not be certain of what had happened in the last few minutes. "No, he's not."

Jenny stared at her a moment then glanced once more toward the prone figure of her husband, visible between the legs of the men who'd carried him out. Paul's right arm, the strength of it showing through the rents in the fabric, hit out at the frail doctor. Doc Partridge staggered back.

Wiping his lips, he said, "Hold him down, can't you?"

"He is alive," Jenny whispered, and then began to cry. Antonia patted her shoulder, wishing she'd remembered her handkerchief.

The stable collapsed inward with the eerie rumble of heat lightning. Sparks fountained high and poured down like burning rain. Antonia and Jenny ducked involuntarily, like everyone else.

The judge shouted, "Get to them sparks, else the whole town'll go!" The children raced about, slapping at cinders, while their mothers shoveled sand and the men kept the bucket brigade moving, despite aching backs and sore arms.

When Doc Partridge stood up, he said, "Head like the *Monitor*—steel plate all the way." Turning, he saw Jenny, still standing in the shelter of Antonia's arm. "You can come up to him now, child. He'll do for a while, but don't you let him use that right arm. He won't be swinging no hammers till that heals up, I can tell you. Who said they'd got a bottle?"

Somebody handed him a flask while Jenny crept up to her husband as if he'd been a sleeping child. Her trembling fingers went out to brush the lock of blond hair from his bruised brow.

Fumbling, Paul caught her hand and studied it. "Don't . . . don't cry now, sweetie. Ain't nothing to cry for."

Antonia turned away, her own eyes wet. Then they opened wide in surprise. Standing between her and the glowing ruin that was once Dakers's Livery, a female figure, all in deepest black, stood like an image from a Grecian tragedy. Mrs. Dakers the elder advanced, ignoring the hail of cinders that still dropped around her.

Antonia advanced to assure Mrs. Dakers of her son's safety. In her heart, however, she imagined that she now knew the reason Jenny Dakers seemed so spiritless. She herself would think twice before marrying any man who brought with him such a mother.

"The doctor has just seen Paul, Mrs. Dakers. He's going to be all right, if laid up for a time."

The other woman didn't even look at her. "It is the wrath and judgment of our Lord. Beware lest it befall you also."

Antonia could only stare after her. She watched as Mrs. Dakers went up to her son and daughter-in-law. Jenny started back, relinquishing her hold on her husband's hand. As though in answer to the look Mrs. Dakers directed at her, Jenny wiped away the tears that had driven clean trails through the grime on her cheeks.

Slowly, in stages, Paul Dakers got to his feet. Supported by the small frame of his mother, and followed by his wife, the blacksmith limped away without glancing back at the destruction of his business.

"Now,"said the doctor from close at hand. "All we can do is hope and pray it don't turn to lockjaw, or that feller will die. I seen it before—it's nothing too pretty." Doc Partridge guzzled again, for a long time, at the bottle.

Antonia had seen it, too, in the slums of Chicago. She began to pray at once, even as she searched for a wet sack to do her part at beating out the embers.

As she passed the bucket brigade, now throwing water directly on the smoldering wreck, her eyes were drawn to a stalwart figure at the front of the line. Her prayers took a new and thankful direction.

Jake's hat and coat were gone. A soaking bandanna showed up brightly against his tanned face and dark hair. Antonia watched him swing buckets along until he became aware of her observation. When it was possible to step out, he did and came toward her.

"I thought you were dead," she said at once.

"Well, that would have been one solution to your problem, Miss Castle," he answered, tugging down the cloth to show a grinning mouth.

How like him to remind her of that now! In another instant she would have forgotten herself completely and flung herself into his arms. She replied coolly, "You're right. I really should be sorry to see you."

"Meaning you're not sorry?"

"I wouldn't wish that"—she nodded toward the remains of the stable—"on anyone."

"Not even your worst enemy." He shrugged at that. "I see Dakers made it. He owes you his life."

"You were there first. He . . . he had a nail in him, That doctor said it may turn into lockjaw."

Jake touched her arm by the elbow. "Blacksmiths are immune to that."

"Are they?"

"Yeah," he said. "Comes from working around horses all the time." He hurried into another subject, before she realized that a dumb-as-dirt marshal knew a word like "immune." "By the way, in case you're still interested, all the horses are safe. They're tied up behind the church and, 'cept for a little burn or two, seem fine. What about you?"

"Me? There's nothing wrong with me. Except that my dress may never be the same. I smell like smoked fish."

Jake lifted his hand and brushed his thumb over her cheek. "Looks like you took a little burn yourself. Culverton's been right hard on your hide, Miss Castle. First tomatoes, now this."

The touch of his hand, in even so careless a gesture, and the tenderness running beneath his flippant words upset Antonia's animosity. She felt a strong yearning to hold on to his hand, to raise it, dirty though it was, to her lips. The depth of this feeling astonished her, so she took immediate refuge in attack.

"You'd better stop slacking off. I have work to do myself."

He grinned. "The fire's all but out, Miss Castle. No reason for you to wait around."

"I won't, then, as I'm not welcome." She pushed her hair, which had slipped from beneath her hat, out of her face and turned smartly about. Feeling his eyes on her back, she marched, though her knees began to tremble with the reaction from her nearness to danger in the stable. Or was it relief at Jake's safety that made her interior feel so weak?

She heard him call her back. It would be impolite to pretend not to hear. Antonia waited for him to come to her. With a ripple of unseemly excitement, the hope that he might kiss her a second time flashed through her. "What is it now?"

"Miss . . . Antonia," he said, giving her a warm smile. "I didn't tell you how much I admire your courage. It was brave of you to stay with Dakers. Not many men would have done that, not with a roof dropping fire all around."

Antonia searched his face. Was he joking? His expression struck her as being somehow less brash and more kind than before. Perhaps he did admire her, a little. Suddenly shy, she murmured, "It was the right thing to do."

"Most people wouldn't have done it. You can be sure the town's going to be grateful, as soon as I tell 'em about it."

"No, don't do that!"

"But it was great!" He seemed to be more enthusiastic as he thought about it, almost boyish. "They'll be lining up to talk to you . . . and—"

"I didn't do it for their gratitude. I don't want their gratitude. All I want is to leave this town." And yet that wasn't precisely true anymore. What she wanted scared her.

"You are the most peculiar woman. . . . All right, I won't tell them. I don't know if the judge or the other men will keep quiet—probably not—but I won't say a word."

"Thank you." She wanted to leave but at the same time longed to stay, gazing into the profound ocean of his eyes. Someone called to him and he glanced away. The spell broke.

By the time she reached Jake's house, Antonia was so tired she felt as though her head floated two feet above her body. She couldn't stand the way she smelled and dared not guess at how ghastly she must look. To go inside and change into her nightgown while in this condition would ruin it.

Too exhausted to figure out what primitive arrangements Jake had for bathing—unless he merely went to the bathhouse in town once a month—she sank down on the steps and waited for him to come home.

With a pang in his heart that he didn't dare examine, Jake saw her sleeping against the door when he came up the lane from the main road. He rode Attila and had two other horses on leading reins. As the livery stable was a complete loss, Jake had agreed to give shelter to two horses, as had several other farmers with the room. Attila never minded company.

Jake turned all three horses out into the fenced field behind the house. Immediately the two livery horses went down to the trough to drink. Green grass, clean water, and fresh cool air were the best antidotes to the hellish hours behind them.

Jake himself felt like sleeping outside, but even that wouldn't have let him escape the reek of smoke that clung to every inch of his body. He wanted a good scrub in the old wooden half barrel that did him service as a bath. It wasn't until he came around the front of the house to waken Antonia that he remembered he now had to share.

Gently he touched her bent back with a cautious forefinger. Hearing her contented sigh, he began to massage her shoulders. She'd cuddled against the door, so he found it easy to rub her back all the way from her rounded shoulders to her waist. He now knew with certainty that she did not, at least for the moment, wear a corset.

Jake could feel the strain slipping from her body as she made small sounds of pleasure. With each soft moan, however, a certain strain increased in his own body. It was either stop or continue in another way. What blissful whimpers, he wondered, would she make then?

When he lifted his hands away, Antonia gave him an affronted glance over her shoulder. "Don't stop," she said. Then she seemed to discover who had been giving her such delight, and she stuttered, "Oh . . . I . . . that is . . . Thank you."

She straightened up and Jake recognized that the austere do-gooder had returned. "My pleasure, ma'am," he said, giving her the slow sassy grin that the ladies seemed to like the best.

"Really, I . . . it was very good of you."

His palms still tingled from their contact with the contours of her back. Hastily he drove both hands deep into his pockets. "I guess you're about ready for sleep."

"I'd like a bath first, if you have one."

Jake felt tempted to tell her he usually bathed in the horse trough, but as he didn't want to prove it, he said, "I'll go fill the tub for you. It'll be cold. Do you mind?"

"Right now the colder the better. I thought I'd never be cold again for a few moments tonight." She returned his grin and then looked around, at a loss. "Er . . . ?"

He led the way around the back of the house. The half barrel sat beneath a lean-to, open on three sides to the air. A bush grew between the house and the tub for privacy. "Here?"

Nodding, Jake studied her face by starlight. He saw her lips tighten and then she said, "I'll help you fill it up."

After pacing behind the bush and peering about often to be certain that Jake could not see her, she could not bear for another second the itchy desire to be rid of these garments. She dropped her skirt and petticoats, kicking away the reeking bundle, and put her hands to the fastenings of her bodice. With a last glance around she pulled that off, too.

She'd never been this close to naked under the open

sky before. Filled with a strange, half-shameful excitement, Antonia seriously considered removing the single
piece of clothing between herself and the night. Her
combinations, drawers and knickers made into one,
clung to her almost as unbearably as her tailor-made
bodice.

"Are you all right out there?" Jake called.

"Yes, yes!" she said, panicking. The fantasy of
wearing only her skin into the tub fled. Still covered from
shoulders to knees in white cotton, Antonia stepped up
onto the low stool Jake had thoughtfully provided.

As she slipped her overheated body into the water,
Antonia half expected to see clouds of steam rise. She'd
been very hesitant about the still depths of the barrel, for
she'd slipped her hand secretly into one of the buckets
and had been stunned by the chill that struck her fingers.
Now, though she gasped and shivered, the coldness
thrilled her.

She sat on the slick bottom of the barrel, the water
lapping at her chin. Several times she dunked her face,
her skin tightening. Shaking off the droplets, she reached
up and pulled the last surviving pins from her hair. She
dipped her head back to wash the long blond mass.

As she soaped it she thought how Mrs. Lloyd Newstead decreed that no unmarried woman should wash her
hair at night, for fear of catching a chill on her internal
organs. Antonia giggled at the thought of how that stern
woman would look if she could but see her now.

"You going to stay out there all night?" Jake called.
She could hear his impatience. Remembering how she
had yearned to be cool and clean, she rinsed regretfully
and stood up. Splashing the foam from her bodice, she
was glad to see that her combinations were now as clean
as the rest of her.

Standing on the stool, she rubbed down her body with
the towel he'd given her. She paused, struck by a
dreadful thought. Not being used to these primitive
conditions, she did not think to plan ahead. She had not

gone into the house since coming back from town. Jake had brought her the towel. How was she to return to the house?

Her wrapper and nightgown were still in the living room, perhaps even in plain view! She would simply call to him and have him bring her those things, although they'd become just as smoky as the clothes she'd shed at his touch. As she shivered in the playful breeze she hated the thought of ever smelling like that again. Even this towel, which he'd barely handled, had still a faint odor. Besides, no proper young lady could ask a man to touch her night attire.

"Marshal?" she called.

The backdoor opened. "What is it, Miss Castle?"

"I wonder if you would mind doing me a small favor?"

"Not at all. I'd even do you a large one, if you want."

"Thank you. Would you mind coming out here?" She heard his feet come rapidly down the steps. Watching him through the leaves, she said quickly, "That's far enough! Now, if you wouldn't mind, close your eyes."

His steps slowed, but he still came closer. "I'm sorry—what did you say?"

"I said—stop!" He halted at the high note, his slow smile beginning to appear. "Now close your eyes."

"Close my eyes? Why?"

Oh, but he was no gentleman! "Isn't it enough that I ask you to?"

"Well, I don't know. You could try saying please, but in my business, it's not so good for a lawman to shut his eyes. Kind of puts him at a disadvantage."

"I'm not going to shoot you, Marshal, although I'd like to."

"I couldn't hear that, Miss Castle," he said, coming closer. In another few steps he'd be able to look right over the bush, all that protected her modesty. Wet cotton did not hide very much, she realized.

"Please, Marshal!" She stepped off the stool and onto

the fresh hay he'd spread around the barrel. "Please shut your eyes!"

Obediently he turned his back. "They're closed, Miss Castle. I've got to trust you, I guess, not to shoot me in the back."

"And I, Marshal, trust you won't open your eyes," she said, stealing out from her shelter. Despite the stones and twigs that rolled beneath her feet, she scurried across the yard.

"Does that mean there's something to see?" He began to turn. Antonia yelped "No!" and dashed up the few steps to the safety of the kitchen. Maddeningly his quiet deliberate chuckle followed her. In a moment she heard a gurgle of running water as he drained the barrel.

During his bath, Antonia had plenty of time to dry her hair. Completely covered by her nightgown, she sat on the sofa, rubbing her hair with a towel. Jake's whistling rendition of "Brown-eyed Sal" kept her company. When it ceased, she lay down beneath her solitary blanket and pretended to be asleep.

The backdoor creaked open and closed. She felt his step shake the floorboards. He seemed to be moving slowly, almost hesitantly. Antonia toyed with the idea of sitting up and shouting "Boo!" if only to see the self-possessed marshal jump.

Glancing up under her lashes, she saw Jake tiptoeing through the room, his boots held high in one hand. He flicked quick looks at her, as though to be certain she really slept. Antonia herself found it prudent to feign sleep, for it gave her the chance to study Jake.

He wore only a towel about his hips, the free ends loosely grasped in his left hand. For the rest, all of his length and breadth was visible. The illustrations she'd studied while training to be a lecturer had left out a great deal!

Jake was pure strength, all muscle, tanned skin, and clean hair. Dark curls spread across his chest, almost exactly where her hands would rest if she were to try to

fend off his kisses. She could almost feel how her hands
would move through that richness, exploring the firm
planes of his torso. From the dip between the well-
defined muscles of his chest, a long narrow strip of the
same hair ran over his flat stomach to the edge of the towel.
His ribs and back were smooth. Antonia felt her cheeks
heating as she wondered at what point exactly did that
provocative strip become mixed with the hair on Jake's
long legs.

Antonia could hardly lie still while Jake crossed the
room to step into his own bedroom. His back showed a
deep channel and she could guess at the strength of his
buttocks from the glimpses she'd had while he was still
wearing his pants. She almost wished he'd taken away
his towel before closing his door. When the door had
shut behind him, Antonia sighed heavily.

What a prurient turn of mind she'd suddenly developed! As a rule she would take no interest at all in what
Marshal Faraday carried beneath his towel. That she was
more than interested—one might even say agog—
indicated a serious deterioration of her moral fiber.

Antonia well remembered the eminent European doctor that Mrs. Lloyd Newstead had invited to address the
Society one spring evening last year. Though she'd
found him patronizing on meeting him personally, the
results of a study he'd undertaken had seemed conclusive. The study had proven that only women of the
lowest possible character found any pleasure in looking
at provocative pictures, excepting fine art, which a
woman of the noblest nature could enjoy.

Antonia tried to concentrate on cultural images to
calm her fevered mind. The Apollo Belvedere, for
instance, a glorious god with a woven chlamys draped
around his neck. Antonia passed her hand over her face,
to wipe away Jake's face on Apollo's figure.

Paintings might be safer. She imagined *The Oath of
the Horatii*, as painted by David just before the French
Revolution. Three brave young men, swearing before

their father on their swords, while wearing what amounted to towels, essentially.

Antonia sat up. She might as well simply paint *Naked Cowboy* by Antonia Castle as pretend anymore. She liked what she'd seen of Jake's person and faced the ridiculousness of pretending she didn't.

She snapped her fingers in the air. *So there, Professor Jouffroy.* She slept fairly well after that.

Chapter 6

The music wove its way into her dreams. She awoke with a smile, which became puzzled when she found that the melody remained, though the dream had passed. She'd been dancing. . . .

Antonia threw off her blanket and stood up, determined to find the violin that played this enchanting song. Already the music came more softly as though it were fading away. It seemed to be coming from the rear of the house, from the outside.

Antonia opened the kitchen door and walked out onto the top step, catching a quick, deep breath of the open air that almost shimmered with music. The gentle strains, of no style she'd ever heard before, whether at a symphony or an opera, held a tender, yet uncivilized magic. She could imagine some savage mother crooning this as a lullaby to her child. Antonia listened, enraptured as the unseen musician played on.

Then, in the middle of a phrase, the music broke off. Antonia heard a rustle in the woods, much like that of the raccoon she'd seen last night. But she didn't think wild animals had violins, at least not yet.

"What are you doing out here?" Jake asked from behind her.

Antonia faced him and the bewitchment of the music shattered under the impact of his maleness. If last night she'd wanted him to stay so she could look her fill, she now had her wish. He stood before her half-dressed, his chest burnished by the golden light of the rising sun. She glanced up into his face, afraid he recognized the look in her eyes for the admiration it was.

"Didn't you hear it?" she asked.

"Hear what?"

"That music; that violin. It was wonderful!"

"I didn't hear anything." Jake studied her. The funny way her hair stood up on one side made his fingers itch with wanting to smooth it down. Her nightgown, though voluminous, was made of some material that let the light come through, silhouetting her body beneath it. Even her small pink toes, peeking out from beneath the hem, seemed to add fuel to his desire for her.

"I wasn't dreaming," Antonia said in response to his look of disbelief. "That is, I was, but the music didn't stop when I woke up. Well, it didn't!"

"I guess you walk in your sleep, Miss Castle. Just don't come a-wandering into my room." Or, he thought, I won't be able to keep myself from helping myself.

"Are we back to that? I've promised I won't go into your room. How many more times must I say it? I'm beginning to wonder what you keep in there?"

"Nothing much. Dirty French postcards, mostly."

"I'm not in the least surprised." She brushed past him to go back inside, but he seized her arm. At the sight of his strong fingers on her white nightgown, a pulsation from deep within took Antonia by surprise. As he drew her in to fit firmly against his sleep-heated body, Antonia did not resist, even when his hand came up from behind to cup her shoulder.

"Ssh," he whispered in her ear, sending tremors through her body. "Look there." He pointed off with his free hand.

Antonia followed the direction he indicated. The dark

woods that backed onto his property were unmoving and silent. "What is it? I don't see anyone."

"There he is, in that black willow. See him—the little blue guy?"

Sitting on a branch, moving his head as though inviting admiration, a small bird with deep blue plumage caught Antonia's eye. She smiled for a moment, until the overwhelming nearness of the man beside her reclaimed all her attention. The scent of Jake's clean body so near her own sent her head swimming. "He's magnificent."

"I think so. I like to watch him while I drink my coffee." A gleam of appetite came into his eyes. "That's what I need," he muttered.

He seemed to realize that he had an arm about her and that a single dip of his head would bring her lips under his. For a moment they read each other's eyes, and then, as if with great caution, Jake released her.

"Do you drink coffee?" he asked politely, with a voice even more deep than usual.

"Yes, please."

Antonia should not have guessed yesterday that she would be sitting next to Jake in his kitchen, sipping at a beverage he'd brewed himself. She could almost overlook his lack of clothing, though she found herself forcing her gaze away from that band of hair gliding over his smooth stomach to the belt line of his trousers. When not sipping the rich, if too hot, coffee, she toyed with the top button of her nightgown, keeping her attention on the floor. To look anywhere else was dangerous.

He put down his cup and said, "Black as the devil, hot as hell, pure as an angel, sweet as . . . love."

"Who said that? Talleyrand, wasn't it?"

"No, my uncle Bert. He gave me my first cup of coffee, God love him."

"Did you come from a large family? You said you fought for the South. Where did you grow up?"

Without replying, Jake stood up and reached out a long arm for the battered pot still simmering on the stove. As he refilled his mug he thought, *Now* she's asking questions. But the urge to overwhelm her with the story of his life had gone.

"It's getting late," he said, sipping from his cup without sitting down again. "You best hurry up if you want to get to church."

"Church?"

"Yep. Mrs. Cotton said I'd better be sure to bring you. They'll be watching to see if you show up."

"Who will?"

"The womenfolk. If you've got to stay here, you better go to church every Sunday . . . Wednesdays, too, if there's something going on." He yawned, showing his white teeth, and stretched. Antonia watched the rippling play of muscles under his skin and forgot the subject of their discussion.

"So drink up, Miss Castle, and get your clothes on. My, but Mrs. Dakers and her friends would purely faint if they could see you sitting here with me, and you in nothing but that nightie." Jake saw her prim up and bit his cheek to control his smile.

"No one could think I am less than adequately covered."

"You bet they could. Keep playing with that button and it'll come off."

Forcing her hand down from her neck, Antonia said, "You could put on a shirt. That would satisfy these women you seem to be so concerned with pleasing."

"I'm not concerned with pleasing any woman, 'cept at night." Jake yawned a second time and scratched his chest.

Antonia saw the way the black hair curled around his fingers. She could almost feel the soft rasping against her own hands, which she promptly dropped into her lap.

Only then did the meaning of his words penetrate her mind. She rose and gave him a scornful look.

"You're awfully coarse at this hour of the morning. I shall go and dress."

"Good. I can't hang around here all day, you know. I've got work to do today."

"Work? On Sunday?" She paused in the doorway.

"The law doesn't take a day's rest, Miss Castle. I didn't like the looks of that fire last night. After church, I'm going to be sifting through the ashes."

"Do you suspect that the fire was set?" Antonia thought of the damage, not only to Paul Dakers himself, but to the hard work and dreams the livery stable must have represented to him and to his family. She'd seen many a prosperous, happy family become miserable and despairing individuals after such a tragedy. "How could anyone do such a thing?"

"I won't have any suspicions until I take a look around."

"I'll hurry."

When she opened her largest valise and pulled out the top and skirt of her serviceable gray serge dress, she realized that she'd left her brown-and-orange-checked ensemble outside last night. With any luck it would come clean, but if not, what with an outfit ruined the night of the lecture, she would soon be out of clothes.

The combinations she'd bathed in were still damp, rolled up tightly in her towel. Fortunately she had plenty of those, but what about outerwear? Her valises weren't that large, as she never expected to spend any length of time in one place.

"Marshal? Is there a laundry in town?"

She heard his chair scrape on the floor. "Mrs. Ransom sometimes takes in washing." His footsteps came closer. "Do you mind if I pass on through, Miss Castle? I'd like to get dressed now myself."

"Ah, yes, of course . . . just a moment." Antonia

snatched up her wrapper and hurried it on, accidentally wearing it inside out. Though he'd spent the last half hour with her, and she in nothing but a nightgown, somehow she felt more secure with the extra fabric about her. She could even manage a civil nod as he walked through the room, and keep her eyes from dwelling on his splendid body.

"That blue's pretty on you, Miss Castle. It brings out the color of your eyes." His hands on his hips emphasized their narrowness and the deep channels running into his trousers on either side of his level abdomen.

Antonia mumbled thanks, knowing she blushed. If only the image of his nearly naked form had not followed her down into sleep. If only she could hide from herself the memory of her dreams. They had danced together, but with none of the fancy clothes a ball requires, or for that matter with any clothes on at all.

"Are you coming down with a fever, Miss Castle?" He stepped closer. Antonia skittered away, until the backs of her knees touched the sofa. Jake lifted his hand and laid it against her cheek. "You feel kind of warm."

"So do you," she whispered.

The warmth radiated from his body, heating up her front as though she stood before a hearth. Her lips were dry, so she shone them automatically with the tip of her tongue. She lost the power to think as his dark eyes fixed upon that curve. He slipped his hand to the back of her neck, driving his fingers through the abundance of her hair.

Antonia didn't wait for him to tilt her head to receive his kiss. She lifted her chin, all but asking him to bend down and meet her offered lips. All her instincts told her that Jake wanted to kiss her. So what was taking him so long?

Jake remembered a lake out in the middle of nowhere. He'd been riding through the heat of the day for hours and his sweat had turned his saddle black. The horse had caught the scent of the water and galloped hard toward it. Jake remembered he hadn't even waited to dismount, but had dived in from the saddle. Antonia's eyes were the deep clear blue of that paradise of water. It would be so easy to drown there.

"We're not going to do this," he said, his voice deep and husky. He withdrew his hand from her hair, took one last plunge into the depths of her eyes, and stood back. The flicker of disappointment on her face almost broke his fragile self-control. Then he saw pride come to her aid.

"Of course we're not!" she said. "Why should we give them the satisfaction?"

It was as if she'd heard his thoughts. "Besides, you've only been here a night and a day. Why let the Cottons think they're right—'specially so soon?"

"Exactly. After all, I am a firm believer that two people who happen to be male and female can live harmoniously together without . . . well, without kisses and all that. This is merely a chance to prove my principles. I should be pleased the judge has placed us in this situation."

"I should think you would be. It's not every day a chance like this comes along."

"And you are really the perfect person to help me, as you are not too fond of women anyway. Why, Mrs. Lloyd Newstead might very well ask you to come and address the Society, once this little experiment is over!"

"Miss Castle, I'd be purely honored." Jake went to his bedroom door and gave her a fraternal smile and a thumbs-up as he opened it.

Oh Lord, he thought, going in, thirty days more of looking at that face, and all the rest of her. I bet she's never been kissed in her life—not the way I want to kiss her. He stamped down hard on his too-eager imagination and thought, Well, her innocence is safe so long as the creek doesn't run out of cold water.

Dressing, he wondered what the hell was wrong with the men in Chicago and Connecticut that one of them hadn't married Antonia a long time ago. A girl like that shouldn't be allowed to run around the country alone. Why, just the look of her could keep a man from thinking about his job and then what would happen to the greatness of America?

When Antonia began to dress herself, she discovered her hands were shaking. She trembled all over, as though with much exertion. It seemed that principles were not strong enough fortification against a man like Jake Faraday.

Passing a hand over her mouth, she could almost feel the pressure of his lips on hers, though nothing of that sort had happened. She had to recapture her self-control. Somewhere in her luggage, unless Evelyn had it, would be a copy of *The Principles of Hygiene,* a book that Mrs. Newstead swore by. After church, Antonia promised herself a dip into that edifying work.

Sometime later, approaching the small white church, Antonia wished she'd brought the book along. Its discourse on the moral benefits of a platonic relationship, not only to the individual but to the community, would have stood her in good stead at the moment. Everyone in town must know about the judge's arrangement for "discovery." What must they be thinking?

Turning to Jake, she said, "Are you certain Mrs. Cotton said I should attend? She might have said I shouldn't go, and you misunderstood."

"Nope. She meant I should bring you to church this morning, so here we are."

"But surely it would be better not to push myself forward. I mean . . . I don't wish to antagonize anyone."

"You should have thought of that before you came out here." Deliberately he took her hand and hooked it into the bend of his elbow. When she tried to tug it free, he fixed her with a glance and said, "Scared?"

"Of course not!" She left her hand where it was and advanced toward the church. How foolishly her stomach was behaving, turning handsprings inside her. She wished she'd had more for breakfast than Jake's hell brew. In a tiny voice she felt certain he would not hear, she said, "At least, not much."

Except for a few adolescent boys and girls flirting inexpertly in the sunshine outside the church door, most of the congregation had already gone in. It was difficult enough to walk past these young people, who stared and giggled at her, or sighed, if female, over the marshal. Antonia noticed that a mere frown from Jake was enough to send the loiterers in.

"By the way," Jake said in a low voice, "you're the prettiest woman here, the prettiest I ever saw."

Antonia gave him a startled glance filled with doubt. Her ears must be playing her false, she decided. He could not have actually complimented her—not the woman-hating marshal!

At her expression, a smile pricked the corners of Jake's mouth. "Stupid-looking hat, though."

"That's more like it," she answered. With a proud lift to her chin and a back as straight as any ruler, Antonia entered the church on the marshal's strong left arm.

The rumbling and hissing began the moment they appeared. Walking between the pews, sometimes Antonia caught a word, clearer than the others, and none of them cordial. She walked with the marshal, paying little attention to where they were going, and hoping her color hadn't risen.

When he stopped, she focused on the backless pew beside him. Mrs. Cotton smiled at her and patted the seat. Feeling genuinely welcomed, Antonia scuttled up the row and sat down. The older woman took Antonia's hand in her cool, dry one and squeezed it lightly, reassuringly.

The judge leaned across his wife and whispered penetratingly, "How's it going, Miss Castle? Jake?"

"Hush up," Mrs. Cotton replied, nodding to where Mr. Budgell had emerged from a curtain-screened room at the front of the church. "Can't you see Preacher Budgell is goin' to talk?"

Antonia had already realized, from the length of Evelyn and Henry's wedding ceremony, that the youthful minister preferred the sound of his own voice to any other. She hoped there would be plenty of singing to make the time pass. Even if the hymns were not those she knew, she enjoyed listening to singing and, in Chicago, never missed a performance at the opera house. Her own voice was light and inconsequential. Nothing, however, gave her a greater thrill than to hear beautiful music excellently played.

Antonia glanced up to Jake's face and revised her thoughts. *Almost* nothing gave her a greater thrill. Though he had seemed to agree absolutely with her reasons for not kissing him, and even thought of a few himself, she found it surprisingly difficult to overcome her disappointment. What would it be like to have this man in her arms?

As the preacher began an interminable prayer Antonia bowed her head. She made every effort to concentrate on the earnest words falling from the pulpit. Jake's thigh lay directly under her eyes. All she had to do was shift her view the slightest degree up that powerful leg and she would see the plenty that filled the front of his trousers. She turned her head to look out the floor-to-ceiling window beside the bench. Concentrating on the view of the cemetery, she still remained aware of the nearness of Jake's thigh.

Closing her eyes, Antonia prayed for strength. She had seen drawings of men's genitalia before and had thought them unwieldy and poorly designed, if one could think in such a way of God's handiwork. Why now did she display an unseemly curiosity about Jake's body? She already knew more of these things than most women. She should, therefore, have more resolution than she'd shown so far.

The service finished almost without Antonia realizing it. She'd stood up and sat down, sang and was silent, following Mrs. Cotton's lead, all without thinking about it. Yet she could remember every restless movement of the man next to her, every sigh that he heaved, every crossing and uncrossing of his powerful legs.

Antonia didn't complain when Mrs. Cotton said, "Now you run along, Jake. You're most likely itching to get at that ruination of the livery. The judge and I will see to Miss Castle's comfort."

Her husband complained, "But I want to go 'long with Jake, Mother. You don't need me. If you ain't gonna be gabbin' at each other like a couple of hens, you can put horns on me and call me a goat."

"I already call you a goat. An old goat. But if you want to run off and get all mucked up with ashes, soot, and mud, you go right ahead. Don't you track any of that into my house, though, or I'll skin you."

As happy as any boy, the judge followed Jake out of the church. Antonia noticed that Jake did not offer her so much as a backward glance. With a don't-care flip of her head, Antonia turned her attention to Mrs. Cotton.

"You'd never know he was an old man, the way he carries on. Could be worse, I reckon. Could be he might chase after women instead of every other blamed fool fuss folks get up to around here. Come to think on it, women might be easier on me 'cause there ain't no way he could catch one. Not that he'd know what to do with one iffen he did."

Listening to Mrs. Cotton, Antonia walked beside her down the aisle. They stopped just inside the church door, where a group of the town's women had paused to pass the time of day. The light dazzled in, illuminating only details until Antonia's eyes adjusted to the change.

"Miz Conway, Miz Fleck," Mrs. Cotton said civilly, nodding to each woman as she said her name. "How's that Amy of yourn, Miz Danton? And Miz Simek—is Rudy's hand healed up yet? If it starts gettin' red again, you bring him to me. Doc Partridge is no more use than a churn without a dasher . . . if as much."

As though the doctor's name were a signal, all the women looked at Mrs. Dakers. Large dark marks beneath her eyes told a tale of a sleepless night. Mrs. Cotton said gently, "I didn't think to see you today, Bettina."

"It's Sunday, isn't it? Paul's got that wife of his to look after him. He don't need me. I'm sure I'm not the only person you were surprised to see, Mrs. Cotton." She looked pointedly at Antonia. "I wonder how long it has been since some people stepped foot inside a holy church?"

At first all the women of Culverton looked alike to Antonia. This one's clothes might be a trifle brighter, or more somber than the others', or she might have a baby in her arms rather than one hanging on her skirt, but their expressions were all the same, set and hard when their eyes happened to fall upon her. Most had turned their backs to her to cluster around Mrs. Cotton, who seemed something of a leader among them.

And then, unexpectedly, one of the younger and more fashionable women said, "You're right, Mrs. Dakers. I've been coming to this church for almost three years— ever since we moved here—and this is the first time I can remember seeing the marshal. How ever did you convince him, Miss Castle?"

"I . . ." Antonia caught Mrs. Cotton's eye. At her approving nod Antonia went on, "I simply assumed he'd be coming, and I went, and he came along."

"Well now, that beats the batter so far as I ever saw," Mrs. Cotton said. "Don't know how I'd talk the judge into it, if he ever took a spite against going to church. 'Course, I reckon he'd rather lie up blowin' smoke rings than do anything. I'll just hope he don't take the notion of giving up Sunday meetings. He's an awful ornery cuss when he puts his mind to somethin'. Oh, my. Oh, yes.''

"He can't be worse than my Jacob," said a pretty girl with a baby asleep on her shoulder. "He said he didn't want to see green beans at the table ever again, and I put up five quarts this year."

"Maisie, do you think he'd take to okra?" asked a woman with red hair peeking out from beneath her straw bonnet. "I got plenty and Mr. McEwan purely hates it like poison. Even the boys won't touch it now. If you want it, I'll trade with you."

"That's the worst of it," someone else said, looking off fondly to where a pair of tall twins stood among a group of their peers. "A husband takes an idea and the next you know, the children take it up and you don't get no peace nohow."

Another girl with a wedding ring almost glaringly new said, "Is it true that all men like tomatoes?"

A short silence fell. Antonia felt all the others were stiffening their necks to prevent their heads from turning in her direction. She said, "Don't tell me you still have tomatoes! I could have sworn you used them all up."

A few lips twitched and the newly married girl giggled. Stepping up to Antonia, she glanced sheepishly around at the other faces. "Miss Castle," she said, and giggled again, on a high nervous note.

"Yes?" Was this her chance to delve into the heart of these women's lives?

"My husband . . . Mr. Lewis says . . . well, is it true what he said about men? That they can't . . ." She faltered and stopped. A hectic flush arose in her smooth, fair cheeks.

Antonia knew all the others had frozen, listening hard and judging. Even Mrs. Dakers seemed for the moment to withhold her wrath. "Go ahead. I'll be happy to answer if I can."

"Is it true . . ." she began with another glance around. "You see, William's mama's dead and my mama's all the way back in New York, and I can't put it in a letter."

"Yes, the laws are stringent."

"Laws? I don't know about the law, but Mama would just die if I wrote her anything like that. What I want to know is . . ." Antonia saw her swallow. She went on in a tiny voice, "Is it true a man can't do much after he . . . we . . . William said it takes an awful lot out of him and he's supposed to lie down and get back his strength afterward. He says he gets so awful tired that if we do it too much, he might die, or somethin'."

The tension dissolved in a flare of laughter. The new Mrs. Lewis looked shamefaced, then scared and finally angry. "You mean it's not true? That's the last time I muck out the pigs in the morning!"

Mrs. Cotton said, "That William of yourn always hated doing that chore! His mama could whale him twice a day and he'd still twist and wriggle to get out of it!"

"Just you wait till you get big," said an older woman with a rounding gesture at her waist. "Then it's your chance to laze around."

"And in a couple years the child can muck the pigs! Children ought to do chores. It's good for 'em."

"Actually," Antonia said, though the conversation had gone beyond the point she intended to make. "Some authorities do claim a man does lose . . ." She heard Mrs. Cotton heave a sigh, but the sound was lost at once in Mrs. Dakers's piercing voice.

"Hussy! Unchaste beast!" Mrs. Dakers all but threw herself between Antonia and Mrs. Lewis.

The young bride stepped back, plainly scared, but Mrs. Dakers had condemnation only for Antonia. "Such low and filthy talk in the house of the Lord! You are without shame and seduce others to be shameless! This innocent girl would never have thought to ask such a question without you here."

Antonia retreated up the aisle, step-by-step, yet still the furious Mrs. Dakers pursued her, shouting. Sunlight stained red and blue mottled Mrs. Dakers's face, rendering the staring, blackly dilated eyes horrible and otherworldly. "Sinful, sinful woman!"

"Ladies, ladies!"

The preacher raced down the aisle toward them, carrying a large black Bible. Antonia almost fell over him. He steadied her with his free hand, his fair face flushing. "Are you all right?"

"Yes, Mr. Budgell, I'm fine."

He glanced between Antonia and Mrs. Dakers. The older woman stood with her arms crossed over her chest, glaring with the air of an Old Testament prophet. Slowly she extended an arm, her forefinger pointing at Antonia. "Jezebel! Are not even men of the cloth safe from you? Throwing yourself into his arms! We all saw you do it!"

Antonia looked past Mrs. Dakers at the other women. They'd clustered together and whispered among themselves. Few of them cared to meet her eyes. Mrs. Cotton stood aside, shaking her head as if all were lost.

Young Mr. Budgell rubbed his hand over the surface of the Bible's incised golden cross. Glancing again at Mrs. Dakers, he said, "I—I think you'd better leave, Miss Castle. We've got to think of our moral tone."

In a voice so cooingly soft that Antonia almost couldn't believe it came from Mrs. Dakers, she said, "You're always so wise, Mr. Budgell. A true inspiration to us all."

"Thank you, Mrs. Dakers. With the Lord's help, I try."

"Do you really mean I should leave?" Antonia said, interrupting.

Mr. Budgell said, "I'm sorry, but we can't have these upsets in church. A house of peace and of gentle humility is what I strive for, always." He held up his hand when she opened her mouth to speak and seemed surprised when the gesture worked. "Now please, Miss Castle, don't feel rejected by God. . . . I know if you pray to him, he will soften your hard heart and make you see the error of your ways.''

"Not her," Mrs. Dakers said. "Her love is given to—''

Mr. Budgell held up his hand again. When Mrs. Dakers fell silent, Antonia saw the young man glance into his palm and give an impressed nod. "We must be kind to those who have strayed, Mrs. Dakers. Take our Lord for your example. When Miss Castle gives up trying to subvert the minds of simplehearted women, I will be the first to welcome her again into my church. But for now I think she'd better go.''

Antonia could do nothing in the face of such sublime, if blind, charity. Mrs. Newstead had warned all her field lecturers not to tangle with the ministers and reverends in the small towns they visited. If these men were interested, they could certainly attend the meetings, which were free to all, but to debate with those who carried a higher authority was useless.

"Thank you, Mr. Budgell," Antonia said. "I will be sorry to miss your admirable sermons. Good day.''

Turning from him, she met Mrs. Dakers's implacable eyes. With a haughty expression she waited for the older woman to step out of her way. In a moment, jerking her skirts out of range, Mrs. Dakers did step back. Antonia went on down the aisle, followed by Mr. Budgell, who seemed anxious not to be left alone with Mrs. Dakers.

She paused to look over the other women. Mrs. Cotton had gone up to Mr. Budgell. Some shook their heads and other wore expressions of distaste. Young Mrs. Lewis dropped her eyes and whispered, "Sorry.''

The most fashionable among the matrons hesitated, glanced back at the others, and then walked over. "I'm Mrs. Wilmot," she said, holding out her tightly gloved hand. Antonia shook it.

"My husband owns the general store. I apologize for Mrs. Dakers. Although I don't approve of your message, Miss Castle, there's no reason for us to sink to . . . rudeness."

Antonia was certain Mrs. Wilmot had meant to say "sink to your level" but had caught herself in time. "Thank you, Mrs. Wilmot. I know I'll soon need to stop in to your store. I haven't enough things to last out my stay."

"We won't have a thing to your taste, Miss Castle. Good day." With a flick of her narrow skirt, Mrs. Wilmot returned to her friends, giving Mrs. Dakers a tight smile as she passed.

Mrs. Cotton finished talking at the young preacher, leaving him paging through his Bible. She trotted over to Antoina. "Danged fool!"

"It's all right," Antonia said. "I don't mind."

"What did Mrs. Wilmot have to say? Something pleasant, I know. She and Mrs. Dakers have been eating at each other ever since the Wilmots moved here, five or six years ago. They used to be sharp but civil until the foofaraw over the curtains. Now if one says black, the other's bound to say white."

"The curtains?"

"The curtains in the church; you must of noticed 'em. The ragging and arguing that went on over them—blue or red, baize or domestic, floor length or short—you'd think Moses was comin' to see 'em and not this bishop from Jefferson City."

Though aware of the disapproving gazes from the other side, Antonia couldn't help asking, "Bishop?"

"Head of the whole district, making his summer tour of all the churches out this way. This is the first time he's been out this way since Mr. Budgell got the call. That's why he's so nerve-ridden. He wouldn't toss you out if it weren't for that. I just gave him an earful about Jesus and collecting the erring lamb. Mrs. Dakers ain't the only one as can quote Scripture! Now, child, you come on to my house for—''

"No, thank you. I wouldn't want your neighbors to turn on you.'' Antonia knew she spoke bitterly.

Mrs. Cotton did not seem to mind. She gave a whinnying laugh. "They know I do what I want to. Ain't I the oldest among 'em except for Mrs. Rogers and she don't get out but on Sunday.'' The older woman looked up into Antonia's eyes. "Well, you run on home now and have yourself a good rest. I expect you're tired after everything. The judge and me'll have you and Jake over to dinner right soon.''

Antonia thanked her and hurried away. Halfway down the street anger overwhelmed her. Glancing around, she reassured herself that no one else would hear her swear. Then firmly she said, "Oh, spew!''

She could think of nothing to do. Going back to an empty house, to where Jake might not return for hours, held no interest for her. She wanted to talk to someone— no, she wanted to talk to Jake.

Thin gray ghosts of smoke still arose from the inundated black carcass of the once thriving business. Half a jagged wall, a blackened twist of iron, and crumbling charcoal still in the shape of a beam poked up from among the wreckage. Nothing could be salvaged here, Antonia knew.

At the rear of the main mass, a smaller structure had burned even more thoroughly than the stable. She heard voices from this area and approached, carefully holding her skirt out of the mingled mud and sodden ash that surrounded the remains of the stable. Jake stood by the edge of the burned-out shed, his black hat pulled down low while he chewed on a piece of hay.

Not far away from Jake, the judge crouched on hands and knees, seeming to sift the ashes through his fingers. He raised a striped face to Jake and said, "What we do is— we take different kinds of combustible stuff . . . kerosene, cooking oil, and burner oil, you know, maybe paraffin . . . and we light up wood and see what kind of ash we got then. Then we compare . . . oh, hi-ya, Miss Castle.'' The judge suddenly looked as guilty as an apple-stealing schoolboy. ''Oh, hell, is my wife with you?''

Hastily he got to his feet and took an ineffectual swipe at the knees of his trousers, which were caked with liquefied gray ash. He'd evidently been pawing at his chin in thought, and had ashy finger marks on the brim of his silk hat.

''No, she's still at the church—the last I saw of her.'' Antonia had to smile. ''If she sees you like that, what you sentenced me to won't compare.''

''Tell me true, Miss Castle. Does it look awful bad?'' Antonia simply nodded. ''I better hightail it on home before she sees me, then. Let me know what you think, Jake.''

Both Jake and Antonia turned to watch the judge running for home, holding on to his hat with both hands. ''He could have outrun jackrabbits when he was young, I guess,'' Jake said in admiration.

''He could now if Mrs. Cotton were after him,'' Antonia added.

Jake squinted sideways at her. ''I thought you'd be gabbing away for hours yet. Did something happen?''

''No, nothing happened. I'm tired and want to go home. I didn't get much sleep last night, remember?'' She waved her hand at the blackness around them.

''Liar,'' he said almost fondly. ''What happened?''

''We were talking together, as pleasantly as you please, when Mrs. Dakers—your star witness—attacked me. She called me the same sort of names she called me the other night. And . . .''

''And?''

''The minister threw me out of the church.''

Jake grinned. ''Did he? Budgell's braver than I gave him credit for.''

''It was entirely unjustified!''

"'Course it was, I guess," Jake said, squatting down to poke among the half-burned timbers with a stick. He frowned, though not at what he saw. "What were you talking about when Mrs. Dakers started in to yelling?"

Antonia smoothed up her hair at the back of her hat. "The usual things women find to talk about when we are together. Children, cooking—"

"Men."

"We may have touched on the subject. Briefly."

"And, naturally, you put in your two cents' worth."

"Someone asked me a question," she replied loftily.

"I guess I take it back. The preacher did the right thing. I am surprised."

"What? I never . . ."

Jake squinted up at her. "You are the beatingest woman! Here's everybody tryin' to make you welcome—"

"Everybody? Who, for instance? Mrs. Dakers? You?"

"We're not talking about me. Great Peter! You've only got to put up with us for a couple of days and then you're shut of Culverton. Can't you act like a lady for that long?"

"I always act like a lady," Antonia said. He grunted in disgust and started investigating the ashes again with his stick.

Squatting on the balls of his feet as he did, he seemed to be off balance above the dross and cinders. A little extra inclination and . . . Antonia surrendered to an impulse. Stepping nearer, she pushed him forward.

Jake whipped around and jumped up, as strikingly fast and lithe as a cat. Antonia leaped back, fear and a new excitement striving for mastery in her blood. What would he do with her?

For a moment they stood there in the blasted yard, a few feet apart. Antonia relived the moment of this morning when it seemed he'd kiss her, and knew he remembered it, too. She saw the same passion in his eyes now, and fear won, this time.

"I—I think I'll go home now," she said.

"You do that." His voice softened. "I'll be back before dark. Try to behave." He forestalled her next statement. "I know—you *always* behave."

===

Chapter 7

_____

The way home seemed much hotter and farther than the walk to the church, perhaps because Jake was not there to point out interesting plants and to talk about living in Culverton. Antonia had wondered why he chose to live so far outside of the main town.

"I like quiet," he'd answered, raising his hand to shield his eyes as he looked out across the field beside the road. "I like the woods."

Antonia didn't understand that. As she stood on the front step, looking out at the dense ranks of the trees surrounding the small house, the air seemed almost too heavy to breathe. Anyone or anything might be observing her in return, screened by the thick trunks and crowding leaves. No longer feeling as if she were alone, Antonia thought there were too many eyes on her. Suddenly unnerved, she went inside.

Unpinning her hat, she laid it on the blanket neatly folded at the foot of the sofa. Without thinking much about it, she went into the kitchen and washed the cups left over from breakfast. Putting them away, she noticed that Jake had only two each of his common household goods. Two cups, two plates, two knives, two forks, two napkins, etc.

Smiling, she remembered visiting Ned, the younger of her two brothers, who had set up bachelor housekeeping with two other medical students. Their opinion, derived from logic or so they'd said, had been that they should have enough dishes for a week, with a grand washup at the end of it. Somehow the washing-up part often slipped their minds, taken up with romps and girls and even, occasionally, studies.

The worst part of living so far from her family was never seeing Ned anymore. They were close in age, he no more than two years older than herself. Always they'd been good friends as well as brother and sister.

Jonathan had been almost seven before Antonia had been born, and away at school for much of her growing up. Then he'd gone to work at eighteen in the shoe factory at the dictates of their paternal grandfather. Her older brother was more like an uncle, and the letters he wrote to her reflected this. Like the rest of the family, Jonathan disapproved of Antonia's mode of life in the wilderness of Chicago. Imagining what he would say if he could see her now in this kitchen, what they'd all say, Antonia gave a small shout of laughter.

Only Ned would have blared "Hurrah for Tony" and thrown his hat into the air. She wondered where he traveled now. His last letter had said Italy but that had been months ago. The distance between Europe and Chicago did not encourage Ned to be more than the indifferent correspondent he naturally was. His year's sojourn in Europe after graduating as a doctor had stretched, so far, to two.

Mrs. Castle did not try to hide from Antonia her fear that Ned would become entangled with some foreign temptress. Antonia wouldn't be surprised if Ned did return to America with an exotic wife. It would be just like him. Her mother, however, could not fathom why her younger son and only daughter did not settle down and be sensible like their older brother.

Jonathan had married a girl from a proper Connecticut family five years ago. Thinking back to that festive occasion, Antonia found she could remember little of the wedding. Only the life-altering aftermath was clear in her mind.

The dancing had gone on half the night, filling the massive stone-and-clapboard house by the shore with so much merriment that it seemed it would float off its foundations. Her friends had chattered about that evening for weeks afterward. Antonia did not talk about it, being too busy with more important matters.

The groom appeared quite the gentleman in his cut-away coat, though he seemed very aware of his new responsibilities. White satin and orange blossom did not flatter Ernestine, though the happiness in her eyes outshone the diamond necklace Mr. Castle had given her as a bride gift.

Innocently vain, Antonia knew her pale pink brides-maid's dress complemented her coloring. Privately she thought she showed to more advantage than any of the other five girls wearing the same thing. The boys clustered around her.

One man had been especially attentive. Lucas Redmond, the heir to Red Coal Oil, shipped to every major port in the world, and Jonathan had been best friends since boarding school. He claimed several dances and stood by whenever she sat out, making a joke of his nearness.

"I owe it to your brother to keep you safe. He's too busy to take care of you himself tonight. We can't have someone stealing you away."

Lucas had been married once, but his wife had died young. The more romantic girls giggled and whispered over his blond good looks, certain he hid an aching heart beneath his smiling exterior. Antonia saw their jealous glances and treasured them. When Lucas asked her if she'd like a breath of air, she went with him, meeting her friends' eyes to be certain they all knew what a trophy she'd taken.

Antonia felt like the heroine of a French novel, strolling along under the moonlight sky with the most

eligible man at the party. He made little response to her
artless chatter, and so Antonia politely fell in with his
mood. On reaching the edge of the copse that ran along
beside the Castles' home, Lucas spread his handkerchief
on a fallen log.

"Won't you sit down, Antonia?"

He'd never called her anything but Miss Castle before.
Her heart beat fast as she seated herself, him beside her.
"It's becoming cooler," she said, and shivered.

Lucas put his arm around her. "Poor little thing," he
said, his voice roughening. His hand moved restlessly on
her arm, which was bared by the fashionable dress. "By
Jove, you're a beauty."

She thrilled. Boys had expressed their admiration,
but this was a *man,* a man who'd been married. Glancing
up flirtatiously, she murmured, "Do you really think
so?"

With an animal growl, he jerked her close against
his body. She could hardly believe it when he kissed
her, so hard, so different from the silly parlor games
she'd played. This was real life as they lived it in
Paris!

Kissing him back awkwardly, she obeyed him when
he ordered, "Open your mouth." His hot hands scrab-
bled against the shoulder straps of her dress as his
tongue plunged into her mouth, too deeply. She choked
a little and tried to draw away, with an incoherent
protest.

"You'll like it once we start," he said, a brutish smile
coming to his lips. "You know you want me to."

Looking back now, Antonia knew she was a naive fool
to have hesitated even an instant in denying what he said.
It was not all her fault, she knew. No one had ever told
her how to resist this wild excitement, or had even
acknowledged that such a thing existed. There had been
a word or two from a spinster teacher about avoiding
polluting thoughts, but none of her friends had understood any more than she herself. No one had even told

her that a man in her own circle could be dangerous, though she'd been warned against strangers and tramps.

Lucas took her silence for agreement. Instantly he put his mouth to hers again and Antonia didn't fight the thrust of his tongue. For a heartbeat, she even met his challenge. Seizing her hand, he forced it down to the small buttons on the front of his evening trousers. Something inside there leaped at her touch.

Was it then that Antonia realized the tingling of excitement had changed to a warning? Even now she couldn't say. All at once she plainly understood that she did not want to be with Lucas anymore.

"Please," she gasped, freeing her lips. "Please!"

"Yes, beg me. I like it. You'll do a lot of it—"

"No! Let me go!" She began to struggle, pushing against his chest and thrashing her head from side to side. From some unknown source she found the strength to push hard enough and he tumbled backward off the log.

Antonia sprang up, flung him a look of utter disgust, and snapped somewhat tearfully, "Never come near me again!"

"It's all right," he said with a return to his gentle-manly manner, somewhat spoiled by his heavy breathing and the leaves in his hair. "Forgive me, Antonia, for jumping the gun. I should have controlled myself until after the wedding, but your beauty tempted me."

"A poor excuse!"

He stood up. Antonia backed away. Lucas held up a pacifying hand. "I didn't intend things to go so far, but by God you'll make a wanton wife! Grace was such a bore—"

Lucas might have said more but Antonia interrupted. "Wife? What do you mean . . . wife?"

"It's all arranged. That's what I brought you out here to tell you. You and I will be married before the end of the year."

"Don't be ridiculous!"

"You'll learn to control your hasty tongue as my wife," he'd said, advancing.

"I don't believe you!"

"Ask your grandfather," he said as he made a grab for her arm. Antonia broke free and ran for the house. After her, she could hear him shout, "Ask him! Ask him!"

Despite the years between that moment and this, Antonia still quailed at the narrow escape she'd had. What if Lucas had behaved himself on the moonlit walk? She'd now be married to a heartless libertine who had so far twice left for different actresses the unfortunate girl he did marry. The present Mrs. Redmond had also been one of Ernestine's bridesmaids. Antonia hated to think what lessons she'd had to learn from her husband.

Breaking into a smoke-filled room, Antonia had sought out her grandfather, demanding an immediate explanation. Usually she had little to say to him, and he to her. His scowl and hard attitude against compromise made him a frightening figure to all the family, even to his own son. Tonight, however, Antonia's blood was up and she would not be tyrannized. Soon they were shouting at each other.

"Lucas Redmond's a fine young man. You've shilly-shallied long enough. You're twenty—how long do you expect to keep us all waiting? I want great-grandchildren!"

"Isn't tonight's wedding enough for you? You'll have your descendants soon enough!"

That was the first time anyone had called her a hussy. "You've no shame!"

"Your Mr. Redmond hasn't any. Do you know what he . . . Never mind. I will not marry him, that's all."

"You will! It's all arranged. You marry him and we get the oil we need."

She bit back her retort to stare at him. "What? You're . . . trading me for oil?"

"Certainly. I've been planning this since you were born. What good is a girl to me otherwise?"

"This isn't the Middle Ages. I'm not some princess you can marry off to cement an alliance."

"That's exactly what you are, my girl, and the sooner you learn it the better. You've been living in a fool's paradise. You'll be Mrs. Lucas Redmond in November, and don't you think otherwise."

At that, a sensation of triumph cut through her anger and alarm. She didn't realize it then, but she now knew that smile silenced her grandfather. He must have recognized it, having seen it on his own face whenever he'd executed a brutally successful business deal.

"I won't marry Lucas Redmond," Antonia said gently. "I don't have to."

"You'll marry him or be cast out of this family without a cent!" Mr. Castle shot back, much of the bluster gone from his voice.

"Do that, if you must. In October, I'll be twenty-one. You've forgotten that. I get my money then, all that lovely money Granny Armstrong left me. I'll be free, white, and twenty-one. You can't do a thing about it!"

They tried. Her mother tried tears, her father sulking, Jonathan sweet reason. Even Ernestine spoke to her sadly and softly about the perils of disobeying one's parents. Only Ned said nothing, but his silent support gave Antonia much-needed strength.

Finally her grandfather tried to get a doctor to say that she was not capable of managing her own affairs. For more than a month it seemed he would win, that she would have to choose between Lucas Redmond and an asylum. Taking legal advice, she fought back with her own doctor. After this scandal she needed to leave Minnaqua and decided that Illinois would be far enough.

All this was now past. Grandfather was dead and she could forgive him. She could even smile when thinking of him. If, in fact, she'd not unexpectedly discovered in herself so much of his character, he might have beaten her down. He had never calculated on finding her as determined as he was himself. Though he had left her nothing in his will, she felt she had his respect at the end. Her mother had written that his last word had been "Antonia," with a chortle.

Antonia regarded what she'd done while thinking of the past. The dishes were clean and put away. After heating a large pot of water, she'd washed what clothes water would not spoil and stretched a clothesline between two trees in the yard behind the house. Her combinations, stockings, and chemises floated in the warm breeze. If she'd been allowed into his room, she might possibly have considered washing Jake's shirts so as not to waste the water. Since he'd made it clear that was a forbidden area, he could just as well do his own.

Content, Antonia picked up her copy of *Principles of Hygiene* and sat down on her sofa bed to reacquaint herself with this laudable work. In essentials, it taught the lessons she'd already learned at Lucas Redmond's hands. Sexual desire was a snare and a trap, leading people to action without thought. Ignorance breeds more ignorance, just as enlightenment in one area makes knowledge in other areas easier to acquire. Fixing one's soul upon higher pleasures than the merely animal helps others rise above the low sensual sides of their natures.

These were her hard-won principles. She'd sacrificed much for them. When alone with Jake, she would have to repeat them to herself. There must be no more heated moments like the one this morning, or that of this afternoon.

With her principles to bolster her, she would be proof against the undoubted attractions of his lean, hard body. Antonia lost herself for an instant, picturing Jake wearing only a towel, remembering how near they'd come to kissing. When she looked up in response to a knock at the door, her self-confidence had been undermined.

"Jenny!"

The young bride stood on the doorstep, a large basket making her bend her backward to support its weight. "I brung you this,'' she said, lifting the basket slightly higher.

"Thank you. It's very good of you." Antonia took the basket from her hand, afraid that the frail arm would break unless immediately relieved. Though the young Mrs. Dakers and herself were about the same height, next to the thin girl Antonia felt like an Amazon. Nevertheless there must be considerable strength there, for Antonia could hardly manage to wrestle the basket into the kitchen.

"It ain't nothin' much—a couple of things I had put by."

Antonia lifted out a plate of sliced ham, half a chicken, two jars of preserves, a dish of butter still oozing liquid, and a loaf of fresh-baked bread. There was also a plate of crispy gingersnaps. "But this is marvelous!" she said. "Mr. Faraday was wondering how he could afford to feed me."

Jenny didn't smile in response to her frivolity. Thinking on it, Antonia couldn't recall even a shy smile lighting the rather pinched if pretty face before her. "Paul told me what you done for him."

"How is he?"

"Resting. His ma's there, so I snuck out."

"You should be sleeping now. You must have been up all night with him."

The girl nodded solemnly. Antonia did not have to be a saint to understand the look of almost holy devotion that Jenny wore. "It was no trouble to me. I had to be up sunrise, anyway. Paul told me what you done for him," she repeated. "I do thank you."

Antonia couldn't equal Jenny's natural humility, so she simply said, "You're welcome. He seems a fine man."

A tinge of rose crept into Jenny's cheeks. "Yes, ma'am. He's a right good provider."

"More than that, I'm sure."

"Yes, ma'am, I reckon." Jenny teetered on the

threshold, not quite all the way into the kitchen. When Antonia tried to meet her eyes, they flicked away like half-tame brown sparrows.

"Well," Antonia said when the silence had stretched on a little. "I suppose you'll be rebuilding the livery stable as soon as Mr. Dakers is on his feet again."

Jenny's thin shoulders moved under the heavy calico of her dress. "Yes, ma'am. I sure wish, though . . ."

Antonia chose to exclaim over the fragrance of the bread, before the silence grew awkward again. She was used to this. Often, at the shelter, a woman would come in two or three times before she could ask the questions on her mind. Worn-down Jenny Dakers seemed very familiar.

After a few moments Antonia said very gently, "You wish?"

Slowly Jenny replied, "He was gonna build me a house as soon as we got a little ahead. A little house I didn't have to share with nobody but him. They was fifteen of us, growin' up."

"Where do you live now?"

"With her. With Mrs. Dakers." As if frightened of her own talkativeness, Jenny began sidling backward. Almost before Antonia realized it, the other woman had slipped out of the house with a mumbled good-bye.

Antonia emerged onto the front step to wave to Jenny. "Please come again," she called after her. "Anytime." If ever she'd seen someone starving for a kind word, it was Jenny Dakers.

Living with Mrs. Dakers might account for that, but Antonia wondered if Paul noticed how unhappy his wife seemed. Probably not. Antonia had no very high opinion of men's powers of observation. Besides, judging from the almost palpable glow that emanated from the girl when her husband's name was mentioned, he never saw the defeated side of her.

Antonia half turned to reenter the house when something stopped her. Weaving its way through the humid, still air came the high haunting song of a violin. It both beckoned to her and commanded her to stay still, hypnotized by the subtle aria. The music seemed to be conjured from the heavy air and the low clouds, existing always, never created. Superstitious chills broke out on Antonia's arms and the back of her neck.

Nonsense, she thought with a mental shake. It has to have a source, a *human* source. She stepped down off the concrete square and crossed the grass to the edge of the woods. The music played on a moment and then drifted into silence.

"Hello!" Antonia called. "Is someone there?"

Jake passed Jenny on the way to the house. Since she shied like a frightened horse whenever he spoke to her, he merely touched two fingers to the brim of his hat and kept on walking. He reached the end of the lane just in time to see Antonia enter the woods.

A temptation reared up before him. Why should he go after her? Let her get lost in the woods overnight. The experience might do her a world of good, and would certainly make her less decided in her notions. If he had wound up covered in ash today, she would have laughed. He had the chance to laugh now.

Jake followed Antonia, chewing himself out as he went. Didn't he have enough to do, he asked, that he had to go chasing after a silly girl? She wouldn't find any of her stuck-up ways were much good if she tripped over a possum or, say, a skunk.

He'd like to see her after she'd tangled with a skunk, all right. She'd have to take another bath, or maybe two. Funny how if he closed his eyes, he could catch a glimpse of a tail as white as that of a leaping deer as Antonia ran again for the kitchen door.

Pushing in past the first stand of trees, Jake could see no sign of Antonia. She had vanished into the dim green dusk under the shifting leaves. He called her name, and the sound fell flat, hardly carrying beyond his mouth.

"Miss Castle!" he called again, moving farther in. If

she kept moving in a straight line, he'd soon catch up to her. The woods behind his house were two miles thick, with hardly another house among them until a person fetched up at Lincoln, a small community founded by freed slaves at the end of the war. If she did not move in that straight line, without woodcraft she would be lost for days.

"Antonia?" he called, walking a little faster. "Damn it, honey, holler back if you can hear me!"

The music had stopped at the same instant she'd stepped from the grass to the muffling rustle of accumulated leaves. Antonia thought of fairy circles and elvish feasts, broken by an intruding mortal. These disturbing fancies only made her more determined to find the secret player.

"Where are you?" she said. Only a faint sighing answered as a high wind tossed the tops of the trees. Antonia felt more abashed by shouting here than she had when thrown out of Mr. Budgell's church. The woods, however, forgave her for her lapse.

A brief burst of song came from nearby. Eagerly Antonia turned toward it. A dark blue bird sat on the low branch of a tree. He flitted his tail and looked at her with an intriguing cock of his head. He sang the same phrase a second time.

"Very nice," Antonia said. "But not what I had in mind."

The bird almost seemed to shrug at her poor taste before flying away. Then, echoing the song, the vibrating notes of the violin came again, tentatively, as if grasping after the bird's natural melody.

"Where are you?" Antonia asked.

"Right behind you."

Spinning around, Antonia practically hurled herself into Jake's arms. He put his hands on her shoulders while she fended off against his chest. "Oh, I'm—"

Jake did not give her time to finish. He'd seen her, a beautiful icon in this grass cathedral, and relief warred with longing. One kiss, he'd told himself, wouldn't do any harm. Even as he approached her he knew he was reasoning like a man dying of thirst in the desert. One sip of water wouldn't satisfy him either.

Antonia, remembering Lucas Redmond, could have dealt with a punishing embrace. Her hands flattened and flexed on Jake's chest as he moved his lips down her cheek and over the sensitive corner of her jaw. Such tenderness could not be rebuked, and she could not find any words to stop him.

He raised his head and met her eyes. Antonia knew that this was the time to draw away. She continued to gaze up into the ever-increasing jade of his eyes. Her eyelids seemed very heavy, but she could see his mouth harden as his hands tightened on her shoulders.

And then, from somewhere, a stifled laugh and the thudding of footsteps hitting hard as someone ran away. Jake spun about, his hand flashing to the holster at his thigh. Antonia saw his long back relax.

"Some kid," he muttered.

He turned slowly back to face her, as if reluctant to do it. "Going for a stroll, Miss Castle?"

"I heard that music again."

"It can't be cabin fever already," he said, looking at the sky as if for guidance.

She couldn't get mad at him, not when they'd been so close to kissing a moment since. "I'm going back to the house," she said, "since you obviously don't believe a word I'm saying."

Walking off, she felt his fingers on her arm. She glanced down and knew heat had come into her face.

"It's this way," he said.

Finding it impossible to trudge along behind him in silence, yet unable to bring up the subject that most interested her—to wit, why was he so attractive when she didn't even like him—Antonia cast about for a neutral subject. "Did you find anything interesting at the stable, Marshal Faraday?"

"What?" He turned his head to look back. She looked like some dang-fool Eastern artist's idea of a pioneer woman with her skirt hiked up in one hand and the bloom of roses in her cheeks. A shame the image didn't reflect reality, although Jake acknowledged a sneaking preference for the picture she made.

"Was the fire at the livery stable set?"

"Yep."

Antonia knew now that the marshal was capable of more than single-word sentences. She caught up to him. "What do you mean, 'yep'? Someone set the Dakers's business on fire, on purpose?"

"You're quick."

"Don't be so . . . Do you have any idea who did it?"

"Somebody in town, I reckon."

"Thank you. I didn't think your congressman came in from Washington for the purpose."

Jake stopped. So did Antonia, the better to glare at him. "You're a pistol," he said. "Look, I found a burned-out barrel, about fifteen yards from the shed, in a stand of tall grass. The barrel was lying on its side."

"It may have rolled there, from the fire. No, that doesn't make any sense."

"Damn right. Between the shed and the barrel was burned grass running in a straight line between the two. I reckon somebody drizzled something that would burn between the shed and the barrel, then lit whatever was inside the barrel. The fire would have followed the trail back to the shed and started it blazing away."

"How big a barrel was it? Huge, like your bathtub?"

"No, a smallish one."

"So anyone could have put it there. It wouldn't have taken much strength to move it?"

"That's right. You're pretty fast, too, when you've got all the facts."

"My goodness, two compliments in one day. You're

turning out to be quite a courtier, Marshal.'' Despite her
flippant answer, Antonia smiled in real pleasure.

Jake just grunted and walked on back to the house.
''There's one more thing you ought to know,'' he said as
they crossed the grass. ''In the last couple of weeks
we've had two strange fires. Somebody in Culverton is
getting to where they like burning.''

Chapter 8

A ntonia caught up to him again at the kitchen door. "What do you mean? What else has burned?"

"Small stuff, mostly. A pile of rubbish at the back of Wilmot's store, a dead smoke tree in the Koers's yard, that kind of thing. Any of 'em could have started with somebody flipping a lighted match, or by themselves, or they could have been set deliberate. There's no saying."

"But the burning of the livery stable was obviously intentional."

"That's more than I know. And anyway there's no evidence as to who it was that set it. People are in and out of the smithy all day. We haven't had any rain in a week. This whole thing could have been set up anytime and nobody would have noticed."

"How horrible!" Antonia tried to imagine the mind that could cold-bloodedly plot such destruction. "Why, Mr. Dakers might have been killed!"

"You, too. And me." He opened the door and went in. Stopping short, he stared in wonder at the food laid out on the kitchen table. "Did you do this?"

"Why, no, I—"

The satin coolness of her face beneath his lips had not satisfied Jake. He continued the kiss that had ended all too soon. Her lips were soft and hesitant, reserving the fire Jake knew must be banked inside her. No woman could be so vibrant and yet be cold.

Receiving his kiss under false pretenses, Antonia could not enjoy it. A slow simmering sensation in her breast, however, told her that she very easily could enjoy Jake's kissing, under the right circumstances. Antonia turned her head away. "I didn't do anything. Mrs. Dakers brought all that."

"Mrs. *Dakers*?"

"Jenny."

"Oh, that makes more sense." Jake grinned down at her. "It's a good thing, though. The school board ought to be here in 'bout half an hour. You should whip 'em up something. I've got to go see to the horses." He brushed past her before she had a chance to say a single one of the words that sprang to her lips.

The horses didn't need anything, though he brought a hatful of oats as a treat. They clustered, poking their supple noses into the hat and asking the man to scratch ears and jaws. Jake examined Dakers's horses for burns. The three small marks on the back of one were clean-scabbed and the other's hardly showed at all. Seeing there was nothing more, the horses danced away.

Jake leaned on the gate and wished women were as easy to understand as horses. Give him one minute to think and he could come up with half a dozen reasons why Antonia Castle did not appeal to him at all. Despite her beauty, she wasn't the kind of woman he preferred.

He liked girls to be sweet and submissive; she was opinionated and stubborn. He thought women should excel in cooking and cleaning, but be helpless and silly when it came to man's business, showing they needed him; Antonia probably couldn't cook, but she certainly had a talent for jumping in and taking over.

He had to admit she proved during the fire she had the kind of valor he admired most, but surely that was irrelevant. He liked girls to pander a little to his dignity, to display to him that they thought he was the most wonderful man ever breeched; Antonia thought he was dumb as a stump and let him know it.

Jake grinned. He'd done nothing to dispel that idea, nor would he. Looking over his list of requirements, Jake realized there was a whole heap of girls who fulfilled his notions. Quite a few here in Culverton had made it plain that they'd be willing to change themselves into his ideal woman. But, he reluctantly admitted, there was only one Antonia Castle. Not that one wasn't more than enough.

The arrival of the judge and two other members of the school board aroused Jake from his musing. "Wilmot's goin' to be late," Judge Cotton announced, dismounting from his fat mare. "He said we should start without him."

"His kids are over at my place," said Mr. Conway. "I'll be surprised if he makes it here tonight at all. I wouldn't go noplace when Mrs. Wilmot takes mine for the evening. 'Cept bed." Conway snapped his galluses with earth-darkened hands. "Yep, it's hard to plow a furrow with eight kids hanging around."

"Jaysus," Mr. Vrecker said and spat. "That is how we get into this trouble. Every time."

Antonia met them with a gracious smile and hurried about the small house, collecting chairs for the men. She showed Mr. Conway and Mr. Vrecker to the kitchen chairs, and the judge and Jake to the sofa. Bringing up the comfortable armchair for herself, she was on the point of sitting down when the last member of the board knocked at the door. She hardly had time to shut it after him before Mr. Wilmot was sitting in the armchair himself.

Jake looked around at her. "Bring in the food now, okay?"

"Certainly, Marshal."

The judge glanced at Jake and gave a soundless whistle. "Pretty good training, Jake," said Mr. Wilmot, smoothing his bushy mustache. "End of the month she'll be bringing you your slippers without your asking."

"Is that what Jane does?" Mr. Conway chuckled.

Mr. Wilmot leaned back, self-satisfied. "Just like dogs. You gotta show 'em who's boss from the start."

"I'll keep that in mind," Jake said. "Now, about this emergency . . . ? Is it the same as all the others?"

Mr. Wilmot nodded disapprovingly. "It sure is. I guess you saw Miss Cartwright wasn't in church this morning. According to Miz McEwan, who's boarding her this month, Miss Cartwright was up bright and early this morning puking into a bucket. Now, one guess what that means."

"Same as all the others," Mr. Vrecker said. "For certain I thought we'd found at last the right kind of woman for the job. Miss Cartwright is thirty, if not more than."

"Who's the guilty man?" the judge asked Wilmot.

"Miz McEwan says it's that good-looking Dutch boy. Says her oldest girl saw 'em together last Friday talkin' by the fence for what must have been near an hour."

"They sure start young these days. Why, Niklaus can't be more'n nineteen. I was still sucking on lollipops at that age," the judge said ruefully.

"I guess you never know about love," Jake said.

"Well, I guess Nick Koers knows now," Mr. Conway added with his loud laugh. He cut it off short as Antonia came in with five empty glasses balanced on a wooden chopping board. With a smile she offered one to each man before returning to the kitchen.

"So, when they are to marry, Wilmot?" Vrecker wanted to know.

"The womenfolk are workin' on it," Mr. Wilmot said. "There's a big meeting at Miz Fleck's tonight. I think my wife said it would be a week from Wednesday. Which leads us to our problem, gentleman. Where are we to get ourselves a new schoolmarm this late in the year? All the good ones from the college is spoken for already."

"Besides," the judge put in, "they said they weren't so sure sending young girls to Culverton was such a good idea. They wouldn't send us no more pretty ones after Grapplin got hold of Maisie, and I don't know what they'll say when I tell 'em about Miss Cartwright. She was our last hope.''

"Just like Nick Koers was hers!" Mr. Conway slapped his thigh.

"Anyway," the judge said, continuing, "they said they were tired of sending us well-trained girls who give up teaching five minutes after they get off the train. I told 'em they were exaggerating—Miss Cartwright's been here near three months—but they said Culverton don't need learning, we need a revival meeting.''

"That ain't right," Mr. Conway said, frowning. "We're the most moral town I ever heard tell of. Didn't we sort out those you-know-whats"—he hooked his thumb toward the kitchen—"as pretty as you please. Just 'cause that highfalutin' teachers' college sent us girls that can't keep their legs closed . . .''

Antonia came in again, this time carrying a covered plate and a large pitcher of opalescent lemonade. Jake leaped to his feet to drag over a small table from the corner. Antonia thanked him and put her burdens on it.

"Now you help yourselves," she said sweetly, "and if you need anything else, just call.''

The instant she'd shut the door behind her, she turned and very cautiously opened it a mere crack. Applying her eye to it, she watched the men.

The judge poured out the lemonade, maneuvering a slice of citrus into his own glass. Jake whipped the towel off the plate to unveil flat, store-bought crackers, adorned with the thinnest scrape of butter she could contrive. The look on his face, Antonia thought, would keep her giggling for days. Grabbing for a dish towel, she bit it to keep her mirth from escaping.

The judge took an injudicious swig from his glass. His round blue eyes all but rebounded from the far wall as he swallowed. Mr. Conway hadn't noticed the judge's reaction. He too took a healthy gulp from the milky-clear liquid.

"Holy cats!" he said hoarsely. "What is this . . . coyote piss?"

Antonia's own eyes were watering now. She watched as Jake, with a caution that well became a lawman, sipped a tiny drop of his lemonade. He tucked in his lips with distaste and then opened and closed his mouth once or twice. Seeing this, Wilmot and Vrecker put their glasses on the table and scooted as far away from them as they could.

Jake stood up. "I'll go get some sugar."

Without wasting a second, Antonia snatched her book off the table and dashed out to sit on the dish towel on the back step. She left the door slightly ajar behind her to avoid slamming it. Holding her book to catch the gilding rays of the sun, she fancied that she looked perfectly innocent of all crimes, especially of the heinous act of serving lemonade without even a grain of sugar. It had been childish, but very enjoyable.

She heard the banging of cupboards in the kitchen and went on reading. "I hope you're proud of yourself," Jake said, appearing above her.

"I beg your pardon?"

"Don't you understand those are my friends in there? Is this how to treat them?"

If she'd turned her head, she could have seen his boots. She turned a page instead. "If they are your friends," she said levelly, "then why did you leave me to prepare for them?"

Goaded and knowing his friends were undoubtedly laughing at him, Jake barked, "Because you're a woman, damn it! That's what women are supposed to do."

Confident, for this was the sort of thing she was trained to meet, Antonia said, "And if I were not here, and your friends came, what would you have done?"

"Cooked 'em something myself, most likely, but since you are here . . ." Jake recalled his plan to put her on the train tomorrow. He now resolved to do it. "What's the use in arguing?"

"Exactly my point. You got along perfectly well without me before, and you'll do just as well now that I am here. I don't want to spoil you, Marshal."

To confess that her skills in the kitchen hardly extended to taffy making would be an anticlimax. She'd always meant to take lessons from her cook, but Mrs. Wiggins, for all her talent, was no natural instructress.

After Jake left her, Antonia waited a few minutes. Then, deciding it wasn't really fair to punish all five of them, she carried in the plate of gingersnaps that Jenny had brought. Jake glanced at her and went on stirring sugar into the pitcher with a long-handled spoon.

Mr. Wilmot was speaking. "Even if you did manage to charm that college out of another girl, Judge, it'd be a month or more till she got here. If Culverton is ever to advance, to take its rightful place among the other great cities in this great state, we can't afford—"

"Okay, Wilmot," Conway said. "We all know your wife wants you to run for mayor."

"But he is right," Mr. Vrecker said. "We gotta have a new schoolmistress fast. My kids forget the English awful fast if not in school. My wife keeps speaking the German and they talk back. I tell her, Mama, they got the English to learn—this is America—but she don't want to learn."

Antonia said, "Why don't you have this Miss Cartwright keep on teaching after she's married? Being pregnant shouldn't interfere with her duties, not for several more months at least. Then you will have had plenty of time to find a new teacher, unless Miss Cartwright wants to carry on."

"She already done her carryin' on," Mr. Conway said, with his yapping laugh.

The other four men looked scandalized, though whether by Antonia's suggestion or her use of the plain word "pregnant" she couldn't quite tell. They exchanged glances. The judge reached out absently for a cookie, then snatched his fingers back as though from a hot stove. He was the first to answer her.

"Miss Castle, everybody knows that a new-married lady isn't goin' to be any good to anybody. Not with her head turned clear around. Add to that being . . . in the family way . . . and it's pretty plain that her mind just isn't going to be on her work. A baby messes women up, you know, inside. Makes 'em scatterbrained."

There were so many errors in this speech that Antonia hardly knew where to begin. "Are you trying to tell me that a woman loses her mind when she gets pregnant?"

The men chuckled. "It sure seems that way," Mr. Conway said. "But I guess you ain't never carried no young 'uns."

"No, I haven't. Have you?"

"Well, I got . . ." His sunburned face took on a deeper tinge. "That ain't nothing respectable to say."

"This isn't getting our problem taken care of," Jake said quickly. "If Miss Castle has no further suggestions . . ."

"But I do." Jake sighed, but Antonia carried on. "As it seems I am to remain in Culverton for the next thirty—excuse me—twenty-nine days, I will become your teacher. Purely on a temporary basis, of course, and provided that Miss Cartwright doesn't wish to continue."

"No!" Jake said. "I mean, you're not qualified."

"On the contrary, Marshal. I attended Mount Holyoke College between the ages of sixteen and nineteen. I hold a certificate from their education department. My grandmother," she explained, "believed strongly in the further education of women."

"Why aren't I surprised?" Jake murmured. More strongly he said, "Look, it's good of you to offer, but it isn't really your problem—"

"You need a teacher?"

"Yes, but—"

"Very well, I am offering to volunteer for the job."

"I like her," Mr. Vrecker said with decision. "She speaks very good English."

"It would save us a month's salary, and nobody's wife'd have to stretch to feed her or have her in the house." Even Judge Cotton nodded in agreement with Mr. Conway's frugality.

Jake said, "Am I the only one who thinks this is a bad idea? You talk of wives, Conway. I don't have one, of course, but how do you think they're going to take this idea? We're talking about a woman here I had to arrest for disturbing the peace, and the judge sentenced her—"

"Why, you . . ."

"Now you know it wasn't a trial, exactly, Jake," Judge Cotton said, forestalling the storm rising in Antonia's eyes. "Miss Castle ain't been convicted of nothing whatsoever. It's not as if we'd have a *criminal* teaching the young 'uns. I don't see what the womenfolk can complain about."

"And you a married man," Jake said.

"I'm kind of the same mind as the marshal," Mr. Wilmot said, looking Antonia up and down, his mustache bristling. "It seems to me we'd be asking for a barrel of trouble if the school board took this step. I move that we quit for the night and talk it over with our wives. See what the majority thinks. The judge here can break a tie, unless he wants to cast his vote now."

"No, I'm willin' to consult with the womenfolk first. Safer for all of us that way, I reckon."

The men decided to break up the school board's meeting. They all shook hands with Jake and tipped their hats to Antonia as they left. She hardly waited until the last one was out the door before saying, "I certainly would have thought *you* would have been delighted for me to be gone all day."

"I'm not often here myself and I'll probably be gone even more now. I got the word a bunch of cattle rustlers may be working their way down here from Illinois. I wish all you folks would stay at home.''

''Oh, we're back to that! I'm such a dangerous sort, I don't wonder you don't want to stay. I might do something violent!''

''It wouldn't be the first time. We've already brawled in the street, and I've got the bruise on my shin to show it.''

''I'll send the doctor over to look at it,'' she said snidely as she reached for her hat. It was not stupid looking, though it had a certain air of being on backward even when worn right side to the front.

''Where are you going?''

''To see Miss Cartwright, of course.'' She pulled on her gloves and reached for the front-door handle.

Jake walked over and shut the door. ''Haven't you gotten into enough trouble for one Sunday? Those women don't want your help, Miss Castle. They've done all right without you for a long time. They can keep on just the way they are.''

''By that reasoning, Columbus would have never left Spain.'' She reached again for the handle, but he didn't release it.

''Some people wish he hadn't.'' He gave her a searching look, one that seemed to find all the secrets she kept buried in her heart. Antonia couldn't bring herself to look away, although she very much wanted to.

''Why did you leave Connecticut, Miss Castle? Why did you leave Chicago to come here?''

She had to clear her throat before speaking, the low ladylike cough she gave before beginning a lecture. ''Ignorance must be rooted out from wherever it lurks, if mankind is to progress. I believe man was meant for better things than brute labor and endless poverty. And if man is of higher stuff than that, so must women be. If all women knew there's no need to wear themselves out with childbearing, until all health and strength has gone—''

"And you mean to tell 'em?"

"I have to try."

He opened the door and stepped out of her way. "God love you, then, Miss Castle. It's a heck of a job you've cut out for yourself. You know, though, folks don't like somebody from out of town telling 'em they're ignorant."

Antonia was keenly aware of his eyes on her as she followed the track that led to the main road. Though he'd made it plain what he thought of her personally, she felt she'd impressed him with her dedication to her cause. Yet it disturbed her that even while talking to him earnestly, she'd been more aware of him as a male animal than as a potential worker for Social Enlightenment. She wondered if it would be worthwhile to be subjugated to such a man.

When she'd fled her family, there had naturally been no complete severance of all ties. Her parents had equipped her with letters of introduction to many prominent persons in Chicago, whom they'd known of through other friends and relations. Though Antonia was certain news of the family scandal had come west more quickly than she had herself, everyone was very kind to her.

She'd stayed at first at the home of Mrs. Roscoe Banneret, a distant cousin of her aunt-by-marriage, Molly Howard Castle. Though Mrs. Banneret, a widow, pressed her to stay at her large home for as long as she pleased, Antonia soon found her own town house, which had been first mentioned to her by Mrs. Windsor, Mrs. Banneret's sister-in-law. Though Antonia had shocked quite a few people by insisting on her own residence, the presence of a cook and a maid recommended by Mrs. Stratton-Douglass, of the Prairie Avenue Strattons, did much to salvage her reputation. It was actually as Mrs. Stratton-Douglass's mansion that Antonia had met Mrs. Lloyd Newstead.

Once she'd furnished her house, and had explored but

by no means exhausted the many thrills of Marshall Field's Department Store, Antonia found herself at loose ends. The parties she frequented were respectable and dull. She went to the theater and the opera far more often than her parents had ever found to be necessary.

Her acceptance into society assured, her name appeared in the Bon Ton Directory—*Names in Alphabetical Order, Addresses and Hours of Reception of the Most Prominent and Fashionable Ladies Residing in Chicago and Its Suburbs.* Even this, to which many young ladies aspired but did not achieve, and the resultant callers did not end Antonia's dissatisfaction.

She accompanied Mrs. Driscoll's daughter Sheila to a lecture at the Art Institute given by Mrs. Lloyd Newstead. Though she'd dropped fifty dollars into a donations basket, she'd not been unduly moved by the speech. Meeting the speaker in person, Antonia had been one of several ladies who had accepted her invitation to visit the shelter her society had established for destitute women. That visit made Antonia realize her vexation was nothing more than the restlessness of a spoiled child.

Once she heard their stories and learned how many young girls had been dishonored and abandoned, she joined Mrs. Newstead's society with her whole heart. She could have so easily been one of these—confused by her own yearnings and the seductive reasoning of some smooth-tongued rascal. Many were ignorant about the processes of their own bodies, even those with children. The obliteration of this ignorance as much as the enlightenment of society became Antonia's main interest.

Surely the women of Culverton could not be more daunting than the sweatshop owners or the factory overseers. These men had tried to intimidate the Society's members to prevent their opening a school and clinic in one of the poorest areas, populated by immigrants and the working poor. The owners had protested that if women had fewer children, it would become

impossible for the factories to stay in business. They'd
go broke paying men and women their proper wages for
work children would do for five cents per hour.

The school withstood two sieges by armed toughs.
Antonia had stood shoe to steel-toed boot for hours in the
blazing heat of a dry summer, her arms linked with
Sheila Driscoll's. Many of her friends gave up the
Society after that day, bribed or ordered off by their
fathers. By the time Mr. Castle heard about the incident,
the school and clinic were well established.

With the memory of this moral victory to shore her
spirits, Antonia asked a passing child the way to Mrs.
McEwan's home. He pointed down the street and ran off.
A moment later he came back, skidding to a stop on bare
feet in front of her.

"Are you the real bad lady?" he asked.

"No, I don't think so," she answered, smiling down
into a pair of eyes as blue as her own, under a thatch of
pure straw.

"My pa said the bad lady was a hot number, and my
ma said not-in-front-of-the-children. What's a hot number?"

"I'm not sure, but I think your mother was right."

She said good-bye to the boy and walked on toward
Mrs. McEwan's house. Obviously there were to be more
challenges to overcome than the women's hostility. If
she convinced the adults to give her the school, she'd still
have to deal with the children's prejudice against her,
prejudice thoroughly ingrained in this short time by their
parents.

Antonia paused, her hand on the swinging gate. The
McEwan home sat wedged between the grocery store
and the druggist. She wondered which business Mr.
McEwan operated.

Wondering over this question allowed her to put off
planning what she was going to say when she went in.
She'd been carried this far by the knowledge that the
town needed her; now she knew doubt. Already she'd

been driven out once from among these women, though by Mr. Budgell's male authority. Would they now let her in?

"Well, this *is* nice!" Mrs. McEwan exclaimed as she opened the door. "Come on in, Miss Castle, and set."

Her red hair half-covered by a lace square, Mrs. McEwan smiled broadly as she let Antonia enter. Antonia, somewhat taken aback by the unexpected warmth of this welcome, stepped timidly in. "I came by to—"

Someone said, "What is *she* doing here?"

The house was similar on the inside to the Cottons', with a parlor through an entry on the right. However, the McEwans hadn't as many embroidered mottoes, seashell frames, or tinkly crystal-bobbled lamps. Everything was taintlessly clean, from the rag rug on the floor to the carved supports of the fireplace.

Those assembled in the parlor were the more mature women of Culverton, some of whom she recognized from church. The young mothers and brides were notable by their absence. Nor were either of the Dakers women present.

Antonia felt Mrs. McEwan's heavy hand on her shoulder and glanced up into the woman's strong face. "She's come here very kindly to tell us what those idiots on the school board said, haven't you, Miss Castle?"

At that, a pale brunette of about thirty, sitting in the midst of the womenfolk, began to sniffle. Judging by her reddened eyes, these were not the first tears she'd shed this evening. From the way she sat with her hand resting protectively on her abdomen, and an air of intense interior fixation, Antonia guessed that this must be the unfortunate Miss Cartwright.

Her heart went out to the poor girl. Before the others had the chance to close ranks, Antonia walked up to her and put her arm about the shaking shoulders. "Here now," she said, offering the clean white handkerchief from her pocket. "A baby is a time for joy, not tears."

"Even when it has no name?" the fashionable Mrs. Wilmot said.

"Many famous people came of . . . irregular liaisons."

"Like who, for instance?"

Antonia didn't care to get into the home life of William the Conqueror or Leonardo da Vinci, the only two examples she could think of at the moment. "Many famous people," she repeated. "Besides, there's no chance of that in this case, is there?"

"The Koers are talking to Niklaus now," Mrs. McEwan said.

"They've been talking at the boy for more than half the day." Mrs. Wilmot sniffed.

"I—I don't want to marry him," Miss Cartwright sobbed.

It seemed to Antonia that all the other women took half a step back. They muttered and exchanged worried or censorious glances. "Don't be silly, child," said an older, heavyset woman Antonia had not yet met.

"Why don't you want to?" Antonia asked gently.

"He's only nineteen—I don't want his whole life . . . to be ruined because of me!" Miss Cartwright put her face against Antonia's waist and let the bitter tears flow.

Antonia looked around somewhat helplessly, even as she patted the disconsolate schoolmistress's back. "Isn't Mrs. Cotton here?" she asked.

"She's in the kitchen, making tea," Mrs. McEwan answered.

"No, I ain't. I done made it." She bustled into the parlor, balancing a tray loaded with pot and cups on her hip. A younger woman took the tray and put it on the table.

"Here you go," Mrs. Cotton said, handing a filled cup of amber liquid to Antonia. "Get that down her. Best thing to stop the colly-wobbles. Deanna, I hope that man of yourn won't mind, but I ladled some of that Scotch

whiskey of his into the pot. Don't look like that, Jane,"
she said when Mrs. Wilmot looked ready to swoon. "I
know you're all for temperance, but a little nip never did
anybody any harm, no ways."

Antonia coaxed Miss Cartwright into looking up and
taking a sip from the china cup. Though she coughed and
choked, her color instantly bloomed again.

Antonia saw that although Miss Cartwright was by no
means conventionally pretty and was at least thirty, she
had a fresh complexion and brown eyes that no doubt
sparkled when not drowning. Her brown hair might even
have a curl, were it not for the inky fingers clutching at
it.

She drew away from Antonia's supporting arm, mur-
muring, "Thank you."

Antonia put the warm cup into Miss Cartwright's cold
hand. "Shouldn't someone go to the Koers and see if
they've finished haranguing their son?"

A new, booming voice said, "That might be a tad
difficult."

Except for Miss Cartwright, every woman there rose
to her feet as the largest woman Antonia had ever seen
came swaggering into Mrs. McEwan's parlor. A vast
structure of elaborately curled and pomaded hair, black
of the deepest dye, supported a swooping Paris hat. A
broad face, so made up as to conceal the natural color,
matched the heavily corseted yet swelling figure beneath.
A red dress, a thousand black bugle beads decorating the
peplum, did nothing to conceal feminine contours taken
to their most extreme.

This elegant leviathan came directly up to Antonia.
"You must be that lecturin' gal. I'm Miss Annie, the
local whore."

"How . . . how do you do?" Antonia offered her
hand, too experienced to goggle at this blunt introduction.

"Couldn't be better, thanks." Despite her size, Miss
Annie's grip was as languid as a Prairie Avenue society

matron's. "Which is more'n you can say for this poor pup. Hon, I'm sorry to have to tell you. That boy of yours lit out of town 'bout an hour ago."

Miss Cartwright only goggled up at Miss Annie as though she couldn't quite believe she was real. Antonia understood her disbelief. From what she could tell, none of Miss Annie's bulk was fat. She deserved the name of giantess.

"Won't . . . won't you have some tea, Miss . . . ?"

"Don't mind if I do," she said, picking up the cup. In her hand, it looked as if it had come from a doll's set.

Antonia saw the fine tremor of the big hand and realized Miss Annie was nervous. She, too, knew what it was like to walk into a hostile room. Wondering whether Miss Annie had ever spoken to any of these women before, Antonia found herself continuing as hostess.

"Pray have a seat, Miss . . . Annie."

"No, thanks. Can't stay long. Good of you, though."

"Tell me, did you see Mr. Koers leaving town?"

"Nope. But he stopped into my place to collect fifty dollars he was owed for work he did on Greening's farm this summer."

Someone in the room gave a sharp gasp.

"Keep your shirt on, Mrs. Greening. Your old man just stopped in for a drink with some friends. My gal at the bar said Niklaus talked about going away and had a shot o' rye."

Slowly Miss Cartwright stood up. "I'm glad you came to tell me, Miss Annie. I won't wait for him any longer."

"That's the stuff, hon. Never mind about him—you got serious problems to think over. Now you listen. You come over to my place. Me and the gals will look after you till your time comes and no . . . no obligations on your part. I reckon we've most of us been in a fix sometime and we oughta help each other out. I got a couple gals that could stand to learn how to read and cipher. I'll say!"

Mrs. Cotton said, "That's a right generous offer, Miss

Annie. It does you credit, don't it, ladies?'' She was answered by a hum that did not sound entirely approving.

Antonia stepped forward to stand beside Miss Cartwright. ''I don't see why she shouldn't go right on teaching,'' she said. ''The school board wants to know if she feels up to it.''

That might not be precisely how the men would have put it, but Antonia couldn't slap Miss Cartwright with another defeat so soon after she'd heard of the defection of her youthful lover.

Again there was a disapproving mutter from the women in the parlor. ''It wouldn't look right,'' someone said, and the others took up this idea at once.

''What kind of lesson would that teach the kids?'' Antonia recognized the woman who spoke as the one with the twin sons. ''I'm right sorry for you, Miss Cartwright, but I don't think your going on with teaching is such a good idea.''

Antonia dropped her bombshell. ''Then I shall have to do it.''

Perhaps her announcement would have had more effect if a young man of almost white blondness had not at that moment appeared in the parlor entrance. He hesitated there, obviously surprised to find so many people looking back at him.

Miss Cartwright's color fled again. She put out a trembling hand. ''Niklaus?''

As if he'd forgotten his audience, the young man took two long strides forward. He seized her hand and pressed his lips to the deepest of the ink spots. When he raised his head, Antonia saw tears in his bright blue eyes. She looked away and found that every other woman there had found something else to look at besides the sight of a man's naked soul.

''Oh, Bunny,'' he said in a ringing voice. ''Can you ever forgive me?''

''Forgive you?''

''I was going to Montana and leaving you behind. I

got three miles down the road and figured out that my
dreams don't mean a thing without you to share 'em.
Please, Bunny. Forgive me for being so thickheaded.''

"I don't blame you for being scared, Niklaus. I'm
scared, too.''

"What for? I'm with you now, Bunny. I'm never
going anywhere without you again." He put his arm
around her waist and held her close.

Shortly after that, the parlor cleared out. Antonia
found Mrs. Cotton beside her. "Bunny?" she asked.

Mrs. Cotton shrugged. "Well, looks like we'll have
another marryin'. And soon. Oh, my. Oh, yes."

"She is somewhat older than he." Niklaus Koers
hadn't even looked the nineteen years the school board
claimed for him.

"Men marry girls more'n twelve years younger every
day. 'Sides, where they'll be goin', it won't make no
difference providin' a gal can shoot a bear and cook it
tasty."

Without thinking, Antonia followed Mrs. Cotton.
Ahead of them, Miss Annie's bugle beads caught the
glimmer of moonlight as she walked. "It was considerate
of Miss Annie to make her offer to Miss Cartwright."

"Annie's a good woman, considerin'. Don't know
how much longer she can keep that place of hers goin',
though. The women don't like it, and the men are afeared
someone'll find out they go. We're gettin' too civic for
that kind of goin's-on."

They stopped outside the gate. Mrs. Cotton looked up
at her house, at a peculiar light that glowed and faded
behind the curtains. "If that old man's smokin' them
nasty cigars in bed, there'll be hell to pay and no pitch
hot, as my granddaddy used to say. You and Jake stop
over for supper one of these nights, won't you?"

"Thank you. I don't know about the marshal, but I'd
be happy to."

"You still callin' him Marshal? I thought he'd was a
faster worker than that! I feel right let down." Mrs.

Cotton chuckled, a pleasant, old-lady sound. "You best scat on home, Miss Castle. You'll have twenty gals calling on you tomorrow tellin' you why it just ain't right you teaching the kiddies. Me, I think it's an idea, all right, but I reckon to be the only one. What does Jake say?"

"You'd better ask the judge. He's on my side, by the way. He thinks it will save money, or was that Mr. Conway?"

"Ol' Conway's been known to squeeze a dollar till the eagle screams. And my old man would agree to cuttin' off his own head if a good looker wanted him to. You best git on home. Take my advice and have that whole place shining like a pin. They'll be lookin' to tear you down over a speck of dust, let alone your funny notions."

Chapter 9

The little house on the edge of the wood was dark when Antonia returned. She let herself in quietly and groped her way to the sofa. Reaching low to touch the edge before her shin found it, Antonia put her hand on a living leg. Though she snatched her hand back at once, she carried away the perception of solid muscle imperfectly concealed by rough cloth.

"Hello to you, too," Jake said softly, his voice deep and slow. His night sight must be much better than hers, Antonia realized, for he effortlessly caught her hand.

He brought it forward. Antonia did not know what he was going to do until she felt his lips warmly roaming over the palm. A tingle like a fired rocket flashed up her arm and struck into her heart.

Her knees seemed to give out. As Jake tenderly bit her fingers she sank down onto the sofa. In the darkness she could not make out exactly where he was, except that he seemed to have discovered a sensitive spot at the joining of her wrist and hand. Antonia knew she should reprove him, but somehow his name came out as a sigh. "Marshal . . ."

"Right here. And I'm Jake." His arm went around her waist. She leaned against its support, yieldingly. He spread his fingers to span her slenderness. "You really don't wear one," he said on a chuckle.

"What?"

159

"Nothing."

She could just make out his silhouette now, against the background of the slightly less intense dark at the window. Though no details of his expression were clear, she felt his wish to kiss her. He seemed nearer. She turned her head, but not away, deciding not to fight her curiosity another moment.

Jake's mouth angled across hers, slightly off. Antonia at once made it easier for him, sliding her free hand over his shoulder. He let go her wrist and clasped her to him with both arms, pulling her against the compact hardness of his chest. She gasped once at the impact, and then gave herself up to him.

Without a moment's thought, she wrapped her arms about his back as tightly as he held her. Instinctively she felt it was wrong that there should be any barrier between them, even air seemed like too much. She opened at once when Jake sought to enter her mouth with his questing tongue, and did not criticize herself for the low sound she made in her throat as he stroked the delicate surfaces within.

Jake lifted his head, clasping her close. "God, oh God," he said. "I never meant . . ."

She felt his chest heaving with his rapid breaths and smiled to consider that it was all her doing. Pressing her nose into his neck, she inhaled the fresh maleness of his skin, and even dared to nip it lightly. Exulting in his groan of goaded pleasure, she looked up into his face. She could not see him, but she could feel how his arms held her as though he never wished to let her go.

Thoughts moved very slowly across the screen of Antonia's mind. She realized, without really thinking about it, that she sat in the curve of Jake's body, that he'd been lying down when she'd come in. The warmth behind her came from his legs, as the warmth within her came from his touch.

Answers to so many mysteries lay but inches from her fingertips. Yet not even the spontaneous passion ignited in her at the touch of his lips had brought her to where she dared explore his body with her hands.

She remembered him nearly naked, and buried her hot face in the hollow of his shoulder. His breathing had calmed somewhat. Antonia was disappointed. The disruption of her own body still continued. Her nipples, for example, were almost painfully tight. Antonia wondered if Jake could do something about that.

At the image this thought conjured up—of him caressing each white curve with tanned fingers—Antonia recoiled in shock. As though she stood outside herself, she saw the two of them fused together in an embrace, she begging for his kisses like any ordinary, uneducated girl.

"Oh, dear," she said inadequately, shifting uncomfortably.

"Antonia." He released her. "Believe me, I never meant for things to go so far. I was just trying to show you why your teaching school is such a bad idea."

"You have original methods."

Exactly as if he could see her, she put her hand to straighten her hair. "I still have my hat on," she exclaimed, taking it off.

"I'm sorry. I thought I could control myself."

Not for worlds would Antonia confess he'd not been the only one. It was ridiculous to continue sitting next to him as though nothing had happened. Regally Antonia stood up.

"You should go to your own room now, Marshal. What were you doing in here anyway?"

"I wanted to know if this sofa was comfortable. Antonia!" He caught at her hand again, but just as quickly let it go. "You've got to see that you can't stay here. You wanted to leave before; I'll help you now. I'll put you on a train tomorrow."

"I'd like to—"

"Good! I'll light a candle and help you pack."

"But I can't."

"What?"

Antonia was glad of the darkness. Explaining motives was hard enough without light to show up the inherent inconsistencies of the human soul. "All I've ever wanted," she said hesitantly, "is . . . well, I want to be needed, to find somewhere I can do some good in the world. Culverton needs a schoolteacher for a while. I can do that and do it well."

"We can manage for a month without somebody to teach them danged kids! Besides, you can't stay *here* after what just happened between us. You've got to see that's impossible."

"No, I don't think so." She heard him sigh, but felt herself to be on solid, even well-traveled, ground. "Now that I think about it, I see this arrangement as a perfect opportunity to prove some of the Society's ideas."

"Such as?" he growled.

"Such as two reasonable, responsible adults overcoming a certain animal attraction by the higher powers of reason and self-control. Simply because I happen to find you—" She stopped, halted by the scraping of a match. A sudden pinpoint of light appeared in his hand.

Jake had moved to the desk by the window and was lighting a hurricane lamp. Replacing the glass cover, he shook out the match and said, "Go on." He turned to face her.

"I . . ."

"You were saying how you find me animally attractive," he said, his unhasty smile focusing on her. Jake came to sit on the arm of the sofa, casually swinging his bare foot.

Antonia realized that this was the first test. If she could not rationally discuss this matter with him with a light on, she might as well get on that train, all the way back to Connecticut.

"Yes," she said. "Why should I deny it? You're easily one of the most attractive men I've ever met. I thought so from the first moment I saw you."

"I'm flattered, purely flattered."

"There's no reason for you to be. Studies have shown this kind of reaction is nothing more than . . . chemistry. One element plus another, causing some kind of reaction."

"I'll say."

If only he'd stop swinging his foot! She was almost mesmerized by the brown extremity. The first time she'd seen him without clothes she hadn't spent any time looking below his knees. He had a handsome foot.

"That doesn't mean I have to act upon these feelings."

"Seems to me you were doing all right a minute ago."

"Really, if you're only going to sit there making rude comments . . ."

"What would you rather I do?"

He eased himself off the arm of the sofa and came toward her, his feet silent on the bare boards. Antonia did not shrink back, knowing this must be the next test. If she could withstand his kiss without going up in flames, that might prove to him a platonic relationship was possible between them.

Jake brushed an errant strand of golden hair off her forehead. Her skin was as smooth and cool as porcelain. He could hardly believe the passionate creature he'd held a moment before was now this composed woman, looking at him with calm blue eyes and an aloof expression. His only regret was that he'd kissed her in the dark. He wanted to see her change from Connecticut snow maiden to Missouri wildfire.

He realized the lamp burned now.

Antonia braced herself for the pyrotechnics to come. She would have to be strong to prove she could disregard the urgings of her body. She only hoped he'd not be brutal.

With exquisite lightness, Jake brushed her lips with his own. Her eyes widened in surprise and he had to clamp down hard on his need to bring her again into closest contact with his body. He tried to forget what she felt like, when she writhed to come closer to him still. Concentrating on feather kisses, he thought with laughing frustration that Antonia could teach him nothing about self-control.

When he began, Antonia almost laughed. Surely it would be easy to remain strong when all he offered were fleeting touches of his lips. Why, he didn't even hold her!

Yet, as he went on, she began to understand what torment really meant. He skimmed over her cheek, breathed against her eyelid, never pausing or lingering to explore more deeply. He pressed an instant against her throat, grazed the angle of her jaw, and returned to taste her lips before finding new areas to tease. Her entire face tingled with new sensitivity.

Antonia found her hands balling into fists at her sides. She could stand it; all she had to do was think of something else. The only question in her mind, however, was which part of her he'd choose to taste next. He kept to no pattern, flitting as randomly as a bird in flight.

When he nipped at her earlobe, a cry tried to issue from her throat. She strangled it. When he found a cord in the side of her neck that made every nerve answer his touch, she couldn't keep back a voiced sigh.

"Marshal . . . Jake!"

"Hmmm?" He flicked his tongue against the awakened underside of her jaw. Straightening, he looked down into a slumberous pair of blue eyes, smoky with fires he'd deliberately ignited.

"Kiss me."

"What was that, Miss Castle?"

She knew he was making fun of her, that he'd forced her to this demand, but she didn't care. Reaching up on tiptoe, she locked her hands about his neck, his hair on his collar curling around her fingers. "Kiss me, gol-darn you!"

Standing-up kissing was better, and worse, Jake realized, than sitting-down kissing. Better because it was all of her against all of him, and worse because he had practically to lift her up to kiss her, which kept his hands from doing what they so wanted to do. Antonia was all woman and he wanted to explore every one of her unrevealed delights.

Nothing that Jake did frightened her. She reveled in the tightness of his arms about her body, and didn't protest when he slipped one hand down to support her bottom. His hand seemed to burn through all the layers of her clothing. Nor did she say one word to stop him when he urged his lower body forward to rest firmly against hers.

But when nothing would content her but to deepen their kiss with her own tongue, Antonia froze with shock. Was she so quickly turned into a creature of depravity? She searched her soul for shame and found none there, which only made her more certain she had been stripped of every moral feeling.

Jake felt the change in her response at once. He let her down gently, grinding his teeth as her body passed over his arousal. Obviously he'd gone too far. He forced himself to remember that Antonia was undoubtedly a virgin, though she responded in his arms like a wild woman.

"I guess I ought to apologize again," he said, stepping back.

"It was as much my fault as yours. I thought I could withstand temptation." Her voice was hoarse. She cleared it. "I was wrong, this time."

"So, you'll be leaving?" It would be better that way, he told himself. Yet he knew, whether she stayed or not, his nights of peaceful sleep were gone. But which torture would be harder to bear . . . Antonia a million miles away, or Antonia sleeping the other side of his door?

"No, I'll be staying."

"But what about us?"

"We simply need to practice . . . restraint." His smile made her heart beat faster without so much as a touch. "After all, Marshal, you don't really like me, do you? I am opinionated and difficult and—what is the word?—ornery?"

"I never argue with a lady. My opinion is you should get the hell out of here, but it's your decision. For now. Good night, Miss Castle."

"Good night, Marshal."

That night it began to rain. Antonia had seen lightning storms come up the shore practically to her parents' doorstep, and she'd been caught out in half a gale, but she'd never seen the sheer concentration of water that fell out of the sky beginning Monday night. It turned the dirt lane into a swirling, milky river, beat down the grass as though it had been trampled by an army, and set the trees to drooping sorrowfully.

It also, as it turned out, kept every child in Culverton at home, except those who labored on their family farms or in the stores. Those children came home muddy and wet, sending their mothers hustling for clean, dry clothes. The older children could amuse the younger ones, and mothers could sing songs and tell stories.

After two days of all but unending rainfall the games started to lose their flavor. Mothers repeated stories and the songs took on an edge. The whining started. Tempers, both child and adult, began to fray. Once, the sun broke through the overhanging clouds, but it was only a momentary gleam, not even bright or hot enough to dry a single union suit.

By the fourth day of this deluge, the women fell behind in the interminable work of caring for their houses and their husbands. That the men tracked in oceans of gluelike Missouri mud did nothing to restore tempers. Many hard thoughts were focused on Miss Cartwright. If only she could have waited one more week to display morning sickness!

Antonia spent the long week staring out the window. She meant to spend it, once Jake had assured her the rain had set in for a spell, writing up an account of her experiences in Culverton for the edification of the Society.

Every day after breakfast, she laid out paper, sharpened her pen, and sat down at his desk. She would begin, looking up casually as he went out to bid him a good day, and then she'd scratch down a few lines, pause for inspiration, and never write another word. Eventually she occupied most of her day with a worn pack of cards she'd found while looking for a clean blotter.

Oddly enough genius always returned the moment she heard the splashing steps of Jake's horse. For all he would be able to tell, she could have never moved from the desk the entire day.

Sometimes, for a change, she tried to read *Principles of Hygiene*. Though she gave the book her customary attention, she found the words fled her mind when Jake appeared, flapping his hat outside the door to remove the wet. When he asked her what her book was about, she floundered trying to describe it, and realized she now *believed* the book to contain wisdom, rather than knew it.

He'd asked her only once if she still wanted to stay. "Nobody's come up to ask you to take the school."

"In this weather? Who'd try to swim this far?"

"I saw the judge today. He said the other members of the board he's talked to haven't heard anybody speak in your favor."

"Which member has he been able to speak with besides Mr. Wilmot? The other two are farmers and must have too much to do now to come into town. Mr. Wilmot was already against me."

He'd shaken his head with rueful respect. "Remind me to telegraph you if I ever get a case I can't figure."

Since Monday night, they had not touched each other. Even in the tiny kitchen, sharing the duties of the day, she carefully nudged condiments across the table when he asked for them, and he never reached past her for anything. Not even their fingers brushed.

Antonia worried about what would happen if they made a miscalculation and one of them touched the other by accident. Would there be an explosion? As a result she behaved with great politeness, offering and receiving more courtesy than she'd known even at one of Mrs. Potter Palmer's grand soirees.

They fixed mostly stew. He saw to the cooking of it while she chopped up the vegetables or meat. Surprisingly Antonia found she did not get tired of the same meal, day in and day out. Jake seemed to have the knack of changing its flavor with new ingredients, although the base substance remained the same.

Saturday morning, Jake stood on the doorstep a moment longer than usual. "It'll clear up tomorrow," he said.

"How can you tell?" To Antonia, the day was as gray and swashing as ever.

He turned up the collar of his coat. "Clouds are thinner. You might even see the sun today."

"The sun? What's that?"

He chuckled and walked out. Antonia peered through the rain-mottled window at him, ready to study the sky if he seemed to be looking her way. Even through puddles, he walked better than any man she'd ever seen, with long confident strides.

He'd spend ten minutes in the shed, saddling the black horse. Perhaps, if he really believed what he'd said, he'd turn the other two out to pasture today. She wondered idly if the horses were as jaded by the rainy weather as she was.

Much later, as Antonia shuffled the cards for another round of solitaire, she was distracted by voices from outside. Had her mysterious violinist come back, bringing an accompanist?

After tossing the cards into the desk drawer, Antonia stood up and peered out the window. A horse and buggy stood under the trees by the lane. Two women, the rain dripping off their black umbrellas, stood in discussion outside the front door.

Antonia opened the door and said, "Won't you come in?"

Two startled faces looked around, pale with cold. Antonia recognized Mrs. McEwan and Mrs. Wilmot. A hint of hope warmed her inside. If the two most esteemed ladies of Culverton (always excepting Mrs. Cotton) had come to see her, what other purpose could they have but to offer her the school?

Especially as Mrs. McEwan held a covered basket in one hand, and Mrs. Wilmot grasped the strings of a bag of apples. Antonia had been in Culverton long enough to understand that food served as a peace offering. If Mrs. Dakers ever baked her a cake, she'd know she had been fully accepted in the town.

"There's a good fire in the stove, if you don't mind sitting in the kitchen," Antonia added when they hesitated.

After sharing a brief glance, in which they expressed much with eyebrows, the two women stepped up into the house. Antonia thanked them for the gifts and said, "My, isn't it wet out?"

Her guests said a few polite things about the weather as they took off their galoshes and shook their umbrellas outside the door. Crossing the living room to the kitchen, Mrs. McEwan said kindly, "We've not had the pleasure of seeing you in town since Monday night, Miss Castle."

Had anyone wished to see her? "I seem to have misplaced *my* galoshes. I think they must have traveled with Evelyn on her wedding trip."

Mrs. Wilmot sat down in one of the kitchen chairs. "We sell a very good brand at the general store, Miss Castle. And they're quite reasonable. Only two dollars the pair. I'd be happy to send you a pair by the marshal. A size-five shoe?"

"Six." Antonia smiled ruefully down at her feet.

"Six?"

"Yes, my brother Ned used to say I must be part Indian because my feet are like birchbark canoes. Heap-Big Boating Toes—how furious that used to make me when I was little!"

"You come from a large family?" Mrs. McEwan asked.

Antonia found herself talking easily about Ned and Jonathan, about the things they'd said, and what they'd done as children, leaving out any hurts or quarrels. While Mrs. Wilmot told an anecdote about her own brothers, Antonia remembered her duty as a hostess and made coffee. Mrs. McEwan brought out a loaf cake with a sticky berry glaze to accompany it.

"I hope you take to this, Miss Castle. It's my mother's own recipe. Some people find it too sweet."

"Oh, I have a terrible sweet tooth. I'm afraid I get a larger bill from the candy kitchen around the corner from my house than I do from the greengrocer's."

"You *buy* candy, Miss Castle?" Mrs. McEwan asked, glancing at Mrs. Wilmot.

Antonia shamefully confessed, "I can't really make anything except taffy and I don't like that nearly as well as chocolate caramels. Those are my real downfall."

Mrs. Wilmot said, unbending, "I'm partial to chocolate drops myself. Sometimes my husband stocks them just for me. He says he can't make a profit on them because I eat them all."

Just as in Chicago, the ladies' visit lasted no longer than an hour. Though Antonia pressed them to stay, and Mrs. McEwan seemed to be willing, Mrs. Wilmot consulted the watch pinned to her bosom and took her leave. She turned back on the doorstep, her umbrella framing her bonnet.

"I hope we shall see you in church tomorrow, Miss Castle?"

"I don't think—" Antonia caught back the words. Surely Mrs. Wilmot wouldn't look at her so mildly if she were offering some sort of snub?

"Yes," Antonia said. "I look forward to it."

"I'm so pleased."

Deciding all at once to risk everything, Antonia said, "And what time should I open the school on Monday?"

Mrs. McEwan answered, "I'm sure if you'll come by to take supper with us tomorrow, Miss Cartwright will be happy to answer any questions."

"How is Miss Cartwright? When's her wedding to be?"

"Not till Mr. Greening comes up with the rest of Niklaus's fifty dollars. He only had thirty with him when Niklaus saw him at Miss . . . before."

Mrs. Wilmot had already scurried across the wet yard to her buggy. She now called to her friend. "Come along, Deanna, or we'll never get supper on the table."

With almost a hunted glance over her shoulder at her waiting friend, Mrs. McEwan said hastily, "I want you to know, Miss Castle, I stuck up for you when we were talking over whether you should take the school. Not that anybody was in too much of a hurry to keep the kids home after what this week's been like. Mercy! But I told 'em I knew you would never pass along any of your funny ideas to innocent babies, no matter what Mrs. Dakers said."

"Thank you, Mrs. McEwan. I'll try to make you proud of your support." She shook hands with her and waved as the other woman skipped over the biggest puddles to the buggy. Antonia waved until the buggy was out of sight. Glancing up, she saw that the sky did seem a lighter blue, though a few minutes later it began raining again.

Jake came home later than usual that evening. He had a pair of black rubber galoshes and a stunned expression. "Mrs. . . . Mrs. Wilmot said I was to bring you these. She's started a credit sheet for you down at the general store."

"How nice," she answered, smiling at his confusion.

"Now I'll be able to go to church without ruining my shoes."

"Church?"

"Yes, I've been invited back. And . . ." She made every effort not to sound as if she were gloating, but she was afraid she didn't hide it very well. "And I'm to start teaching class on Monday morning."

"I know. I heard all about it from the judge. Congratulations." Jake walked toward his bedroom door.

"Thank you." She stood up, pushing back the desk chair, and followed him across the room. Jake turned and faced her, his fingers already hooked into his necktie.

"Marshal," she began, and then paused, uncertain how to continue. She'd been planning what to say ever since the ladies left, but when he spoke to her, all her rehearsed speeches vanished.

"Marshal, now that I've been put in a position of such great responsibility, there's no reason to go on with this nonsense."

"Which nonsense?" His eyes showed dark gray, and Antonia looked away beneath the weight of his steady gaze.

"My living here, with you." She hurried on. "Obviously I'm not any of those things the judge suspected I was, or no one would let me teach. Certainly they wouldn't think of allowing me near their children if anyone suspected that you and I . . ."

He tugged loose the ends of his cravat and stood there, winding the dark band around his fingers in an endless loop. "That you and I what?"

It was just like him to make things more difficult for her. She raised her head proudly. "No one would allow me to teach if they thought we were illicit lovers."

"Oh, you're right about that." He shoved his necktie into his coat pocket and wrenched open his collar. The rain must have driven under his hat as he was riding home, for drops of water trickled down from his dark hair and clung to the sides of his neck. Antonia wanted to wipe each one away with the soft end of her braid.

Instead she concentrated on his eyes. He had thick black lashes, softening a gaze that tended to be stern when fixed on her. "I don't see that I need to live here any longer."

"You may see it that way," he began.

"You mean that you don't? I thought you'd be happy to see the last of me."

"I still have my duty to do. The judge didn't say a word to me today about ending this 'nonsense.' If you try to move out, I'll arrest you again."

"What? That's outrageous!" Her exclamation was halfhearted.

More outrageously still, Jake was slowly slipping the buttons of his shirt free of their holes. Antonia watched each step as he moved one hand down his front, leaving a trail of visible skin behind it. When he reached the two buttons on his waistcoat, she thought he'd stop. But he opened it, pushing the sides away and pulling his shirt out of his woolen pants. His shirt hung open either side of his naked chest and his hands rested on the brass belt buckle, his thumbs tucked away inside the waistband.

Antonia's own hands itched with wanting to run wildly over the distinct planes and rises of his body. Would that long line of his hair feel soft or crisp? Would it catch at her fingers the way the hair on his head had curled around them when she'd kissed him back?

Standing this close to him, she could see a thin white scar tracing over his right ribs, but it only emphasized the smooth unmarred brownness of the rest of him. If he'd been magnificent at a distance, what word would describe him close to?

"Is something the matter, Miss Castle?"

Hearing the devilishly innocent tone of his voice, Antonia caught herself up. She'd been watching the movements of his brown hands like a dog waiting for a tidbit from the dinner table. Everyone knew that women could not be aroused by the sort of gross visual stimuli that men required. Why then did her lower body feel heavy and tense, and her heart beat with this new and dangerous rhythm?

She caught her breath, and the scent of his warm, rain-touched body filled her senses. Her voice shook as she said, "Nothing in the world, Marshal Faraday. Since you insist, I must stay on here."

"Are you sure you don't *want* to stay?"

"Of course I want to stay." Did he move toward her or was it her fevered imagination? "Mrs. Fleck's boardinghouse was most uncomfortable. The walls were very thin; I could hear every word the man next door said in his sleep. You at least don't talk at night."

"Sometimes you do."

"I do not!"

"Sure you do," he said, his voice low and amused. "Almost every night. You want to know what you say?"

"I suppose you listen?"

"You bet. You might say something incriminating. As a matter of fact . . ."

Antonia knew she'd turned red. She flung around so he could not see her face, saying, "I've never heard of anything so low!" She wanted to storm away, but he seized her arms by the elbows.

Off balance, she could not stop him from bringing her back against his chest. Immobilized by his touch, but not by force, Antonia stood still, with no desire to fight. She let her head fall back against his shoulder, and his heart thrummed beneath her ear. His warmth spread through her.

"You say my name . . . Jake . . . and then you sigh like this." His whisper lifted the tendrils at her temples, and deepened the spell he'd cast. "Sometimes you give a little whimper, like this . . . as if I'd run my hands over you."

"I don't," she whispered. "I couldn't. . . ."

Jake looked down at her. Antonia's eyes were half-closed and he could feel in his own body the tremors that ran through hers. With no effort at all he could turn her around and take sweet advantage of her lips. Then, he knew, she'd come into his arms willingly and his bed was only three steps inside the door.

Very carefully, as if he were handling pure nitroglycerin, Jake set Antonia on her own feet. "I'm going for a bath," he said, his throat rasping when he spoke. He pretended not to see her confusion as he stepped back into his own room, shutting the door in her face.

It had been a bad day. He was weary and saddle sore. Almost as soon as he'd gotten to the office, he'd been greeted by bad news. A friend, Carroll Richey, who lived on a ranch to the north, had wired for his help.

Rustlers had struck the day before at a small ranch, only taking a few head but killing the thirteen-year-old boy who'd tried to stop them. Jake and Pete rode for two hours to reach the Griffith place, arriving in the middle of the funeral.

Jake had attended too many graveside services ever to be untroubled by another person's grief. However, he could never think of anything comforting to say. The words he wanted to say, heartfelt and true, would only cause more tears. Words are useless and you couldn't put your arms around total strangers to comfort them.

As soon as he decently could, he left the meal the Griffiths had pressed on him, and rode with Richey and Pete to the pasture where the crime had taken place. When Pete was sober, he had an Indian's eye for a track.

"It's kind of muddy—that's only to be expected, I reckon. I'd say there were five men, pretty well mounted, and a packhorse, on the light side. There's a lot of trampling—I'd guess that was the two that were down here ridin' herd. Don't know, though. Seems like a lot of tracks for just them two."

"Thanks, Pete. I wonder if the other kid saw anything

of the rustlers. It would be something if we could figure out which one pulled the trigger.''

''I'd sure like to get these guys,'' Richey said. He sat heavily in his saddle, his big freckled hands crossed on the horn. ''Roy was a good boy—worked like a black to keep this place going when his dad hurt his leg last year. I'd sure like to get these guys.'' He sent a long stream of tobacco juice out across the wet grass.

''We'd all like to get 'em,'' Jake said, turning Attila's nose toward the smoke rising from the sad white house.

Going back, Jake questioned Joe, the surviving boy. He was nine, and torn between shocked unhappiness and a kind of guilty excitement in being the center of attention.

Jake remembered when word had come that his own brother had been killed while on picket duty. He'd only dimly understood that Stuart wouldn't be coming back and been distressed by his mother's tears. At the same time he'd liked all the extra hugging that came his way and how their cook, Xylina, didn't scold when he stole a piece of cake from under her very nose. Within a week, he was again playing with his friends, pretending to shoot ''Yanks'' in the woods.

Joe hadn't seen much. Roy had sent him hotfoot for home the minute he'd decided the strangers were up to no good. Joe had heard yelling and the shots that had killed his big brother as he galloped to fetch his father. He could, however, describe the rustlers well enough so that Jake felt certain in his own mind that this was the same gang that had fled Illinois.

''If they're smart,'' Richey said to Jake, when the boy had gone back to his mother, ''they'd head west, into the territory.''

''They aren't smart. If they were, they wouldn't have come this far down—lots easier to cut through into Kansas. I'd guess they want to go down into the mountains. Maybe one of them's from the Ozarks. I'll wire every lawman south of here to be on the lookout,'' Jake said, kicking at the dirt.

Richey spat again. "I don't know why these bastards couldn't just pass through without killing. That boy wasn't doing 'em any harm."

"If you could think like one of them, you would be one of them," Jake said.

"I guess you're right. You want to join the posse I'm getting up?"

Jake shook his head. "If they're heading south, I better get back to Culverton. With any luck, they've already passed us by, if they are heading for the mountains." Catching his friend's eyes, Jake said, "Do me a favor, Richey."

"What is it?" Richey flushed, though the sun had disappeared behind a wall of clouds.

"If you do catch up with these men, and if you capture some alive, don't hold a rope party. Bring them down to Culverton and we'll have a trial—Judge Cotton needs the practice and I don't care to arrest you for murder."

"Now, would I do a thing like that?"

Jake's hope that the bastards wouldn't come to Culverton grew into a prayer as he and Pete headed for home. Though he tried to block the pictures from his mind, he knew full well what a group of evil-minded men could accomplish. He'd seen so many burned homes, murdered men, and weeping wives and children. Not even Culverton had been immune; it had burned once before over a matter of fifteen dollars the previous blacksmith had tried to collect from the wrong debtor.

Missouri had been a hellish haven for every kind of ruffian ever since the close of the war. Some were just out for whatever they could get, failed farmers or ruthless Easterners booted out of their own states. Some, like Jesse James, had been guerrillas fighting dirty for the Confederacy who, with peace, turned their talents to crime.

Though he hated to remember it now, he'd ridden with

a group like that himself for a mad month once he'd seen there was nothing for him at home. His mother had died of heartbreak and hunger and his sister had married a four-eyed carpetbagger. There'd been nothing to go back for—not even his father's dream of sending his sons to one of the great Southern universities.

The gang had left him in a nothing town on the Texas–Arkansas border after he'd taken a bullet. Healed up, he'd changed his name and headed farther into Texas, where he'd joined the cavalry. A lot of former Confederate men had done it; he couldn't have chosen a better hiding place.

Once a lawman, he'd kept track of his former accomplices. Most had died, violently. One had become the operator of a Wild West show, doing very well in Europe. Still another was a congressman.

After sending telegrams to every county south and east of Culverton, Jake headed for home. The galoshes had been sitting on his desk with a note from Mrs. Wilmot when he'd come in. He'd no sooner read it than the judge had stopped by, talking about how the womenfolk had changed their minds, though still carrying a grain of salt, about Antonia. Judge Cotton hadn't stayed more than a minute. He ducked out before Jake could react.

Jake hadn't expected the town to soften toward Antonia. Rather, he'd thought that his time with her was nearly at an end. A grin had crept onto his face when he realized that she wouldn't leave now.

Finding Pete staring at the sight of him holding a pair of rubbers in his hand and grinning like a fool, Jake had coughed gruffly and said, "Hold down the fort, till I come back. I'm just going home to fetch a bath and a clean shirt."

"Right, Marshal."

He urged Attila to move more hurriedly than his usual gentle glide, and after a whickering sigh, the horse worked up to a trot. Jake promised himself that he would continue to keep his hands off Antonia. He only wanted to see her, to make sure she was all right.

Then when he got there, she'd been all aglow with excitement at taking the school, at being needed. He'd seriously thought about kissing her gently—sort of by way of congratulations. Then she'd begun to talk about moving back to the boardinghouse.

At that moment, stunned, Jake realized as though lightning had struck him how much having her in his house meant to him. He didn't want her to leave. Instinctively he'd threatened her with the first thing that came to his mind, namely his power as marshal. Then he'd tried to influence her with his power as a man. Jake knew she'd give in to one or the other, but he didn't want to force the issue. So here he sat, stripping off his tired clothing, thinking of Antonia.

He liked coming home to her, liked her when she sat restfully on the sofa, liked her when she argued with him. Most of all he liked the nervousness she displayed whenever he came too close. During this week of rain, he had often wondered what it would be like to have the right to kiss her when he came in the door and to keep on kissing her.

It scared the hell out of him.

Chapter 10

"Good morning, children. As you know, Miss Cartwright isn't going to be your teacher anymore. My name is Antonia Castle. Until another teacher arrives, I'm going to be here with you."

Antonia looked out over the young, scrubbed faces. They squinted back at her from benches and tables, their books and tablets under clasped hands before them. Her desk stood on a small dais at the end of the rectangular building, flanked by the flag of the United States and the broad red, white, and blue stripes of the flag of Missouri.

A small girl, with thin blond plaits falling onto the shoulders of her red-and-brown calico dress, raised her hand.

"Yes, dear?"

"Can I go to the bathroom?"

"Of course." She wondered if this first question was an omen for the rest of her scholastic career. As the girl scurried out Antonia said, "If any of you need to be excused, simply go out quietly and come back quietly. You don't need to ask for permission."

"All the others teachers always had us raise our hands and ask," an older girl said on a complaining note.

"I'm sure they had their reasons, but as long as not too many people leave at the same time, I don't think it will be a problem." She'd always hated feeling under another person's control in that regard.

"Now," Antonia began with a small cough. "If you'll open your readers, you may go on from where you left off last week." Thuds and rustles echoed around the plain walls of the tiny building as the students opened their books.

Going behind her desk to sit down, Antonia gave a tiny, sincere sigh. She'd faced hostile crowds made up of contemptuous females and laughing males, but she'd never been more nervous than when she stepped outside with the wooden handle of the large brass school bell in her hand. It had been surprisingly difficult to lift it and harder still to ring it.

When she first appeared, the boys were chasing each other through the muddy schoolyard while the bigger girls sat on the steps, keeping their skirts out of the mud while they thumbed a *Harper's Bazaar*. The younger girls stood on either side of the walk while a local artist repaired a hopscotch pattern with small white stones. No one had looked around when Antonia had stepped out, even though she'd nearly stepped on one girl's hand.

The moment the bell clanged, there'd been an influx of children, laughing and screaming, and then dead silence. She'd entered the building to find the lively crowd turned into effigies, still and absolutely quiet, the boys on one side, the girls on the other. She'd said good morning and with one voice they'd replied, "Good morning, dear teacher."

Now she had leisure to look at them. They did not seem to be armed, even with a lowly tomato, although every child had a container of some sort with them. Some had galvanized lard buckets and others had some kind of tin box, with *Superior Snuff* or *Mojave Java* emblazoned on the side and a wire loop inserted in the top. These, Antonia surmised, carried lunches.

They dressed very much as their parents did—the girls in gingham or calico dresses, mostly dark in color, the hems shorter or longer depending on the age of the girl; the boys in dark woolen pants and white shirts, some with coats, but most with just suspenders, and a few of the older boys in waistcoats, some without a shirt underneath. Everyone, boy or girl, wore heavy shoes if not boots.

The more dapper among the boys had hung hats on nails in the back hall. Most of the girls had long hair, either plainly dressed or curled in the front. Two girls, possibly sisters, had close-cropped hair that heightened their resemblance to each other and to a boy on the other side of the classroom. She recognized him as the boy who'd asked if she was a bad lady.

Antonia had reached this far in her observations when she heard the door at the far end of the schoolroom open and slam. After a moment a boy slouched into the room. His hands were stuck in the pockets of his pants, and mud clung liberally to each knee.

Smiling, Antonia said, "Please find your seat and open your book."

"I ain't got no book, and I carry my seat with me, anyhow." Two or three of the girls giggled, hiding their mouths in their hands. A couple of boys choked.

"Please sit down," Antonia said.

He sauntered over and stood beside a bench. "Scoot on over, Lily-Belle. I like sittin' next to you."

The girl might have been as old as sixteen judging by her ripening figure. She crouched over, her arms protectively around her book, and seemed to pretend not to hear. Antonia saw red dye her skin as giggles broke out afresh.

Though Antonia carried in her heart the firm belief that separating children by sex made them prudish and led to undesirable curiosity later in life, she also knew that young boys were barely civilized. "What is your name, young man?"

"Ernie," he answered casually. "Come on, Lily. If I was Rip Koers, you'd let me sit next to you."

Laughter broke out from all but the very youngest children. Nobody paid any attention to their work, only to the torment going on at the front of the class. Antonia stepped down from the dais, slightly alarmed to learn there was another Koers boy with apparently the same charms as Niklaus.

She hovered over the troublemaker. "Ernie what?"

He glanced at her. His light hair pricked up all over his head, not slicked down like the other boys. "Ernie Ransom."

"Go sit on the other side of the room, Mr. Ransom. I will lend you a book." She glanced around as the boy took his seat across the aisle from Lily. "The rest of you please go on with your reading."

Antonia handed Ernie the schoolmistress's copy of *McGuffey's Fourth Eclectic Reader*. Perhaps one of the hard-hitting moral messages would touch a productive chord in the boy. She returned to the desk. Very quickly, however, it became obvious that the quiet air of study had evaporated.

Muttered talk and muffled giggles came from the back of the room. A girl on the end of the middle row gave a sudden "ouch!" and half stood up, rubbing her arm, to glare at an immediately angelic boy. A few minutes later it was his turn to yelp and hers to raise soulful eyes to the ceiling. Someone brought out a white mouse while a lollipop passed from lick to lick.

None of it, of course, was Ernie Ransom's fault. Yet, irrationally, Antonia had felt all was under control until he walked in. Somehow his immediate disrespect had percolated throughout the entire class. She rapped out, "Will Lily, Greta, and Susan please come here?"

The three oldest girls left their places and approached, Lily's cheeks flaring into rose at the muted wolf whistle that filled the air. Antonia shot an swift glance at Ernie, but he appeared entirely engrossed in the rhyming alphabet.

The girls in front of her now, so Miss Cartwright had said, were to be applying for their third-class teaching licenses the next time the district inspector came by. "If you'll take the younger girls," Antonia said, "I shall deal with the boys. Lily, if you'll take the mental arithmetic group, Susan the grammar, and Greta U.S. history. I believe you left off with the Crossing of the Delaware?"

Antonia dragged herself out of the schoolroom at three o'clock. She'd stayed to clear up, wiping off the blackboard with a wet rag and making futile swipes at the bare wood floor with the broom in the cloakroom. Locking the door behind her, she stepped blindly down the steps.

"How'd it go?" Jake asked.

He leaned up against the dark bole of the tree that shaded the well. Antonia blinked in surprise and suddenly realized she must look as though she'd been rumpled by hasty hands. Smoothing her hair at the temples and setting her hat straight, she said, "Perfectly well. What well-behaved children!"

"That's good. Glad to hear it." He came toward her. "So, no problems?"

"None at all."

He nodded as though he believed her, but went on doing it for a little too long. "For instance," he said, "Ernie Ransom give you any trouble?"

"Ernie?" Antonia rumpled her brow as though trying to remember which boy Jake meant. "Oh, he was fine."

"Fine? Well, you must be a heck of a teacher, Miss Castle. Every other one we've had found him to be a handful."

"Oh, really?"

"Sometimes I wonder if they don't get pregnant so they don't have to teach him anymore."

"I doubt it, but you need have no fear of such a thing happening to me." She meant that she would never run away, but the sudden light that flared up in Jake's eyes made her wonder if he put a different meaning in her words. What would it be like to feel the child of the man she loved moving in her own body?

Quickly, as she began walking toward the main road,

Antonia added, "I mean, Ernie was very well behaved."

Jake fell into step beside her. "You surely do surprise me. The word around town is that Ernie will wind up playing the fiddle so the devil can dance."

"I beg your pardon? The fiddle?"

"Yep. He's not worth much, that kid, but he can sure charm a bow. You heard him play when your friends got hitched."

"That boy plays the violin? How old is Ernie?"

She had so little experience with children that she had no clear idea, just by looking at one, of age. An eight-year-old and a five-year-old seemed very much the same, although once they were in the teen years, the accuracy of her guesses improved.

"Ernie? He's about eleven, I guess. I can't really tell, unless I've been told. All kids look alike to me."

"You, too?" Antonia smiled up at him and asked the question she promised herself she would not ask, wincing as soon as she heard herself speak. "Do you think you'll be coming home tonight?"

He regarded her with raised eyebrows. "Why? You been missing me?"

"Certainly not! I'm only asking." Antonia could feel the prickling heat of a blush starting beneath the high collar of her blouse. In a moment it would flood her cheeks and he'd know the awful truth.

She did miss him. He'd not spent the night in his own home since Friday, though he returned to change clothes and to escort her to church yesterday. The little house echoed with loneliness when Jake was not sitting across from her, sipping thick coffee, or arguing with her, or standing in the doorway removing his clothing piece by piece. Heat flamed in her face.

Jake, however, had turned his head to scan down the road. "I wonder what's up," he murmured as his hand dropped, seemingly of its own, to the gun at his thigh.

Antonia saw a figure coming toward them. In a moment she saw it was one of her students, running as fast as he could toward them. Aaron, who'd asked her about being a bad lady, came to a panting stop beside her.

"I . . . there's . . ." he gasped.

"What's up, Aaron?" Jake asked with a frown.

Placing her hand on the boy's shoulder, Antonia sent the marshal a quelling glance. "Do you want a drink of water, Aaron?" The boy shook his head. Antonia said, "Take a deep breath, and another. Now, what is wrong?"

The boy choked, sniffled, and said, "Nothing. There's a big shipment come to the depot."

"Is that all?"

"It's for you. Got your name all over the boxes in the biggest lettering I ever seen—even bigger than the wanted posters."

"Aaron helps me around the office once in a while," Jake added.

"That must be where he learned to read so well." To the boy she said, "Let's go and see what has come for me."

The boy set off at a run. In a moment he was back, saying, "Don't you want to hurry, Miss Castle? The man said he's got to leave on the train but he can't go till you sign the paper."

"What man?" Remembering that Henry and Evelyn were supposed to send help, she asked, "Is he a lawyer?"

"No, he's respectable. C'mon." He took off again.

Antonia, without so much as a glance at Jake, picked up her skirt and ran after Aaron. She thought for certain she'd left Jake far behind—for she used to be able to outrun even Ned, the fastest boy in their set—but when she saw the depot ahead, he was no more than half a step behind her. When he lengthened his stride to pass her, Antonia yelped a protest and began to run faster still.

Glancing around, she saw his intensity. Commotion flared in her heart at the thought of being caught up again in his powerful arms. She stumbled. Laughing, she regained her balance and ran on in a flurry of petticoats.

Though he leaped up the station steps, two at a time, she managed to touch the front door a finger snap ahead. Winded, she still had breath enough to crow in triumph.

"I won!"

The answer in Jake's eyes had nothing to do with the race. "Maybe I will come back tonight," he said, covering her hand against the door. "You deserve some kind of trophy for beating me. What would you like?"

When his voice dropped low, Antonia found herself unable to concentrate on anything but the warm caressing sound. Gazing up into his deep emerald eyes, she didn't remember the question, but she knew the answer could only be an enraptured yes.

The piercing double toot of the nearby train brought her back to the present. "Oh, my delivery," she said, and pushed the door open.

No Mr. Grapplin looked out from the ticket window, but a murmur of many voices filled the station. "Everyone's out on the platform," Jake said, leading the way.

The two of them stepped outside and the crowd fell back to reveal a stack of crates. One was fully six feet long and about three feet wide. Mr. Wilmot stood over this one, inspecting the label as a child looks at his own name on a wonderfully wrapped Christmas present.

On noticing Antonia, he asked in a whisper, "Is this *the* Marshall Field's?" At her nod he gave a sigh, blowing out his mustache. "I was there, once. The most magnificent emporium . . . the lights . . . the showcases . . . the variety of goods." He clasped his hands and sighed again, happily, as though looking back on a transporting dream.

"I'm supposed to sign something?" Antonia asked.

A young man, faultlessly dressed in a black suit, complete with red carnation, appeared like a genie. "Miss Castle? I'm Mr. Dodson, of Marshall Field's. If you could just sign here . . . and here. Thank you, Miss Castle."

"I didn't expect them to send anyone along."

Mr. Dodson smiled deprecatingly. "All part of the service, Miss Castle. Charming town. I wasn't sure about arranging transportation to your home?"

"We'll take care of it," said a big, deep voice.

"Mr. Dakers!" Antonia exclaimed, pleased. "How are you?"

The blacksmith shook her hand solemnly. "Very well, Miss Castle. I'm glad to see you're still around."

The train sent up a billow of white steam and the impatient whistle split the air. Mr. Dodson said, "Thank you for your business, Miss Castle. I must run. I have fourteen red parlor lamps for delivery in Independence."

He leaped aboard the slowly moving train and waved his gloved hand to the townspeople. One or two waved back. Some of the children ran alongside the train until it got up speed. Most people, however, lingered on the platform, inspecting the big boxes and trading guesses on what Miss Castle had received.

While Antonia asked after Mr. Dakers's health and Jenny, Jake strolled up to them. "How do you intend to carry this stuff home?" he asked her.

As it turned out she had plenty of help, both with loading the wagon Paul Dakers found for her and with unloading. All the children, freed for the afternoon, followed the wagon to Jake's house. The women accompanied the children, and most of the older men who were not otherwise occupied followed the women.

Paul brought out a crowbar but had to give up prying out the nails because of his arm. So he handed the iron rod to Jake and stood by, his wife supporting him. Antonia saw Jake glance around as though looking for someone else to do the work. With a shrug he began to open the crates, the biggest one first.

"Oh, my God," he said when one side fell away.

Mrs. Wilmot took a look inside. "Gracious! Isn't that a lovely color?"

Antonia said, "Let's see how it will look in the living room. Jake, what should we do with your sofa?"

"Throw it in the backyard, or in the creek!" He pushed the crowbar at Mr. Wilmot and stalked off.

Mrs. Wilmot said to Antonia, "Never mind him. Men hate moving day."

Though Antonia couldn't help craning her head to watch him walk away, the other women's enthusiasm was catching. They each had suggestions for the best location for every item. Even Mrs. Dakers arrived later, drawn by curiosity, though she sniffed disapprovingly more often than she praised. The rest couldn't say enough. Antonia had to stop three or four of them from entering Jake's room.

She asked herself if he'd come back tonight. He had not promised her that he would, but his expression had told her that he might. Standing back, looking at the newly decorated room from the doorway, pretending to be him, she could not imagine him being less than thrilled with what they'd done.

"I can't believe you did this."

Antonia awoke to see Jake standing in the doorway of his room, holding up a candle and still shaking out the burning match with which he'd lit it. She sat up, remembering to clutch her new sheet and blanket to her chest. He did not look her way. Slowly he paced around the room, peering past the candle's flame at her improvements.

"Don't you like it?" Antonia asked.

"I can't believe it."

"Of course it's not the same without wallpaper. You can't get the full effect—"

"Thank God for small favors."

"You don't like it? Perhaps it's a little overwhelming, but they didn't have any measurements. Maybe if you lit some of the other lamps, you could get a better impression of the whole thing."

"No, thanks. I prefer my nightmares in the dark."

Antonia thought about laughing at him and telling him he was merely a Philistine without a soul. However, looking at the room in the flickering yellow light, she could see Jake's point. The strange bronze greens and bright reds of the Japanese style were really best by daylight.

"How did you do this?" Jake asked, recoiling from the sight of a large painting of a suspiciously coy blond woman in a floridly patterned kimono and parasol.

"I sent a telegram."

"Oh, yeah. Who is Marshall Field?"

"Marshall . . . ? It's the biggest department store in Chicago. They sell *everything*. I sent them a telegram, saying I had a studio to furnish and could they send me all I would need in the latest mode."

"Mode?"

"The Japanese style is very popular now. All the best people . . . It's from England."

"I could guess it wasn't from Japan." He set the candlestick down among the knickknacks on a rickety bamboo table that had been lacquered a greenish gold. He began to sit on a matching chair but stopped himself as though afraid it would collapse beneath him. Crossing the room, he sat on the edge of her new chaise lounge.

Antonia shrank inwardly. The crimson chaise was broad and deep, very comfortable for sleeping and much wider than his sofa. The letter that accompanied her furniture had described the chaise as being wide enough for two, "should a friend wish to stay the night." Antonia had taken for granted that the writer had meant a female friend. Now she wasn't so sure.

Jake fought to capture her gaze. Finally he reached out and took her chin between his fingers. Staring down, he said, "You're rich, aren't you?"

"Not rich, exactly," she said, still managing to avoid his gaze. "I'd say I was in . . . comfortable circumstances."

"Comfortable? That's what all rich people say. Don't tell me this store would send you all this stuff on the strength of a telegram if you were poor."

"They have liberal credit policies." She never in her life thought that she'd be on a bed with Jake, discussing her finances.

"Nobody's that liberal."

"I don't understand why you are making such a noise over this. It's only furniture. I'll take it with me when I leave. You won't be troubled. . . ."

Her words died away as he released her chin. What had she said to make him look so formidable? His jaw was set hard and his eyes were the color of a rainy day at sea. It couldn't just be furniture that made him look that way.

"I was angry that day, remember? I ordered what I thought would make living here bearable. But I can do without it. If you really hate what I've done, I can send it all back. All but this chaise. It's not nearly as lumpy as that old sofa and I need the rest." Antonia smiled, trying to call up an answer on Jake's face.

He sat very still, his big shoulders slumped. "How long is it now?"

"How long is what?"

"I thought you were keeping a running total of how many more days you've got to be stuck here."

"Oh, I am." All the same she had to think a moment. "Twenty-one, no, twenty days. It must be after midnight."

"Yes, it's late. Later than I thought."

He rose heavily and turned away from her. Offering no more than a muttered good night, he picked up his candle and went into the other room. Antonia saw an insubstantial light glowing beneath the door. In a moment she heard the by-now-familiar groan of his bed as he fell onto it. The light went out. She heard him sigh and shift.

"Antonia?" he said after a long time of nothing but the sound of her own heart beating.

"Yes, Jake?" She propped herself up on one elbow to listen. He didn't answer. Deciding he was only talking in his sleep, she listened again, hoping to hear her name a second time. She wondered what the moral position was on eavesdropping on an unconscious person. When, after a long time, she heard nothing more, she let her head drop on the pillow. Soon she fell asleep.

Jake lay in the dark with his arms crossed under his head, a picture of Antonia as he'd last seen her glimmering in his mind. Her hair had fallen from its knot, lying in waves over the covering she held to herself. Many blondes were washed out, or always looked as though they were about to cry, but Antonia shone in the candle's glow, shone like a good deed.

How he wished she were only beautiful. Then he could understand the way his heart leaped when he saw her. He confessed to the darkness that a random fantasy would once in a while cross his mind about coming home to her and being greeted with a kiss and a smile. Sometimes she even offered him a hot dinner, which grew cold while they made love.

Jake quashed a groan. He'd said her name before, not even knowing what he'd say if she answered. Her reply had come so quickly that he'd been alarmed and drawn back.

Now he knew he'd wanted to tell her that she could do whatever she liked to the house or to him, as long as she'd stay. Did he want her to stay for always, to marry him? Jake didn't know, but a suspicion lived in his heart that he might enjoy finding out. But, he reminded himself, her money added another complication, putting her right out of his reach. He groaned aloud this time, pulling the pillow over his head.

The next morning a heavy mist hung in brooding festoons among the tree branches. Antonia, muffled against the damp chill in her robe, hurried across the dew-dripping grass from the small house in the back. She'd not stopped to button her shoes and the tops flapped. Half tripping, she paused to wiggle her foot back inside when she heard the violin.

It was a slow song, in keeping with the weather, but not sad. The music danced up a few notes, played and rearranged them, and then skipped down. Though the soft calling music repeated, it did not grow tedious, any more than did the song of a bubbling spring.

Antonia called, "Ernie?"

The sound of her voice did not carry. There was no change in the endless little tune. If it was Ernie, he was not prepared to trust her yet.

Ordinarily Antonia would have been tempted to snuggle back in bed after awakening earlier than usual. Today, charged with responsibility, she dressed at once. Folding away her sheets and blanket, Antonia put them in their boxes and looked around with satisfaction. Now she could receive guests without feeling as if she were entertaining in her bedroom.

"Good morning," she said from the desk about an hour later when Jake appeared, yawning in the doorway. She proclaimed herself happy to see that he had on all his clothing, except for his coat, and sternly repressed the pang of disappointment that he was fully dressed.

"I made coffee," she added.

"Coffee!"

A few minutes later he reappeared, both eyes open and his hands wrapped around a steaming mug. "Not bad. A little weak."

"I made it exactly the same way you do."

"I guess you don't have to make your own, in Chicago."

"No, I don't."

"A maid, huh?"

"And a cook."

He puffed out a sigh. " 'Comfortable,' " he muttered.

Antonia finished writing her notes for class. "Are you going into town soon?"

"I was going to go in later, get caught up on the chores I've been neglecting around here. Why?"

"That reminds me. Why were you spending your nights at the jail? If it was because of me . . ."

Jake found himself telling her about the rustlers. "But I heard last night from the sheriff of Cedar County that four men passed through there yesterday. They tried to rob the bank but were scared off. I can tell you it relieves my mind to think they're moving south. The last thing I need is more trouble."

Antonia flushed when he glanced at her, knowing she was his first trouble. "Are you certain it is the same group?"

"How many gangs do you think there are around here?"

"In Missouri? I can't imagine." His smile encouraged her to go on. "I have a favor to ask you. I want to take this box to school with me today and it's heavy. Could you carry it for me on your horse?"

As they entered, the children were not very interested in the strange metal contraption on the teacher's desk. Finding the marshal in the schoolroom when they arrived caused more comment and considerable banter.

The older girls eyed Jake and giggled, Lily turning as bright a red as Antonia's new chaise.

"Your shooting days are done, Jesse James," one boy said to another, a yellow magazine poking up from his back pocket.

"You'll never take me while I can hold a gun," was the reply. Though many shots were fired, every single bullet missed, though each shooter claimed multiple hits.

"Momma told you not to spill your milk, Jessica. Now the marshal's gonna arrest you and lock you up like he did Daddy."

"No, no!" Several of the smallest children started to cry, the burden of their paltry crimes too much for their consciences.

Antonia stood back and watched, fascinated, as the big

man went on his knee to talk to weeping infants. They looked up at him, each and all, with wide eyes as he explained that certain offenses fell outside his jurisdiction. She saw him reach into his coat pocket and bring out candy, pressing it into plump hands. Why was she so surprised to find that he could be gentle when he'd never been anything else with her?

Caught off guard, and a little ashamed of herself, Antonia did not have sense enough to rearrange her features when he glanced up at her. She knew her expression was soft as butter. They stared at each other for a long moment while the sounds of the classroom faded.

"Hadn't we better get started?" he said somewhat gruffly.

"We're not all together yet."

Exactly as it happened yesterday, she heard the door to the schoolhouse slam. Late, his hands stuck in his pockets, Ernie Ransom slouched into the room. Then he saw Jake.

His hands came out of his pockets in alarm. He spun and ran for the door. But the marshal's long legs made short work of the distance and he caught Ernie before the boy got the door open.

Antonia stepped into the hall to find Ernie twisting in Jake's grasp, held by the slack of his shirt. "Ouch! Lemme . . . lemme go! I ain't done nothing."

"Bring him in here, if you please, Marshal. His seat's down in the front, by my desk."

While Jake brought Ernie in, Antonia stepped up onto the dais. She turned the handle, moved the arm, and violin music poured forth from the short horn, a simple rondo by Mozart. It filled the room, clean and harmonious with a lilting laughter that seemed very natural.

The children gasped. Ernie stopped fighting the grip on his collar and leaned forward. Jake let him go.

Catching Antonia's eyes, Ernie sat upright at once, his arms folded across his chest. His face drained of all expression, he gazed up at the ceiling. In that one moment, however, Antonia had had her question answered. Ernie was a born musician.

After the cylinder stopped spinning, Antonia spoke briefly about the phonograph, how it worked and how Edison had come to invent it. She explained that this was a special machine, newly invented, that would play music and speech, where the very first phonographs could only record speech.

"There are only a very few of these, and we're lucky to have one of the first models with us today. But who can say but that one day every home will have one!"

From there, it was easy to turn the subject to the writer of the piece they'd just heard. She found she did not need to refer to her notes. There were many incidents in Mozart's life that would appeal to children, like his proposal to Marie Antoinette when he was seven.

Though Antonia tried to keep the other children diverted, her real message was directed at Ernie. Mozart had begun playing and writing music as soon as he could walk. He'd been world famous before his thirteenth birthday. She tried to let Ernie know there had been other prodigies, other virtuosos. He was not alone.

Jake left at about eleven. "Thanks for the concert," he said, coming to her desk. "I'd never heard of a machine like that before. It's darn near a miracle, isn't it?"

"But did you enjoy the music?" Antonia asked brightly.

He grinned and lowered his voice. "You know me, Miss Castle. If a pretty girl isn't singing it, it don't seem much like music."

"I wish I had you in my class all the time—" she began fiercely.

"I bet you could teach me anything you wanted to. I bet I could teach you a few things, too."

She couldn't blush, not right here with the students lifting curious eyes from their papers and slates. "I've never learned how to shoot a gun," she said levelly.

"Is that all you've never learned?"

"Marshal, please," she said with a glance past him. The older girls were staring and whispering.

"Have I said something wrong? And by the way, you really ought to get used to calling me Jake." He went out whistling a tune he occasionally sang in the bath, about a brown-eyed gal named Sal. The giggling broke out again as he left.

Antonia played a few of the other black cylinders, including Edwin Booth giving a shortened reading of "To be or not to be" from his ground-breaking portrayal of Hamlet. Regrettably the cylinders did not play for very long. The children were fascinated. They all wanted to examine the machine, filing past her desk to peer at it.

Ernie alone pretended indifference. When he didn't leave his seat with the others, Antonia stepped down to invite him forward.

He said, "Who cares about a phonograph? It's just a machine. It's not like there's a person standing there playing the music."

"Why is there a difference between a recording and a performance, Ernie?" Antonia asked, delighted because the boy was stating his opinion instead of sitting in sullen silence.

Ernie rolled his eyes and sniffed, dismissing her for her ignorance. "There just is, that's all."

"I'd like you to stay for a few minutes after class, if you wouldn't mind. I want to talk to you."

The boy eyes narrowed. "What about?"

"Music."

Antonia was taken aback by the sudden leap of hunger she saw in the boy's face. It was as though she'd offered him the whole world. He seemed, however, to suspect her and her gift, for he almost instantly settled back into his pose of apathy.

"You like music, don't you?"

"It's all right."

When she dismissed the class, Ernie rushed out the

door with the others. Disappointed, Antonia washed the blackboard and decided the floor could wait until tomorrow. On her way home she stopped into Wilmot's store to pay for her galoshes and to look over their stock of gloves, as the pair she had on were not wearing as well as she'd hoped they would.

The general store smelled exotic and mysterious, the last thing Antonia would have expected. Spices stood in bottles and tins along the back of the counter, their fragrances mingling with that of warm leather and the sea smell of pickles. On wall was stocked with fabrics and other dry goods and the other with items for the home, everything apparently from bootjacks to lamps to cheerfully painted china chamber pots. More items dangled from the ceilings, and the entire back wall was taken up with even more. Big barrels and kegs occupied much of the floor space and both counters were thick with display cases and assorted canisters.

"Good afternoon, Miss Castle." Mrs. Wilmot bustled forward to greet her.

The interior of the store being very dim, Antonia could only make Mrs. Wilmot out by the brightness of the apron she wore over her clothing. She had already noticed that Mrs. Wilmot dressed very close to the fashion, unlike the other women of Culverton, who wore what was simple and reasonably comfortable. Reaffirmed in her adherence to Rational Dress, Antonia wondered how Mrs. Wilmot managed her tight skirt and ruffles without sending things crashing down in the crowded darkness of her store.

While Mrs. Wilmot brought out samples of gloves from beneath the counter, Antonia said, "Robert and Martha seem bright children, Mrs. Wilmot. You must be very proud."

"If they grow up to be good Christians, that's all I want. You don't have my oldest boy in school. He helps Mr. Wilmot and me here. Such ideas he has for expansion! Mr. Wilmot says the boy's a dreamer, but I'm not so sure Jerry's wrong. What about these? White kid-skin.''

"They're lovely," Antonia said, smoothing the fine leather. "But not very practical. I wanted black or dark brown."

Someone cackled behind her and Antonia turned. Her eyes had accustomed themselves to the gloom, so she could make out Mrs. Cotton almost at once.

"What do you think," the older woman asked Mrs. Wilmot, "she's going to a ball? Bring out them nice leather ones like you sold me last spring."

"Them's the ticket," she said when the gloves were produced. "They'll wear a good long time, winter and summer. Now, what's this I hear tell about you having a machine that makes music?"

"Yes, I heard about that," Mrs. Wilmot said. "It's a phonograph, isn't it? I told Mr. Wilmot we should think about carrying one, but he tends to lag behind the times when it comes to stock. Why, one day everyone will have one, and so I told him, but he never listens to me."

No longer surprised at the speed with which news traveled in Culverton, Antonia explained to Mrs. Cotton how the machine worked.

"Well, if that don't beat all," the older woman said, marveling. "You ought to invite the adults along to hear it, Miss Castle. Make 'em sit up and stare!"

Antonia waited after paying cash for her purchases while Mrs. Cotton inspected some lace. She did not buy any, but she kept Mrs. Wilmot busy fetching and carrying. Finally she said, "If I could see that watch again . . ."

Mrs. Wilmot brought out a dark velvet box. Proudly Mrs. Cotton said, "There. What do you think of that?"

Lying on the satin padding, a gold watch winked up at Antonia. She brought it close to her eyes and the chased pattern of an American eagle became discernible. "It's splendid."

"Do you think the judge would like it for an anniversary present? Forty-five years."

"Any man would be proud to own such a watch."

"That's what I think." She nodded at Mrs. Wilmot. "Put it away again, and I'll keep on mulling it over." Taking Antonia's arm, Mrs. Cotton confided, "Our anniversary ain't till next July, but I don't reckon that watch is going nowhere. It's thirty-five dollars and fifty cents, no trades accepted."

Outside she said, "I couldn't say it in front of her, but the judge's always hankered after one of them fancy tickers. I would have figured Cedric Quincannon would leave him his, considerin' how they were partners and all, but he left all he had to his wife. Poor woman."

"Is this the same Quincannon for whom the city hall is named?"

"That's right. It was Vernon's doing. The rest of 'em wanted to name it Culverton City Hall, but the judge said everybody knows where they are, and if they don't, we'd rather not have 'em in town. Except for Poot Harvey. He never knows where he is."

"When did Mr. Quincannon die?"

"Matter of three years ago. Funny, it don't seem that long. He would sure have taken to you, Miss Castle. He had an eye for the pretty ladies, always. There wouldn't have been any cause for you to be arrested if he'd been here, and if you had been, he would have brought you flowers in jail. I'll say this much for Cedric—he had a flair."

Antonia parted affectionately from Mrs. Cotton after accepting a dinner invitation on Jake's behalf for the next evening after a middle-of-the-week church meeting. She stood for a moment outside the store. Across the street the livery stable's blackened boards served as a reminder of the darker side of this sometimes pleasant town.

Passing the marshal's office, she hesitated and then went in. Remembering the grizzled man behind the desk from her single night's stay in the jail, she colored as she asked, "Is the marshal in?"

"Nope, Miss Castle. He surely ain't. Any message?"

"No . . . no, thank you. I'll see him tonight."

"Right," Pete said, putting his feet back on the desk and tilting back in the sprung chair. His snores reached her before she put her hand on the door handle.

The sleepy stillness of the afternoon filtered down through the dull sky. A dog slept in the middle of Main Street. Antonia found herself patting away several yawns as she strolled down the uneven sidewalk.

She waved to Jenny Dakers when she saw her taking down laundry from a line strung in the backyard of their clapboard house. The girl looked as though she'd like to speak to her. As soon as Antonia crossed the street, however, Jenny picked up her basket and went inside.

Antonia did not take the snub to heart. Probably Mrs. Dakers watched from nearby and Jenny dared not risk her mother-in-law's anger.

The general store was on the opposite end of town from the schoolhouse. She had passed the Silver Spoon Saloon before, hearing the jag-time music, but had been on the other side of the street. Though she did not slow down as she passed it, she couldn't resist throwing a glance in the plate-glass window.

Except for the piano player, it seemed fairly peaceful, but then she hadn't expected an orgy at three-thirty in the afternoon. All the same Antonia felt slightly disappointed that there were not at least two drunkards and a soiled dove in evidence. Remembering Miss Annie's kindness to Miss Cartwright, Antonia reproved herself for her flippant thought.

An alley separated the saloon from the house next door. Passing this gap, Antonia smelled smoke. She stopped and called out, "Is someone there?"

She heard a unintelligible voice. Was the saloon to be the next target of the firebug? She started down the alley.

"Who is it? Answer me!"

As though she'd flushed a covey of grouse, boys came rushing past her. The leader slid in a patch of mud, half falling. Though he saved himself, a corncob pipe dropped from his clothing. A friend helped him up and they vanished around the corner, hotly followed by two or three others. Antonia thrust out a hand and caught a skinny arm.

"Ernie!"

"I wasn't doing nothing!"

That seemed his standard answer.

"You show me," Antonia said.

She marched him back to where they had come from. Judging by the pipe that lay still smoldering where some boy had dropped it, an abandoned keg by the wall seemed to be the center of their activities.

"Now what were you doing here?"

"Just smoking. Honest, Miss Castle." He cocked at her an impudent look, which Antonia recognized as one of Ned's stock expressions when caught in a naughtiness.

"What else?"

He tried to twist free, but Antonia had a firm grip on his arm, not his ragged gingham shirt. After a moment's look around, Antonia saw there was a knothole in a shutter about three and a half feet above the keg. Standing on tiptoe, she applied her eye to the hole.

On the other side was a room with a iron bedstead, a commode, and a screen painted with a gaudy bouquet of unrealistic flowers. Two figures occupied the bed, each an obvious example of gender-controlled secondary sex characteristics. Fortunately for her blamelessness of mind, a red-and-black blanket covered them both below the waist.

"Oh, gracious."

Dropping down, Antonia looked into the face of the boy. "Don't you know that . . . you come with me. We're going to see your parents."

With a violent effort Ernie broke free. "Everybody in

this town hates you! You're nothing but an inter . . . interferin' old maid. Everybody says so!''

He darted away and ran directly into Jake's solid frame. ''Here now!'' Jake said, fending the boy off with a firm hand. ''You can't go talking to Miss Castle like that. You apologize.''

''I won't!''

''Then I guess I'll have to blister your britches.''

''No!'' Antonia said, starting forward. ''Don't strike him!'' She looked down. ''Run on home, Ernie. I'll speak to you tomorrow.''

''I won't come to your old school no more.''

''Then you won't hear any more music. I have more cylinders at home, you know.''

In Ernie's eyes she saw a yearning quickly stifled. ''I ain't coming no more,'' he said, but she could tell he didn't mean it. Perhaps he wouldn't come tomorrow, if only because he was male and had to prove himself, but she knew he'd be back soon.

''Run home,'' she repeated.

''Now wait a minute,'' Jake began, but Ernie didn't stay for the incalculable whims of grown-ups.

''You can't go around beating children,'' Antonia said.

''That isn't fair. He's a holy terror and needs a lesson. Aren't you mad about what he said to you?''

''He told the truth, as he sees it. Not very many people in this town do like me.''

''They would if you'd act like a reasonable woman every now and then, just for a change.''

Antonia dismissed that. ''Anyway, Ernie's parents must be the ones to discipline him. I shall call on them.''

''I wouldn't do that if I were you. He's only got a mother and she's drunk half the time.'' Jake instantly looked guilty for speaking.

''That's terrible! What has been done about it?''

''I knew I shouldn't have said anything; I knew it. Now, look here, Antonia, don't go stirring up more trouble. People out here don't like folks interfering in their business. What are you doing?''

A backdoor was set into the wall a few feet deeper in the alley. Antonia knocked on it and looked back to answer Jake. ''See, even you agree with Ernie that I interfere. Well, someone has to and it might as well be me. Excuse me,'' she said to the woman who opened the door, ''is Miss Annie in?''

''Who wants to know?'' the woman said, shaking back her loose dark hair from her face.

''Tell her it's Miss Castle.''

The woman saw the marshal behind Antonia and alarm flickered in her eyes. ''Wait a minute.''

In less time than that, Miss Annie's Junoesque form filled the doorway. Her face was painted very high and she wore an eye-popping tight green velvet gown. ''Oh, it's you. And the marshal,'' she said, looking over Antonia. ''Howdy, Jake.''

''Miss Annie,'' he answered, tipping his hat.

''I'm sorry to bother you,'' Antonia said, ''but I felt you ought to know about this knothole.''

''What knothole?''

Chapter 11

"You're amazing, you know that?"

"Why, thank you, Jake."

"It wasn't a compliment!" He stalked on ahead, stopped, and waited for her to catch up. "Most women cut her dead on the street and you offer helpful hints on home repair like some jeezeldy bride's magazine. Didn't your mother teach you how to act like a lady?"

"Of course she did."

"When are you going to put what she taught you into practice?"

"When are you going to learn I'm not like other jeezeldy women?"

"There's no call for you to swear."

"I didn't . . . this is ridiculous. I'm tired. I'm going home."

"It's not home, Antonia. It's jail, remember?"

She stopped and looked up at him, knowing that hurt darkened her eyes. "There's no need to remind me."

"Dang it," he muttered. Jake shifted his weight from one leg to the other, glancing up and down the street. Then, with a swift sureness that startled her, he caught her hands, pressing them to his chest. She could feel his heart beating under her hands and lost the will to pull away.

"You scare me," he said, his words faltering. "You

rush in without any more thought than a baby. So far everything's gone your way. Even the womenfolk are starting to like you.''

''Well, then . . .'' she began, but he wasn't finished.

''One of these days, you're going to get yourself into trouble and I'm scared to death I won't be around to pick up the pieces for you. If you'd only be reasonable . . .''

His gray-green eyes were far from cool and the vibration of his deep voice told her how much he felt the things he said. Antonia knew she was weakening, that in another moment she'd be willing to sit in his house with her hands folded just in case he gave any thought to coming home.

She'd had dreams lately where she did exactly that, dreams in which she baked perfect cakes and made elaborate dinners on his old cook stove. Somehow, though, they never ate those utopian meals. In dreams, she could kiss him and cling to him and never worry about what he'd think of her.

Very slowly, as though she were a phonograph badly wound, Antonia said, ''I'm always reasonable.''

Her mind wasn't on what she said. Already he stooped to kiss her. It didn't matter that they stood in the open street, that probably a hundred people were watching from behind curtains, or that in a minute they'd draw a crowd. Antonia wanted him to kiss her, wanted him to so badly that she could already taste him on her lips.

When his eyes lifted past her and he straightened, Antonia could have ground her teeth in frustration. Maybe she did, for he gave her a polite, meaningless smile. Hardly moving his lips, he said, ''Here comes Mrs. Dakers and Jenny. Watch yourself.''

More loudly he said, ''I don't know if I'll be coming back tonight after all, Miss Castle. I'm not going to be comfortable in my mind until I hear for certain that bunch is captured down south. Afternoon, ladies.''

Antonia said, "Your diligence does you credit, Marshal," before turning around. She had a polite smile for Mrs. Dakers. If Jenny had lifted her bonneted head, Antonia would have increased the warmth of her smile for the girl. But she stood behind her mother-in-law as though wishing herself elsewhere.

Mrs. Dakers said, "Miss Castle, I hoped to see you today."

With an effort Antonia hid her surprise at being addressed by the black-clad woman without a single denunciation. Resisting the urge to glance toward Jake to see how he was taking this startling about-face, she replied, "Did you, Mrs. Dakers?"

A becoming tinge of pink arose in her sallow cheeks. "I have heard you are doing well with the school. That being so, I wanted to ask . . . my daughter-in-law could hardly read when she came to me a few months ago. I have been teaching her using the Good Book."

Jenny never moved, not even when Mrs. Dakers gave a false, self-deprecating laugh. "Though I can't think of anything worth knowing that isn't in there, there's no doubt many a thing exists in our modern world that isn't mentioned in the Bible. She still cannot read the labels in the stores. I send her for navy beans and she comes home with rice. She is too shy to ask for what she wants. She points." Mrs. Dakers laughed again, not at herself.

Writhing for Jenny, Antonia said, "I will be happy to help Jenny learn to read more modern words."

"Oh, there's no need to put yourself out. If you will lend her two or three of the schoolbooks; improving works, no novels or any of your evil—I mean, nothing that might take her feet from the path of the right."

Mrs. Dakers's careful avoidance of Jenny's name made Antonia uneasy. She spoke to her directly. "Jenny, come with me to the school and we can pick out something. I saw an abridged version of Miss Strickland's *Lives of the Queen of England*—I liked that one very much!''

But Mrs. Dakers clutched Jenny's arm. ''We cannot leave my son alone for too long, Miss Castle. There's still supper to get. Maybe tomorrow after school lets out?''

''Right after school I'm going to church and then the marshal and I have been invited to the Cottons' for supper.'' She glanced at Jake. ''I'm sorry, Marshal. I forgot to mention it till just now.''

Jake nodded and said, ''The judge asked me yesterday to ask you if it would be all right. I guess I forgot, too.''

''*You'll* be in church tomorrow, Marshal?'' Mrs. Dakers asked.

''Uh, most likely not,'' he answered, turning his hat in his hands. ''Sundays are about as often as I can stand to listen to Mr. Budgell.''

Antonia thought for certain Mrs. Dakers would be unable to maintain her pleasant bearing after this slap at the young preacher. Her smile became sharper and she squinted at him as though to see if he was serious. ''Then I shall not look for you,'' she said.

''How is your husband? I was grateful for all his help yesterday,'' Antonia said hurriedly, directing her words again toward Jenny.

A shy smile lit the girl's face. ''His arm's still sore but gettin' better every minute. He can't wait to be clearin' the land so we can rebuild the stables.''

''Paul never has known what's best for himself. I must go home now, Miss Castle. Thank you for your offer to help.'' Mrs. Dakers turned away and walked down the sidewalk, her dress hardly moving with her rapid steps.

Jenny looked intently at Antonia, as if there were

something she wanted to say. When she still hesitated, Jake said gently, "She's waiting for you."

They stood together silently, watching the two women turn toward their house. Then Antonia sighed. "Perhaps you're right," she said. "Maybe the women are starting to like me."

"She probably heard about what you did for Paul."

"No more than what you did," she mumbled, not meeting his eyes.

"I wasn't wearing a dress that could catch at any second. Give me a little credit, Antonia. I know bravery when I see it." His voice was dry. She could have imagined the moment when it shook with worry on her account.

"I hope Mrs. Dakers doesn't know. I almost prefer her to be shouting at me."

"Well, she sure was cooing at you this time. What else could have caused a change like that, except her knowing about you saving Paul?"

Antonia looked down the street at the Dakers house. "How long have Jenny and Paul been married?"

"Matter of six months. Why? Don't tell me you're going to get mixed up in their lives, too?"

She didn't dignify that with an answer. "And how long has Mrs. Dakers lived in Culverton?"

"Why do you want to know?"

"Womanly curiosity. You said I should act more like other women. So, gossip with me."

"I know what I'd like to do with you."

"I beg your pardon?"

"Never mind. I've got better things to do than stand on a street corner with you."

He couldn't think of anything but he'd see himself warming his backside at Satan's stove rather than give in to the sole impulse he had left. When Miss Annie had opened the door, it had taken all his self-control not to hustle Antonia inside and demand a room. Even now, with her eyes sparkling at him from beneath that silly hat, he wanted to kiss her and go on doing it, street corner or no street corner.

Antonia tried to take herself in hand. She should not feel as though she were drinking champagne when Jake scowled at her. When he was charming, she couldn't be certain he hadn't practiced his enticing smile and flirtatious ways on a hundred other women. But when he became annoyed, she knew all his feelings were bound up in her and no one else.

"Oh, Marshal," she called sweetly as he retreated. "If I could ask you one more question before you go . . . ?"

"What is it?" he asked over his shoulder.

"Which way to Mrs. Ransom's house?"

He spun around with a speed that thrilled her. "Hell and damnation, woman! You could make a temperance meeting take to straight rye!"

"And you think *I* swear!"

Jake marched up to her. She thought he would take her in his arms, but he merely spun her around and pointed over her shoulder. "You go back down that road as if you were going to my house. Then cut back between the start of the woods and the wheat field. Go straight as you can and cross the creek. After a little while you'll get to a clearing full of stumps and that's her house."

"Thank you, Jake."

Antonia set off with a light heart. He had walked away, shaking his head as though holding a private conversation. She knew he was thinking of all the firm, dominating things he should have said, arguments which would have made it clear that he put his foot down.

She herself thought of a few things he might have said, words that would have reduced her in a moment to an elemental female yearning for his touch. Making note of them, she promised herself she'd not give in. But her promises rang hollowly in her own ears.

As her way lay very close to Jake's house, she could not resist stopping for a few minutes to freshen up. In accordance with the customs of Culverton, she wrapped some of Mrs. McEwan's baking in a clean napkin to take to Mrs. Ransom. She felt a pang of guilt over not making her own gift, but she wanted Mrs. Ransom to be on friendly terms with her, not an instant enemy.

When she came out, she couldn't imagine how the sun had dropped so far. She wasn't worried about the dark. Jake's directions made it sound as though she hadn't a long way to go. Shutting the door, Antonia walked toward the wheat field a few hundred yards up the lane.

Finding the creek was not a problem. Crossing the creek turned out to be a different story. The water in the narrow bed, swollen with last week's heavy rain, churned and turned white as it ran. Rocks, scattered across the creek to serve as stepping-stones, were drowned in fast-rushing foam.

Antonia wished she had thought to put on her new galoshes, as she'd ruined two pairs of shoes already. Ernie, however, mustn't be left in a state of suspense too long. She'd risk her shoes. She could always buy a new pair. Wilmot's store probably stocked her size, and if not, she could buy men's.

The water ran very fast here, as it poured down from a slight rise. Antonia walked along the bank, looking for a level section. Where there was no stones or branch-woven dams to roil the surface, the water seemed both clear and distorting, like the original glass windows in very old houses. Brown, flat stones lay along the bottom and black fish, no longer than a finger, kept their places among the streaming water weeds.

Antonia found a spot that seemed acceptable. The bottom was lined with flat small stones that wouldn't turn as she stepped on them, and the pace of the water seemed slower. Though the water wasn't deep here, she thought it would rise right over the tops of her shoes. She had no choice.

As she started forward, a wild thought occurred to her. What if, she thought, glancing around to see if anyone was there, what if she took off her shoes?

She had never run barefoot in her entire life. From infancy, partly because her family owned a shoe manufactory, partly because only heathens went unshod, she'd been laced into boots as though the safety of her soul depended on their stoutness. The added savagery of removing her stockings out-of-doors would have sent everyone she knew reeling in horror, and when she tucked her gray serge skirt and petticoats to keep the hems dry, she did it knowing the sight would have buried half her relations if any had been present.

Dead leaves crunched and crinkled beneath her toes. The dirt clung warmly to the soles of her feet. Where thin grass grew beneath the shade, Antonia giggled as it tickled. At first she walked tenderly, afraid of stubbing her toes or of stepping on something squishy.

She stepped down from the low bank. The touch of the fresh, cold water sent a shivering shock through her body. After the initial jolt, Antonia began to enjoy the sensation of the swift-flowing current over her hot feet and up her ankles. It seemed a shame to hurry. With a glance at the sky she decided she had time to linger.

She tossed her shoes, stockings, and gift onto the far bank. Her gloves followed. She opened her sleeve buttons and pushed the material up to her elbows. The water bubbled around her legs, tugging as though urging her to trust it to keep her afloat.

The stones looked so bright and clean that she leaned over to pick one up and came as close to losing her balance as she would have if she'd been pushed. Give the water the slightest excuse and she would be bobbing up and down in it, a soggy mess with no option but to squelch in disgrace back to Jake.

"That's enough of this," she said aloud. Very carefully she negotiated her way across the rest of the creek. Wiping off the water that clung to her skin as best she could with her hands, she sat on a fallen log to replace her stockings and shoes. She tucked her gloves into her waistband.

Promising herself that she'd come back to splash in the water when the level was lower, Antonia set off to look for the clearing Jake mentioned. Glancing up again, she was surprised to see that the flat white clouds visible through the branches had begun to turn to gold.

The sun must be setting. She had noticed that this time of year tended to have long dusks. There would be plenty of time to reach Mrs. Ransom, talk to her, and come back.

The dark, however, did not depend on the setting of the sun. It seemed to well out across the ground, as though released from the roots of the trees. She'd been aware of birds ever since she entered the woods. Their calls were softer now, as if afraid.

Antonia told herself she was being silly. The birds were simply preparing to roost. All the same she found herself walking more quickly and, at the same time, trying to be quiet. A strong feeling, which had nothing to do with sense, grew in her. It was as if by crossing the creek she had entered into a new domain, less friendly and more watchful than the woods on the other side.

Surely she should have reached the Ransom house by now. Jake hadn't said how far it was, but it couldn't be much of a walk or he wouldn't have let her go alone. A suspicion whispered that Jake had been angry, that maybe he was teaching her a lesson by letting her get lost. Then he could rescue her and make her realize how helpless a woman could be without a man.

Remembering when he found her in the woods before, Antonia vowed she'd not throw herself into his arms a second time. Beside, Jake wouldn't mislead her. His instructions were undoubtedly correct. All she need do is continue in a straight line. . . .

Antonia stopped and tried to remember. She'd walked along the creek for a little way, trying to find an easier place to cross. She'd not kept to a straight path.

Putting her hands on her hips, she scolded herself for being so stupid. At least the solution was near at hand. All she needed to do was go back to the creek, find the stepping-stones, and return to the house. It was too late to pay a call now, anyway.

Turning around, Antonia listened for the sound of the running stream. It had been part of the landscape for such a long time, both as she approached it and as she went away from it, that she could not at first believe that she could no longer hear the rush and gurgle. The creek couldn't be far behind her; after all, it cut through the entire wood. She was bound to run into it if she went back the way she'd come.

Until she realized she was lost, she'd thought these woods pleasant and hadn't minded walking through them. As soon as she knew she was not going to find the creek or the clearing, panic began licking like a flame at her nerves. A twig snapping behind her sent her spinning around.

"Jake?"

Only silence and the flutter of a bird answered her.

"Oh, spew."

She sat down on the humped root of a huge tree. Though not hungry, she began to be pleased that she'd thought to bring food along. Those slices of cake might have to be dinner, and breakfast.

In the morning, no doubt, she'd find her way out of the woods. She could smile, thinking of herself as one half of Hansel and Gretel, until a low mournful howl broke out from somewhere nearby. Did wolves still prowl in Missouri?

She shrank back against the rough bark of the tree trunk. "Oh, Jake," she whispered. "If you are planning to find me, now would be a very good time."

How long had she been sitting here? Awakening from a doze she hadn't intended to take, she dimly realized that some loud noise had broken the stillness. Instantly she thought again of wolves. And hadn't one of the schoolbooks said something about primeval giant elk? Perhaps one had survived the coming of men.

She did not leave her meager shelter. Whatever was there, it would pass her by if she did not move. The moon's ethereal light turned all the woods to black and white, darkness and brightness mingling into a misty gray. Detail blurred except where the vaporous light fell through a rent in the canopy of branches and tossing leaves. There every particular stood out, as if she could see things more clearly than anyone was meant to.

As long as she stayed still, Antonia knew she would blend into the trunk behind her. Already she felt as though she'd grown to be a part of it.

A shape moved into a brighter patch of light. A man, broad of shoulder and tall, stood on the edge of the shadows. Antonia recognized that silhouette. Suddenly her limbs were no longer made of wood.

"Jake!" she squealed, exploding from her hiding place.

Completely unprepared, Jake staggered backward, Antonia's weight in his arms making it impossible to correct his tilt. His boots slipped on some leaves, still wet underneath. He fell back, managing to keep Antonia on top so she wouldn't be crushed. At once he bent his knees to get up, but she did not move.

"I thought you'd never find me," she said, kneeling over him. It was too dark to see his face, so she leaned closer, one palm flat on the ground beside his head and the other by his shoulder for support. "Are you all right?"

"No, damn it, I—" He cut off his complaint.

Though she couldn't see his eyes, she could feel their gaze in the same way she could feel his hand slip up behind her head. Her locked elbows trembled as he gently urged her downward. One bent. She kissed him, offering everything she owned of pride. She'd sworn to herself that she wouldn't do this; she betrayed herself without a second thought.

When standing, he towered over her. Yet when they lay down together, the difference became unimportant. As she savored him she freely touched his face, discovering a long-hidden yearning to do so, smoothing his frowning black brows, running her hand over his beard-roughened jaw. She pushed her fingers through the cool hair at his temple and flirted with the edge of his ear.

Jake growled and nipped delicately at her lower lip. Freeing her mouth, she whispered, "You like that? No?" Nipping in her turn, she repeated her fingertips' feather touch.

He heaved his shoulder off the ground, his strength and speed preventing any check. She yelped in surprise as he altered their positions. Now he lay propped up on his elbow beside her, his head and shoulders blocking the sky above her.

"See how you like it," he said.

Antonia laughed in an intimate, provocative way she had never practiced with another man. Reaching up for him, she answered, "I think I'll like it fine."

Jake kissed her with a steadiness and a gentleness that Antonia recognized as the marks of great restraint. As a girl she had imagined there could be no greater pleasure in life than eating sun-warmed strawberries with fresh cream. Then she'd discovered chocolate caramels and wondered why this pleasure was not sung of as poets sang of love. Now she knew. Instinctively, however, she realized that kisses, even those that made her toes curl in her shoes and sent her senses swimming, might be like strawberries.

If only it were possible to let him know how stirred up she became when he kissed her. She moved her hands restlessly on his back, trying to interrupt him so she could tell him. At once Jake increased the pressure of his mouth on hers. She preferred his strength to his gentleness.

For a moment she luxuriated in this new delight. Slowly it occurred to her that he'd enjoyed her touch before. She felt very foolish that it had not dawned on her before now that the golden rule applied to kissing as well as to every other human endeavor.

Remembering how he'd explored her face and throat with his lips, she found a moment to essay a voyage. She inhaled the warm spice of his skin, reveling in this knowledge of him. At the same time she ran her hand out along his arm. When she found his hand clenched into a fist at his side, she raised her head, wounded.

"Don't you want to touch me?"

"Antonia, I shouldn't even be doing this!" He leaned down to give her a last kiss.

Earlier that day he had seen where each pearl button lay on the cambric-and-lace bodice she wore under her man-style jacket. Only by the exercise of all his self-control had he kept himself from undoing those buttons. He'd told himself that holding her and kissing her was to come closer to heaven than he ever thought he would. To ask for more—to steal more—would be blasphemy.

He tried to sit up, but she brought him down to her again with more strength than he'd realized she possessed. No man could have bested him in a contest of brawn; she threw him with a smile and two words.

"Touch me."

She helped him work the buttons free, helped him by arching her back to tug her blouse out of the confining waistband. Only the crocheted lace at the top of her combination covered her now. Though she yearned for him to undress her, she could not find enough boldness in herself to give him the hint. His hand rested warm and heavy on the cool skin at the base of her throat, his thumb on her collarbone. She could feel it shaking.

"Jake?"

With a constricted moan he brought his mouth down on hers, claiming her with his urgency, his need. Antonia opened her lips to him to meet his thrust with her own. Caught up in his arms, she ardently pressed herself against his body, her skirt hiked up recklessly high. His virility settled strongly along her thigh. She knew what that hardness was, and what purpose it had; she'd never guessed that the knowledge would arouse her to the point of senselessness.

Her principles scattered like rabbits. She swept her hand along the front of his hips, testing the contour of his phallus. He sucked in his breath, caught her hand, and forced it away. Lying on her back, his weight immobilizing her, she looked up at him with widened eyes nearly black in the dim light.

"You don't know what that does to a man, Antonia. Can't you see you're playing with fire?" He rolled away, his arms over his face, his chest rising and falling to a frustrated rhythm.

Antonia sat up, pushing her tangled hair back, plucking out a leaf from among the pins. "Everything makes much more sense now," she said. "The women at the shelter . . . some of them didn't seem to be oppressed by the sexual desires of their husbands."

He chuckled as if against his will. "I wonder how the husbands felt about it."

"You don't see. I've always felt at a disadvantage because I'm a virgin."

"Antonia, for God's sake, not now."

"There's no reason to be embarrassed. I'm quite pleased this happened. Now I can face the women we try to help."

Jake sat up. "Are you trying to tell me this was an experiment?"

"No, I didn't plan any of this—it was spontaneous—but I do feel more capable now of—"

"Button your blouse," he interrupted sharply.

"I beg your . . . oh, yes." Her fingers fumbled with the tiny pearl studs. "As I was saying, I do now feel more capable of talking to other women about these kinds of experiences." She knew she was talking too much, but a great ocean of embarrassment threatened to swamp her the moment she fell silent.

"You're going to talk about me? About this?"

"I meant *generally*."

"I wouldn't do that if I were you. You don't know everything." He lifted his hand and brushed a clinging leaf from her shoulder. Proud of himself for being able to touch her so casually, Jake tried to convince his body that his want for her had lessened. The thickness between his legs was a powerful argument in favor of continuing to touch her.

The only thing that had saved her from even greater "experience" had been a dim remembrance of her chastity. He wanted her so much that kissing her was not enough, that touching her was not enough, that taking off her clothes and exploring her with hands and lips was not enough. He would not have been able to stop there. Better to deny himself these pleasures utterly than take her completely.

Antonia watched him rise to his feet. "Let's go home," he said, picking up his hat and knocking the leaves off it.

"Do you know how to get back?"

"Of course. Miss Ransom's house is about five minutes' walk that way."

Surprised, she asked, "Are you certain? I can't believe I was so close, and so lost."

"That's the way it is in the woods. Even a little one like this is mighty confusing if you're not used to it."

"What time is it, do you think?"

"About six-thirty, I reckon. Why?"

"Oh, good. It's not too late to call."

"You can't . . ."

She stood up, her hair riled every which way. She patted it, rearranging the curls into a semblance of neatness. "Do you see my . . . there it is."

She leaned down to pick up her straw hat. Jake tried not to watch the curve and sway of her hips under her skirt. He already regretted the protective instinct that had kept him from loving her. He could have at least touched the softness of her breasts. Self-control could have waited another moment or so. Now he couldn't even carry the memory of what she'd looked like without one of her prim blouses.

With a harsh sound of frustration he turned away from her. Everything worked out for the best. If he'd carried away that picture, it would then become impossible to see her clothed without wishing to see her naked. His imagination did not require any more food.

As she came up to him he said harshly, "None of this happened. We won't talk about it. We won't even think about it."

"If that's how you want it," she said, surprised.

"It is. It's best. But—" He couldn't keep from looking at her forever. Stiffly he faced her. "It *did* happen. And what's to stop it happening again, and again, until we do what we both want to do?"

"I—I don't know what you mean."

His chuckle was not silent, but sharp and unkind. "You do know. You can hide from it, order it to go away, but this passion between us is going to be resolved, one way or the other."

"Passions can be fought. They should be fought. That is the secret of progress."

"Then you and I are doomed to be backward. This passion is very strong. It demands surrender. Yours. And mine."

Chapter 12

"Is this it?"

"Yep. Not very grand, is it?" He'd led the way, never looking over his shoulder to see if she kept up. He didn't dare for fear a flash flood of desire would overtake him again.

They stood on the edge of a clearing, the hacked stumps of trees clustering around a slant-walled shack. Some smaller buildings surrounded it, laid out in no particular plan or with any specific use. The clear twilight showed every appalling detail. The hard-packed dirt, without a shred of grass, was marked by broken crockery, sinkholes ugly with slimy water, and piles of deadwood.

Her experience of the tenements and slums of Chicago did not prepare her for this squalor, somehow all the worse for the fresh greenery of the woods around them.

"Somebody's home," Jake said, nodding toward the thin column of blue smoke rising from the makeshift chimney. No light, however, showed in any of the papered windows. "Are you sure you want to go on?"

"Certainly," she said, lifting her head. "I told Ernie I would see his mother tonight, and I will. He mustn't be left in suspense. That would be cruel."

Jake muttered, "I'm in suspense and you don't—"

"Excuse me?"

"Nothing. Come on."

"Wait! Do I . . . look all right?"

"Just tell Mrs. Ransom leaves are being worn in Paris this year."

"Oh dear." Antonia took his meaning at once. She bent her arms, awkwardly trying to sweep the dead leaves from the rear of her skirt and her back.

"Here, let me." As impersonally as if he had no notion how she collected her foliage, he walked around her and brushed her off, thinking of snow, ice floes, and blizzards. When she was straight, he stepped back but caught the edge of her smile.

"Apparently leaves are the fashion for men this year as well."

Not even arctic images could kill the flames that burned inside him when she did him the same service. He steeled himself against the flicking touches of her gloved hands. Grinding his teeth seemed to help when she plucked a leaf off the back of his thigh.

"There," she said. "Now we are fine enough to pay a visit on the president, as my mother used to say."

"I'm sure Mrs. Ransom will appreciate it."

Antonia walked across the muddy yard, Jake thought, as if she were approaching the executive mansion. Her attitude did not change even when a hissing gray goose came tearing around the corner of the shack. She simply stopped, as though challenged by a uniformed guard.

Jake knew how hard that orange beak would be if it struck her. The goose waddled back and forth in front of Antonia, snaking its supple neck to peer at her with tiny suspicious eyes.

"What a good watch . . . goose!" Antonia said. The animal only opened its beak in another hiss. She looked back over her shoulder and said, "I guess flattery has its limits."

"Watch out!"

Antonia jumped back just as the goose struck out. It advanced and she retreated. She tried to remind herself that this was a dumb animal. It should not have her on the run. Jake must be laughing at her, but she didn't have the attention to spare to find out.

"Do something!" she said.

"I'll distract it. You run to the door and knock."

He took off his hat. Stepping even with Antonia, he flapped it at the goose. The long, liquid neck turned, the mean eyes following the black circle.

Antonia sprinted among the puddles and trash. The entire house seemed to rattle as she rapped on the door of weathered gray boards. She glanced back at Jake, who seemed to be holding his ground against the winged defender. Knocking again, she at last heard sounds from inside.

"What do you want?" The door was jerked open and a woman in a greasy print dress stood there. Her eyes burned a dreadful red in her brown face, half-masked by stringy graying hair. Antonia recognized the sharp, raw smell of alcohol.

"Would you mind calling off your goose?" Antonia asked.

Mrs. Ransom peered past her. "Who's that? Faraday? What's he doin' here?"

Jake had shrugged off his coat. With a quick thrust, he threw it over the goose's head and left it there, squawking. His shirt sleeves gleaming in the sun's last light, he came up to the house. "Evenin', Mrs. Ransom. Can we come in?"

The woman made no move to let them over the threshold. She stared at them, her rough hands hanging by her side. Antonia could see that Mrs. Ransom had noticeably regular features. She had probably been attractive once, perhaps when Ernie was still a baby.

"I'm Antonia Castle. I'm teaching in Culverton now and I want to talk to you about Ernie."

"I ain't got money to pay damages."

"Nothing like that. I want to talk about Ernie's music. He has a very great gift and—"

"Music!" Mrs. Ransom's mouth moved as if she wanted to spit. "If it hadn't been for that—"

"I've heard Ernie play the violin. I think with training he could be a very fine musician."

"Musician! Is that what you call it? His father was a *musician* and what good did it ever do him? I'd want Ernie to be a murderer before—"

She put her hand to her mouth as though holding back the words. As she stared at Antonia her voice dropped to a whisper. "He was a good husband to me. I'd of stuck by him no matter what he did. I didn't even mind the other women, you know? He always came back to me."

"Mrs. Ransom," Antonia said, stepping forward with her hand held out. "I want to help Ernie. There are schools that can teach him so . . ."

The older woman stepped away from her hand, scorning the touch. More loudly she said, "Faraday, you've been a good friend to me and my boy, but you get out of here!" Mrs. Ransom slammed the door.

Antonia would have knocked again, but Jake shook his head as she raised her hand. "She's had kind of a lot to drink and doesn't want to talk. Leave her alone. I wonder if the kid's around," he said.

She followed him around the yard as he poked in the various buildings. They seemed to house mostly broken tools and old sacks covering mounds of dirt or hay. One of the buildings was a dilapidated chicken coop with a few skinny hens who protested at being disturbed. A wash house, set up with tubs and a clothesline, had an disused look and smell. Antonia took one look and backed out.

Jake disappeared into this for a few minutes. When he came out, he carried a preserving jar half-filled with a clear, yet oily liquid. "Kerosene," he said. "I found it behind an overturned tub. There's a big mount of rags in there, too."

"So?" She didn't understand his interest in common household necessities.

"Do you remember about the fires?"

"You can't arrest anyone with kerosense. It's used all over the world."

"Still, it's a little odd to find the stuff hidden with two fancy marbles and a set of cracked conkers. There's already a lot of talk about Ernie. He's a troublemaker, and wouldn't be the first kid to take to burning property in revenge."

"And kerosense," Antonia added, "is often used to clean clothes. You did say Mrs. Ransom sometimes takes in washing."

He curled his lips at her, but acknowledged she might be right. After putting back the jar and looking through the other buildings, he said, "Wherever the kid is, he's got his fiddle with him."

"Both of them could be in the house."

"Doubt it. If Ernie'd been home, he would have answered the door and said his mother was sick, most likely. And Mrs. Ransom wouldn't have a fiddle in the house."

"She's very bitter about her husband. What became of him?" Antonia asked, looking back at the crooked house.

"He left town about five years ago. I hadn't lived here long, then. I was still living at the boardinghouse. He up and grabbed every dime they had in the bank and took off."

Antonia said sadly, "Every state should have a Married Woman's Property Act. Then things like that couldn't happen. I've known so many women in the same situation. Even money they've earned by their own labor can be taken, because according to the law, it belongs to their husbands. It makes me long for the vote."

"God forbid. Anyway, Ernest takes off. She doesn't worry about it at first. Like she said, it wasn't the first time and so she'd squirreled away a few dollars for safety. But after a couple of weeks he still hasn't come

back and now she's flat out of money. So I start asking
for the law in some of the bigger towns to keep an eye
out for him. Runaway husbands usually head for the gay
life, you know.''

"Thank you, I'll remember that if I ever have one.
What happened to Mr. Ransom?"

"I got a message from the police in St. Louis. A man
answering Ernest Ransom's description lost a whole pile
of money in a card game at the place where he was
working, playing the fiddle for the dancing girls. He
wrote an IOU, went up to his hotel room, and wrote
another note. Then he swallowed a store-bought prepa-
ration of laudanum. Lady Somebody's something or
other. It's sold in lots of respectable stores but isn't
meant to be drunk by the bottle.''

"I know of women who swear by Lady Carlotta's
Nerve Tonic. I haven't ever used it—I don't need to. I
believe it has a very strong sedating effect. It killed Mr.
Ransom, I take it.''

"He never woke up, that's for sure. In addition to his
suicide note, affectionate letters from Mattie were found
in the room.''

"Oh, so that's how—" Antonia began.

"Mrs. Ransom's name is Jean. But it was Ransom all
right. The St. Louis Police sent back his personal
belongings, including a violin. Mrs. Ransom smashed it
the minute she saw it.'' He remembered her, with a face
of fury, lifting the highly polished instrument above her
head and bringing it down against a supporting beam at
the jail.

"The reasons behind Ernie's behavior are becoming
more clear.''

"Ernie doesn't know anything about it. He was just
told his father had gone away.''

"But that's terrible! All the authorities on child
rearing tell us that we shouldn't lie to a child in these
matters.''

"Maybe Mrs. Ransom hasn't read the same books as

you. Besides, how do you tell a six-year-old—or an eleven-year-old for that matter—that his father's too much of a coward to face living?''

Jake leaned down and snatched his coat off the goose. The bird scuttled away, hissing angrily, obviously wounded in its pride.

Antonia followed him back into the woods. As she stepped out of the clearing she glanced once more at the run-down, lonely house. Catching up to Jake, she said, ''I can't believe the citizens of Culverton allow a boy and his mother to live under these conditions.''

''It's like I said. People around here don't like to meddle in other folks' business.''

''You can't expect me to believe that. I have seen a good deal of *meddling* since I've come here. You can't tell me that some of your good people couldn't have helped this woman repair her roof!''

''Nobody wants to offend her by offering charity,'' Jake said. Even to himself it sounded like a lame excuse, but to his relief Antonia dropped the subject with a disgusted sigh.

As she trudged along behind him Antonia was busy with plans to help the Ransoms. Ernie had too much talent to waste his youth making trouble and peeking in bawdy-house windows. Mrs. Ransom had to be brought to see that music did not make for evil, that Ernie's talent properly trained could mean a wonderful life for him.

There were marvelous conservatories in the East that could not only teach Ernie how to harness the music within him but could teach him a discipline and self-assurance that would take him far in whatever he chose to do. Walking through the woods, Antonia began to make a list of the music-loving millionaires she knew who might be willing to contribute to Ernie's schooling.

At the house, Jake crossed into the kitchen and lit a lamp. ''I bet you're hungry,'' he said. ''I sure am.''

Antonia slapped her hat onto the desk. ''Oh, spew!'' she said.

"What was that?" She could hear amusement in his voice though she couldn't see him.

"I forgot the cake I was taking to Mrs. Ransom! I must have forgotten it when . . ."

She could not think of a way to finish her sentence without bringing up a delicate subject. If she had not hurled herself into his arms, she would have remembered her gift. If she had not been so aroused by his body on hers, she would not have lost all sense of her mission.

During the quick supper he fixed, she hardly dared to look at him or reply to his conversation. This emotional riotousness must be dealt with firmly. There was a time and a place for everything. She had always believed in saving oneself for the sanctified marriage bed, and not in giving herself on a pagan chaise longue. Antonia shook her head to dispel the memory of Jake's hands on the buttons of her blouse.

He stood up and removed the dishes. "You must be tired. If you're not careful, you'll fall asleep right here on the table."

"On the table?" she echoed.

The quick motions of his hands as he scraped the plates stopped. Antonia could almost feel the effort of will it took for Jake not to turn around. After a second's hesitation he went on clearing up. "I think we'll leave washing 'em till morning."

Had the same image—of the two of them locked together, rolling across the scrubbed tabletop—flashed through his mind as it had through hers? Antonia found the picture frightening in the same way that skating on thin ice was frightening. How did he think of it?

"No," Antonia said, striving to keep her voice level. "No, I'll be glad to do them." She pushed her chair back and stepped over to the sink.

"I'll say good night then, Antonia."

His gray eyes locked on hers, and she could not look away. With a craving that came from her soul, she wanted him to kiss her, if only once more. She swayed ever so slightly nearer.

He stooped down, his hands hard on her upper arms. All in one motion, too quickly for her to do anything, he swept a kiss across her cheek. Letting go, he almost ran from the room. She heard his door close an instant later.

Resolutely reaching for a dirty plate, she tried to think of him as a hostile yokel with the manners and sophistication of a human spittoon. Even as she thought it she knew it wasn't true. He did not even speak the same way he had when they'd first met. He hardly ever said "yep" anymore or allowed that dull glaze to enter his eyes. She knew now he'd only acted that way because she'd let him see that was how she'd thought of him.

Trying to think of him as he was then, all Antonia could remember was the gentleness and understanding he'd offered to crying children this morning. She realized she stood smiling tenderly at a rinsed coffee cup. Then she had to clutch hard at the rounded edge of the sink as the storming memory of his kisses overtook her again. It was as if she could feel them all over again—slow, warm, and devouring.

Quickly drying her hands, Antonia carried a light into the living room and picked up her copy of *Principles of Hygiene*. There was a passage she recalled that might help her shake off these alien feelings. She paused for an instant at the depiction of the male organ, then, mortified, paged on.

Although matrons report certain mildly pleasurable sensations connected with the preliminary stages of marital relations, conclusive evidence proves that only the most abandoned females of the lowest kind admit to convulsive intoxication through the physical act. These poor abandoned wretches become so fixed upon their degradation that they may actively solicit—even demand!—

such contact and even confess to dreaming of the gross satisfaction of their animal natures.

The passage continued with some description of the demises of some unfortunate females that the learned writer had studied in the course of his researches.

Antonia put the book down, very depressed in spirit. Having been once threatened with the asylum, she did not care to risk it again. She resolved to put away her thoughts of Jake. It wouldn't be easy, not while she lived with him. However, a regime of plain food, cold baths, and long walks, according to the book in her hand, should help defeat these troubling thoughts.

Her mind made up, Antonia prepared for bed. She had not knelt beside her couch to say her prayers in years, but she did it now. Then she climbed under the covers and closed her eyes. Instantly a picture of Jake lying in the other room with his eyes wide open sprang into her mind. She drove it out by thinking of what she meant to do in class tomorrow.

A moment later he was again in her thoughts. Details became clearer. He had his arms crossed under his head. He did not wear a nightshirt or anything else. Moonlight poured in through a window, lighting up the contours of his muscles. Antonia curled her nails into her palms.

She searched her mind for another subject. All she could think of was how lonely she became waiting for him to come home at night. How had she known this evening that if she reached his arms, she would be safe? If only her heart did not leap so high whenever she saw him, whether in a dark alley or in the broad light of day.

Antonia began to hope she had a low, promiscuous nature. The alternative was far worse. She did not know when or why it happened, but she was forced to acknowledge it.

She loved Jake Faraday. She loved everything about him, from the way he smelled to the way he smiled. She loved his silent chuckles and even the way so many of them were at her expense. She'd love him now if he began eating with his knife.

Sitting up, Antonia thumped her pillow hard and flopped down on her face. "This is the worst night of my life," she muttered into the pillow.

"What's the matter?" Jake asked the next morning. "Didn't you sleep well?"

Antonia tried to speak normally, as if the revelations of the night had not happened. "I slept excellently, thank you. The chaise is very comfortable. You should . . . that is, I would recommend one to anybody."

"No, not for me. I like my bed hard—more restful than struggling with a soft one half the night. Rolling down to the middle and fighting your way back to the side . . . there's lots better ways to get your exercise!"

Antonia knew she looked tired. If she had dared, she would have used a finger's-end worth of rouge, from the tiny pot she kept concealed at the bottom of her case, to brighten her dull complexion. Knowing that would shock the town for certain, she tied a red ribbon through her hair instead.

"I'm sure you'd find my bed adequately restful."

"Would I?"

She glanced at him sharply, but he did not appear to have a second meaning. Pouring herself a cup of coffee, she sat down at the table.

Jake said, "I sure hope somebody comes to call on you soon. We're about out of baked goods. Next time you come to stay, you better bring that cook of yours. I don't know where she'd sleep, though. Maybe out in the barn. Attila likes company." He slipped a couple of slices of toast on a plate.

"Attila?"

"I never did think to ask. Do you ride, Antonia? A horse, I mean."

"Attila? You named your horse Attila?"

Remembering Psyche MacDougal of blessed memory,

Jake said, "That's right. After an old friend of mine, Attila Feinbaum. He darn near saved my life during the war."

"Attila Feinbaum?" Antonia repeated with a sideways squint.

"Yeah. A real sure-shooter, never missed with a gun or a lady. Soft-spoken kind of gentleman, though. I don't think I ever heard him raise his voice."

Except for the first name, he gave a perfect description of a fellow soldier, who hadn't been a day over seventeen when Jake had joined up. "I remember once he sweet-talked a widow into giving us a whole bushel of corn—free. We lived off it for a week—the first food we'd had in I don't know how long. I think he wound up marryin' her, come to think of it, once the war was over. What was her name? Charlotte, Charlene . . . ?"

"Are you certain it wasn't Scheherazade?"

"You don't believe me? I'm hurt."

She smiled, lowering her eyelashes, and said, "Yes, I do ride."

He gave her one of his more charming smiles. "You should have said something earlier. I don't guess Dakers would mind if you borrowed one of his horses. Save you a lot of time getting to school in the morning. You could leave her at the jail while you're teaching."

"I don't think so. I don't have the right clothes and—"

"What's wrong with what you got on?"

Antonia ran her hand over her brightly checked dress. The worst of the smoke smell from the fire at the livery stable had vanished when she'd aired it, and the dirt had sponged off. "I don't want to spoil one of my only dresses on horseback. I'll walk. But . . . thank you for thinking of me."

He stood up and drained the last drops of coffee from his mug. "I guess I'll see you tonight, at the Cottons'." She watched him as he left, her cheek propped on her hand.

Wednesday dragged. Ernie did not appear for class. When school let out, Antonia went home again to try to take some of the rest she'd missed last night. It was more difficult to get up after a brief hour's nap than it had been after finally dozing off at the first dawn.

Even before the tingle of the cold water she'd splashed on her face had stopped, she'd yawned half a dozen times during Mr. Budgell's sermon. No one noticed as several other people seemed to be having trouble staying awake, too. The fire and brimstone that made his preaching last Sunday so inspired did not appear.

Mrs. Cotton poked her in the ribs. "I bet it's that Mary Lou Ginnis," she hissed.

"Mary Lou?"

"Her with the cherries all over her hat. And if she didn't rub her cheeks with one, call me a Dutchman."

Antonia managed to look at the black-haired girl in a pew two or three back without appearing to look at all. Certainly the young woman's face had a very good color, yet Antonia thought it was because Mr. Budgell seemed to be talking straight to her.

"You mark what I say," Mrs. Cotton went on in a low voice. "He'll be going to supper at her house this evenin'."

"I thought she was interested in Jake . . . the marshal."

"Oh, they're all after him. But if he won't look at 'em, they've got to find somebody who will."

Antonia could sympathize with this attitude. After all, there was only *one* Jake Faraday. She could not, however, imagine transferring her love to a man like Mr. Budgell. A good man, of course, but too thin and too young for her. And too serious. She doubted he could crack a sly joke and be talking of something else before she had the chance to smile.

Jake waited for them outside the church, to one side of the stream of emerging people coming down the path. Mindful of Mrs. Cotton's sensitivity to the warmth between unmarried people, Antonia greeted him carefully.

"Good evening, Marshal. What a nice day it was today. I was worried it might rain."

He took off his hat. "Evening, Miss Castle. You're looking mighty pretty this evening."

She gave him a fierce, quelling look from under her lashes, but he'd already begun talking to Mrs. Cotton. "I was real glad to get this invitation to supper, ma'am. The food's kind of monotonous at our place lately. Antonia's not much of a cook, but somehow a man doesn't mind that, looking at her."

Mrs. Cotton all but danced with excitement. "After all, a gal can always learn to cook; you can't do nothing about a face."

"Exactly what I thought."

"Marshal Faraday," Antonia said through her teeth. "If I could have a word with you in private?"

"Certainly, but I reckon you better talk to Mrs. Larrabee first." He nodded at someone behind her, and Antonia turned around, hearing her name called.

During the ensuing discussion on whether Mrs. Larrabee's son Bud should advance from *McGuffey's First Reader,* Antonia's attention divided in half. On the one hand, she tried to understand Mrs. Larrabee's opinion of her son's genius; on the other, she strained to hear what horrible things Jake said to Mrs. Cotton.

"Both Miss Cartwright and the present Mrs. Grapplin agreed that Bud is an exceptionally bright boy, if lazy. His interest must be caught and held if he is to do better in class. His father wants him to be a farmer; I want him to go to Harvard. Or even Yale."

"Oh, Yale, definitely. It's in Connecticut." Straining her ears, she heard Jake say, ". . . all over me . . ." and Mrs. Cotton's titter, but the rest was lost.

"I'm just so worried that he'll lose interest. I already have enough trouble keeping him away from the cows. You know"—Mrs. Larrabee tittered—"I shouldn't boast, but Bud can say all the pieces in the *First Reader* practically by heart.''

''I'll test him, Mrs. Larrabee. If things are as you say, I'll be happy to advance him right away.''

''Oh, thank you.'' She looked around and dropped her voice. ''He's very curious, you know. I hope you'll refer him to me if he asks . . . embarrassing questions.''

''Please don't worry about it.''

''My husband says I should take the strap to him, but I don't want to discourage Bud from the sciences. Perhaps he'll become a doctor one day. However, I don't think he needs to know *everything*.''

Mrs. Cotton asked, ''What did you do then?''

''I gave her exactly what she'd asked for!''

Antonia realized Mrs. Larrabee had stopped speaking and was standing there looking at her expectantly. ''I beg . . . oh, I'll . . . Um, I'll keep what you've said in mind, Mrs. Larrabee. Now, if you'll pardon me . . . ?''

The other woman said archly, ''We mustn't keep the men from their suppers, must we?''

When Antonia turned hesitatingly around, she expected to see Mrs. Cotton glaring at her in condemnation or worse, giggling helplessly into her handkerchief. Actually she was speaking animatedly to Mrs. McEwan and two or three other women.

''After all, a pageant ain't that much work. A couple of white dresses for the girls and keeping the boys' hair slicked down'll be the hardest part. I don't guess the bishop will be too picky. He's probably seen plenty worse young 'uns than ours. And we've got Miss Castle to school 'em in their pieces. You're willing to help us, right?''

Antonia stammered the correct reply, without being certain what she'd just agreed to. She looked around for Jake.

He stood apart from the women, watching her with his head tilted to one side. Antonia felt the slow burn of a blush rising in her face. She could not see his eyes, but she knew somehow that he remembered last night. When he motioned for her to come closer, she obeyed without thinking.

Before she could reach him, however, Mrs. Cotton threw out a hand to hold her. "Look," she whispered. "What did I tell you?"

Mr. Budgell locked the church door, talking all the while to the fresh-faced, black-haired girl Mrs. Cotton had pointed out earlier. Then they walked together down the path, apparently unaware of the fascinated gazes that followed them. Mr. Budgell had his hands clasped behind his back, walking like a scholar, while Mary Lou Ginnis trotted alongside, listening with the face of an acolyte to what he said.

Going out the gate, she chirped, "I've often thought just that. Fancy!" She paused an instant to give a pert nod to the group of women, with perhaps an extra wrinkle of her upturned nose at the marshal. Then she hurried away to catch up to the preacher, who'd gone on ahead, still talking.

"That explains the two different kinds of pies Mrs. Ginnis baked this afternoon," Mrs. McEwan said with the air of solving a most perplexing mystery.

"*And* why her best tablecloth was airing on the line all morning!" another woman added, nodding like a proven prophet.

Maisie Grapplin said, shifting her baby to her other arm, "I don't think much of *her* as a preacher's wife. She always seems flighty to me."

"Say all you like," Mrs. Cotton said, summing up. "At least she can play the harmonium. Not much, but she can play it." The other women muttered in agreement. "We don't sing nothing but 'A Mighty Fortress' and the 'Old Hundred', you know."

Mrs. Cotton could not wait to tell the judge all about what they'd seen. She rushed Jake and Antonia along and burst into speech the moment they entered the house. Judge Cotton hadn't even a chance to welcome them.

When he'd sorted out what his wife said, he rolled his twinkling blue eyes at Jake. "I wonder if anybody ever counted how many weddings it takes to satisfy a woman."

"More than her own, that's for certain," Jake said, smiling.

"Too true. She ain't goin' to be happy till every male and every female's hitched up. Sometimes I think I'm married to Noah. Everything's got to be two by two."

"If I was Noah, I wouldn't take you on any ark I built. There isn't and never will be a lack of wicked old men."

Antonia stepped forward to stop the warfare. "I wonder if I could wash my hands?"

"Lands, yes. Come with me and take your hat off." Antonia followed Mrs. Cotton but heard the judge say, "How about a tonic before dinner? Get your blood moving."

"Thanks, I will. But I haven't noticed too many problems with my circulation lately."

"Prevention, my boy, prevention."

Mrs. Cotton showed Antonia to the white room at the top of the stairs. The last time she'd seen it, Evelyn had been preparing for her wedding.

"Let me take your hat. Do you care to freshen yourself? The church was hot enough to bake a cake."

Antonia splashed her face and washed her hands in the cool water set out in a pitcher and basin of the palest robin's-egg blue. When she complimented Mrs. Cotton on it, the older woman said, "It was my mother's. She had the prettiest yellow-gold hair, kind of like yours, 'cept longer. She could sit on hers, oh, my, oh, yes. Many's the time I helped her brush it out and coil it up. I used to wish I had a little girl; she might of got it. Them brushes are hers, too. We had to throw a power of things out of the wagon when we come west, but I kept what I could."

"Have you always lived in Culverton . . . since you came west?"

"Lands, no. Culverton ain't been here but maybe twenty years. And hasn't looked like it does now but for five. We used to live farther south, but that friend of the judge's—Cedric Quincannon—moved here to be near his sister and we come along. They were partners at law, you see." Mrs. Cotton shook her head. "Cedric would of been so tickled to see his name on the city hall. He would have signed the order for his own hanging, just to see his name on something!"

"I confess," Antonia said with a sparkle, "that I was a little disappointed that I didn't get put into that jail my first night. The building is so grand."

Mrs. Cotton looked arch. "You couldn't have. There's something wrong with the doors in the jail. They swing open the second you shut one. The locks don't fit. Figures, don't it—a man fashioned it."

The men stood out in the back, taking nips in turn from the judge's silver flask. "So, you gettin' on all right, Jake?"

"No complaints."

"What about her?" the judge asked, hooking his thumb toward the house.

"She's your problem."

"I don't mean my wife. I mean yours. That is . . ." His bald head glowed red.

"I know just what you mean. Consarn it, you're just as bad as the womenfolks. Maybe worse. With women, wanting to see folks get married is natural, like they can't help themselves when it comes to watching and wondering which one's goin' to be next. But you ought to know better."

"Nothing wrong with wanting to see your friends as happy as yourself." Jake looked at him in disbelief. "Anyway," the judge added, "you ain't gettin' any younger."

"Thank you . . . lad."

"You know what I mean. If you're goin' to enjoy your young 'uns . . ."

"I'm not even married yet, but you're already talking about kids!" He took a swig of the whiskey.

The judge dropped his hand on Jake's arm. "All fooling aside, son. You gotta think about it. A wife's more than a duty to watch out for. She can help you. A burden shared is a burden halved, as my old daddy used to say."

"There are some burdens I can't share, Judge. Things that happened before . . ." Jake stared at his past and blinked. "No, I could never share them."

"So don't."

"What?"

"Nobody ever said you got to tell a wife everythin'. Mostly you face what's going to happen together, not what's happened before. Soon you've forgotten there ever was a before. Look at me. I can't hardly remember what I was like before I was married. 'Cept a whole lot better lookin'." He patted his overhanging stomach.

Jake grinned involuntarily. Then he said, "I can't conceal the things I've done, and been."

"I'm not saying *lie* to her, but you don't have to drop your whole life on the girl like a thousand tons of brick! You tell her slow, over ten or twenty years. You'll be talking about nothing and then you start telling her about the ol' swimmin' hole, or your first gal. Maybe you say something about an Indian fight you was in one time."

The judge stared straight at Jake, his baby-blue eyes serious for once. "Some things maybe she'll find out for herself, like how there weren't no Jake Faraday before around 1866, or about how fine a man can grow from a wild boy."

Jake stood there with his mouth open, as stunned as the first time he'd been shot. He'd realized then what a fragile bubble the world could be and how carefully a man must walk to preserve it. His hands balled into fists at his sides. Twenty years ago he might have hit out and run. Now he stood still, feeling the earth crack under his feet.

Judge Cotton held up the flask. "You want any more of this?"

"No, thanks."

He watched dully as the judge knocked back his head for a last, long swallow. The older man sighed with pleasure and shook his head in wonder at the powerful medicine that is whiskey.

"I wish we had time for a cigar," the judge said in the tone of a man yearning to return to paradise.

"What are you going to do?"

"'Bout what? Oh, that. Nothing. 'Course not. I reckon plenty of men had cause to take a new name after the war. Makes sense, come to think of it. Maybe one of these days I'll change mine, just to make conversation." He began to walk toward the house.

Jake caught up. "Wait a minute. If you know that much, you must know . . . what else do you know?"

The judge shrugged. "Nothing. And it wouldn't matter if I did, either."

"Why not?"

Giving him a disgusted glance, as if he could not believe Jake's stupidity, Judge Cotton said, "Don't you get it? Well, it's the first time I ever thought you a fool! This is your home, boy. Nobody's gonna care much what you did twenty years ago. And it ain't just sentiment. We know you. And so, I reckon, does Miss Castle. Now come on. I'm hungrier than a bear in spring." He opened the backdoor and hollered, "Woman! Where's my supper at?"

After the meal Antonia helped to clear the table, but Mrs. Cotton wouldn't hear of her doing the dishes. "You've never seen how careful the judge is. He's never dropped a cup in all the years we've been married. Not while washing 'em, anyway. Come on, honey lamb."

"I don't want . . . oh, yes." He smiled around at the younger couple. "Dishes," he said, clapping his hands together as he shoved back his chair. "I can't wait to roll up my sleeves and get sloshing in there."

Jake and Antonia exchanged laughing glances across the white-swathed table. Mrs. Cotton popped her head back around the door. "Take your time over your pie, y'all. Our stereoscope's in the parlor. The judge gave me a new set of pictures of Europe for my birthday. It's like being there!"

When they were alone, Jake moodily ate the point off his quarter pan of pie, Mrs. Cotton's idea of a moderate helping. "I guess pictures seem mighty small to you. You've been to Europe, most likely."

"No, though, I've always wanted to go. My grandfather promised me a trip to the capitals there for my wedding journey."

He toyed with the crust on his pie as though it were not as flaky and brown as any housewife could want. "So there was someone you wanted to marry?"

"There was someone Grandfather chose for me to marry, but I didn't want to go to Europe that much." She took a bite and the cinnamon sweetness of dried apples burst sweetly on the roof of her mouth. Sighing with pleasure, she took up another bite on the end of her fork before noticing that he wasn't eating his. "Don't you like it?"

"No, the pie's fine," he said, digging in with renewed enjoyment.

"Actually," she said, lowering her voice, "I ate so much at dinner I don't know if I can finish this whole piece, although it's delicious. But I don't want Mrs. Cotton to think I didn't like it."

He glanced around slyly, even lifting the edge of the tablecloth as if he wanted to look underneath it for eavesdroppers. Antonia bit her lip to keep from laughing.

He said, "If you can't finish it, I will. I think I can find a place for it, somewhere. Listen, if I fall asleep while looking at the stereoscope, just poke me when you want to leave. You'll have to borrow a wheelbarrow to take me home.''

"I wasn't planning to make you run. Anyway, you have your horse.''

"I've left him with Pete. I'll be proud to walk you home, Antonia.'' He reached across the white expanse of the tablecloth to touch her hand. "Right proud,'' he added, and returned to his dessert.

Antonia had lost her appetite. She wanted to end the evening so that she and Jake could be alone on the road home. He'd kiss her again tonight if she had to dredge up every feminine trick she'd ever heard of or read anything about.

Most authorities would condemn her as a deranged woman, and maybe it was true. Maybe love could not be reduced to lines on a chart, to temperature gauges, and to theory. Sooner or later, Antonia thought, every theory must be tested!

In the kitchen Mrs. Cotton stood by with a dish towel while the judge splashed around in the washbasin. "That's it. Nothing else in here.''

"There's got to be. They're still talkin'.''

"They could be talkin' half the night. I ain't goin' to stay in the kitchen all night. Anyhow, you don't know. At least Jake and me talked about her.''

"Well, we didn't need to talk about him. It's written all over her. A gal don't keep lookin' at a man to see if he's lookin' at her unless it's something mighty like love.''

"Seems to me he just makes her nervous.''

"There, you see? I'll go and find out if they've headed on into the parlor yet.'' She went to the door. "Yep, they've gone in. I say he'll put his arm around her while they're lookin' at the Colosseum, kiss her at the Arch of Triumph, and propose before the Ringstrasse.''

"How do you know?''

"'Cause that's the order I put the photographs in.''

Sitting on the parlor sofa with Jake beside her, Antonia

somewhat self-consciously held the viewer to her eyes.
"That's the Colosseum in Rome. Ned wrote me a letter
about it. He said he could almost hear the roars of the
lions, even through all the centuries."

"Ned?"

"My brother. He's in Italy now. Or was, the last time
I heard from him."

"How many brothers and sisters have you got?"

She lowered the viewer. "Just the two. Ned and
Jonathan. I'm the youngest. What about you? Where
does your family live?"

"Right here."

"In Culverton? Who? You never said anything."

"It's them," he said, hooking his thumb toward the
kitchen door. "They're my family. As close to one as I
have anymore."

"Yes, I understood that the first time I met them," she
said with a rueful smile.

Jake leaned forward, his hands clasped loosely between his knees, his eyes challenging hers. "Are you still
angry about that? Do you still feel tricked and cheated?"

"Sometimes I . . ." She'd thought that she had
heard a knock before. It was now repeated. Reluctantly
Antonia stood up from the horsehair sofa. "Perhaps I
should answer that."

He threw out his hand as if he'd restrain her, but then
dropped it. Perhaps a thought of the walk home, they two
alone, occurred to him, for he smiled and whispered,
"Don't be long."

Jenny stood on the doorstep, a roughly knitted woolen
shawl over her head and shoulders in place of her bonnet.
She carried a lantern, throwing strange shadows around
the covered porch. In the light from the open door, her
face was as pale as a nun's.

"Miss Castle," she said breathlessly. "Do you have
time now?"

"Won't you come in, Jenny?"

The girl shrank back. "No . . . I guess this is a bad time."

"A bad time for . . . ? Oh, yes, the books!"

Antonia wanted to go back into the parlor to sit with Jake. She could have sworn she'd felt his arm along the back of the sofa, as if he were about to place it around her shoulders, while she was looking at the Colosseum. However, she knew that if she rebuffed Jenny now, she would fail in doing her best.

"Let me get my hat," Antonia said. "Come in. I won't be a moment."

The girl came over the threshold as cautiously as a stray cat. "I left Paul asleep. Mrs. Dakers is there, but I daren't leave him long. I thought that if I had a book, it might be easier to stay awake."

"Is he so ill you have to stay up all night? I had no idea."

"No, he's much better. She thought it would be best for one of us to be there all the time, in case he wanted something."

"You do rest during the day?" Antonia asked, thinking that even the girls who worked eighteen-hour days in the meat-packing plants looked healthier than Jenny.

"I don't need much sleep," Jenny answered, straightening her back.

"I'll hurry."

When she came down the stairs, Jake stood in the hall talking to Jenny. Antonia heard him say, "I'll come by and see him tomorrow and talk to him about it."

He glanced up and Antonia found herself concentrating hard on placing her feet just so on the steps. At the bottom she fussed a moment with a stubborn button on her new gloves. Jake took her hand. Holding it palm up, he gently eased the loop over the tiny button. "Perfect," he said.

She didn't quite manage to meet his eyes. "I won't be long."

"Try to remember where we left off."

After the girls had left, Jake sat down again in the parlor. His foot tapped restlessly and he drummed his fingers on his thigh. Suddenly smothering under the weight of the parlor's trimming, flounces, figurines, and filigree, Jake sprang up and headed out to the kitchen. Maybe he and the judge could sneak away for another swig.

Mrs. Cotton stirred cocoa on the stove. When he told her where Antonia had gone, she said, "If she ain't the sweetest thing! How she tries to do good everywhere she goes! I was sayin' just yesterday—or was it the day before? Never mind. I was sayin' to some of the girls that even if you don't agree with her, you got to give her credit for tryin'."

"You don't have to convince me," Jake said. "I admire Antonia's good qualities very much."

"You do?" Mrs. Cotton's interest reminded Jake of a dog's interest in a cat's dish of fish heads. Pleased for the other person, but looking for what he could get out of it.

"Yep. I also admired Abraham Lincoln, but I didn't want to marry him either."

Mrs. Cotton shook the dripping spoon at him. "You don't know a good thing when you've got it, boy."

The judge looked up from the newspaper he had spread across the kitchen table. "Does this mean we can go sit in the parlor?"

His wife was about to retort when a furious banging on the backdoor shook the house. Someone called for the judge on a high frantic note. Then a face appeared in the window.

"Judge! Thank God you're here, Marshal!"

"What's the matter, Wilmot?" Jake asked, throwing open the door.

"The schoolhouse is on fire!"

"What?" Jake seized the man by his jacket and hauled him into the room.

Twisting in Jake's grip, Wilmot said, "It's burning

like crazy. I saw the whole thing! I was walking out that way when—"

"Never mind that!" Jake said, dropping him. "Antonia and Jenny are in there!"

Chapter 13

"I don't know, Miss Castle," Jenny said, putting down the red-backed book on the teacher's desk. "It looks kind of hard for me. And I just gotta learn to read good!"

"Please call me Antonia. Why not give this a try?" She handed Jenny a school copy of a mustard-yellow and Dutch-blue book, opened to a poem.

Jenny frowned and began slowly, "Speak gently to the little child / Its love be sure to gain / Teach it in—" Looking up, she smiled ruefully. "I don't know this word."

"Look at the next page. Some of the harder words are broken down and defined."

"'Ac-cents. Speech, tones.' Oh, accents!" The pale girl's face pinkened in pleasure. "Speak to it in *accents* soft and mild / It may not long remain." Her brow rumpled with puzzlement and distress. "Does that mean the child will die? How awful. I don't want to think about nothing like that!"

"Have you really only been reading a few months, Jenny? Even the girls who have been all through the *First* and *Second Reader*s have trouble with the *Third*."

"I had some schooling before I left home. I remember these books. We had 'em in Kentucky." She put her hands behind her back and recited, "Mary had a little lamb / Its fleece was white as snow / And everywhere

251

that Mary went / The lamb was sure to go. I never forgot that, despite everything.''

"But Mrs. Dakers . . ." Antonia saw Jenny's pleased expression fade. "Go ahead and borrow that one first. If you want more, feel free to come and get them.''

"Thanks . . . Antonia." Jenny cradled the rigid cover against her breast. "I'm real grateful. I guess I could tell you why I gotta learn all the stuff I never did. It ain't for me, in a manner of speakin'.''

"If you'd like to. I haven't made very many friends in Culverton. Yet.''

Jenny leaned closer. "I'm so excited about it I could just bust! I think . . . I think I'm goin' to have a . . . you know.''

"A baby?''

The girl nodded eagerly. "You and Paul are the only ones I've told. You ever get where you just have to tell folks something?''

"Sure. But never anything this big! I'm so pleased for you. When do you think . . . ?''

"I don't know exactly. I ain't showing yet, so it can't be too long, can it?''

Antonia asked, "When did you last have your menses?" Jenny only looked at her like she'd suddenly begun speaking a foreign language, which Antonia guessed she had, in a way. She sought for another expression. "Your monthly flow?''

"Oh, the curse! Not for a couple of months. Two, maybe three.''

"Then you are most likely two or three months pregnant." She squinted at the ceiling and counted on her fingers as she said the months. "May?''

"I'd purely love to have a spring baby!''

"You've gotten your wish, it seems. I imagine Paul is thrilled.''

"Oh, him! He walks around like he's done something special, or did until this happened to him. But like I told him, he didn't have hardly nothing to do with it! It's me that's got to do all the hard work."

Antonia hesitated before asking, "Have you told Mrs. Dakers?"

Jenny shook her head guiltily. "I don't know how she'll take it. She don't like me much."

"Paul is her only son."

"There's that. Maybe a grandbaby will make her happy, wouldn't you think it?"

"I'm sure it will." She patted Jenny on her thin shoulder. "I know it will."

"You been awful nice to me, Miss . . . Antonia. I sure wish I could do something for you."

Antonia felt close enough to Jenny to take the plunge and trust she wouldn't be laughed at. "There is something. Ever since coming to Culverton, I've realized how silly it is that I can't cook. If I ever had to fend completely for myself, I should be in trouble. As it is now, I can't even offer a friend a cookie of my own baking."

"But it's so easy," Jenny said, staring at her in wonder. "I've done it since I was old enough to hold a spoon."

Ashamed of herself, Antonia hurried to explain. "I never had to learn, you see. And when I moved to Chicago, I found so many women were never free of serving three meals a day in addition to working long hours, that cooking seemed like drudgery, just another form of slavery. But it's different for me. I should know how."

For the first time Antonia saw Jenny laugh. Then she said, "I don't deny I can get powerful tired of the kitchen, but you don't seem to mind so much when the work's for your man."

"My wanting to learn to cook has nothing to do with men," Antonia said a bit too hurriedly.

"I thought at first they were just tellin' tales on you,

Miz Wilmot and Miz McEwan, when they said you couldn't cook nothing but taffy.''

''I'm afraid it's true.''

''I'll come on over tomorrow after you're done here and I'll show you—''

Her words were lost in a shatter of glass. Antonia turned to see a broken window and shards of thin blue glass on the floor. She started forward. Surely those curved fragments looked familiar? Then she recognized them. Someone had hurled through the window a fire-extinguishing bomb, such as had been used at the livery-stable fire.

Suddenly Jenny grabbed her arm. ''Smell it! That's coal oil!''

The upper half of the window broke inward like a fountain of sharp ice. A second bomb broke on the floor. It had something around its neck that had blazed in an arc as it flew. Fire leaped up, like a burning river between the women and the door.

They fell back, their arms over their faces. The heat shimmered in a wall before them. Everywhere the kerosene had splattered, fire arose. The children's benches were already blistering. Air blew in through the smashed window, driving the flames toward the opposite wall. A foul smoke billowed up.

''Can we run through it?'' Antonia shouted over the roaring.

''Our skirts'll catch for sure! We need something to beat it out with.''

The dais was behind them. Antonia reached out and jerked down the two flags hanging on poles beside the desk. She pushed the Stars and Stripes into Jenny's hand.

''I can't,'' she shouted, staring with glazed eyes at the colors.

Antonia stepped forward and tossed the flag of Missouri down on the burning aisle. That part of the fire smothered, but the edges of the heavy cotton began at once to smoke. Reaching back for Jenny's arm, she dragged her forward between the burning benches.

"Look!" Jenny said, pointing behind her.

The fringed edge of the flag showed a devouring ribbon of fire. Antonia snatched the second flag from Jenny and tossed it down. Without the heavy fringe that adorned the state flag, the wind carried it farther, setting it down crookedly across the aisle. Though the flames under it died at once from lack of air, there was still a good foot of liquid fire between the edge of one flag and the other.

"Our skirts will protect us that far," Antonia shouted over her shoulder, and then flinched as the window on the far side exploded outward. When she glanced back to see if Jenny was ready, she saw her pointing downward, her mouth open in a scream Antonia could not hear.

Antonia twisted to look behind herself. Pinpricks of orange red clung to the weighted hem of her skirt, like rubies on a ball gown. Even as she looked down, the fire began to spread. She stared at it, fascinated. It did not seem to have anything to with her, this line of fine stitches sewn in fire.

Then Jenny knelt down, beating at Antonia's skirt with her rough shawl, her own skirt in danger of catching. Antonia blinked and came out of her daze. She pulled Jenny to her feet, pointed, and shouted, "Hurry!"

Coughing, Jenny nodded.

They leaped across the intervening space one at a time. The flames snapped at their heels like ravenous beasts. Once on the flag, they had only to take two steps and they stood panting in the cool quietness of the cloakroom.

As they hustled through, Jenny shouted, "Stop!" She tried to turn back but Antonia kept a firm hold of the other girl's shoulders.

"You can't go back in there!"

"I dropped the book!"

Antonia looked back through the open door. The

Fourth Reader lay open on the striped state flag, its pages ruffled by the greedy fingers of the flames.

"I'll order you a complete set tomorrow. Come on."

They ran down the front steps, choking as the fresh air filled their lungs. In the flickering light that poured from the side of the building, Antonia caught a glimpse of someone—a man—running like sixty along the road toward the town. She stared hard after him. He glanced back once, stumbled, and ran on.

"Who was it?" Jenny asked.

"From the mustache, I'd say Mr. Wilmot. Let's get away from this."

Walking on to where the schoolhouse lane joined the main street, Antonia found herself having to struggle for words. "Thank you," she said at last. "I don't know why I froze like that. If it hadn't been for you . . ."

"If it hadn't been for you, I'd be hidin' out under the desk, helpless as a kitten."

"We're even, then."

Jenny shrugged and smiled. "I've been thinkin'. What do you say we start out tomorrow with gingerbread. It's easy as can be, and men like it just about as well as anything."

Laughing for no other reason besides being alive to laugh, Antonia said, "I told you—"

She started as a series of double shots rang out in the distance. "What on earth was that?" They came again, and a third time.

"It's the alarm to bring out the menfolks. Nothin' like a rifle shot to stir 'em up."

More than the men had been roused. Coming toward them in a concerted human wave was the entire town. Children, the younger ones still in their nightshirts, ran ahead of the rest, clutching to their chests fire grenades exactly like the ones that had started the blaze. Many of their mothers had forgotten to take off their aprons but carried brooms and sacks. Dogs, barking or tongues lolling, ran with their young masters.

Antonia heard Jenny gasp. "Paul!" she called, then picked up her skirts and ran to the big man's side. He still had one arm strapped across his chest, but he swept the other about her waist and lifted her off the ground to kiss her soundly.

Alone, Antonia moved through the crowd as unnoticed as if she'd been a ghost. A core of people who appeared more organized than the rest moved along in a body in the center of the crowd. Judge Cotton seemed to be in charge, giving orders right and left.

"Now let's hurry!" he said, clapping his hands. "An' the next time I tell you we need a fire engine, you vote the funds to buy it without handing me an argument. Gol-darned shortsighted idiots!"

"Judge?" she said, falling into step beside him.

"Well, I swan!" He stopped short and the rest went on toward the schoolhouse without him. "We thought you was burned up for sure. Mother's goin' to be tickled— yes, sir, tickled!"

"You ought to know . . . it's a kerosene fire."

"Right! We've got sand buckets and rugs." He peered ahead as if counting up his arsenal.

"Where's Jake?" she asked, putting her hand on his shirt sleeve. His black coat was missing, but he still wore his watch chain looped over his vest buttons.

He toyed with it now, looking off toward the glow of the fire with the same eagerness as any of the smaller boys. "Jake? Last time I saw him he was killing the messenger."

"Killing who?"

"Wilmot—same as those Greeks used to do. Well, he didn't really kill him, just rumpled his face some. 'Course, with Wilmot the hero of the day, we'll have to have an election now instead of me being mayor sure as preaching."

Antonia did not take time to puzzle this out. She repeated her question. "Where's Jake right now?"

"He went to the depot. Something about a telegram."

"Wait a moment. I'm almost killed and he goes to send a telegram? To whom?"

"I don't know," the judge answered, starting to walk on. "Maybe to your folks."

"Good heavens, no!" Antonia began to run in the other direction.

She burst into the depot just as Jake turned away from the counter. Mr. Grapplin stood behind the grille, reading a piece of yellow paper. "No," she gasped. "Don't send it."

Jake supported her elbows in his strong hands and all but carried her to a seat. "You got any water back there?" he called.

In a moment Mr. Grapplin shuffled out, a glass clutched in one hand. He gave it to Jake, who helped Antonia hold it and tip it up.

"Not too much," Jake said. "Cramp your stomach."

She looked up at Mr. Grapplin. "Don't . . . don't send it."

The men's eyes met and there was a shrug hinted at. "Hold it for a couple of minutes?"

"You bet, Marshal. Sure to get there first thing, if I send before midnight." Mr. Grapplin disappeared again into his world behind the counter.

Antonia had recovered her breath and her composure. "Aren't you surprised to see me? Or are you disappointed?"

"That hurts, Antonia. I knew you weren't dead. Wilmot saw you and Jenny Dakers come out of the building while he was running to get help."

"That was Mr. Wilmot? I saw him. I thought it might be the arsonist running away." She saw his gaze change focus. He still appeared to be staring into her eyes. She knew, however, that he wasn't admiring their beauty. Instead he pictured Mr. Wilmot in the role of a fire setter. The storekeeper might be setting the fires in an attempt to scare up a wave of panic, which he could ride into a mayoral victory.

Then he shook his head and smiled. "I don't see how it could be him." She could pinpoint the instant he stopped thinking about the storekeeper and began concentrating on her.

"So you weren't worried about me at all." She had meant to sound humorously defiant, yet her voice somehow came out soft, as if she needed reassurance. She didn't get it.

"Nope. I knew you'd make out all right. I have faith in you, Antonia."

He wasn't going to stumble through an explanation, for there existed no words in any language to tell her about the fear that had paralyzed his entire body and mind in the instant he had first thought she was dead. He lifted his hand and brushed at her cheek, marveling that she permitted him to touch her.

"A little soot," he said in explanation.

"Oh. Do I have any more smudges?"

He tilted her face to the light overhead. "A few," he murmured as he pressed his lips to her forehead.

"Where else?"

"Here. And here." He felt her relaxing, her eyes fluttering closed, the tension draining out of her. In a minute he'd have to ask her questions about the fire, but not now, not yet. He swept his lips over her cheekbone and down to the softness of her lips.

"Good thing I like charcoal," he said on a laugh as he lifted his head. "You taste like range bread. Take the raw dough and bury it in the ashes. Then brush off the ash—least you're supposed to. They get mightly attached to one another."

"They do?"

She wasn't listening to a word he said; it was enough that his arms were around her. Leaning against his strength, she said, "Who were you telegraphing?"

Jake raised his voice. "Mr. Grapplin? Read that message out, please."

Antonia sat up, pushing herself away from Jake when Mr. Grapplin opened the door.

Standing in the doorway, the stationmaster read, " 'To Marshall Field's Department Store, Michigan Avenue, Chicago. Please send one Crane-Neck Rotary Steam Fire Engine this address stop. COD. Your firm highly recommended Antonia Castle stop. Marshal J. Faraday.' "

"Go ahead and send it," Jake said.

"I don't think they carry fire engines—at least I've never seen one in the store."

"You did say they sell *everything.*" He cuddled her closer. "I wouldn't recognize you without the smell of smoke."

"Yes, but a fire . . . !" She caught herself up. "They might be able to do it."

She rose and walked to the barred window. "Could you add something to that? Also two complete sets *McGuffey's Eclectic Readers.*" She glanced back at Jake. "The town can charge them both to me, though one set's for Jenny Dakers." She returned her attention to Mr. Grapplin. "When you've finished, I'd like you to send one for me, please."

"Go ahead," Mr. Grapplin said, licking the tip of his pencil and holding it poised over the form.

" 'Miss Grace Finster, 1023 Chester Street, Chicago. Please send pilgrim dress'—yes, that's right," she said in answer to the older man's questioning glance. " 'And claret tailor-made this address.' Oh, you better add something. 'Don't worry.' Sign it Miss Castle." Antonia walked toward Jake and said, "To my maid."

"Of course."

"Wait," she called to Mr. Grapplin. For a moment she hesitated, but decided it was better to be safe than sorry. Grace tended to be thorough, yet perhaps she should spell it out. "Please add 'Also all necessary items.' "

"Where should it go?"

"After address."

Mr. Grapplin read it back. " 'Please send pilgrim dress

and claret tailor-made this address. Also all necessary items'?'' She nodded and he went on. '' 'Don't worry. Miss Castle.' ''

"Marvelous! If she packs quickly, I'll have new clothes in a few days. I'm so sick of everything I brought along. What's left of it.''

Jake had come to stand behind her. "Looks like this skirt's shot. What happened?''

"It caught on fire. Please send that telegram right away, Mr. Grapplin. I'm really desperate.''

"Sure. You pay in the morning.''

"Thank you.'' She turned and saw that Jake had a very strange expression. "Are you all right? You look . . . pale?''

His lips moved once or twice before any words came out. "You mean you were *inside* the schoolhouse when it was on fire?''

"Yes. Someone threw those fire-extinguishing bombs through the window. You know, like the ones Wilmot's store sells. Only they were filled with kerosene.''

"My God,'' he whispered. "Wilmot said he saw you outside. When he told me that, I assumed you weren't even in the building when it . . .''

Ignoring the bright, engrossed eyes of Mr. Grapplin, Jake dragged Antonia into his arms. He embraced her so tightly she could barely breathe. Her face pressed against the rough wool of his coat, she felt as comfortable as ever she did in her life. The deep trembling that went through him told her, more than words, of his fear and his relief.

It affected her strangely. If being in his arms comforted him, then she would happily stay there for life. Sighing, she held him closely. She could feel herself dwindle, turning into the clinging female he claimed to want. The temptation to become that woman, someone he could put in his pocket, overwhelmed her. Instead of being instantly certain of the right path, Antonia had to ask herself what would a strong, independent woman do and then force herself to do it.

"I'll take you home," he murmured.

"You should go to the schoolhouse."

"They don't need me. You do."

"You have to look for evidence."

His hold slackened. "I'll see you home first."

"You don't have to. I'm surprised you're here, as a matter of fact. I would have thought you'd be first at the fire."

He stepped back. "I can't look into anything until the fire's out."

"I guess that's true. I just thought you'd want to find out who's doing all this."

"I *do*! If you must know, the judge sent me here to send that telegram."

"It couldn't have waited until morning, I suppose."

"I figured he was trying to be tactful with me. If you were dead, I don't think he wanted me to see you that way. Not knowing, of course, that I'll most likely kill you myself."

Antonia gave him a haughty glance. "Well, I . . ."

"Go on, Miss Castle!" Mr. Grapplin said, leaping out of his chair. "Give him what for!"

She gave the stationmaster a polite, automatic smile. To Jake she said, "I'm going home."

"I'm going to walk you."

"I don't want you to," she said, halfway to the door.

He stepped in front of her and opened it. "I'm walking you and that's final. There's a lunatic runnin' around loose somewhere. He's already had one crack at you. I'm not giving him another free shot."

"I doubt the arsonist even knew anyone was in the schoolhouse."

"You had a lantern, didn't you? He could have seen the light in the window. The school doesn't have curtains. Did you see anyone, or hear anything?"

"No, Jenny and I were talking." She continued to march down Main Street. The dark sky ahead seemed like the ceiling of a huge forge, reflecting back the orange glow of fire.

Jake kept up easily, his steps hardly lengthening. Antonia would have had to run to outpace that ground-swallowing stride, and she knew from previous experience that he could keep up with her then, too. Perhaps if she told him everything he wanted to know, he'd go off and do his duty. She wanted to be alone, to bathe, to rest, to cry.

They halted in the middle of the street, and the silence wrapped around them. "Is there anything else you'd like to know, Marshal?"

He knew she only called him that now when she wanted to annoy him. Her face still bore traces of her ordeal. If she were scrambling to find solid ground again after facing death, she might assume this mood as a defense against the further chaos his nearness inflicted. He hoped he made her as crazy as she made him. However, no one understood more than he how important being true to oneself was. Jake backed off.

"No, I think that covers it. If you come up with anything else, you let me know, all right?"

Wasn't he going to pursue the matter? Argue with her? Antonia realized she wanted him to. When his shoulders straightened and he glared into her eyes, she could remember how ill-suited they were.

"Did Mr. Wilmot see anything? Or were you too busy strangling him to find out?"

"I reckon the judge told you about that. I was a mite worried. But, yeah, Wilmot claims he saw someone hanging around the schoolhouse when he set out on his evening . . . constitutional."

"Constitutional?"

"Everybody but Mrs. Wilmot knows he likes to slip out of town for a drink over in Handfast, the ex-slave town down the road. He can't very well go to the Spoon."

Antonia shook her head over the deceit. "So who does he claim to have seen?"

"You're not goin' to like it. You've become real concerned about that kid."

"Which kid? You don't mean . . . not Ernie?"

"'Fraid so, Antonia."

She thought about it and then said with decision, "No, it can't be Ernie."

Trying to control himself, though this was the sort of woman's trick he disliked the most, he asked, "Why, 'cause he plays the violin sooo beautifully." A syrupy intonation spoiled his good intentions.

Antonia walked on, leaving him behind. Just before she turned to walk away from town, she called back, "I simply don't believe it."

She repeated this to herself at intervals as she walked along. Ernie was disobedient, which she knew from her own experience could be a constructive thing. He had a tendency to show off and could be flippant, but she knew what that was like. She also shared with him a love of beauty, and although a fire could be spectacular, she couldn't believe Ernie capable of setting one any more than she could have believed it of herself.

Slowly it occurred to her that her back and shoulders ached. If the stove had not completely died down—some hope—she could heat some water. Even a lukewarm bath would be better than cold. Jake hadn't lied when he said the stove was temperamental. She hoped Jenny would be able to cope with it. Imagining Jake's face when she offered him a cake freshly baked by her own hands carried her the rest of the way home.

Antonia paused with her hand already turning the front doorknob. With a sigh, for she had almost been able to feel the hot water, she walked around the outside of the house and sat on the back steps. It was her clear duty to wait for Ernie. She nearly nodded off there before she heard the music.

It welled up from the night, as though the breeze had

found a voice. The music had no sadness in it tonight, nor even much wildness. Elegantly harmony and counterpoint met in a dance. The laughing capriccio reminded her of Mozart, but the tune was "Brown-eyed Sal."

Taking care, Antonia rose from the back step and slipped silently toward the woods. The moon's dim light, she hoped, would not show her to the unseen player. She heard no faltering in the working of the bow.

Until, that is, she tripped over an unseen root and fell sprawling into the dirt.

When she raised herself up, spitting out leaves, she did not hear the sound of flying footsteps. She heard laughter. Somewhere nearby, a boy rolled on the ground, roaring. Paddling the loose dirt from her face, Antonia realized what a picture she must make. As she sat up she began to laugh, too.

Violin and bow clutched in one hand, Ernie leaped out from hiding. "Gee," he said, coming up to her and sitting down on the ground a few feet away. "You sure looked funny falling down."

"Like London Bridge, my fair la-dy."

"Sing that again."

"Don't you know 'London Bridge'?" He only looked intently at her. Obligingly Antonia sang the ancient ditty. Before she'd reached the third "falling down," Ernie had swung his violin into place and had begun tentatively to sketch in the melody.

He played with it, turning it around and inside out, until it was hardly itself anymore, but something rich and strange. Antonia listened, feeling privileged to attend this concert for one. Ernie's face was transformed with the song, losing its wry, secretive look. He seemed to be playing the music he heard from some source other than his own instrument.

After a few minutes he lifted his chin from the violin. "My dad taught me."

"He must have been a good teacher."

Ernie pointed. "That used to be my house, you know?"

"No, I didn't. The marshal bought it from you?"

"Yeah, when Dad went away. He told me to practice, every day if I could."

"But your mother doesn't care for it?"

The thin shoulders lifted in a shrug. "I don't know," he said, but his eyes shifted under hers. Antonia understood that nothing would make this boy say a word against his mother.

"I've always enjoyed hearing you play, Ernie. You played at the picnic when my friends got married."

"Yeah, I play at dances a lot. Sometimes somebody'll give me a nickel. Once a cowboy gave me a whole half-dollar! But they always want me to play the same songs. 'O Susanna.'" He seemed to throw something away, a gesture compounded of disdain and deprecation.

"You liked the music in school yesterday?"

"It was all right."

All at once Antonia realized why the boy had been at the schoolhouse. "You were trying to see if the phonograph was still there! Ernie, did you see anyone else at the school this evening? It's important."

He wanted to run. She could see him grow tense. "No," he gasped. "I didn't see nobody. Is . . . is it all right?"

"What? The phonograph? I don't know. It was still in there when I left and the fire was pretty bad."

"I knew I should of stole it," he muttered, but Antonia heard and repressed a smile.

"One day maybe you'll hear a real orchestra."

"What's that? Some kind of phono-thing?"

"In a way. It's a hundred musicians all playing right in front of you. People go to big houses to hear it."

"Reckon you'd have to, with a hundred folks all playing. Do they all play the same thing?"

"Ideally." She wanted to help this boy who contained within his soul such power over music. Culverton couldn't do him any good; perhaps Chicago, Baltimore, or Vienna could.

"Ernie, I'd like to see your mother. Will you take me to her?"

"You can't," he said slowly. "She's . . . sick."

"I don't mind that. I do need to talk with her again."

"When'd you see her?" His voice held wariness.

"A few days ago."

He stood up. "I gotta go."

"Please, wait!" She came to stand beside him and put her hand on his shoulder. "If you'll let me, I can send you to a school that will help you learn more music than 'O Susanna.' But we need your mother's permission to send you there."

"Could I?" She could see his eyes in the pale moonlight. The longing there struck her heart and told her that she held his dream in her hands. Then she saw his young face harden. By some trick of the uncertain light Ernie seemed to age before her eyes into an adult carrying heavy burdens.

He shook his head with a too-brave smile. "I gotta go home now. If he comes back, tell him where I am."

"The marshal?"

"No," he said as if she weren't very bright. "My dad." Ernie turned and sprinted away.

Chapter 14

She had still not taken her bath by the time Jake returned. Pulled out of her thoughts by his entrance, she gazed up at him blankly. He had to repeat what he'd said. "Any more of that coffee going?"

"It isn't coffee; it's tea. But I'll heat some more water."

"You sit still." He crossed the kitchen and shook the kettle experimentally. Pouring what was left into Antonia's cup, he rinsed the kettle and set it on the stove to heat. "I've got bad news for you, Antonia."

Used to reading him by now, she could tell by the glint in his eye that it wasn't very terrible, quite the opposite. "What is it? Anthony Comstock's in town to suppress vice? And me, while he's at it? Or has Professor Prospero come back?"

"Nothing that drastic. When Dakers heard how you helped Jenny this evening, he ran around telling everybody what you did for him. I hate to break it to you this way, but you're a heroine. Even the ones that don't like you want to shake your hand." He'd expected false modesty, or a hint that she was actually pleased to have her bravery discussed. He was surprised by the earnestness of her reaction.

"That's dreadful! I didn't want them to like me for that reason. Now they'll never listen to me."

"Are you kidding? They'll be lining up to hear you talk on any subject, even sex."

"But they won't learn anything. Mrs. Lloyd Newstead particularly warned me that our message should be serious and straightforward. If they only come because they like me . . ."

"Mrs. Lloyd Newstead—there's a name I haven't heard you mention in a while. One of these days I'd like to meet her. She must be a remarkable woman. Of course, she's wrong about a lot of things, if that book you've got is any clue."

"What book?"

"*Principles of Hygiene.* I kind of looked through it the other day while you were out."

"A quick flip through the pages cannot begin to reveal . . ."

The kettle whistled and Jake turned to make himself coffee. "Now, I don't object to everything in there. I saw a couple of notions I invented on my own."

"Oh?" she said, as nastily as possible.

"Yeah. Like how a person's face doesn't necessarily have anything to do with her nature. I can't tell you how many women I've met that's true of. Why, I know a gal who could make a man sit up and howl, and she doesn't know it."

Antonia couldn't meet his eyes. Did she really make him feel that way? "So you approve of—"

"Not everything. Some of it was kind of simple-minded, like how a married woman ought to follow her husband's lead in the bedroom and not try anything herself."

"You did read it!" Antonia exclaimed, surprised.

Jake didn't react to her surprise. "On the other hand, I thought the advice that a man and a woman should take time over every stage of a courtship was pretty good— not two or three years between meetin' a girl and kissin' her like the book said—but a while."

"I hadn't noticed that you took very much time," she said, and could have bitten her tongue.

He turned around, sipping from his mug. His gray eyes held an emerald tint that Antonia knew was a danger signal. Putting the cup down, he said, "Come on, honey. I didn't kiss you for almost a week. That was considerable patience considering you were flirting with me just as hard as you could go."

"I never flirted with you! I've never flirted with anyone!"

"Maybe not," he said, backing down in a way that irritated her. She could have done with a fight. Suddenly she seemed to have enormous energy and could hardly sit still in her chair.

He continued, "Every time you sassed me, I wanted to kiss you, so you can see I spent most of my time wanting to. I really look forward to coming back here at night. By the way, the schoolhouse is going to be closed for a while. The damage isn't too bad, but it's going to need paintin' and airin'."

She didn't care about the schoolhouse just then. However, she wasn't about to goad him into continuing the subject she was interested in. All those tricks for garnering compliments that other girls indulged in were degrading.

She lifted her cup to her lips. The warm tea strengthened her, so she could say calmly, "Thank you for letting me know. I'll have to find something else to occupy my day, or perhaps we can find another place to hold class. Quincannon City Hall is still empty, isn't it?"

"That's right. And there's a courtroom big enough for everybody."

"Right, that problem's solved. I'll declare tomorrow a day off from school, though. I remember how I used to wish our school would burn down. It wouldn't be fair to the children not to let them enjoy what every child dreams of."

Her smile faded as she thought about Ernie. Was it just

that he didn't care to leave Culverton, believing that his father couldn't find him if he went away?

"Hey now," Jake said quietly. "Don't go fallin' asleep in your cups."

She blinked. "I was just thinking."

"What about?"

"Ernie. Do you think he's setting these fires?"

Jake couldn't meet her eyes. "I don't know. He's been trouble for a long time."

"Since his father 'went away,' in fact. Give a dog a bad name and hang him."

"Look, I'm doing my best to be fair. Wilmot doesn't like the kid—he's hooked a few too many sour balls. From what I've been able to tell, Wilmot saw a boy and thinks it was Ernie, but he couldn't see much from where he was. And most people know Wilmot doesn't see so good at long distance."

"People seem to know quite a bit about Mr. Wilmot."

"He's running for mayor, sort of unofficially, against the judge. Everybody keeps an eye on him. There's been a whole lot of credit extended at Wilmot's this year."

"What about the fire grenades? Are they the same kind as he sells?"

Jake nodded. "Everybody's either bought some in the last two months, because of the new fire regulations, or has the chance to get ahold of them in other ways. Someone could have even walked off with a pair when the livery burned down, as nobody was keeping count."

"So really you're as much in the dark as before?"

"Not quite." He leaned back against the sink and crossed his long legs in front of him. Antonia could see herself in his shiny gun-belt buckle. "The livery fire could have been set at any time. All it needed was a match. At the school he had to be there—on the premises—to throw those bombs in the window."

"He?"

"Or she . . . they? How about 'it'? Maybe a dog did it."

"Never mind the pronouns. What does that prove?"

"Most people were still at dinner when the fire started, or sitting in the parlor like we were. You left at quarter to seven, and Wilmot came in at five after, leaving twenty minutes. Now, this is where I bring out my heavy artillery."

"And what is that?" she prompted.

"Mrs. Cotton." He enjoyed the way she gaped at him. It gave him a pleasant impression of his superiority, though he knew a word could put her on an equal footing with him, where she belonged. "She's going to find out where people were when the fire started and who saw 'em."

"Jake, I'm truly impressed. Did you think of that yourself?"

His fingers clenched on his coffee mug. Very slowly, controlling himself, he put it down on the drain board.

"No," he said. "I read about it in *Dead-Eyed Dick's Magazine* for very young cowboys. I'm not stupid, you know, Antonia." Even as he said it he knew it was the typical protest of witless people everywhere.

"I didn't mean it like that," Antonia protested, getting up and stepping closer to him. She held out her hand, palm up, but he didn't take it. "I know you're very sharp-witted, even brilliant. It stands to reason you couldn't be a marshal without some intelligence. I mean, a great deal of intelligence."

"Don't put it on too thick," he said, a reluctant smile tugging at one side of his mouth.

Encouraged, Antonia stepped a little closer still, her hand flat against the buttons on his shirt. "If you were really smart," she began, her voice dropping into a carnal register that surprised even her.

"Yes?" he said, his hand covering hers.

She looked at him from under her lashes, trying hard not to smile. A flicker of nerves came and went in the area of her stomach and she could have easily given in to a fit of nervous giggling.

He had always kissed her before. Now, though she wondered what it was like to be the instigator, she couldn't bring herself to cross over the limits she'd set on herself. If she lifted her face and pressed her lips to his, she would know beyond doubt that she was a truly abandoned woman.

"Why don't you show me what I'd do if I were really smart?" he asked, no teasing in his voice at all.

Abandoning her dignity, Antonia threw her arms around his neck, risking everything in one moment and relishing it. Jake staggered back, stopped by the sink, and put his arms around her to keep upright. "Whoa, honey," he began, but she caught the rest of his words on her lips.

She kissed him without refinement, barreling in. She felt his hands slip up to her shoulders, and knew in a moment he'd take control, leading her to the delights his kisses always promised.

"Slow down, Antonia," he said, prying his lips free. "Remember the *Principles of Hygiene*!"

"I'm not doing this right, am I?" she asked, backing away. A hot, hateful blush sprang up, flooding her throat and face. Kissing had never taken up much lecture time, except for the required warnings against it for fear of where it might lead the impressionable.

He followed her into the living room. "It's all right. You've done it before. I had no complaints."

"No, I haven't done it before. You always kiss me!"

"You're right. Well, that's not a problem, if you'll stand still. I can show you exactly what to do."

"Please stop following me. I'm smoky; I'm tired; I just want to go to bed. Sleep! I want to go to sleep."

"Sure. After you kiss me again." He was grinning now, his arms spread out to either side to herd her into a corner. "Practice makes perfect, you know."

Up against the wall, Antonia only wanted that he should stop looking at her, so she could die in peace. She supposed her clumsy embrace had its funny side, but at the moment she didn't wish to laugh. He came closer, the green in his eyes deeper than she'd ever noticed it before. She closed her eyes, wanting to disappear into the paint.

"Now, what you do is—you've got to watch me. How you going to learn anything with your eyes shut?"

She screwed them, if anything, more tightly closed. His fingers combed through her hair, removing the pins and freeing the silky masses to cascade over her shoulders. The calluses on his hand caught the strands and rasped faintly as he slowly followed the smooth river of her hair over its length. When the flat of his palm reached the curve of her bosom, he stopped.

"Look at me, Antonia." His voice held a ragged plea.

Gazing up into the deep seas of his eyes, she did not hesitate. She pressed her own hand over the rough back of his and give him a small quivering smile. His arm around her waist tightened.

Their lips met in a kiss that neither of them began but that they equally shared. It was Antonia, however, who first hunted for a fuller closeness, still pressing his big hand against her softness.

Her reaction to him in the woods, when he'd first realized the passion that lived inside Antonia, had haunted Jake. As she now slid her hands up his arms and opened her lips invitingly, he knew he should stop. She didn't know what she was doing to him; she was merely experimenting again, gathering more experience for her society work. He had to stop her before he became a willing partner in that work.

"Antonia," he began.

"Is this how I should do it?" she whispered, reaching up as high as she could to bring his head once more down to hers. His hair was coarse and alive, like fur. She wiggled furtively nearer to his warmth.

"Is this right?" she murmured against his mouth.

He wanted to say "No!" But he couldn't deny that she had all the talent in the world for lovemaking. Nor could he say she had no idea what she was doing, after all the books she'd read on the subject.

"Antonia, we should stop."

"Yes, yes. In a moment."

For an instant Antonia broke free of the ardor that clouded her mind and asked herself why she was behaving this way. Having been as near to death as she hoped ever to come, she was now alive to every sensation. And the one sensation she wanted more than anything was to experience again Jake's exciting touch.

A single doubt rose up, and she wondered if she weren't surrendering to base animal passion. Standing on the points of her toes, she kissed Jake, forgetting everything except her need to be near him. Dimly aware that he held back, she tried to impart all she felt in this one embrace.

Jake responded. He groaned as though pushed to the limits of his endurance. Putting his hand behind her, he brought her into the closest possible contact with his body, considering that they were still clothed. He took full advantage of her waiting mouth, plunging into its mysteries with abandon. What was the use in denying how much he wanted her?

A sigh of pure pleasure wafted from Antonia's throat. Even so, this was not enough. Recalling the weight of his hand on her breast, she wondered if he would consider doing that again.

His fingers were tilting her chin, stroking the tender underside of her jaw. Frustrated, though his touch was wonderful, she boldly wrapped her hand around his and dragged it downward. "Oh, Jake, please." She sighed, rolling her shoulder.

In a moment he was on his knees before her. He tried to remember gentleness and consideration, but the third button of her blouse tore off in his hand. When he thrust aside the concealing fabric, his mouth went dry.

Antonia, her hands on his shoulders, chortled at his expression. Her smile faded when he looked up. He

looked almost disapproving. "You wear silk under-
wear?"

"I'm all out of cotton."

The celestial whiteness of her breasts showed through
a lace insertion in the center of the ruby-red silk. Jake
had never seen anything so decadent on the most
accomplished whore. If this is what Chicago ladies wear,
I'm moving, he thought. He knew, however, that no
other woman would challenge and arouse him even a
tenth as much as innocent Antonia in her scandalous
combinations.

Antonia began to fidget, embarrassment sprouting up
like a dragon-seed army. Her fingers slipped from his
shoulders and crept up to cover her exposure. Jake
caught them, kissed them, and holding them down,
leaned forward to taste the firm point pushing out against
the red silk.

She'd never known anything as hot and tantalizing as
the swirl of Jake's tongue over her skin. Antonia went
rigid. She couldn't move, and wanted to move in new
ways.

As though something stretched and awoke, a tightening began deep within her. She groped along the wall,
searching for something to anchor her to this planet. As
Jake slid her blouse off her shoulder and pushed down
the lace edge of her bodice, Antonia locked her knees to
keep from falling.

Suddenly Jake stood up. Wordlessly Antonia protested. In an instant he'd gathered her into a strong
embrace, the impression of his thigh driving through her
skirts to settle against her most intimate part. He raised
his wide thigh so that she all but straddled it as he lifted
her off the floor. Bending his head, he again drew the tip
of her breast into his fervent mouth.

Antonia lost all control. There was no time to think,
only an instant to grab onto him, her sole prop when all
her other foundations crumbled. She returned to herself

with the memory of her own cries still sounding in the air.

She stood again on the ground, her arms tight around Jake's waist. His hands were flush against the wall as he held the both of them up. Shaking back her hair, Antonia looked up into his face without shyness. She opened her lips to speak, but he interrupted.

"I guess you're probably tuckered out after all you've been through today. I won't bother you anymore tonight." With infinite care, he stepped back from her slackened embrace. "Good night." Moving as fast as a mountain cat, he shut his bedroom door behind him.

"Bother me? Jake!"

Reaching for the doorknob, she turned it and stumbled into Jake's room. Instinctively she shut the door and put her back against it, to keep him from escaping. But the room was empty. The plain muslin curtains blew in the breeze through an open window.

But she was no longer thinking about the fiasco in the kitchen. Before her, like the jewels in Aladdin's cave, were books. Stack upon stack and shelf upon shelf. From where she stood she could see Scott's *Waverly* and Macaulay's *Lays of Ancient Rome,* lying beside Carlyle's *French Revolution.* The Americans were also there, including Mark Twain's newest book, which she'd been unable to find in Chicago, it having sold out.

Her embarrassment flying before her anger, Antonia ran to the window and looked out. But Jake, playing the coward for what she knew must be the first time in his life, was nowhere in sight.

Chapter 15

Walking into town the next morning, Antonia went over in her mind what she was going to say to him. After reviewing her behavior of last evening, she had discovered her mistake. Men needed to have things spelled out clearly. She had expected him to infer from her actions that she loved him. When he had not, or more properly, when she'd given him no chance to put the evidence together, she had suffered unnecessary embarrassment. And so had he.

If she could have five minutes alone with him, all their confusions would be over. Today she would be brave. She would say "I love you," out loud and kiss him.

Perhaps he'd laugh in her face, or worse, be kind. She had little hope that he would tell her he loved her, too, though she could be certain he desired her. Antonia kept walking toward the jail, her feet two heavy blocks of ice.

She heard the rumble of voices, like distant thunder, before she turned the corner. A crowd made up of most of the men in the town clustered around the jail. Many were smoke-bleared and red-eyed from fighting the schoolhouse fire. Horses lined the street, tied to every available hitching post.

Judge Cotton faced the crowd, standing on a box so everyone could see his portly figure. His round face was unusually grave. He waved his arms for silence, but the roar did not diminish until Jake stood up behind the judge.

The stern, authoritative man she'd first met closing down her lecture had returned. She could tell his eyes were cold as he pushed back the side of his coat to reveal the gun at his thigh.

"That's enough, boys," he said, hardly raising his voice.

The crowd quieted. The judge said, "Thanks, Jake. Now, you fellows listen here. This ain't goin' to be no hanging posse. We're goin' to do things legal or I'll prosecute for murder. Get that through your pumpkin heads. That said, I want to tell you that Nick Koers is goin' to be all right, according to Doc Partridge, and you all know what his word is worth."

"Gosh darn, the kid's deader'n a doornail, for sure!" cried an anonymous wit. There was some scattered laughter, but most of the faces Antonia could see were far from smiling.

"What about Conrad?" someone else called out.

The judge answered reluctantly, "Not so good."

The roar became a growl. Antonia was more afraid, standing on the periphery, than she'd been when she'd faced many of these same men in the Hall. She wished another woman were here, to hold hands in the face of so much male wrath. This kind of assembly was outside her experience. The men seemed to be losing their individual personality, melding together into one entity in a way that women never do.

The judge was speaking again. "Now, the marshal will tell you what he wants you from you." He stepped down and Jake took his place.

He stood there, magnificent in his size and strength, saying nothing until they'd quieted again. "The first thing is I don't want any of you to spook. We'll care for Culverton first. That's why I want some of you to stay here, guarding the town.

"Stay alert. Watch out for trouble, but don't shoot unless you're dead certain of who it is you're shooting at. Keep the wives and kids at home. And I want this street patrolled regularly to prevent another fire. Mr. Wilmot and Judge Cotton will handle that part of it. The rest of us will split into three corps, one under me, one under Caleb, and the rest under Pete."

He waited again until the comments and grumbles had ceased. "We know that these men are dangerous. They're also desperate to get wherever they're going, so I don't want anybody taking stupid risks. If they get by us, there's a posse at Greensboro waitin' to take 'em on, so no heroics either. That's all."

He stepped down from the box and cut through the crowd of men. Many stopped him to talk, maybe trying to convince him that they should go out with the posse. Sometimes he simply shook his head, but he would pause to speak to the youngest among them. Antonia recognized two or three of her older students, all of whom went away from the marshal with dejected faces.

She waited for him to come to her, preparing a last time for what she would say. All her fine phrases were dust in her mouth, as her legs began to shake.

Jake didn't take off his hat. "I want you to sleep at the Cottons' tonight. The house is too lonesome out there, unprotected." As she opened her mouth to agree he said savagely, "For God's sake, Antonia, do what I say once without arguing!"

"I wasn't going to argue," she said. The faint lines around his eyes were intensified and she knew he could have had no sleep. She wanted to touch him, but he seemed to have traveled to some region beyond her reach.

"It's been hell," he said. "The rustlers hit the Koers' place late last night. Nick and his father were both shot. The neighbors heard the ruckus and ran 'em off."

"Was it the same men you told me about?"

"I think so. They should have been miles away by

now, but it looks like they holed up somewhere. I should have been riding guard instead of . . ." He looked at her, and Antonia understood how he would have finished his sentence. She let it go.

"Did they take cattle?"

"They weren't after that. They attacked the house, maybe looking for money or food. They've been on the run a long time now." He spoke absently, looking across the street. The men had divided into four silent groups. Every face in one group turned toward the marshal and the woman.

"I gotta get back over there," he said.

"Of course. I . . . wish you the very best of luck."

"Thanks." He looked down into her eyes for a long moment. Perhaps he could read there all the words she could not now say. They would sound hackneyed and false in this setting, and she dared not risk distracting him from his duty with sentiment.

As he walked away her feeling rebelled. They would not be satisfied with so cold a good-bye. Antonia started impulsively forward. "Jake!" she called, making him turn. Under his gaze she faltered again. "I . . . I'll have some gingerbread for you when you come back."

"My favorite," he said seriously.

Antonia smiled with relief. There was no need to tell him at this particular moment that she loved him. The words would keep. He already knew. Jake touched his hat to her and went across the street.

She watched until the posses rode out. The street patrols had adjourned to the saloon to discuss the roster. When nothing was left behind in the street but some swirling dust, she saw several of her students standing around.

"You boys had better go home and help your mothers," she said. "They need you now."

"Shoot," said Bill Lewis. "Nobody needs you when you're twelve. If I was eighteen now, I'd show 'em something."

"Yeah," Aaron agreed from a full heart. "I can already shoot a rifle—sort of."

"Ah, who can't?" Peter Vrecker, the third of Mr. Vrecker's boys, spat into the dirt. "Ain't nothing more to see. I'm goin' home."

"When's school goin' to start up again, Miss Castle?" Aaron asked. The other two paused to hear her answer.

"Let's leave it until Monday, boys. Tell everyone we'll hold it at Quincannon City Hall." Bill and Peter grinned, showing a few missing teeth. Aaron, on the other hand, moved uneasily from foot to foot.

"Don't seem a lot of point to it, somehow," he said. "We're changing teachers again right quick. Don't know if I want to go on with schooling—Mr. Danton said he's lookin' for a boy to 'prentice."

Bill made a face of disgust. "Who'd want to be an undertaker?"

"He carves headstones, too! I can learn that!"

Before warfare could break out, Antonia said, "If I were you, Aaron, I'd stay in school a little longer. You're only in the *Second Reader*. Try to finish the *Third*. If you really want to work with Mr. Danton, ask him to wait until then."

"But George Russell's out for the job, too, and he's older'n me, even if he ain't done with the *First Reader* yet."

"Then you tell Mr. Danton that a better-educated boy will learn faster and work harder than an ignorant one. And then prove it."

Aaron looked thoughtful. "Mr. Danton would most likely think I was sassing him, Miss Castle. It's a shame you can't stick around to teach a little longer. He'd listen to you, 'cause you're pretty. I heard him say there weren't nothing a blond lady couldn't do with him. Mrs. Danton got real mad—she's got black hair."

"Go home, Aaron," Antonia said with a playful swipe at his fair head. He ducked and came up laughing.

More seriously she said, "And, boys? Please be

careful and stay off the streets. The men who are patrolling the town might shoot before you can call out. Tell your mothers to keep the children home.''

Mindful of Jake's orders, Antonia went along to Mrs. Cotton's. Approaching the backdoor, which stood open, she could hear heartbroken sobbing. Gingerly Antonia peeked in the open door, not wanting to intrude. Mrs. Cotton stood beside a girl whose face was buried in her arms while she cried. Surely Antonia had heard those sobs before, and had seen that narrow back shake in just that way.

Mrs. Cotton saw her and held up a hand to stop her coming in. ''Now you sit quiet, Miss Cartwright. I'll be back before you can say 'lickety-brindle.' ''

She gave the girl a firm pat on the shoulder and came down the backstairs. Taking Antonia by the arm, she led her out of earshot.

''I heard about Nick Koers,'' Antonia said.

''Would you believe that little girl was as brave as can be? Set right there and held her man's hand the whole time Doc Partridge was cuttin'. Nick nigh broke her fingers. Then she came back with me to get some medicine and whatnot and broke down. It's the shock, I reckon.''

Taking a few steps closer to the backdoor, Mrs. Cotton called, ''I'll be there in a minute, child. You drink that tea now.'' Returning to Antonia, she said, ''Hot sweet tea's the best thing for her. I seen it quiet men shot through with arrows, let alone weeping from nerves.''

''You'll be going back to the Koers' place, Mrs. Cotton?''

''Sort of have to. Constanzia Koers ain't no more use than a headache in an emergency. Sitting there in her rocking chair, screaming and laughing fit to bust somethin'. I had to slap her to shut her up.''

Antonia couldn't drop another load onto this remarkable woman's shoulders. Obviously Jake had assumed

Mrs. Cotton would take her in, and no doubt she would, if asked. But Antonia couldn't bring herself to ask.

Mrs. Cotton went on. "I'm kind of glad actually to have something to do besides worryin' over the judge. Not that he ain't having more fun than a boy with a new toy pistol, playing law the way he is. 'Course, it's a mighty important job they're doin', but if there's any enjoyment to be got out of it, men will surely find it."

"I don't understand," Antonia said. "According to Jake, there are only four or five of these desperadoes. Why is the whole town mustering?"

"I guess 'cause of what happened—oh, five years ago it must be, I reckon, as Jake had just come here. The war'd been over a long time, but them danged raiders didn't seem to know it. Sometimes it would be quiet for weeks and then they'd come again, roaring and fire raising. That's why the town don't look twenty years old, and why some of the buildings are kind of spread out, stragglylike. A good half the town burned one night—a couple of folks were killed. If it hadn'ta been for Jake . . ." The wrinkles in Mrs. Cotton's forehead deepened as she looked into the past.

"What did Jake do?" Antonia asked breathlessly.

"Mrs. Cotton?" Miss Cartwright appeared on the back steps, using the corner of her apron to wipe away the tears from her face. "We better think about heading back. Hello, Miss Castle."

"Hello. I'll be happy to go to Wilmot's for you if you need anything. Antiseptic, bandages, food?"

"I reckon we got everything," Mrs. Cotton said. She patted Antonia on the arm and whispered, "I'll tell you later."

They drove off in an unpainted wagon behind a gray-muzzled horse, Mrs. Cotton holding the reins. Antonia waved to them. When they were no longer looking back, her hand dropped limply to her side.

She could just go home. There was plenty to do there, and she could always find companionship in a book. She had lots to choose from now. She smiled, thinking how surprised Jake was going to be when she didn't get angry over his deception. He'd literally acted the fool, and so had she. That charade was all over now.

Jake wanted to protect her, which warmed her heart, but the danger must be illusory. The thieves were unquestionably miles away from Culverton and the scene of their last battle. No reasonable criminal would stay, knowing the hunt must be up. She could go home. What harm could come to her?

Then she remembered her promise to him. She hadn't seen any cookbooks in his collection. The only way to learn was for someone to show her. Resolutely she set out for the Dakers' home, hoping Mrs. Dakers would not be hostile to her. Their last meeting gave her some hope, but not much. Though it was spineless, Antonia wanted Mrs. Dakers to be away from home. Being called a "brazen woman" would strike a little too close to home today.

The whitewashed gate stood open. Looking toward the front door, Antonia could see that it, too, hung ajar. Stepping on the smooth cement stepping-stones that made a path to the house, Antonia called out, "Hello? Is anyone home?"

No hand pushed the straight curtains aside. No answering voice made her welcome. There was only silence, and a door that did not open further to admit her.

One of the red-flowered geraniums that grew with cupped leaves to either side of the path had dropped a few petals on a white stone. She'd noticed this impurity the moment she stepped inside the gate. As she came closer she could not dismiss the petals. The stones had been scrubbed, recently by their look, and yet here lay this flaw passed over by the careful scourer.

Each step spanned an unbearable amount of time. The red petals seemed to swell as she came nearer. It hurt her head to think, yet she could not keep herself from thinking. "If Mrs. Dakers and Jenny went out, leaving the front door open, why didn't their skirts brush these off. . . ."

The blood was fresh, red droplets still, not yet dried to drab brown stains. Her own blood drummed in her ears and darkened her eyes, yet she could not lose the petrifying sight. Antonia felt she would never move again.

Then her vision cleared. She saw more blots on the lowest step leading to the Dakers' house. Without entirely realizing it, she stepped over the low flowers and continued toward the open front door, her serge skirt whispering over the grass.

She nearly slipped on the highly polished floor. All the surfaces, from the tables to the stair railing, gleamed with forbidding immaculacy. Mottoes hung on every wall, two and three grouped together. Moving closer to read one, Antonia nearly stepped in more blood. A little pool of it had collected near the door, as if someone waited there some time.

When she called out again, the sound of her own voice seemed to shatter the fear that gripped her. Suddenly in a panic to know what was happening, she ran through every room, opening every door, calling, "Jenny? Mrs. Dakers? Paul?"

Remembering the sick man, she hastened up the red-carpeted stairs. Mottoes marched up the wall, keeping step. The first door at the head of the steps was locked. Afraid with an icy terror that threatened her each second with a relapse into paralysis, Antonia threw herself against the door. It did not move. Gathering herself to try again, she heard a noise.

Whirling around, she ran recklessly for the sound. Any horror would be preferable to the torment of the unknown. Bursting into a hot, sunny room, she saw a big man stretched out on an iron bedstead elaborately patterned with wrought hearts and flowers. His stertorous breathing reassured her, though she saw how still he lay.

"Paul," she said, shaking his heavy shoulder. "Wake up!"

Looking around for water to dash in his face, she saw a deep purple bottle with a garish label on the washstand. She'd seen it before, in the homes of women too poor to buy liquor. At a dollar a bottle, a very small dose of Lady Carlotta's Nerve Tonic and Regulator sedated even the most unhappy woman, lifting her out of her troubled life into strange dreams. Remembering the story of Mr. Ransom's suicide, she wondered how much Paul Dakers had taken, or been given.

Antonia could do nothing for him except prop open the door to allow some breeze into the stifling room and throw off the heavy winter quilt someone had placed over him. As she did so a piece of paper fluttered to the floor. Antonia snatched it up. Dense black writing covered both sides.

With a flaming sword I have tried to save you. Man is born to trouble as the sparks fly upward. The lips of the strange woman drop as a honeycomb, and her mouth is smoother than oil: but her end is bitter as wormwood, sharp as a two-edged sword. Can a man take fire into his bosom, and his clothes not be burned? I was glad when they said unto me, Let us go into the house of the Lord. Shall I suffer a witch to live?

There was more, along the same lines. The handwriting grew more compressed and more difficult to read. Frowning over it, Antonia realized that "fire" seemed to leap out at her with appalling regularity. She held in her hand the key to the mysterious arsonist and would have given much to know if Jenny had spent any time in the blacksmith's shed on the night it burned down.

Where was Jenny?

Antonia's feet on the steep, highly varnished steps were as uncontrollable as her thoughts. Where would

Mrs. Dakers take her hated daughter-in-law? What had she done to her already? Each question brought a series of horrible pictures, as lifelike as though she held them to her vision with a stereoscope. As she all but fell the last four steps, Antonia prayed to God the gentle father to delay Mrs. Dakers's wrath.

Reaching the street, Antonia called frantically for help. Had everyone gone deaf? Where were the patrols Jake had talked about? Still in the Silver Spoon, no doubt, she thought bitterly, cursing the criminals who'd taken so many citizens out of Culverton. They'd cause another death today unless she were quick, quick!

In the distance she saw a boy and a woman. Hating the skirts that constricted her, she ran toward them. "Mrs. Ransom? Ernie! I need you. Run as fast as you can to the marshal's office. Find Judge Cotton. If he's not there, try the saloon. Tell him Miss Castle said that Jenny needs help. Exactly like that and they'll believe you."

"Miss Castle says Jenny needs help. Where should I bring 'em?"

Suddenly, with the question, Antonia knew. "To the church. Hurry! As fast as you can!"

With no more than a single glance upward at his mother, Ernie took off like a bullet. Antonia seized Mrs. Ransom's hand and ran the other way, towing the confused woman behind her. "But . . . what . . . where?"

"Faster!" Antonia shouted as her hat fell off. "God knows if we're too late."

When they reached the church fence, Antonia stopped abruptly. Mrs. Ransom stood gasping through her open mouth, her palm pressed to her heart. "Are you tryin' to kill me?"

"Hush," Antonia said, flapping a hand at her.

"What the tarnation do you think you're doin'?" Mrs. Ransom did at least speak more quietly.

"I think Mrs. Dakers is inside, preparing to kill Jenny, if she hasn't already." Said out loud, it savored of the ridiculous.

"That's the stupidest idea I have ever heard. You dragged me—"

"I'd rather look stupid and be wrong than do nothing and let someone get hurt," Antonia said sharply. "Let's see if we can get in the back."

"I'm not goin' nowhere near any loony. I had my share."

"But it may take both of us to overpower her! I believe Jenny is already wounded."

"That's her lookout. I just come up here 'cause my boy wants all them fancy things you were offerin' him. You might as well take him. I ain't doin' him no good."

Antonia didn't hear what Mrs. Ransom said. As soon as the other woman refused to help, she no longer contemplated her. Only the note of self-pity broke through, irritatingly like the whine of an unseen insect. Antonia looked blankly at her and then sneaked across the churchyard. She tried to look in one of the tall windows at the side, but the long red drapes were closed.

Pulling open the backdoor with all the caution in her, Antonia found herself in a small room at the back of the church. A cushion and a large book of Henry Ward Beecher's sermons showed where Mr. Budgell prayed for inspiration before services. There was a strong smell of lemon furniture polish mingling with the damp mustiness of a stack of hymnals.

Leaving the outside door open, for she did not think she could close it quietly enough, she crept toward the opening to the main body of the church. A voice came through the curtain, a voice that faltered and sobbed, only vaguely recognizable as Jenny Dakers's.

"I'm sorry. I'm sorry I've been a bad girl. I didn't want to be. I was poor and . . . alone. They made it sound like I'd be all right if I just do what they said. After I done it once, where could I go? I had to stay."

Antonia started forward impulsively, drawn by the need to soothe the dreadful pain and unhappiness she could hear in the girl's words. She thrust aside the curtain. A dim red light filled the interior, marked with blue where the sun fell through the round stained glass above the lectern.

Jenny knelt in the aisle, her hands pressed together in prayer. Blood, black in the red light, dripped from her elbow onto her skirt, tucked and twisted under her legs. She had not bowed her head, though; she cringed away from Mrs. Dakers, who stood beside her with a torch flaming in one uplifted hand. Bitter gray smoke roiled against the ceiling.

"Pray for the souls of the men you've led into hell!" Her voice rang sharp and clear, as merciless as a bitter wind. She slowly lowered the gleaming blade of a knife before Jenny's staring eyes. "Pray for his forgiveness, for the way of the transgressor is hard!"

"Mrs. Dakers!" Antonia called, stepping out into the church. "Mrs. Dakers, please put down the knife."

The woman's eyes reflected the fire. The pale blue had shrunk to a mere rim, and her pupils were huge, black as a sunless pool in the depths of a lightless cave. Antonia felt they did not see her, though they shifted at her voice.

Raising the knife in her right fist to her eyes, Mrs. Dakers stared at it, moving it back and forth so that the light of her torch danced on the surface. She began to mutter, " 'I will say of the Lord, he is my refuge and my shelter. . . .' " She continued the psalm, sometimes in a whisper, sometimes shrieking at the limits of her voice.

Antonia motioned to Jenny. The girl's face was pale as she cradled her wounded arm against her body. She struggled to get to her feet. Stumbling a few steps, she sank down, clutching at the end of the first pew to save herself from falling to the floor.

Going to her, Antonia attempted to lift Jenny up. "Help's coming," she whispered. "Hurry."

" 'A thousand shall fall at thy side, and ten thousand at thy right hand. . . .' " Mrs. Dakers turned and seemed to see Antonia at last. Smiling, she advanced, the knife and the torch held out at the full stretch of her arms.

The quality of her smile, warm and yet fractured, prickled the hairs on Antonia's nape.

Antonia rose to her feet, shielding Jenny behind her skirt. The mad eyes followed her. She said gently, "Hello, Mrs. Dakers. Isn't it a beautiful day."

"'This is the day which the Lord hath made,'" she agreed.

"Let's go outside, shall we?" Smiling stiffly, Antonia urged Jenny to stand. But the girl was a deadweight. Looking down, she saw that Jenny's eyes were nearly closed and she looked as drugged as her husband had.

Some burning bits dropped from the torch onto the floor. Mrs. Dakers said, in her ordinary voice. "'Every man's work shall be made manifest; for the day shall declare it, because it shall be revealed by fire.'" She gazed blankly around at the benches as if she were addressing a congregation only she could see. "Yes, by fire. 'And the fire shall try every man's work of what sort it is.'"

Antonia shook her head, trying to snap the fascination Mrs. Dakers wove. A sensation took hold of her that Mrs. Dakers made perfect sense and that it was she herself who was mad. If only the other woman did not look so normal. No wisps escaped from the prim bun, her black dress bore no trace of disorder, even her cameo brooch was neatly fastened to the high neck. Only the flaming torch and the knife detracted from the sane picture she made. They belonged to the medieval fanatic looking out from her deranged eyes.

"Let's go outside," Antonia repeated, walking forward. Mrs. Dakers fell back, and for a moment Antonia hoped that she could persuade her to leave the church without harming Jenny.

Then Mrs. Dakers stopped and raised the knife above her head, the torch held out at arm's length. "Pray!" she demanded. "Pray for forgiveness! You who led men down into the pit! You who are without mercy! You betrayed your husband with base desires for another man! Down on your knees, Jezebel, and pray!''

The knife flashed down. Antonia twisted away with a yell, and the blade sparkled through the stuff of her skirt. Mrs. Dakers ripped it loose, and swung her torch at Antonia's head like an Amazonian gladiator with net and trident.

Dodging, Antonia fell sideways, hitting her right elbow on the edge of a bench. Pain shot down her arm, immobilizing her fingers. She knew she'd met a task that was beyond her. If only Jake were here!

Mrs. Dakers stepped over her legs and approached Jenny, still struggling feebly to get up. Looking at the figure of wrath standing over her, Jenny sank down again, whimpering, her hands over her face.

"Thomas is a good man. 'Behold, I am vile; what shall I answer thee?' He never reproaches you for your wickedness. Instead of washing his feet with your tears, you cast your eyes on another and rejoice in your heart at your deception."

Jenny dropped her hands and stared upward. "Thomas? But your husband is dead," she said slowly. "Paul said he died when the raiders burned the town."

Mrs. Dakers did not seem to hear. She wandered in the nightmare of her past. "You meet behind the stables, while Thomas labors. Labors for your good while you kiss and caress behind his back! You wanted him to die, and lo, he did die! The blame on your head, harlot. Your head! Not mine!"

She flung down the torch. Antonia barreled into her just in time to spoil her aim. Instead of landing on Jenny, the torch bounced away to land beneath a window. The long red curtain fluttered in the draft of sudden heat.

Without an instant's pause, as swift as a striking snake, Mrs. Dakers bent to stab Jenny. The girl scarcely flinched as the knife drove down. She sighed like a tired child and fell back, losing her grasp on the edge of the bench, just in time to miss the silver blade.

Mrs. Dakers drew back her arm for a second strike. "Curse God and die!"

Antonia sprang for the upraised arm. At the touch of her hands Mrs. Dakers began to scream, a high thin wail that went on and on without breath. Staggering backward, Antonia strove to break Mrs. Dakers's grip on the knife, forcing her arm down at an awkward angle. The knife fell, point down in the wooden floor, quivering.

In relief, Antonia slackened her clutch. The black silk sleeve slipped through Antonia's fingers as Mrs. Dakers jerked free. She gasped and began to laugh. "Behold, the Lord in a pillar of fire! How great a matter a little fire kindleth!"

Seeing flames reflected in Mrs. Dakers's dilated pupils, Antonia involuntarily turned to look. The curtain billowed in the wind of its own destruction as fire raced up it. Fragments flew wildly, catching all the other drapes.

"Oh, spew," Antonia whispered.

Suddenly she was on the floor, Mrs. Dakers's weight on her back and her arms wrapped almost lovingly around her throat. Antonia clawed at the stubborn silk sleeve, unable to find a purchase, while a mad giggle went on chanting, "'Honor thy father and thy mother. Thou shalt not commit adultery. Thou shalt not steal. . . .'" The rest of the commandments were lost in the roaring that had begun inside Antonia's head.

As a bubbling blackness rose before her eyes she thought, She's left out "thou shalt not kill." She tried to force her fingers to continue searching for a hold, but they did not seem to belong to her anymore. She no longer had any idea what the oppressive weight on her back was. The only thing of which she was aware was the iron band ever constricting around her throat.

Then the band was loose and she could breathe. The first air brought tears of pain to her eyes. She choked and coughed and began crawling out from beneath the cruel immobile weight. The air was sweet, if smoky. Antonia sat up and saw Mrs. Ransom, outlined by the burning wall behind her, holding Beecher's bound sermons in both hands.

"I hit her," she said, amazed.

"Thank God," Antonia croaked.

Mrs. Ransom stepped around Mrs. Dakers's fallen body to help her up. Coughing, Antonia said, "We'd better get them out of here. You get Jenny."

Wearily, she rolled Mrs. Dakers onto her back. Taking her by the heels of her stout shoes, she dragged the inert figure toward the rear of the church. Ahead, Mrs. Ransom supported Jenny, who could walk, though her head lolled and her body sagged loosely.

In the temporary safety of Mr. Budgell's private room, Antonia said, "Take Jenny outside, then come back. I can't go on."

She sat down on the leather cushion, her head on her knees. Mrs. Dakers began to snore softly. Antonia did not want to look at her, for she seemed as innocent as any matron, and if she could be insane, what else might be possible?

Mrs. Ransom had to awaken Antonia from a half doze. "Don't just sit there," she cried, shaking her violently.

"Has no one come?" Antonia asked, coughing as she bent down to take Mrs. Dakers's feet again. Dizzy and sick, she felt the effort to be almost beyond her.

"Not yet," Mrs. Ransom answered over her shoulder. "They're all out huntin' them rustlers, I reckon."

As they carried Mrs. Dakers out Mr. Budgell suddenly appeared. "What is going on here?" he demanded, his fair skin flushing.

"Well," Mrs. Ransom said, "your church is on fire, for one."

Mr. Budgell gave her a horrified look and dashed inside. Antonia paid no attention. Someone had told her it was her duty to carry this woman, and she always did her duty.

She said it later, when a large brown hand came down

into her vision, holding a dipper of water. "I always do my duty," she muttered, squinting up into the sun that glowed like a halo around her benefactor's head.

"I know you do," Jake said, squatting down beside her and guiding the cup to her lips. She drank thirstily, half the water dripping onto her dress. Jake glared, thinking that one of the people running around brainlessly might have thought to bring her something.

He took the dipper away when it was empty. When he put his arm around her shoulders, she leaned against him, seeking his strength. He'd never felt a keener pride. Leaning against the church fence, he cuddled her close. Whatever the future could hold for him, this ranked as his supreme moment. Antonia needed him.

In a few moments she said, as though in the middle of a thought, "It's not true, though, is it? Or maybe I just don't have a life, and that's why . . ."

"Why what?" He couldn't see her face, only the top of her ear and the pins in her smoky hair. Her voice came muffled.

"I've always heard your life passes before your eyes when you're about to die. It's not true. I didn't see anything, and I know I was about to die."

"Since it didn't happen, you couldn't have been in that much danger," he said, though Mrs. Ransom had already told him how close Antonia had actually come to death.

"No, I think I don't have that much of a life." She raised her head, shaking back her falling hair, to look at him with tearful eyes.

"You do now," he said.

They shared a kiss as gentle and pure as the holy kiss that binds a new husband and wife. Sweet with ripe promise, it required neither passion nor furor for its meaning to be clear. They said, "I love you," in the same breath, and laughed, close to tears.

Antonia put up her hand and traced his jaw. She

blinked and shook her head to clear it. "What are you doing here?"

"That's a fine question to ask your financé."

"Are you?"

"You don't think I'd get away with kissing you in front of the whole town without marrying you?"

"Oh, yes. I forgot this was Culverton, the Quick Wedding Capital of the World. But you rode out after those bandits? What time is it?"

"My posse found one of 'em hiding in the woods not far from the Koers' place. It seems old Conrad's a hell of a shot. He's going to be fine, by the way, should be on his feet in time for Nick's wedding. So anyway, we brought in the one we caught, just in time to hear young Ernie trying to tell anyone who'd listen a wild story about you and Mrs. Dakers. Knowing you the way I do, I saw he was telling the truth and hightailed it up here."

From the safety of his arms Antonia looked around them. Mrs. Ransom sat on the ground, talking earnestly with her son. The boy nodded as she spoke, looking at her with adoring eyes not entirely free from traces of tears. Antonia wondered if employment might be found for Mrs. Ransom at whatever school Ernie would attend. Who did she know on the governing board of the Chicago Symphony?

Nearer to hand, Mrs. Wilmot dressed Jenny's lacerated shoulder. The girl hardly winced, her heavy lashes low on her colorless cheeks. A few feet away from her Mrs. Dakers lay on the ground. Though someone had crossed her arms on her chest in the manner of the dead, her chest still rose and fell. Jenny did not look at her.

Antonia sat up. "I forgot about Paul! He's at their house, drugged!"

"Doc Partridge is trying to wake him now. Don't you remember? You told Mr. Budgell about Paul half an hour ago. You've explained the whole story to me. Never mind," he said, drawing her close again. "It's been kind of a shock. You rest quiet."

Obeying, she lay back in his arms. She became slowly aware of a loud and constant noise. She realized it had been in the background for some time without her hearing it, like a continuing sound in another room while one is asleep and dreaming.

Lifting her eyes, she saw that the church still blazed, roaring like a furnace. The walls remained upright but all within was flame. The doors stood wide as Mr. Budgell, at the head of the bucket brigade, hurled useless water inside.

"I didn't think it was so bad," Antonia said.

"It's old," Jake answered. "Probably the oldest building in town. The first settlers built it before anything else. They lived in canvas tents, but they had a church."

"You'll build a new one. Your great-grandchildren won't care if it's a hundred years old or one hundred and ten."

"*Our* great-grandchildren," Jake said, tightening his arms.

The calling of the bucket brigade went on as Antonia sank again into a stupor. As long as Jake was willing to hold her, she was willing to stay just as they were, though the ground was damp. She resigned herself to wearing gunnysacks until her clothing arrived from her maid.

Antonia was not immediately roused by the sharpened note of the voices. Not till Jake pushed her aside to jump to his feet did she sit up and look around. Everyone, even Jenny, stared in shock as a figure clad in tattered black silk ran toward the burning church.

"Stop her!" Jake shouted as he followed her, and others took up the cry.

Mrs. Dakers ran with the free stride of a young girl. Those who saw her face said later that she seemed to be singing with great joy, though none could swear to the words.

Mr. Budgell threw himself at her feet, trying to intercept her. She leaped nimbly over him and ran to the opened door. Her speed did not lessen as she entered the inferno. She never glanced back. If she screamed, no one heard her.

Chapter 16

Antonia woke to find the sun slanting in the window at a peculiar angle. The ceiling sloped in a way she'd never noticed at Jake's house. She stared upward for what seemed a long time before she decided this meant she was not *at* Jake's house.

Heaving a sigh, she realized an arm lay over her, resting heavily just below her breasts. Jake lay not a foot away, on his side, his eyes closed, his breathing steady. His coat and boots were off, and his holster hung on the wooden post of someone's spare bed.

Antonia decided she was too relaxed to get up and explore. Dropping her head back down on the soft pillows, she looked over at Jake and found his eyes were open. He smiled as he moved his arm away and asked, "How are you feeling now?"

She coughed once or twice before her voice would work. "My throat hurts."

"It's going to for a couple of days. Then you'll be fine."

The high tight collar of the nightdress she wore chafed her sore neck. Absently she undid the constricting buttons and spread the collar wide. "What are you doing here?"

"I sneaked up the back steps. I didn't want you to wake up alone and be scared." His eyes winced away from the bruised skin at her throat, but his gaze dropped helplessly to the plump cleavage that an extra opened button revealed below.

"Thank you. What time is it?" She stretched, her breasts straining against the open placket.

"I don't know. Three-thirty, maybe."

"No wonder I'm so hungry."

Jake chuckled. "I better get up and find you something, then. I promise it won't be stew."

"No," she said. "Hold me for a while?"

Pushing aside the soft blankets that covered her, they came together, helped by the distinct valley that ran down the center of the mattress. Antonia needed to feel every warm inch of his living body against her own, to remind her of what she'd so nearly lost. They lay very close together until she could almost feel herself fusing with him.

"Comfortable?" she asked against his shoulder, a long time later. He hummed an answer, shifting his hips away from contact against her body. Antonia smiled tenderly, knowing he couldn't see her face. "Whose nightgown is this, anyway?"

"Mrs. Wilmot's. This is her spare bedroom."

"You know, she's smaller than she looks. This gown is too tight." She took a big breath and held it, pushing out the bodice to press against his chest. "Look," she whispered. "I'm about to burst my seams."

"Antonia . . ."

Taking great pains, she traced a path from his waist down over his smooth leather belt to the top metal button of his trousers. "Looks like I'm not the only one."

"And people were afraid you'd corrupt Culverton," he said through his teeth.

"If they only knew." She put back her head and smiled up at him, intimately and enticingly.

He kissed her, almost growling with the effort of restraint. As she wriggled closer to him he felt his control slipping. He couldn't claim she didn't know what she did to him or that he was taking advantage of her innocence.

Not when she ran delicate fingers inside his shirt where it had come untucked in sleep.

Drawing his breath in with a hiss, he said with forced calm, "We're not going to do this. We're going to wait until we're properly married."

"Oh, absolutely," she agreed. One last time she kissed him, his prickly stubble titillating her lips. Primly she withdrew her fingers from his heated skin. "I had better get up anyway. I can't spend the entire day in bed with you."

"I'm glad you're going to be sensible." He rolled over onto his back, striving to calm his breathing. Every time he inhaled he could smell the airy freshness of the bed linens and the clean soap she'd used when she'd washed herself in a tin hip bath.

Briskly Antonia sat up. Before he could move, she threw her arm over his broad shoulders, holding him down. As she leaned over him, supporting herself on her elbow, the freed tendrils of her hair caressed his face. She grazed her fingers through the shining hair above his forehead and lingeringly she brushed her lips over his, again and again, until his hands came up, not to push her away, but to hold her in place while he kissed her in return.

Recklessly she fumbled with the bone buttons of his shirt, not looking, for she did not want to end the deepening kiss. Without a blush she plunged her tongue wetly into his mouth at the same instant she swept aside his shirt.

Then the world turned upside down. She laughed as he tipped her over onto her back and settled himself on top of her. His eyes were pure green with a steady light shining in their depths.

"You've got about one second to say you don't want to do this," he said. "I might not be able to stop later. . . ."

"I don't want you to ever stop." She could tell she wore nothing beneath her borrowed nightgown. There was no hiding from his hardness, not in this bed, not in her mind. It was time to learn everything she could, for she would have years to put her knowledge to good use. What would happen, she wondered, if she rocked her hips ever so slightly?

"Antonia . . ." he groaned, though with a note of exasperated laughter.

"What?"

The first experiment was so satisfactory that she did it again, adding a slight sideways roll. Glancing up in his face, she saw him staring down into hers with an intensity that humbled her. "What should I do now?" she asked shyly.

"Exactly what you're doing, only . . . could we do without this?" He pinched up the stiff white cotton.

"Yes, if we can do without this." Running her hands over his pants, she discovered the firm muscles of his buttocks and wanted to repeat the action, especially when he thrust forward reflexively. A gasp of surprise and wonder broke from her throat as her heart began to beat in a crazy tempo.

They scrambled to be free of the confinement of clothes and at last gazed at each other with awe. Antonia realized there was nothing graceless or unhandsome about the design of a man after all. She reached out with a natural wish to touch. The smoothness of it was far softer than any surface on her own body, but reinforced with a might that was purely male.

Jake caught her hand after she'd no more than skimmed him. "Don't. . . ." He saw the briefest flash of hurt in her eyes and hurried to explain. "I can't stay . . . rational if you do that."

"Oh." She smiled at him in a way she knew was wicked, lying back under his gaze on the cool sheets. "Never mind rational."

A rush of pride filled her when Jake took her in his arms. With one callused finger, he followed her spine from the nape of her neck, tracing the division of her backside as delicately as if her were painting her. Antonia arched her body at that touch, pressing forward against his rigidity.

"Oh, my. Oh, yes," she said, for everything she'd ever read suddenly made perfect sense.

He laid her on her back and sought out the tender pinkness at the tip of her breasts with his tongue. Her ardent yes was his reward as her fingers entwined in his hair. He felt her tense as he smoothed his hand over her rounded stomach and continued down.

Pausing at the very top of her feather-soft curls, Jake again tasted her nipple. He knew from before that she could achieve a certain release from suckling alone. Though he ached to fill her, he would wait for her readiness, if it killed him.

Antonia screwed her eyes shut as the unbearable tightness began again deep within her. It was more intense than yesterday's, as though the thing awakened within her now knew its proper role. When Jake's fingers sought her hidden cleft, she did not at first realize it, caught up in the spiraling ecstasy that spared none of her. Then her energy broke loose, freed by his mouth and, above all, his hand.

She found herself clinging to him, as a shipwrecked sailor holds to the only spar among pounding waves. "I'm sorry," she said, letting go her clutch.

"What for?"

"I've heard . . . that is . . . nice girls aren't supposed to feel 'convulsive intoxication.'"

Jake laughed, right out loud. Antonia stared up at him. She'd never seen him do that before. Meeting his eyes, half shyly, she saw that he smiled down on her with such love and happiness, she knew he'd never reproach her for her wantonness.

"You know," he said, "that was only the beginning. There are some things I didn't see written up in your *Principles* book."

He gently pushed her down so she lay once more on

her back. Taking infinite time, he strew tiny kisses over her shoulders, her breasts, and lower in a line over her navel. Though Antonia guessed the destination he had in mind at once, and trembled with consuming anticipation, she stopped him.

"I want . . ." she began.

He looked up, his eyes a rare shade of emerald. "You must always tell me what you want."

"I want . . . you."

Straightening out, he lay with his head by hers. He stroked her face, the only place he could touch without being driven crazy. His thumb stroked her lower lip, which was a mistake, especially when she nipped at his fingers. Fighting to keep his voice steady, he said, "We don't have to do more than this. We have a whole lifetime in front of us."

Certain now of what she wanted, she placed her hand, firmly yet cautiously, over his virility. He sucked in his breath, his eyes closing in pleasure. "How long were you planning to wait?" she asked.

They rolled together, already one. Supporting himself with locked arms, Jake held back. Between gritted teeth, he said, "I hope . . . I don't want to hurt you."

Instinctively she raised her hips to meet him, taking him to the edge of consummation. His way eased by the balm that nature had given her, Jake entered her easily. Antonia cried out, her body flexing, as elation flooded her soul.

"Oh, God," Jake said, pausing. "I've hurt you."

"No, no." Her voice was muffled by his shoulder, but he could hear her happiness. "It's the most . . . you're so magnificent!"

She rocked her hips in an innate rhythm, new to her, but old as the promise of heaven. In a moment she'd lost it, as another outburst of irrepressible passion shook her. Her entire body called to him.

Jake took up the cadence at once, driving her to as-yet-undreamed-of heights. She held him with a strength he'd never expected. He was not even afraid of crushing her. Though he made every effort, he couldn't withstand the living fulfillment of his dearest wishes.

As he shouted her name, as Antonia felt the first wave of his seed inundate her body, she knew a release that made all the others seem as nothing. Though in time she might forget the horror of this day, the bliss of this moment was hers for eternity. A loving smile came to her lips as she remembered that she could repeat this moment often in the approaching years.

Her laughter rippled through the sunny room. Jake, still clasped within her, raised his head and demanded, "Share the joke." When she told him her thought, he said, "Often's a pretty indistinct time. I think we ought to figure out just how often *is* often."

"What did you have in mind?" she asked with a suspiciously pleased smile.

"Twice a day? 'Course we won't get a heck of a lot done otherwise, but I've been thinking about giving up marshaling, and we can always eat stew."

"Ugh, no more stew. Would you really want to do this twice a day?" She ran her fingernails lightly down his back, feeling him withdrawing and not wanting to lose him.

Jake tugged at her earlobe with his teeth and then said, "Twice a day seems kind of scant to me. What do you say to three times? And, of course, there are the nights." Lifting himself up, he gazed down into her lake-blue eyes and answered her unspoken question. "I could love you forever and never want you a whit the less. You're perfect."

Tears filled her eyes. "I am?"

"Yep. Don't let anyone tell you different. I'm one hundred percent in favor of book learning for women, if it makes them all like you." He kissed her lips and felt them curve into a smile beneath his own.

"Could we really make love three times a day?"

With a comical groan Jake rolled over onto his back.

Closing his eyes, he said, "Give me a little time to nap, honey, and I'll show you."

She wriggled onto her stomach and propped her head up on her hands. After watching him for a few moments, reveling anew in his stern good looks, she said, "Did you mean it?"

He opened one eye. "I need more than two minutes, Antonia. Oh, you mean giving up my job? Yep." He shut the eye. Despite that, he instantly trapped her hand when she raised it to slap at him. He began to tug at her fingers, playing with the sensitive inside edges.

"Nobody's got more respect for the judge than I have. But I decided it's about time Culverton's had more than one man who can say what the law is. I figure if I study, I can get a lawyer's diploma in next to no time."

"You wouldn't have happened to decide this about two weeks ago, did you?"

"Why, Miss Castle. I don't know what you are referring to!"

She left her hand in his and soon drifted into a doze. Somewhere in the distance a lonesome train whistle blew. In a few minutes she felt him sit up and drag Mrs. Wilmot's spare room quilt over their naked bodies. Snuggling up to Jake's warmth, she fleetingly hoped they'd not be disturbed for a long time. They had to nap to build up their vitality for later. "Twice a day," she whispered, deeply content.

When she awoke again, it was with the fading memory of a dream. She'd been doing something . . . that part had gone . . . but everywhere she went she could hear footsteps. It should have been frightening, but she'd somehow known that she heard the echoes of all the shoes she'd ruined or lost since coming to Culverton. She still regretted the loss of her elastic-sided boots, though they'd gone in a good cause. With any luck Grace would send shoes, too, or she'd have to go barefoot in her gunnysacks.

There'd been whispering in her dreams, too, remote

yet familiar voices. She turned to Jake, wanting to share her dream with him. She'd never slept with anyone before, with the chance to murmur such enigmas and hear another person's views. But Jake was still asleep. Antonia was bringing up the quilt to cover his chest and her shoulders when the door opened.

"Antonia!" Familiar voices indeed! Her parents stood aghast in the doorway.

Startled, Jake leaped out of bed, grabbing for his gun. Antonia's mother screamed and covered her eyes with her gloved hands. Mrs. Wilmot stared goggle-eyed over Mr. Castle's shoulder while in the hall Ned went into whoops of laughter.

"Oh, my God," Jake said, his face as red as a ripe tomato. He turned his back and snatched his shirt from the bedpost. Holding it in front of himself, he confronted the crowd.

"Blasphemy, too!" Mr. Castle said, his brow as stern as a Puritan's.

At that moment Antonia pulled the quilt over her head. She heard Jake ask, "Who the hell are you people?" and her father's reply, "That, sir, is my daughter."

"Oh, my God," Jake said reverently.

Antonia decided she should show some guts, or at least poise. Clutching the quilt to her shoulders, she sat up. "Jake, I'd like you to meet my father, my mother, and . . . that's Ned. You'll remember I told you about him. This is Marshal Faraday, everyone."

It was by no means easy being gracious while her father scowled like an Puritan about to start a witch-hunt, her mother looked as though she'd been dipped in boiling oil, and her brother barked with laughter in the hall. Mrs. Wilmot had remembered modesty enough to cover her eyes, but Antonia glimpsed the liquid gleam of her eye between two of her fingers.

Trying to smile, Antonia could feel her lips twitching with incipient hysteria. She said, "I'm very surprised to see you all. I didn't expect you."

"Obviously," her father said, looking at her directly for the first time. "I begin to see Father may have been right, Antonia. You do belong in a home for the deranged."

"Now, Mr. Castle," her mother said, still with her hands over her eyes.

"What's that supposed to mean?" Jake demanded, stepping forward. Though his shirttails flapped around his knees, Antonia thought him glorious, admiring even at this moment the native power of his defined muscles. She saw some she'd not seen before, like the smooth hollow at the side of his behind, and could hardly keep from speaking her tribute aloud.

"It's all right, Jake," she said. "Father's upset. He doesn't mean it. Ned, why don't you take Mother downstairs and wait for me? I'll only be a few minutes and then we can talk everything out."

Wiping the laughter-forced tears from his cheeks, her brother took their mother's arm and led her away. "Oh, what does it mean, Ned?" Antonia heard her ask quaveringly.

"I'd say a wedding, at a guess," Ned answered in the deep voice that assorted so oddly with his boyish appearance.

Mr. Castle stepped into the room. "Well, sir, I am awaiting your explanation."

"What explanation?" Jake said, beginning to chuckle. "I'd say circumstances speak for themselves."

"Father," Antonia interrupted, before the stiffly starched Easterner could speak again. "Father, wait downstairs."

"Kindly do not use that tone with me, Antonia. I am already seriously displeased with you. Your rudeness in not waiting for us in Chicago has put your mother through a difficult and exhausting journey, not to mention the difficulties entailed in reorganizing that ridiculous mess formerly known as the Society of Social Harmony. I might have known. . . ."

"Father, I have no idea what you're talking about. But I really think we could wait to sort it out after Jake and I put our clothes on."

"I promise you I would not stay to hear the details of this infamy were it not that there seems to be a noticable dearth of trains to this misbegotten hobnailed town!" He walked out, pushing past Mrs. Wilmot, who hadn't moved.

Jake glanced at Antonia and said, "Hobnailed?"

"He makes shoes."

He nodded and went over to shut the door. Mrs. Wilmot said nostalgically, "Those are my best sheets, you know."

Antonia was ready to apologize when Jake said, "Just think of the story you'll be able to tell." He closed the door on her thoughtful expression.

Jake looked at Antonia, his blush fading. "I don't suppose you could climb out this window."

"I probably could."

"We could borrow one of Dakers's horses for you and we would be in Kansas City in a couple of days, if you wouldn't mind riding rough."

"I wouldn't mind."

"Then we'd find someone to marry us, head west, and . . . ah, heck. Mrs. Cotton would never forgive us." He flung away his shirt and sat beside her on the bed, putting his arm around her.

Antonia kissed his shoulder and leaned her head on it. "The story will die down in ten or fifteen years, most likely."

"If we're lucky." He felt the gentle nips and nibbles of her even white teeth and began to cheer up. "I guess it's not so bad. Around here there's sure to be another scandal pretty quick. We've got a new schoolteacher coming in and she ought to be good for gossip. Antonia!" he said sharply as she explored the puckered brown circles on his chest. "Antonia, they're waiting for us."

She promised herself she'd save what she'd been doing for later as the rewards were so tantalizing. Daring to run her hand over the crisp hairs on his thigh, she said, "So it is possible to indulge more than once a day!"

Jake gritted his teeth. "Where are my pants?"

"I don't know. Did you have them when you came in?"

About half an hour later they descended the stairs, Antonia avoiding Jake's eyes, for she could not help giving a tender smile whenever she did meet them. She had to take his arm, for there was a slight sting present when she walked. "Let Father talk," she said. "He works himself up until he's astounded by his own brilliant oratory and that puts him in a reasonable mood."

Ned met them outside the parlor, carrying a tray for Mrs. Wilmot. Getting her first clear look at him, Antonia almost didn't recognize him. He now wore his fair hair rather long and slicked back, and he'd grown a luxuriant mustache. Jake looked a little sideways at Ned's large, negligently knotted silk tie.

But then Ned grinned and he was Antonia's own lively brother again. "Cicero's waiting for you by the fireplace," he confided.

Walking in ahead of them, he said, "Mr. Faraday and Antonia are here, Father."

Mr. Castle had chosen his position wisely. As the focal point of the room, he compensated for the greater height and solidity of the man who had, so far as he could tell, completely debased his daughter. He drew breath to speak, but Mrs. Castle, spoiling his moment all unaware, held out both hands and said, "Come to me, my poor darling!"

She sat on a hard chair, her skirt wrapped around her as though she were afraid of mice. Antonia crossed to her, pressed her cheek to her mother's discreetly powdered face, and said, "How are you, darling? I'm awfully surprised to see you."

"Not so surprised—" Mr. Castle began.

His wife's soft little voice ran on. "But I wrote to you, telling you Ned had come back from those foreign countries and that he'd talked to us about coming out to see you. He wouldn't let us wait for a reply."

"A most inconsiderate—"

"Then we came to Chicago after a thoroughly pleasant train journey—Mr. Pullman was kind enough to lend us his car as it had to go back to Chicago anyway. He doesn't hold it against you at all that your little society persuaded him to fix up those workers' homes. So really we were very comfortable. Your father hardly had dyspepsia at all and traveling always upsets him so."

"Dora, if you please—"

"And when we arrived, we went right to your house. Oh, it's so lovely! How ever did you manage to decorate it so nicely?" She continued without waiting for an answer. "Your father had a long talk with the cook after he dismissed your maid, and no one knew where you were. So he went to see Mrs. Newstead—oh, I forgot . . . it's Mrs. Parisi now. She didn't have any idea where you were and your father called her . . . a fluff-headed old fool." A pretty blush rose in her still-youthful face.

Antonia squeezed her mother's hand gently. "Wait a moment, darling. You think so fast the rest of us can't keep up. What's this about Grace? And Mrs. Newstead is married?"

"A disgraceful business! I'm not surprised you allowed yourself to get mixed up with that sort of person. You always were—"

"Here, Father," Ned said, bringing him a glass of lemonade. "You better take one of your pills."

"I don't want—"

Jake pushed his shoulders off the wall. He'd leaned there as soon as Antonia had left his side, and appeared to be enjoying the family reunion very much. "Why don't we step outside, sir? Wilmot keeps a good brand of cigar and we can have that talk.''

Mr. Castle threw a triumphant glance at his family. Seeing they appeared properly cowed at this example of his worth in the eyes of strangers, he said, "Certain, Mister . . . er . . . ?''

"Faraday. I'm the marshal of Culverton, almost retired. I wouldn't want you to think Antonia's marrying a man who could leave her a widow at any minute. Not that crime's much of a problem in Culverton—not since this morning.'' As he ushered Mr. Castle out Jake turned and gave Antonia a wink.

Antonia returned it, and had the satisfaction of seeing that she could still surprise him. Giving her attention to her mother as she sat down near to her, she said, "Now explain everything. Slowly. I've been through a lot today.''

"Oh, I don't know if I can. Let Ned.''

Bestowing a fond kiss on his mother, he said, "Father liberated your maid because she had a man in the kitchen. Somehow I knew you allowed your servants followers, so I gave her fifty dollars' wages in lieu of notice when Father wasn't looking. Don't forget to pay me back.''

"I won't,'' Antonia promised. "And Mrs. Newstead?''

Her mother said, "I don't know if it's fit for your ears, dear. She's married a Persian gentleman whom she'd only known for a very short while, it seems.''

"No, no, Mother. They'd known each other as Caesar and Cleopatra, remember? And, apparently, as Charles the First and Henrietta Maria, I think it was. For all I know, it might have been Punch and Judy.''

"That doesn't sound like Mrs. Newstead.''

Ned just shrugged. "Love does strange things to people, as you should know. Or am I being indiscreet?''

Antonia made a face at him. "What did Father mean by reorganizing the Society?''

"Things were in a shambles at your headquarters. Rather like a beehive when the queen dies. According to the second in command, your Mr. Gringley, who was very nearly in tears, Mrs. Parisi hadn't paid much attention to the Society since meeting her spiritual lover."

"Oh, Ned, really," said his shocked mother.

"There was even some talk that she may had given society funds to him, though Father pretty well disproved that when he checked the books. I tell you, Antonia, I never had more respect for Cicero. He listened to no excuses, inspired the lazier volunteers, and formed a new board of directors within the first week. Of course, he was impatient to clear things up so he could come after you."

"You mustn't feel that he was neglectful," Mrs. Castle said quickly.

"No, I don't," Antonia said, squeezing her hand. "I understand that Father couldn't have my name associated with anything the least unsavory. I still don't understand one thing, though. You say Mrs. Newstead didn't know where I was? But I sent her a telegram explaining everything."

"You must make allowances for new brides. At least she knew where you'd gone on this lecture tour," Ned said. "So we followed your itinerary, hoping to cross your trail, as they say. I still can't imagine my sweet sister stirring up so much trouble in these little Western towns. One place Father was nearly ridden out of town on a rail when he told them you were his daughter."

"Winston, Illinois?" Antonia asked, cringing.

"You remember it. They certainly remembered you."

"I still don't understand. Even if she didn't receive my telegram, Henry and Evelyn should have told her where they'd left me and why. Come to think of it, they were supposed to send me a lawyer to get me out of this town." She shook her head at the strange inevitable tide of events.

"Would that be Mr. and Mrs. Layton?"

"You did meet them, then?"

"Oh, yes," Mrs. Castle said. "At a hotel in a charming town two or three stops away from here. They were so very surprised to see us, but a delightful couple."

Ned saw Antonia's confusion and said, "They seemed to be on their honeymoon. Mrs. Layton wrote you a letter. It's with my valise at the boardinghouse."

Pressing her fingers to her forehead, Antonia said, "I can't make heads or tails out of this. I feel I've been gone for a hundred years, not two weeks."

When Jake and her father came back, Mr. Castle pulled out his watch and said, "Two minutes, Jake."

"Yes, sir." Jake steered Antonia out of the room. "We'd better humor him, Antonia. They're only going to be here long enough to see us married, so we might as well make him happy."

"Happy about what?"

"You're staying at the boardinghouse." Seeing her disappointment, he swept his arms around her. "I understand, honey. I can't guess how I'll get through the nights, now I know how sweet you are. The days have been tough enough. I can't tell you how many times I just plain didn't want to leave you before you got the school and came to where I could see you sometimes."

"Couldn't you climb in the window, or something?" Antonia asked, leaning against his body.

"I have a feeling you're going be sleeping in your mother's room. Your father's a very intelligent man. It won't be so bad. He said I can come and sit in the parlor every evening seven to nine."

Her father's decorous cough told them time was up. She wanted time to tell Jake all her feelings, but there was only a moment to kiss him and to whisper, "I love you."

Mrs. Fleck's boardinghouse might not have met Mr. Castle's stringent requirements, were it not that Bishop

O'Donnell, Mr. Budgell's district superior, was also staying there. Having met on the train, they became solid companions. Antonia could only hope her father did not confide his daughter's waywardness to the bishop, for she did not want Mr. Budgell's standing to suffer. His misery over the loss of his church on the same day as he was to have it inspected was soothed only by Mary Lou Ginnis's compassion and the bishop's enthusiasm over her apple pandowdy.

Jake and Antonia hadn't even their daily two hours in the parlor. The sheriff at Greensboro had captured the remaining outlaws, and Jake took his prisoner there under heavy guard for extradition back to Illinois. She waved to him while he rode out, and blushed under the eyes of the town when he touched his hat to her.

The bishop, the Castles, and the Dakers were asked to dinner at the Cottons' house on Friday night. Mrs. Ransom was invited to make up the numbers, and looked neat and sober in her newly washed dress. The bishop was very kind to her, and Mrs. Cotton got that matchmaking twinkle in her eye until Mr. O'Donnell began talking of his peerless wife.

After the men went out to look at the horses and smoke, and the three older ladies found they had a common interest in flowers, Antonia found herself alone with Jenny.

The girl's arm was still stiff under the mourning she wore, but she had a peace in her eyes that Antonia had not seen there before. She no longer held herself with stilted posture and had laughed and smiled through dinner. Now she looked across the parlor at Antonia and said, "Paul's comin' through it just fine. He'd seen her gettin' a little strange, but he didn't know what to do about it, and didn't want to burden me, not with the baby on the way."

"He's a good man."

"The best." Jenny leaned forward. "I guess you got some questions about the things she said."

"No, not really. She was deranged."

"I don't mind you knowing. Come over here, where I don't have to shout."

Obligingly Antonia sat beside Jenny on the sofa. She remembered the last time she'd sat there, but gave her attention to listening to Jenny. "You don't have to say anything if you'd rather not."

"I know you won't look down on me." She took a deep breath and began quickly, "I met Paul in St. Louis. He'd come there to buy stock. I was working in a—well, a house. You know, like Miss Annie's. Not really like hers. She treats her girls fair, no cheatin' 'em, or slappin' around if they don't take enough customers a day."

Antonia could only reach out and cover Jenny's hands in mute sympathy. The girl shrugged. "Paul never should've told her, but he couldn't lie any more than he can dance. So when she asked him where I'd come from, he told her."

"Men do sometimes have more respect for truth than is wise."

"You can say that again! 'Course, that's one of the things I loved about him right away. Everybody tells lies in a house. He kept on showin' up every evenin' payin' his money just to talk to me. When his money was gone, he asked me to marry up with him. I had to trust him to do it—that was the hardest part—'cause they weren't gonna let me go, 'specially as I done bought all my clothes from 'em."

"You were very lucky to find Paul."

"I'd begun to wonder if I was. She kept on niggling at me—dropping hints before company, keeping me workin' long past Paul's goin' to bed, and the praying! I feel like I done enough kneeling for the next twenty years. And I didn't like sayin' nothing against her to Paul. He knew she was gettin' strange. He didn't have no idea she was being mean to me. She was clever, powerful clever, and men don't notice nothing."

"Some do," Antonia said, thinking of Jake's changing eyes. "I still don't understand one thing. She knew all this—I mean, about you—for months. What set her off?"

Jenny put a protective hand to her midriff. "Paul told her about the baby when she was watching over him last. She gave him a dose of that tonic she always took. He shouldn't of taken it, but I don't guess he thought she'd give him anything that'd hurt him. When she came downstairs, she looked awful strange."

"I think she must have taken some of that 'tonic.' I noticed her enlarged pupils."

"Yeah, and she was talking like she couldn't stop. She made me something sweet to drink. I guess there was something in it 'cause I got real foggylike. But I could hear what she said, right clear. She kept tellin' me to move, and when I didn't, she run that paper knife into my arm. It didn't hurt exactly, but I was scared of it. It seemed a whole lot bigger than it was. . . ."

"Don't think about it anymore, Jenny. You have to think about the future now."

The older ladies came back. There was no time to tell Jenny that her story made no difference to their friendship, except by another clasp of their hands.

The subject changed to clothes when Mrs. Cotton admired Antonia's dress and wanted to see how it was made. "I don't know how Mother knew to bring me dresses. This trip's been so hard on my clothes," Antonia said, standing up and turning around.

Mrs. Castle said, "I thought if I'd been traveling for a long time, what would I want most?"

Later that evening Antonia volunteered to help Mrs. Cotton in the kitchen. After scrubbing a few plates, Mrs. Cotton said, "I reckon you've got some questions to ask me about Bettina Dakers."

"You knew her for a long time."

"Sure did. Since coming to Culverton. You'd never think it, but she was the prettiest little thing you ever saw. Prettier even than you, which is sayin' a piece."

"Thank you."

"Pshaw."

Antonia said, "She talked about a man she was seeing before her husband's death. She felt terribly guilty about it. Mr. Thomas Dakers died when the town burned, didn't he?"

"That's right. Jake shot most of the varmints that did it, but they'd trapped Tom in his stables, just for sheer devilment. I can still hear them horses screaming. Tom killed a few raiders himself, but he didn't have enough ammunition. When they found him, it turned out Tom had saved one bullet for himself. Bettina thought suicide was a sin, but what could the poor bastard have done?"

"Do you know . . . ?" Antonia hesitated. In truth, it was none of her business.

"Who the man was? I can guess." Mrs. Cotton's expression became grimmer if anything. "Cedric Quincannon was the smoothest-talking, shiniest-smiling, sweetest-smelling devil I'd ever seen. Beat my old man hollow, but Vernon never tried to charm everything in a skirt. Cedric had to move here 'cause he got some poor married gal in trouble. His wife left him and his practice went to hell. Not even Vernon could save it."

"And yet he moved you to Culverton to be with this . . . Mr. Quincannon?"

"He was a friend. Besides, the only time he tried anything on me, he was singing high for a week."

Antonia laughed. Then she asked. "If Mr. Dakers died eight years ago, why didn't Mr. Quincannon marry Mrs. . . . did his wife ever divorce him?"

Mrs. Cotton splashed the water around. "No, she didn't. She's still alive, last I heard. And he went right on making up to every woman he saw. Bettina had her hopes, I guess, but I think she figured out what he was. If she'd gone on dreamin' about him, she wouldn't have felt half so bad. It's the truth that gets you, every time."

"What wise words," Ned said from the kitchen door. He held a spoon in his hand. "I found this under the table. I bring it, dear lady, with all my warmest affections.'' He bowed and flipped the spoon into the dishwater.

"Antonia, whip off that apron and give it to him. I'd rather have a good-looking feller helping me any day."

Ned bowed his head for the string. "I hear and obey."

"Don't you give me any of your sass! I know your kind," Mrs. Cotton said, shaking a soapy finger at him. She turned to Antonia. "And don't you worry none. That man of yourn will be back before the moon can change her shape."

Antonia was about to thank her for her kindness when a frantic tattoo came at the backdoor. Mary Lou Ginnis burst in, breathless. "Mrs. Cotton," she gasped, holding on to the table.

"Lands, child, you should know better than to run when you're all laced up! Sit down and catch your breath! Now what's the matter?"

"Mother wants to know! With the church burned to the ground, where should Randolph and I get married?"

On Sunday, the citizens gathered under a sky of crystal blue to hear services preached by Mr. O'Donnell. His voice carried over the gurgling of the creek, the ebullient singing of the birds, and the soft whispers of a cooling breeze. Drifting flotillas of fat clouds, dazzlingly white, seemed like feather beds for harkening angels.

Under the picnic tree, its leaves now celebratory gold, stood a sawhorse table, literally groaning with bridal offerings of food and drink. There were two wedding cakes. When Nick Koers heard that O'Donnell himself had agreed to perform the wedding for Mr. Budgell and Mary Lou, nothing would do but that he get out of bed in time for Sunday and his own wedding. His father was there, too, in attendance on a pallet but grinning widely.

Antonia had just handed Miss Cartwright a third handkerchief to mop her happy tears when a hard arm stole about her waist from behind. She was swung up into the air and exhaustively kissed.

"Jake!"

He'd recently shaved, and his hair still lay in wet ridges where the comb had passed. "I wanted to come right to you," he said when he put her down on her feet. "But Mrs. Cotton insisted I take a bath. I could see her point after two days' hard ridin'."

"Remind me to thank her." She stood up on tiptoe to press her lips against his smooth chin. If it hadn't been for Ernie Ransom starting his introduction of the wedding march, she might have pursued the matter. "I'm sorry to tell you that your former sweetheart has found another."

"Not the Widow Nichols?"

"Would that bother you?" she asked with a toss of her head. She knew her hair looked particularly nice today and she hoped he noticed. When he didn't answer immediately, she pushed him and said, "We'll talk about the widow later. Anyway, Mary Lou and Mr. Budgell are getting married."

"Just like a woman. Turn your back for five minutes . . ." He snatched a kiss as people hushed them.

In a quieter voice he said, "If it's Mary Lou's weddin' day, why is Miss Cartwright all gussied up? Her, too?" At Antonia's nod he looked thoughtful. "You know, you're lookin' mighty pretty yourself, Miss Castle. Do you reckon the bishop might be up to a third ceremony today?"

Antonia thought about all that had happened in the last two weeks and how her entire outlook had changed. She now knew the best way to serve society was to aid those nearest to her, and let love spread out to the world as rings spread out in a pond.

She looked up at Jake and said, "I reckon."

Later, as the musicians took a deserved rest and the dancers staggered off to eat another helping, Antonia saw her father taking solemnly to Ernie. She pointed out the sight to her mother.

"Your father's developed a real interest in music ever since he decided to attend the opera with me last season. He gave a substantial gift to the Naugatuck Conservatory this year."

"How substantial?"

Ned, after swallowing a large bite of Mrs. Cotton's special angel food cake, said, "It should be enough to guarantee any young violinist's training. Especially one like that. And there might even be an accommodation and position for a widowed mother in the Castle Dormitory Wing."

Antonia ran to tell Jake the news. He turned from umpiring a discussion between the judge and the bishop on eternal versus temporal laws. "Hey, that's wonderful!" he said loudly. "Let's get out of here," he said, whispering in her ear. Antonia blushed as a warmth spread through her body.

Kindly hands had hitched Attila to a decorated gig. Looking back to wave to her family, friends, and cheering neighbors, Antonia recognized an elastic-sided boot tied to the back. She'd last seen it when she'd clouted someone over the head with it. Facing front, she laughed, sharing the joke with her husband.

"We'll keep 'em all for later. You never know when you might want to throw something at me."

Snuggling up under his arm, she smiled and said, "That's true."

As they reached their house Jake swung Antonia off the gig. He didn't let her down but carried her into the house. As they crossed the threshold she pulled his head down to touch her lips to his.

Kicking the door closed behind them, he placed her on the chaise and stood back. He eased off his coat and dropped it on the floor. As she reached up to unbutton his black silk vest, she said, "By my calculations, we ought to continue our platonic arrangement for another week at least. It would be an excellent test of our compatibility.''

"Not to mention self-control.'' He continued taking off his clothes, slowly unbuttoning his clean white shirt.

Antonia felt her mouth grow dry as Jake let his shirt fall on top of his jacket. Then, his bare chest within reach of her fingers, he reached out and untied the blue ribbons of her best straw hat. Gently removing it, he touched the sensitive side of her neck with his fingers.

"Glad to see this is better,'' he murmured, before he teased the most susceptible spot of all.

She could hardly remember to breathe, her fingers spreading out to cover his upper chest, the silky hair there intensifying the torrent of sensuality about to overwhelm her. Feeling his fingers at the pins in her hair, she reclined on the chaise, taking him down with her.

"So much for self-control,'' she said, covering his mouth with her own for the first of a lifetime's kisses.

If you enjoyed this book, take advantage of this special offer. Subscribe now and get a

FREE
Historical Romance

No Obligation (a $4.50 value)

Each month the editors of True Value select the four *very best* novels from America's leading publishers of romantic fiction. Preview them in your home *Free* for 10 days. With the first four books you receive, we'll send you a FREE book as our introductory gift. No Obligation!

If for any reason you decide not to keep them, just return them and owe nothing. If you like them as much as we think you will, you'll pay just $4.00 each and save at *least* $.50 each off the cover price. (Your savings are *guaranteed* to be at least $2.00 each month.) There is NO postage and handling – or other hidden charges. There are no minimum number of books to buy and you may cancel at any time.

Send in the Coupon Below

To get your FREE historical romance fill out the coupon below and mail it today. As soon as we receive it we'll send you your FREE Book along with your first month's selections.
